P9-DFB-145

AN UNOFFICIAL MINECRAFT-FAN ADVENTURE

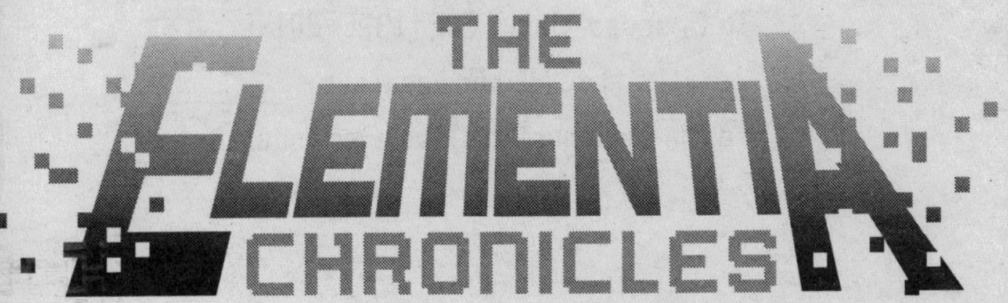

BOOK TWO:
THE NEW ORDER

by SEAN FAY WOLFE

HARPER
An Imprint of HarperCollinsPublishers

To Grandpa "Jack" Fay (1936–2014)

A gift to all who knew him

and the strongest man I've ever known

The Elementia Chronicles Book 2: The New Order
Copyright © 2015 by Sean Fay Wolfe
All rights reserved. Printed in the United States of America.
No part of this book may be used or reproduced in any manner whatsoever without written permission except in the case of brief quotations embodied in critical articles and reviews.
For information address HarperCollins Children's Books, a division of HarperCollins Publishers, 195 Broadway, New York, NY 10007.
www.harpercollinschildrens.com

Library of Congress Control Number: 2015946544
ISBN 978-0-06-241634-6

Book design by Victor Joseph Ochoa
15 16 17 18 19 CG/OPM 10 9 8 7 6 5 4 3 2
❖
First Edition

This book is not authorized, sponsored, endorsed, or licensed by Mojang AB, Microsoft Corp., or any other person or entity owning or controlling any rights to the Minecraft name, trademarks, or copyrights. Minecraft is a registered trademark of Mojang Synergies AB.

"These are the times that try men's souls.
The summer soldier and the sunshine patriot will,
in this crisis, shrink from the service of his country;
but he that stands by it now, deserves the love
and thanks of man and woman."

—Thomas Paine

CONTENTS

PART III: NIGHTFALL

PROLOGUE

Leonidas gritted his teeth and shook off his discomfort. Having been raised in the desert, he was foreign to the frigid wind and snow that now racked his body with shivers. He resented that, of the three generals of the Noctem Army, Lord Tenebris had assigned him to oversee the construction of the tundra base. Leonidas turned and looked at the marvelous stone complex rising from the snow-hardened earth. He couldn't help but take a little pride in the fact that the Noctem Alliance's first true base was now in its last phases of construction.

It dawned on Leonidas that it was probably time for another patrol. He pulled out his watch to confirm this. He had to squint to see the golden clockface through the heavy snowfall, but he could still make out the time as midday. It was time to send two of his ten men out to circumnavigate the construction zone, searching for trespassers. Leonidas found these patrols to be pointless. They were in the middle of the most expansive and desolate biome on the server, so the chances that anybody would run into them out here were slim to none. However, on Caesar's last inspection of the base, he had made it very plain to Leonidas that Lord Tenebris felt the perimeter patrols were vital.

Ever since it had been founded on Spawnpoint

Hill, the New Order had gathered almost a hundred and fifty followers, and had since been renamed the Noctem Alliance. Lord Tenebris, however, remained in a foul mood. He refused to let go of his anger that Element City had been so successful since King Kev had fallen. He had expected the city to struggle to support itself under the rule of Stan2012. However, Element City was now thriving to a level not experienced since the Golden Age of King Kev's rule, and Stan had only been president for a few months. Tomorrow was the day of the second election of the Republic of Elementia, and Stan was expected to win in a landslide.

Given Lord Tenebris's foul mood, Leonidas reasoned that his own head would be on the chopping block if Lord Tenebris somehow found out he had missed a patrol. Therefore, Leonidas called out to the two nearest workers, "Corporal! Private! Get over here!"

Immediately, Corporal Emerick and Private Spyro pocketed the stone bricks they were building with and hastily hustled over to Leonidas.

"Yes, sir, General Leonidas," the two soldiers responded in full salute.

"It's twelve hundred hours now, and it's time for the midday perimeter check. Ya know what to do," said Leonidas.

"Sir, yes, sir!" said the players. They spun on their heels, drew their bows and arrows, and marched off until they disappeared into the heavy snowfall.

Leonidas sighed. With two players gone, work would be slower for the next hour. He turned back toward the construction, about to continue his work, when something caught his eye. There, approaching from the general direction that Emerick and Spyro had just disappeared, a light flickered through the snowfall, getting brighter and brighter. Leonidas briefly wondered if one of his men was coming back, but he quickly realized that this was neither the corporal nor the private. A figure adorned in flowing white robes came into view, a jack-o'-lantern clutched in his hands.

"I need food, Leonidas," came Caesar's battered voice, breathing heavily from his long trek through the barren plains. Leonidas was taken aback, seeing his comrade and equal-in-command here when Caesar was supposed to be catering to the personal needs of Lord Tenebris. He pulled two pieces of bread from his inventory and quickly handed them to Caesar.

"What brings ya here, Caesar?" asked Leonidas, showing Caesar into the modest dirt-block shack, lit by torchlight. The structure served as Leonidas's personal quarters during the construction of the new capital. "I thought Lord Tenebris told ya to stay with him, and help with whatever he needed."

"He did, and I am," replied Caesar. Even through his

mouthful of bread, his upper-class Element City accent was prominent. “Lord Tenebris is displeased that he has not received word of the completion of Nocturia. He wishes to know why you have not completed our new capital yet, and how long it will be before it is completed. He has sent me to ask you this.”

Leonidas sighed. “Don’t actually say this to Lord Tenebris, Caesar, but if it weren’t for these stupid perimeter patrols, we would have completed the capital a week ago. With only ten guys workin’ on construction, the patrols really slow down the work.”

Caesar gave a slow, emotionless nod.

Leonidas finished his report. “Nevertheless, we’ve entered the final phases of the construction of Nocturia. We should be done by the end of tomorrow.”

“Now, that is what Lord Tenebris will want to hear,” replied Caesar, standing up. “I shall give him the report.”

“Do ya really have to leave so soon?” asked Leonidas. Since all the players out here were subordinate to him, Leonidas found himself with nobody to talk to, and he was truthfully becoming a little lonely. “Can’t ya stay for at least a little while?”

“No, I’m sorry, Leonidas. Lord Tenebris made it very clear that I am supposed to survey the premise hastily and report back to him, no delays. Otherwise, I would be quite content to stay, but you know how Lord Tenebris is when he gets angry."

In fact, Leonidas had never seen Lord Tenebris angry. The one and only time he had seen Lord Tenebris was on Spawnpoint Hill, the night they had lost to the Grand Adorian Militia in battle. On that day, desperate and with nothing to lose, Leonidas, Caesar, and Minotaurus had pledged themselves to a new leader. Since that day, Lord Tenebris had ordered Leonidas to build the Noctem Alliance's capital city of Nocturia out here in the Southern Tundra Biome. His only contact with the founder of the Noctem Alliance since then had been through messengers.

Leonidas rarely saw his fellow generals. Lord Tenebris had ordered Caesar to act as his own personal adviser and servant, and what he had ordered Minotaurus to do, Leonidas could only guess. Regardless, Leonidas was well aware of what Lord Tenebris was capable of, and he did not imagine he would be very agreeable when angry.

"Then have a good return trip, Caesar," Leonidas responded, handing his friend three cooked pork chops for the hike back to Lord Tenebris's base. Caesar nodded his thanks, and was about to exit through the wooden door when three players burst into the dirt shack.

The three players were covered in snow, so it took Leonidas a moment to distinguish two of them as Corporal

Emerick and Private Spyro. They had their bows raised and were nudging a third figure forward. This player, Leonidas did not recognize. It appeared to be a girl, dressed in a full snowsuit with a red ponytail running down her back. The moment she entered the building, she fell to her knees, overwhelmed with fatigue. Leonidas stood up.

"Who is this?" he asked his corporal harshly.

"We found this player wandering around, not far from our border, General," replied the corporal. He seemed quite proud that he had led the effort of capturing a trespasser.

"What's your name?" Leonidas asked.

The girl seemed unable to respond. She whimpered. It was then that Leonidas noticed the arrow protruding from her left shoulder. One of his men had shot her.

"Answer him, you pathetic worm. He asked you a question!" bellowed Caesar, and all in the vicinity jumped from his sudden outburst. "What are you doing here?"

The girl gave an almost inaudible whisper, and Leonidas thought he heard the words "lost" and "community" in her answer.

"So there's a community out here? Where? I thought the colony of the king's banished criminals died out a long time ago," inquired Leonidas.

Another dubious whimper escaped the girl's mouth, and Leonidas heard the word "survived" in her response.

"So the community still exists? And you are a member of this community?" Caesar asked gruffly.

The girl, still kneeling and unable to stand, gave an almost imperceptible nod before her head sank to the floor and she dissolved into desperate sobs.

"That's all I needed to know," responded Caesar with a sly grin. An instant later, there was a flash of diamond. The girl fell backward, a slash across her chest and her items lying in a ring around her. Caesar slid his sword back into its sheath.

Leonidas opened his mouth in horror, but quickly closed it again. It was necessary, he reminded himself, trying to keep his breathing steady. She knew too much, and she was a danger. Still, Leonidas couldn't bring himself to look at her body, and he felt unable to look back toward Caesar until he heard the faint noise indicating that the girl had vanished.

"I'll tell Lord Tenebris not to expect the capital completed for a few more days," said Caesar, a smile appearing on his face. "But when I receive the next report, I expect that not only will the building be finished, but every member of the old community will be dead."

Caesar threw back his head and laughed, and before Leonidas could open his mouth to object, he had swept out the door.

Leonidas stood looking at the floor for a moment, then realized that Corporal Emerick and Private Spyro were still looking at him, waiting for a command. He cleared his throat and, trying to keep his voice steady, gave the order.

"Private, you're stayin' with me and finishin' this capital. Corporal"—Leonidas took a deep breath—"take half the men and find the village. Leave no survivors."

"Yes, sir," came Corporal Emerick's response, and he left the room without another word.

There was silence as Leonidas stood in the room lost in thought, Private Spyro standing beside him. After a minute, the private spoke. "Is it really the right thing to do, General? Those players, they're not hurting anybody, so how can it be right?"

Leonidas, ignoring his own strongly conflicted feelings, gave Spyro the response he was supposed to give. "It doesn't matter if it's right or not, Private, it's what has to be done." Leonidas let out a raspy sigh and fought the urge to vomit. "Come on," he said, "we have a base to finish.

And with that, General Leonidas and Private Spyro of the Noctem Alliance left the dirt shack.

PART

THE NOCTEM ALLIANCE

CHAPTER 1
THE SECOND ELECTION

Stan knew that technically, this was Elementia's first real election for president. There had not really been a vote when he first became president. Everybody had been so euphoric at the downfall of King Kev that they had immediately wanted the one responsible for their freedom to be the new head of the Minecraft server Elementia.

Now, however, it was time for Elementia's first true presidential election. The entire voting population was crammed into the square of Element City. Over three months ago, King Kev had stood above this very courtyard and made the announcement that it was time for the lower-level citizens of Elementia to leave Element City. Stan's all-consuming rage at King Kev's proclamation and the arrow he'd sent at the king to show it were the reasons he stood on the bridge of Element Castle now.

That fateful arrow had started an uprising among the lower-level players of the Minecraft server Elementia, and their rebellion had resulted in the death of the tyrannical King Kev. The majority of the king's supporters were now dead or imprisoned, with the rest living as fugitives of the law. In their joy at the fall of the evil king, the citizens of Elementia were quick to jump on Stan's idea of Elementia being turned into a republic. Stan was unanimously elected to be its first president.

Now, however, his first term was up. He had been president for four months, and it was time for another election. The councilmen, who assisted Stan in making the laws of Elementia, had already been elected. Stan's good friends Kat, Charlie, Jayden, Archie, Goldman (aka G), DZ, and the Mechanist had all been unanimously reelected to the council.

The eighth seat on the council, however, was now filled by the former mayor of Blackstone, Gobbleguy. The seat's previous holder, Blackraven, was running against Stan for president of Elementia. The majority of the players believed that Blackraven had been stupid to give up his seat on the council, as they believed there was nothing he could ever say or do to convince them to elect him to office over Stan.

Stan, however, felt Blackraven was a formidable opponent. He believed Blackraven was wiser than he was. If Blackraven played his cards right, Stan thought that his seat as president of Elementia may well be in jeopardy. This idea made him nervous as he sat on the bridge of Element Castle, preparing to give one last speech to his people before they voted.

Stan and Blackraven would both be asked five questions. These five questions, dealing with the most important problems in Elementia, would be Stan's last chance to assure the population that he was the right player to continue leading them.

Stan's stomach was in knots as he was called to step forward and begin to speak. As he walked out onto the bridge of Element Castle, the crowd received him with hoots and cheers. Stan's anxiety vanished. There was nothing to be nervous about, he realized. As long as he answered the questions honestly, he believed that the people of Elementia would agree with him.

The first question rang out, echoing around the spacious courtyard. "Stan2012, if elected president, how do you intend to handle the diamond shortage we have in Elementia right now?"

Stan, whose views on this matter were firm, responded confidently. "I know that diamonds are a very important resource for creating the best gear possible. However, I don't think that diamonds are nearly as important as iron ore, which is way more common and equally useful. Right now, we don't have access to a good diamond mine. If we find one, then Elementia will have more diamonds to go around. Right now, though, I think that we're much better off mining more iron ore, rather than searching for diamonds."

There was general applause as Stan finished. Although the players of Element City certainly did like their diamonds, they felt that Stan had a very reasonable view of the issue.

As the applause died down, the next question sounded out.

"Stan2012, if elected president, how do you intend to fulfill Elementia's coal needs now that the mines of Blackstone have been declared unsafe?"

Stan smiled. One of his most recent acts as president had been to close down the coal mines in the mining town of Blackstone after inspecting them firsthand. He had found that the entire mining system was situated around an underground lava lake. Though he was quite happy with the decision, one of the biggest concerns was how Elementia was going to keep up with the ever-present demand for coal after the city's reserves ran out. Stan now, once again, shared his plans to resolve this issue.

"Well, let me first say that I have no regrets whatsoever in declaring the mines of Blackstone unsafe. The safety of our miners is much more important than any coal that we may find. However, because we do need coal to fuel our ever-growing population, let me tell you about a new opportunity that has come to light. Councilman Charlie has recently started exploring the Southeastern Mountain Range, trying to establish an Elementian outpost in the far reaches of the server. During his exploration, he found extensive coal veins inside and beneath the mountains. It would not be difficult to extend the Blackstone railway to reach these mountains. We're currently putting together plans to do just that, and so I see plenty of coal in Elementia's future, even without Blackstone."

The applause to this response outstripped the last round by a mile. Stan had received praises for closing Blackstone and for supporting exploration of the Southeastern Mountain Range.

"What are your thoughts on the recent ideas of taxing the NPC villagers, now that they can grow carrots and potatoes?"

"Oh, no way!" cried Stan. "I will never put any sort of tax or quotas on the NPC villagers! I've lived with the villagers before, but they typically just want to be left alone. I do think that we should get carrots and potatoes from the NPC villagers, but we should do this by offering them a fair trade. We know how to grow crops. If we trade with the NPCs, they'll be happy, and we'll have our own carrots and potatoes to grow. If we're honest with ourselves, we know that we're smarter and more powerful than they are, so it's our responsibility to make sure that nothing bad happens to them. We certainly can't put taxes on them!"

There was healthy applause for this statement. Almost none of the citizens of Elementia understood NPC villagers the way that Stan did, and they knew that. All they saw was that Stan was trying to stand up for those who could not stand up for themselves.

"Stan2012, what are your thoughts on the emerging organization calling itself the Noctem Alliance?"

In the past month, there had been a growing number of protest rallies in Element City staged by members of a group called the Noctem Alliance. Despite the fall of King Kev, they still believed that the lower-level players of Minecraft didn't deserve the same basic rights as the older, upper-level players.

"The Noctem Alliance is, as of right now, just a protesters' group, so I have no control over them," Stan said calmly. "Everyone is free to voice their own opinions, regardless of how I, or anybody else, might feel about it. However, I'll definitely be keeping an eye on them. Any group that threatens the equality of the players of Elementia won't be tolerated. The Noctem Alliance can say what they want, I won't stop them, as much as I disagree with them. However, if the Alliance acts on any of their views, there will be no hesitation in putting the group to rest."

The applause shook the courtyard. Although all present were aware that Stan was vehemently opposed to the views presented by the Noctem Alliance, it was encouraging to know he believed in their laws to a point where he would not actively stop the Alliance unless they took action.

"Stan2012, here is your last question: What are your thoughts on tracking down and neutralizing any of King

Kev's remaining allies?"

"Well, I think my thoughts on that should be pretty obvious," replied Stan with a chuckle, and a charged laughter rippled through the audience.

"I don't know where King Kev's remaining supporters are, or what they are doing. Our army has devoted almost half its resources to catching any of King Kev's followers who are still out there. I think that we are giving all that we possibly can to the search right now, but I'm ready to send more soldiers out if the traitors don't reveal themselves soon. Rest assured, however, as long as I am your president, there is no danger in Element City from King Kev's supporters."

The applause the crowd was barely holding back now surged forward as they sang the praises of their president who they fully trusted to keep them safe and happy. Stan was elated. The applause was still strong as he left the platform and entered the side tower to watch Blackraven's interview.

Blackraven had always had somewhat different views from Stan. Personally, Stan believed that Blackraven was in favor of putting resources where they were not necessary, and taking them from where they were. Although Blackraven did have a following among the citizens of Elementia, it paled in comparison to Stan's.

One thing Stan gave Blackraven credit for was that, although Stan may not agree with them all, Blackraven was firm in his beliefs, and he made that plain. Respectable a quality as that may be, Stan still did not feel that Blackraven should have run for president. Blackraven had had to give up his seat on the Council of Eight to do so, and he almost certainly would lose, as very few players agreed with his ideas.

For example, Blackraven believed that investing resources in diamond mining was of supreme importance, even if that meant less effort went into looking for King Kev's remaining followers. He also believed that people with similar views should band together into political parties. This was unsettling, as the shady Noctem Alliance wanted to become a political party. Perhaps the view that Stan most disagreed with was that since the NPC villagers lived on the Elementia server, they should pay taxes the same as the players.

After Blackraven finished answering his questions, he walked over to sit next to Stan as the polite applause died down. Stan turned to wish Blackraven luck, but a pensive look had crossed the old player's yellow-and-black-feathered face, so Stan looked away. Instead, he looked out the window of the tower at the voting machine.

The machine was an ingenious contraption of the Mechanist's design. One by one, the citizens of Elementia lined up and walked into a room, inside of which there were two buttons: one to vote for Stan, and one to vote for Blackraven. Press a button, and pistons ejected you gently from the room, and the door opened for the next voter.

By the time the sun was setting, the last voter had entered the booth. As the door swung shut for the last time, there was a moment of silence as one of the officials checked the records of the voting within the machine. Then, a frizz of white hair appeared on a platform atop the machine as the Mechanist climbed up and read the redstone circuitry that sat before him. Stan saw him give a slight nod and a tiny smile before turning to address the crowd.

"The votes are all in," the Mechanist announced, his Texan accent deep and pronounced. "The winner of the election for president of the Grand Republic of Elementia is Stan2012, for his second term!"

Stan tried to look dignified, but he couldn't stop the uncontrollable grin that had spread over his face. Blackraven didn't seem to mind, though. He offered Stan congratulations, which Stan returned, shaking Blackraven's hand for good measure. As Blackraven headed down the stairs to leave the castle, Stan looked over the bridge to tumultuous applause.

"Thank you, citizens of Elementia! Together, we will make this server the best place that it can be! Thank you for giving me the chance to continue to prove myself to you! It is my job to serve you, so I hope that you find yourselves happy, healthy, and safe under my leadership. Good night, and thank you again!"

The applause shook the ground beneath his feet as Stan walked back into the tower. He was quite content that he was president once again, but he felt exhausted, and was eager to finally get some sleep.

CHAPTER 2: THE VOICE IN THE NIGHT

Stan could not deny that he was very happy he had been reelected, but right now, he could not hide his annoyance. He had explicitly told the guards of the castle that he would talk to anybody who needed him the next day, but not tonight. Yet he had still been woken up four times, by DZ, Kat, Charlie, and DZ again. His friends only wanted to congratulate him, but Stan was far too tired to appreciate it. Stan ordered the guard firmly to tell everybody to leave him be for the rest of the night, and slammed the door irritably.

Stan got back into bed, glad that the campaign was over and that he could now get some real sleep for the first time in days. He pulled the covers up, closed his eyes, and was about to fall asleep when a faint voice caught his ear.

"Stan . . . hey, Stan, are you awake?"

"Whoever you are, GO AWAY!" barked Stan, hiding his head under his pillow in his angst.

"Oh, okay then. I thought that you'd be rather happy to hear my voice again, noob, but if you'd rather sleep, I get it . . ."

Suddenly, Stan was wide awake. He glanced wildly around the room, daring to hope that it could really be true, that the voice could really be that of . . .

"Sally?" Stan asked tentatively.

"Yeeeees?" came the sarcastic, smirky voice.

"Oh my God. It's you!" cried Stan, his eyes brightening in delight. "You're alive! But how . . . where are . . ."

"No, you idiot! I'm not *alive*, Minotaurus cut me open with an axe, remember?"

"But . . . wait a second . . . ," said Stan, his elation suddenly shifting to a sudden-onset headache. "If you're . . . but then . . . Sal, how are you talking to me if you're dead?"

"Well," came Sally's voice, the source of which Stan still could not distinguish, "ever since I died, I've been trying to find ways to get back onto the server. I've gotta hand it to King Kev, he really did his research. I've tried every method of rejoining, of hacking my way in, of bypassing the blacklist . . . you know, the list of people who have been banned from Elementia. But what you hear now is the closest I've been able to get."

"So . . . can you see me?" asked Stan.

"Yeah, I see you," she replied. "It's weird, my view of you keeps shifting around the room, though, and I have to really focus on you to keep my sight there. Frankly, you're not too much to look at, so I think you owe me an apology there."

Stan chuckled. "Well, death hasn't changed you much, Sally. Is this the first time that you've managed to do this . . . this . . . well, whatever this is?"

"No," Sally said. "I've been able to do this for about the past week or so, and it's so strange, I really don't have that much control over where I get to see. It's like I see flashes of things that are happening all over Elementia. Sometimes I see trees in the forest, or pigs in the plains, or buildings in the city. Anyway, if I don't focus on what I'm seeing really hard, I lose the connection."

"That is weird," said Stan, thinking about what might cause this but drawing a blank. "So, have you talked to anybody else?"

"No, frankly, most people are too boring to focus on," replied Sally, and Stan could almost see the sarcastic simper on her face. "I just happened to have the luck of teleporting directly into your bedroom. By the way, it was cute when DZ tried to come in twice to congratulate you. And also, congrats, Mr. Two-Term President. Not bad for a noob who can't even flop down onto a pillow correctly."

"Are you ever going to let that go?" Stan whined, but he was laughing. Even though he couldn't see Sally, this was as close to old times as he could possibly get.

"No," replied Sally simply, and Stan chuckled some more, but when Sally spoke again, her voice was as serious as Stan had ever heard it. "Actually, there is something important I have to tell you. I saw Caesar and Leonidas."

Stan's eyebrows shot up. "Wait, you saw those two?

Leonidas is alive?" he asked in shock.

Sally grimly continued. "Yeah. One time, I tried to join, and I went to this place I didn't recognize. It was really dark, and I could barely see anything, but Caesar and Leonidas were there. They were saying something I couldn't hear to a big group of guys that seemed to be listening to them. I tried to focus in, but I lost the connection."

"So they had people with them? How many, Sally?" asked Stan, panic creeping into his voice as he began to contemplate the possibilities of what this development could mean.

"There were probably about twenty-five, total. I couldn't tell, but it looked like Caesar was giving some sort of speech, and they were cheering for him."

Stan gulped, sweat breaking out. "So . . . does that mean . . . that Caesar and Leonidas are gathering followers? What about Minotaurus, was he there? Did they have weapons?" Stan was talking very fast now, panic rising in his throat. "What were they doing there, Sally? Can you tell me anything else?"

"I don't . . . oh, wait . . . oh, no . . ." Sally's response was suddenly punctuated by static, like a radio signal was being jammed. "I'm . . . losing the con . . . the connection, Stan . . . I've got . . . got to go . . ."

"No, Sally! Don't go!" Stan was on edge now. With his

fatigue, the knowledge of an organization headed by Caesar, and finding out that Sally could still speak to him, Stan was in a very unstable state. He was desperate to find solace in the now fading voice of Sally.

"Go . . . go to sleep now . . . Stan, you're exhausted . . . be careful . . . I promise, I'll contact . . . contact you again . . . again very soon . . ."

And then there was a static crackle, and the voice ceased. Overwhelmed with exhaustion and despair, Stan gave a moan of dejection and passed out on his bed.

"I'm telling you, it was the weirdest thing!" said Stan, pulling back the ceremonial presidential gold helmet to wipe away the sweat accumulating on his brow. All the councilmen and the president were required to wear them around the town, and they were the only ones by law allowed to do so. They were also each equipped with a golden weapon of their choice, for the sake of ceremony as well as self-defense. Stan had a golden axe strapped across his back, and Charlie, who was walking next to him, had a golden pickaxe latched to his waist.

"Stan, listen, I get that you really miss Sally," said Charlie. "But there is no way that she telepathically contacted you or something. Trust me, I've read pretty much every book in the library about this game and the stuff in it, and there's no way that it's possible. I'm sorry, Stan, but Sally's dead."

Stan sighed, his tolerance wearing thin. "Charlie, I am positive of what I heard. Sally was speaking to me, and she told me that she had seen Caesar and Leonidas talking to a whole group. And personally, I think it's very possible that the remnants of King Kev's army have banded together."

"Stan, stop!" Charlie butted in. Having lost his cat, Lemon, in the Ender Desert during their quest to take down King Kev, Charlie understood what Stan was going through. However, he felt Stan's grieving had reached a point of crazy obsession. That Stan was having this kind of hallucination three months after the fact made Charlie seriously question Stan's mental state.

"Stan, listen to me very carefully. You were dreaming. Sally is dead and she is not coming back. You miss Sally very much and I get that. But do me a favor, and don't talk until we get to the arena. On the way there, I want you to ask yourself if you really heard Sally talking to you last night, or if you were just hearing things because you were very tired after a long campaign."

Stan followed his friend's instructions. And the more he thought about it, the more he realized that Charlie was probably right. Stan certainly had done his fair share of grieving over Sally, but he realized that his exhaustion after the campaign may very well have caused him to hear voices. By the time Stan, Charlie, and the throng of players around them had crossed the grassy courtyard and entered the Element City Spleef Arena, Stan had dismissed his late-night conversation with Sally as nothing more than a delusion.

CHAPTER 3

THE SPLEEF QUARTERFINALS

There could be nothing better said about the Element City Spleef Arena than that it was the crown jewel of the metropolis. It was expertly constructed with elegant patterns of blocks of diamond, gold, lapis lazuli, and brick. The large building was ringed by the ornate courtyard, which was more often than not packed with fans, hoping to hear anything to indicate what was happening inside.

When Stan defeated King Kev in battle and became president of the Grand Republic of Elementia, it was less than three days before an enormous petition surfaced, requesting the reinstatement of Spleef in Elementia. After consulting briefly with the Council of Eight, and particularly with DZ (who was an experienced Spleef player from back in the day), Stan had decreed that the sport of Spleef be allowed back into Elementia. He had ordered the construction of a new Spleef arena equidistant from the upper-level and lower-level districts of Element City, so that citizens of all levels could easily come and watch the Spleef matches.

Under the new mandate, a new schedule of Spleef games was carefully set up. There were also variations to the game put in place to make the sport more interesting. All these changes made Stan very excited to see what today's quarterfinal match would hold. He was even more excited, though, to see how DZ, Kat, and Ben, as the three members of the competing Zombies Spleef team, would handle it.

Kat pulled the green leather helmet onto her head and fastened the strap under her chin. She grumbled to herself, not liking this new feature. Although leather armor had become much more lightweight in the last update of Minecraft, it now also required additional straps. Kat personally would have preferred the heavier but simpler leather cap, tunic, pants, and boots that she was used to.

She was sitting in a cobblestone room with a chest, three chairs, and an iron door on both sides. The two chairs were occupied by Kat's teammates, DZ and Ben (who, alongside his brothers Bill and Bob, was now a chief of police in Element City). The chest contained their gear, which they were now putting on. While one iron door led to the corridor through which they had entered the room, the other led to the Element City Spleef Arena. On this square field, the three players were expected to battle another team of three for the amusement of six hundred spectators.

"I still can't believe that Stan makes us wear this stupid armor," complained DZ in his heavy New York accent as he struggled into his green leather pants. DZ had played Spleef back before King Kev had banned it, when no armor was required. He was so used to playing without armor that, to this day, he refused to wear it, even in combat.

"Ah, be quiet, DZ," retorted Ben, who was already suited up and pulling his diamond shovel out of the chest. "He only added it so that we can whack each other with shovels now!"

"Oh, please, don't you remember the old days? People used to hit each other with shovels all the time! They weren't supposed to, but the refs didn't stop it. The crowd liked it, and it was freaking awesome!" DZ replied as he finally managed to tie the straps of the leather pants.

"As a matter of fact, I never did see any of the old Spleef matches, because my brothers and I—"

"Come on, guys!" exclaimed Kat, standing up. "We've got to focus, okay? We almost lost to the Ghasts during that last round!"

"We did not *almost* lose, I had that match the entire time!" retorted DZ, snatching up his diamond shovel.

"DZ, you taking out one guy while the other guy gets knocked into a pit by a snowball is not 'having the match!'" said Kat. "I get that you're probably the best Spleef player in the league, but if the dispensers hadn't started to fire snowballs, you would have gotten destroyed by those two!"

"How do you know that?" DZ snapped. "As I recall, you and Ben were floating in a lake twenty blocks below the arena when this happened!"

"Ah, lay off her DZ," said Ben, reaching into the chest and tossing the last diamond shovel over to Kat. "It doesn't matter, okay, guys? That was the last match. What matters is that we're still the best team, and those Blazes aren't gonna know what hit them!"

"Oh yeah!" cried Kat as she caught the shovel and pumped her fist in the air.

"You're right, Ben! We're gonna win 'cause we're awesome, unstoppable, and, most important, we've got *me*! So let's go!" cried DZ, just as the mechanical door swung open. DZ rushed out, followed quickly by Ben and Kat. All three of them were hyped up, and the crowd greeted them with raucous applause. Kat's eyes adjusted to the bright light of the open-skied Spleef arena, and her jaw dropped.

Inside the fifty-by-fifty-block arena, surrounded on all sides by screaming fans, was a bona fide forest. Trees sprouted from the flat dirt ground, which Kat knew to be only a block thick. The trees covered a good portion of the arena. It would lead to various trapping and ambush techniques by the two teams.

Kat was shocked. It was her third official Spleef match, but this was by far the most complex arena she had seen. In their preliminary match, the arena had been the standard level surface constructed of snow blocks. Kat had liked that arena. Breaking the snow blocks had yielded snowballs, which Kat had thrown to great effect, knocking two of her opponents into the pit below.

The object of Spleef was pretty simple. In a fifty-by-fifty-block arena, with the floor only one block thick, two teams fought to knock each other into the pit below by destroying the floor and knocking their opponents into the holes using shovels and snowballs. The last team with a player standing won.

Kat, Ben, and DZ, the three members of the Zombie team, had easily managed to take out the Wolves in the qualifying round. However, they had barely notched a victory against the Ghasts on a tundra field in the preliminary round. Now, in their quarterfinal round against the Blazes, they would be fighting in a forest.

Kat heard the telltale creak and click of the iron door swinging shut behind her, indicating that the match had officially begun. As was her pregame strategy, she focused on the environment around her, completely ignoring the open blue skies above and the cheering of the fanatic crowds. She only allowed herself to be aware of the woodland that had been constructed around her and the two players at her side. They were now the only players she could trust until she left the arena.

Suddenly, the sky turned black, and all was silent. She had tapped into some primordial survival instinct, and now imagined herself standing in a silent forest at night. Somewhere in these woods were evil monsters, all working for a team called the Blazes. The only way for her to escape was to take them down with the help of her friends beside her.

Kat realized that DZ was motioning her and Ben forward. As he was their team leader, Kat followed his order. She trailed DZ into the maze of trees, aware that Ben was watching her back. Kat was confident following DZ into the arena. He was a fantastic leader and had a ton of knowledge about Spleef strategy, built up from playing professionally back before the game was banned. While the other teams used the strategy of spreading out, DZ had explicitly told them that the best strategy was to stick together and watch one another's backs.

Suddenly, Ben cried out in alarm, and Kat spun her head toward the source. A player, clad in bright orange leather armor, had burst around the side of the nearest tree, bringing his shovel down onto the dirt block beneath Kat's feet. She leaped backward as the block broke, revealing a pit of water below. Ben lunged forward and swung his shovel across the assailant's chest.

As Kat regained her footing, she became aware of DZ locking shovels with a second member of the Blazes and quickly overpowering him. Kat turned and saw both Ben and the other Blaze fall to the ground at the same time. Kat stepped forward and drove her shovel into the block beneath the fallen Blaze, sending him tumbling into the pit below. She quickly turned back to DZ and saw that he had caught the other Blaze off guard, opening a hole in the ground behind him and kicking him into it.

Kat was jubilant. They were up three to one, with only one more Blaze standing between them and the semifinals. As the applause died down, Kat followed DZ's motion for a team huddle.

"All right you guys, good work so far, but I think it's time to switch our strategy. Execute Operation Zombie Swarm."

"Right," replied Kat and Ben in unison, and they spread out around the edge of the arena and eventually lost sight of one another. In Operation Zombie Swarm, they would all hunt the remaining Blaze separately. If they found him, they would play defense and call in their teammates for backup.

Kat quietly snuck forward through the trees, her ears perked up, tuning out the roar of the crowd to listen for any unnatural noises that indicated an impending attack. Her eyes scanned the gaps between the trees. Suddenly, she caught a flash of orange behind one of the pillars of wood before it hastily disappeared. Wasting no time, Kat called out to her teammates and sprinted after the orange form. Kat burst into the clearing where she was sure the player had gone, but it was deserted.

Kat only had a moment to consider what to do next

before someone crashed into her side, and she hit the ground tumbling. Dazed, she pulled herself up in time to see the dirt beneath Ben's feet bursting into nothing as he fell into the pit below. An orange figure was standing there, shovel in hand. It was Ben who had knocked Kat out of the way, even though it meant falling into the pit below himself.

Kat hopped up and attacked the remaining Blaze with a shovel, just as DZ burst from behind a tree and did the same. This Blaze was exceptionally skilled, as he dodged both attacks and then swung his shovel into DZ. By the time Kat had recovered from her missed attack, the Blaze had tricked DZ. He took one wrong step and plunged into the same hole that Ben had fallen into.

Kat gritted her teeth, determined not to lose, and rushed at the remaining Blaze. She leaped into the air just as the player destroyed the dirt block beneath her. Kat reached out her left hand and tackled the Blaze to the ground, pinning him beneath her. In his daze, the player was powerless to stop Kat as she brought her diamond shovel up in her right hand, and in two jabs destroyed the dirt below them. Kat kicked off the player's stomach, forcing him downward to join Ben, DZ, and the two other Blazes as Kat landed safely on the soil above.

The match now over, Kat took in the tumultuous applause from the crowd around her. She waved to them all, a huge grin breaking across her face. From the pit below, she heard the hoots and cheers of Ben and DZ, praising their teammate for her victory.

Oh man, thought Kat as the glow of victory radiated from her face like sunbeams. *Three matches down, two to go!*

Stan was now well below the stands, but he could still hear the sound erupting from the crowd above. Stan and Charlie had to push their way through gaggles of fanatic Zombie fans to get to Kat, DZ, and Ben.

"That was easily one of the most awesome things I've ever seen," said Stan, images from the match still flashing through his head.

"I know, right?" said Charlie. "I mean, I get that we're busy and all, but was that really the first time you've ever come to one of these matches? Stan, you signed the paper that made the place!"

"Well, I'll tell you this, Charlie, I'm definitely coming to every one of these matches from now on."

Charlie laughed. "Man, you haven't seen anything yet! You know, last time they played, in the match against the Ghasts . . ." And Charlie and Stan spent the rest of the walk down the corridor talking about the previous matches.

"And right as DZ was about to— Hey, guys!" shouted Charlie as he entered the room and rushed over to greet his friends. Stan followed closely behind. G and Kat released each other from their hug and beckoned the two new arrivals over to them, while DZ, Ben, and his brother Bill walked over, followed closely by Bob, who sat on the back of a pink pig.

Stan, like all his friends, felt that Bob was very lucky to be alive at all. During the battle in which Stan had defeated King Kev, which was now commonly known as the Battle for Elementia, Bill and Bob had engaged Caesar, who had been King Kev's right-hand man and was an exceptional swordfighter, in combat. They had failed to defeat him, and Caesar would have killed Bob had Kat not intervened. Instead, the sword strike intended to kill Bob destroyed his kneecap and severed his leg from his body.

Luckily, Bill and Ben had used their entire supply of Potions of Regeneration to reattach Bob's leg, and he had regained very limited use of it. However, it had quickly become evident that Bob would never walk again. That didn't stop Bob from serving alongside his brothers as a police chief of Element City, though. He now followed Ben, Bill, and DZ over to Stan, Charlie, Kat, and G on the back of Ivanhoe, his trusty war pig, which had been saddled and was controlled with guidance through carrots.

Although one might think Bob wasn't the same warrior he'd been, nothing could be further from the truth. He could shoot his bow just as well on pigback as he could on foot, and the pig was swift and adaptable to rough terrains. Bob had quickly gained renown as the fastest and most pliable officer on the force, a nightmare to any criminal who gave them chase.

"Nice match, guys!" said Charlie.

"Yeah, guys, that match was one of the most awesome things I've ever seen," added Stan.

"Eh, thanks, guys," said Kat. "Nice of you to finally come down to see one of the matches, Stan," she added with a smirk.

"Hey, you know I've been up to my neck in work since the campaign began," said Stan, being playfully defensive. "I tell you, though, from now on I'm making it a priority to come to each and every one of these matches."

"Good to hear," said Ben, butting in between them with DZ and the other two police chiefs at his side. "Now is it just me, or did I hear someone say party at the castle courtyard?"

"Nobody said that, Ben," added Kat with a laugh.

"Oh, well then, I guess it was just me thinking it," said Ben, grinning. "But now that it's out there, we might as well go and do it. Come on, guys!" He led his brothers and DZ out of the room and into a corridor that would take them into the courtyard to be received by their adoring fans.

Kat gave a laugh and called out, "Wait up, Ben!" She ran to catch him, followed by G, who had been at Kat's side the whole time and was now following her at a determinedly close distance. Stan and Charlie glanced at each other, and both rolled their eyes at G's clinginess before following the other five players.

Stan never failed to be amazed at how fast the Imperial Butlers prepared meals at his whim. Even now, when Stan ordered them to prepare enough cake, cookies, and pumpkin pie for a victory party, it was all prepared and set out on ornate tables within a matter of minutes. Stan had personally been in favor of getting rid of the Imperial Butlers, as the organization had originally been created for catering to the desires of King Kev. However, the council had surveyed the people of the city and voted that they deserved the service of the butlers, provided the butlers were paid well.

Stan was certainly glad that the butlers were here, now that the festival was shifting into full gear. He looked around and saw that his people were in the highest of spirits, with more players streaming into the courtyard and immediately partaking in the dancing and feasting. Stan saw Ben and Bill cheering on Bob, who had somehow managed to teach Ivanhoe the pig how to do the moonwalk as the music blasted from the nearest jukebox. Kat and G were mingling with people, Kat holding a feather quill in her hand and signing autographs for fans of the Zombies. She seemed to be thoroughly enjoying her newfound fame as a Spleef athlete.

"Eh, this is a nice little shindig ya got goin' here, Stan," came a voice from behind him. DZ had come up to Stan, pumpkin pie in both hands, with Charlie following.

"Yeah. I wouldn't be surprised if people supported the Zombies now just so that there are more victory parties like this," Charlie said.

"Very true," said Stan. "So, DZ, how does it feel to finally get back in the Spleef arena?"

"Awesome, man!" came DZ's enthused reply. "I mean, I think it's been coming for a long time, but I really owe you one, Stan. I think the new rules for Spleef are a million times more fun than the old ones—even if you do make us wear armor," he added with a smirk.

"It's a necessary evil, DZ, you know that. I made the shovel techniques legal, just like you asked, but the council—"

"Yeah, I know, the council insisted on armor," DZ finished for him, waving his hand. "I'm just joshing ya, Stan, you know how grateful I am for you doing all of this. And I gotta say, I am very, *very* happy with my new teammates."

"Yeah, they do seem to be enjoying it," said Stan, jerking a thumb toward Kat, who was now being approached by two boys and a girl, all of whom were wearing green Zombie uniforms and asking her to sign them.

"Okay, okay, don't worry, plenty of me to go around," said Kat with a laugh as she pulled out her quill and brought it down toward the chestplate.

Stan felt a chill on the back of his neck, and he knew immediately that something was wrong. He could tell by the widening of G's eyes that G could sense it too. As a sword appeared in the fan's hand, G whipped out his pickaxe and knocked the blade aside. The fan's sword, which would have pierced Kat in the stomach, instead stuck into the ground, and G's pickaxe slammed across the fan's head, knocking him to the ground.

Kat's sword was out of her inventory in a flash as the second fan-turned-assailant whipped out a bow and arrow. Kat slashed the bow in half before the player could fire, just as the third assailant pulled a green potion out of her inventory and threw it at G's head. Kat struck the flying bottle out of the air with her sword and the bottle exploded, spraying G and herself with poison. Two slashes later, all three of the fans lay unconscious on the ground.

Stan's senses kicked into overdrive as all over the courtyard, figures hastily pulled black tunics and caps on. Fifteen figures throughout the crowd pulled swords from their inventories, which swiftly changed to the same color as their tunics. In unison, the figures raised the black swords in the air and belted out, "VIVA LA NOCTEM!"

Stan immediately recognized that, whatever this was, it was not random. This was planned, this was organized, and this was dangerous. The figures surged forward and converged toward the center of the courtyard. The party-goers sprinted away from the black-robed figures, screaming in terror. Stan reached into his inventory and slung his bow across his back, put his quiver of arrows at his side, and held his diamond axe in his hands. He saw that two of the figures were rushing toward him, and he prepared to engage their black blades in combat.

However, Stan was totally caught off guard when the two figures jammed their black swords into their sheathes and whipped out more potions, both green and dark purple ones. Stan realized in horror that these were Potions of Poison and Harming. In a matter of seconds, four potions flew through the air toward Stan, and he was forced to hop and skip backward to avoid being caught in the blast radius of the shattering bottles.

Stan was uneasy, never having fought against players who used potions as weapons before. Taking what he found to be the logical approach, Stan drew his bow. The string of his bow twanged twice, and an arrow flew into each of the dark figures' tunics. Unfazed, the two players drew bright red potions from their inventory and in one swig downed the entire bottle. The effect was instantaneous. The arrows popped from the chestplates, leaving only a small hole in the tunic in their places.

Stan was shocked. What was this? Who were these players, where did they get all these potions, and how did they learn to fight with them so well? Stan, desperate as more Potions of Poison and Harming flew his way, looked around for help. He realized with a jolt that all the high-ranking officials of Element City, all his friends, were now engaged in combat with these players. He was equally alarmed to see that all the mysterious players fought using potions, keeping even master sword fighters like DZ from getting in close enough to use their skills.

As Stan drew his axe to engage his attackers at close range, he reminded himself that he had to be careful. He had no idea where these players came from or who they were, but they were clearly in the order of assassins. That meant that besides escaping the attack and staying alive, Stan had an obligation to take these players prisoner. If he killed the players or let them escape, they would never be interrogated and Stan would never find out why they had attacked him.

Stan ducked another Potion of Harming, and he slammed the butt end of his axe into the thrower's head. The player, whose eyes were barely visible under a ninja mask and black leather cap, looked stunned. He fell to the ground at Stan's feet, just as Stan felt a sting on his unarmored back. As he cringed, Stan realized that he had been hit with a Potion of Harming from another assassin. Stan spun around just as the attacker was about to throw another potion. Stan ducked the bottle, and he swung his axe blade under the attacker's legs, knocking him to the ground. Stan surged forward and stepped on the player's chest, pinning his throwing hand to the ground with his axe.

"Okay," said Stan, breathing heavily. The potion stain on his unprotected back was burning, intensifying his rage. "Who are you people, and why are you attacking us?"

There was no hesitation. The attacker, with his free hand, drew a purple potion from his inventory at light speed and poured the entire contents down his throat. There was a quick shudder, and the attacker's hand went limp, the empty bottle rolling to the side. His items burst about him in a ring, a sure indicator that the attacker had died.

Stan looked around and saw that like himself, all of his friends had bested the attackers. The black-robed forms now all lay on the ground. In the hands of each of them were the glints of empty glass bottles.

Stan was stunned. What motivation could these players possibly have had that they would rather die than be captured? Stan looked down and realized that one of the attackers was not dead, just unconscious. *Well, I'm sure he'll be able to explain this to us*, thought Stan as he dragged him by the knees over to the others.

Kat and G were each drinking a Potion of Regeneration to counter the poison that had exploded in their faces. Kat was using another potion to heal her dog, Rex (who had appeared from nowhere to defend his master). Bob was using a Potion of Healing to mend a burn that a Potion of Harming had left on Ivanhoe's side. Besides that, everybody seemed fine.

Five players were rushing over the Element Castle drawbridge. As they approached, Stan recognized them as Blackraven, Councilman Jayden, Archie, the Mechanist, and Gobbleguy. They looked around in shock, disgust, and horror at the black-clad corpses that littered the ground, and the empty potion bottles beside them.

"What happened out here?" asked Gobbleguy, his face stricken with worry.

Stan explained, "We were having an after-party to celebrate the Zombies winning the Spleef match, when out of nowhere a few of the fans tried to kill Kat. Then a bunch of other players pulled out black caps, tunics, and swords, and tried to kill the rest of us."

"Wait, they yelled something before that, didn't they?" asked DZ.

"Yeah, they yelled 'Viva la Noctem,'" said Charlie.

Jayden's and Archie's faces morphed into alarm. "Did you say . . . they yelled 'Viva la Noctem,' and then they tried to kill you?" asked Archie.

"Yeah," said Kat. "Why? Does that mean anything to you guys?"

"Oh, boy . . . yes it does," said Jayden, pressing his hands together, sweat accumulating on his forehead. "You know how Archie and I said we had business yesterday?"

"Yeah . . . ," said G slowly. The two of them had had to leave the council meeting early because of it.

"Well, we went to a Noctem Alliance rally in the Residential District," said Jayden.

"You did *what*?" shouted Stan, taken aback.

"Yeah," said Archie. "We went undercover there. We wanted to know more about the group, you know, check out whether or not they were just a protesting group, or something more threatening."

"And what did you find?" asked Bill. Stan was dreading the answer.

"The guy speaking there said that the upper-level citizens of Element City deserve better than to share the streets with what they called 'lower-level trash,'" said Archie.

"Yeah, well, we know that's what the views of that group are, they've made that very clear from the get-go," said Charlie. "But what does that have to do with what happened today?"

"That's just it! The guy at the rally said that the Noctem

Freedom Fighters—that's what he called them—must be willing to go to any lengths to preserve their ideals. The rally finished with the leader doing that chant. The entire rally started chanting." A shadow crossed his face as he said the phrase once again.

"*Viva la Noctem*. The motto of the Noctem Alliance."

CHAPTER 4
VIVA LA NOCTEM

There was stunned silence. Stan could not believe what he was hearing. The attempts to kill him and his friends . . . the black tunics . . . the chant . . . it seemed clear to Stan that the players who had tried to kill them tonight were working for the Noctem Alliance.

"Are you serious right now?" wailed DZ in despair.

"Hold up, DZ, don't jump to conclusions," said Gobbleguy quickly. "It is very possible that these attacks were a result of the Noctem Alliance, and at this point it may seem like that's the only explanation. However, let me remind you that we cannot know this for sure until the attackers have stood trial. For all we know, these people could have been trying to frame the Noctem Alliance."

"How are they going to stand trial?" asked Blackraven, gesturing to the corpses around him. "They all killed themselves rather than allow themselves to be captured."

"Not all of them," Stan and Kat said at the same time. Stan looked down at the would-be-assassin who he had knocked unconscious with the butt of his axe.

"Four of them weren't killed," said Kat. "Stan knocked one out, and G and I knocked out three more. When they come to, we can have them stand trial in the name of their co-conspirators."

"We'd better strip them of their stuff, though," added Ben, "or else they'll just try to kill themselves when they come to."

"Good idea," said Kat, giving him a smile, which he returned. Stan noticed G instinctively edge a little closer to Kat.

"Okay then," said Stan. "Charlie, come with me and clean up the items these guys dropped. Bill, Ben, Bob, and DZ, you take these four." He jerked his thumb at the four remaining black figures, the others having vanished. "Bring them down to the jailhouse, but strip them of their items first. The rest of you, go down to the courthouse and let them know that we have four assassins who attempted to kill us, and we need to have an emergency trial. Okay, let's go."

And with that, Rex, Ivanhoe, and all the players went off in their respective directions.

By that evening, the Elementia courthouse was prepped for what people were calling the biggest trial of all time. Indeed, since Stan had come to power on the server, this was the first attempt by anybody to attack him. The trial of those responsible was extremely important.

All those necessary for the trial, which was to take place in the Avery Memorial Courthouse, were present. The four surviving conspirators sat side by side, inside a machine designed by the Mechanist that restrained their movement.

Stan sat in the middle chair of the Panel of Judgment, with four members of the council on each side of him. Bill, Ben, and Bob stood at attention at the base of the podium on which the Panel of Judgment was sitting. As the chiefs of police, it was their job to call in their forces if anything bad should happen.

Ben stepped forward and, after opening statements and taking a roll call of the council members, he spoke out. "You four players before me, who have given their names as Arnold S, Stewart, Lilac, and Roachboy, you are hereby charged with the crimes of attempted murder and terrorist activities. Do any of you plead innocent to any of these charges?"

"No," came the reply. Completely in unison.

Stan's eyebrows flew up. The Mechanist had designed the machine holding the suspects so they could hear the members of the Panel of Judgment, but not each other. Somehow, though, they had all answered Ben's question at exactly the same time.

"In that case, I find you guilty of all charges. You are to be interrogated by Mecha11, and then, depending on how you cooperate, you will either be given a painless death by lethal consumption, or be imprisoned for life in Brimstone Prison."

"We will not speak," came the reply, again in complete synchronization. "And we would rather die than bear witness against our noble leader, Lord Tenebris of the Noctem Alliance."

Stan leaped to his feet. "So you *are* with the Noctem Alliance! Where are you organized? Who is Lord Tenebris?"

The reply never came. All four of the co-conspirators smiled, again in perfect harmony. Suddenly, in a rush of clicks and whirs, the whole detainment machine sunk into the ground, freeing the four players. The Mechanist's jaw dropped. He had been standing by the levers that controlled the machine the entire time, and he hadn't touched them. More incredibly, the four players, who had previously been searched thoroughly and were holding nothing, drew Potions of Harming out of their inventory and raised them to their mouths.

Stan bellowed in rage, and the police threw a storm of Potions of Slowness at the assassins to knock them out before they could drink their potions. But it was too late. The four assassins downed their potions in one gulp, and gave out one last valiant shout of, "VIVA LA NOCTEM!" The four hit the ground face-down at the same time. To be safe, the soldiers and police surrounded the four bodies, weapons at the ready should they be faking death, but when the four assassins disappeared, all doubt vanished.

As the panel started buzzing like bees, urgently discussing the implications of this latest turn of events, Stan's face showed only grim resolve. He was mortified that this chain of horrific events should happen to him, to his people. He was furious that a new threat had arrived even before the last of King Kev's supporters had been caught. Stan would not allow the Noctem Alliance to grow into an organization similar to the reign of King Kev. This time, Stan was determined to nip it in the bud.

The next day, Stan, on his first Proclamation Day of his second term as president, did just that. The court had decided with no doubt that the Noctem Alliance was supporting these assassins, and after a hastily organized council meeting, the Noctem Alliance had been pegged as a terrorist organization. When the citizens had gathered at the foot of Element Castle, Stan announced the new law, which had been implemented unanimously by the council.

"From this day forward, it is illegal for anybody in Elementia to be a member of, or to be associated with, or to be sympathetic toward the terrorist group called the Noctem Alliance. This organization has tried to kill me as well as your councilmen, and they are opposed to equality for lower-level players. Any information regarding the Noctem Alliance and its members should be given to a soldier or policeman, and your help in defeating this threat is greatly appreciated."

The cheers that reverberated over the packed courtyard seemed hollow and empty to Stan. He couldn't help but wonder how many of those in the crowd were really advocates of the Noctem Alliance, whose applause of adulation were nothing more than facades, hiding true feelings of hatred, malevolence, and spite.

Across the server, away from the fertile plains and forests of the motherland of Elementia, past the jungle, across the vast Ender Desert, sat the tundra, a dark plain biome of frigid badlands where no civilization had ever taken hold. There, deep in the most inhospitable stretches of the barren wasteland, another proclamation was imminent. If you looked hard enough through the snow that whipped the face and stung the skin, that kept the sky black even at high noon, you could see it. Indeed, there was a society out in the tundra, which at the moment was nothing more than one grand building, constructed of the finest stone brick and spruce wood. Makeshift dirt shelters speckled the permafrost surrounding the one ornate structure.

A total of about a hundred and twenty players stood clustered at the foot of the brick building. The wooden balcony above them sheltered them from the snow, and the torches on the walls provided heat. Though the warmth was faint, it was still a welcome break from the cold that these players had endured for months on end.

As they heard footsteps on the wood above them, the

rabble of a hundred and twenty frozen players quickly rushed out from below the balcony, forming the rows they were expected to be in when addressed by their superiors.

Now that they had left the warm haven of the balcony, the players could see the three players standing on the balcony. These were the three generals of the Noctem Alliance, the organization to which all these players had pledged themselves. Barely visible in the torchlight, the players could make out the brown face and ornate armor of General Leonidas at the back right, the giant, hulking shape of General Minotaurus at the back left, and the white-robed form of General Caesar, head of the Noctem Freedom Fighters, at the front. Caesar opened his mouth and spoke.

"My brothers and sisters of the Noctem Alliance, I address you today bearing good tidings. The fifteen of our own that we have sent into Element City have submitted to the leaders of Elementia. They revealed their allegiance to our great leader, Lord Tenebris, before sending themselves in the same way as our great martyr, King Kev of Elementia. The beginning phase of our plan to retake Element City for our own is a success!"

As they were preprogrammed to do on such a rare occasion that news as good as this came their way, the hundred and twenty members of the Noctem Freedom Fighters gave the Noctem Alliance victory chant in perfect unison: "VIVA LA NOCTEM!"

"Furthermore, our spy within the hierarchy of the Element City government has informed me that Stan2012 has declared affiliation with the Noctem Alliance illegal. In their noble sacrifice, our brothers and sisters have instilled a germ of fear of the name of the Noctem Alliance. This germ shall multiply and spread within the populace, and shall before long infect the entirety of Element City!"

Again, the chant rang out in unison through the whistling winds of the never-ending blizzard: "VIVA LA NOCTEM!"

"Besides this, I bear news of even greater importance: our beloved leader, Lord Tenebris, has informed me that the construction of the Specialty Base is underway. In time, this shall spell doom for Stan2012 and the rest of the leadership of Element City, leaving the plot of land called Element City, which is rightfully ours, ripe for the picking!"

"VIVA LA NOCTEM!"

"It is in light of these joyous developments that I announce it is time to put our second phase of warfare into action! I now call all members of the second battalion of the Noctem Freedom Fighters to mobilize, for tomorrow, you follow General Leonidas into combat in the motherland of Elementia. The rest of you are dismissed. Good night, my brothers and sisters! Long live Lord Tenebris! Long live the Noctem Alliance!"

"VIVA LA NOCTEM!" the Freedom Fighters belted out for

the last time, before running into their dirt shacks to prepare themselves for battle.

Caesar turned and retreated to the warmth of the building, followed by Leonidas and Minotaurus, who had to duck to enter the room.

It was pleasant inside. Books sat on shelves all over the walls, and a fire roaring on a Netherrack base projected warmth into the room around them. The walls were of stone brick, and the three generals' prized weapons—Leonidas's bow, Minotaurus's double-ended battle-axe, and Caesar's diamond sword—hung in frames on the mantel.

Leonidas and Caesar sat down on chairs facing the fire. Minotaurus spoke, "Excuse me, Caesar, but I will be back. It is time for me to tend to my potato farm," and walked out the side door to attend to his hobby, accidentally breaking the wooden door off its hinges as it slammed behind him.

As Leonidas and Caesar stared into the fire, neither of them conversed, but both knew that there were unspoken words hanging in the air. It was a full minute before Caesar turned to his colleague and spoke, "Well, Leonidas, you clearly have something on your mind. What is it?"

Leonidas said nothing at first. He was lost in a train of long, confusing, and never-ending thoughts. At last, he turned to Caesar, and voiced the most pressing of his concerns.

"Caesar . . . do ya remember the prisoners' village?"

Caesar stood up and threw back his head. "Oh, for heaven's sake, Leonidas, don't tell me you're still on about that village!"

"No, of course not," said Leonidas quickly, quite unsure of whether he was lying not only to Caesar but also to himself. "We did what had to be done, I wouldn't have done it any other way, except for . . ." Leonidas chose his words carefully; he did not want to see Caesar upset. "Why is it that we didn't even ask those players if they wanted to join us? I don't know, but it's kinda possible that we may have killed some potential allies."

"Rubbish, Leonidas," spat Caesar, shaking his head in contempt at Leonidas's apparent foolishness. "There was nothing for us in that village. Those people in the prisoners' village had been living on nothing for longer than was worth it. Trust me, we did all of them a mercy."

"Yeah, yeah, that's right," said Leonidas, his voice falsely cheery. "Yeah . . . there just woulda been more suffering if we'd left any of 'em alive."

But the more Leonidas thought of his corporal's reports of the carnage and slaughter the Noctem Alliance had committed in the prisoners' village, the more Leonidas was reassuring himself that that was not true.

CHAPTER 5
THE TENNIS MACHINE

Although Stan did not know exactly what the repercussions of the attack by the Noctem agents would be, he certainly did not expect that life would carry on as usual. And yet, that's exactly what happened. The only significant difference in the daily flow of things was the cessation of rallies and protests by the Noctem Alliance.

"Don't you think it's weird?" Stan asked, a week after he'd banned the Noctem Alliance, as he walked out of the castle courtyard and onto the bustling main road lined with stores alongside Kat and Charlie. "I mean, these guys in black try to kill us, and they say they're with the Noctem Alliance before committing suicide, and then there's nothing for a week? What sense does that make?"

"It is odd," replied Charlie slowly. "You'd think there would be some aftermath. But it's like the Noctem Alliance completely vanished off the map. You don't think they're plotting something, do you?"

That thought sat unpleasantly in Stan's stomach, and he was about to respond when Kat cut him off, and said in a superior drawl, "I think you two are reading too much into it. The Noctem Alliance was just a bunch of stuck-up, rich brats who didn't like that they had to share with the lower-levels. They whined and had a tantrum about it, but some of them took it a step too far."

"Well, if that's the case, why haven't they retaliated yet?" asked Charlie.

"Because they're a bunch of cowards," replied Kat, a note of disgust on her tongue. "They couldn't get what they wanted through protesting, so the twenty or so of them who cared more than was good for them tried to attack us. They were okay with dying, because they didn't think life would be worth it if they couldn't get what they wanted. That's why they were willing to kill themselves, and that's why they had such good supplies, because they're spoiled upper-levels. And now that those few radicals are dead, none of them left care enough to die for the cause of the Alliance."

"I guess that makes sense," said Stan, nodding. "It is true that it's really only the rich and upper-level people in this city who are against equality now. Well, besides the war prisoners we took from the battle."

"And they're not in any position to do anything about it, they're all locked up in Brimstone," added Charlie. He was referring to the highest-end prison in Elementia, situated in the remnants of the Nether Fortress that RAT1 had blown up before the Battle for Elementia.

"Exactly," said Kat. "Trust me, Stan, I think now that you've made it illegal, we aren't gonna be hearing any more from the Noctem Alliance. On the other hand, there are probably going to be more rich people sulking in their houses about equality now that they can't run around in black tunics whining about it."

Stan chuckled. "Yeah, you're right, Kat, I'm just overthinking it."

Charlie agreed. "So, what are we gonna do on our day off, guys? Let's make it count."

"Ooh, ooh! I know!" said Kat, jumping up and down in excitement. "How about we borrow Ivanhoe and have him defecate on the steps of the Avery Memorial Courthouse?"

"Kat, I built that courthouse as a memorial to my friend who sacrificed his life to save me from King Kev! I am not going to let a pig poop on the front steps!" said Stan in exasperation as Charlie laughed. Stan seriously wondered whether she was joking.

"Fine. Ooh! Better idea!" said Kat, her mouth wide open in an elated grin. "Let's go over to the Apothecary Memorial Fountain . . . and have Ivanhoe defecate in the water!"

"NO!" cried Stan as Charlie clutched his sides in his hysterics. "The Apothecary saved my life too!"

"Good point. Ooh! I know!" cried Kat, her face glowing with amusement as she glanced at Charlie.

"Does it involve a pig taking a dump on something I built to honor my dead friends?" Stan asked, taking in just how ridiculous it was that he should have to ask such a question, as Charlie rolled on the ground laughing. Prolonged exposure to Oob the NPC villager had made Charlie susceptible to laughter at these kinds of jokes, a fact that Kat used to her advantage often.

"Wait, you have more dead friends? Well, I suppose we could go down to the Adorian Village or to Steve Memorial Farm . . ."

"Do you have a real idea, Kat?" Stan asked as Charlie pulled himself up and regained his composure.

"Okay, okay. The Mechanist told me he's unveiling his new machine today!" exclaimed Kat.

"You mean the one he's been building in the park?" Charlie asked. "That's being finished today?"

"That's the one," replied Kat. "I'm thinking we should spend the first part of the day seeing whatever that is."

"Sounds like a plan!" said Stan, and Charlie nodded his approval. Together, the three friends turned and walked in the direction of the park where the Mechanist had spent all his free time for weeks, building a mysterious contraption. On the way, the talk turned to the Spleef Tournament.

"Oh, there's no doubt about it, DZ is the best player on our team," Kat assured Stan. "He was brought down by a lucky shot in that last match, I would be shocked if something like that ever happened again."

"Regardless of who's the best player, there's no denying you three are the best team, right?" asked Stan. "I mean, you guys did those combo attacks like they were second nature, and the other team barely did anything!"

"Yes, and you'll notice that we moved on, and they didn't," said Kat with a grimace. "We've got a long, hard road ahead of us, Stan. We only have two matches left, and we're gonna have to put our noses to the grindstone if we want to have a chance of beating our next opponent."

"Who is your next opponent, by the way?" asked Charlie. "I know that the only teams left in the tournament are the Bats, the Skeletons, the Ocelots, and you guys. But who are you up against next?"

"The Ocelots," replied Kat. "I think that of the four of us, they're probably tied with us and the Skeletons for the best. I don't think the Skeletons will have any problems beating the Bats."

"You can't know that," said Stan reasonably. "There's always a chance the Bats get lu . . . oh, man," he breathed as the three of them walked into a shadow and paused.

They were standing in the shadow of a giant box in the middle of the public park. The front was a square, nine blocks high by fifteen blocks long, composed entirely of redstone lamps. Protruding from this was a black box that extended twenty blocks back and probably contained the redstone wiring of the machine, which Stan assumed extended far underground. The machine was the only thing that extended up from the flat ground of the sunlit courtyard, besides the now dark lampposts that lined the sides of the gravel roads that crossed the grass park. As such, the machine commanded a good deal of attention from those strolling through the park.

"Beautiful, ain't she?" came the smooth voice that Stan recognized as the Mechanist's. He was leaning on a black wool table in front of the machine. On this table were two levers and a button.

"Man, Mechanist," said Charlie as the trio walked over to him. "I don't even know what this thing does yet and I'm already impressed!"

"Thanks, Charlie," said the Mechanist, looking up at the towering electric marvel with a smile. "This thing's my baby. Easily the most impressive thing I've built since the redstone supercomputer."

"What does it do?" asked Stan, his interest piqued.

"Well, how'd you like to test it out? Stan, you take the lever on the left, Charlie, the one on the right," said the Mechanist, and he gestured to the two levers, which the boys ran over to and enthusiastically clutched.

"Now, press the button, and let the magic begin," said the Mechanist, stepping back next to Kat as the two of them prepared to watch the invention on its maiden run. Stan watched in awe as the screen of the mechanism flashed on and off at strobe speed before settling on what could only be the game screen. A single light shined in the center of the screen, while two vertical lines three lights high glowed on opposite sides.

From somewhere within the mechanized obelisk, a series of note block chimes rang out in a catchy melody, and the Mechanist said, with glee in his voice, "Push the levers up and down."

Stan pushed up on the lever on his side, and the effect was instantaneous. The line on his side of the screen moved to the top in a fluid animation. Stan saw the line on the other side of the screen move downward. Charlie had pulled down on his lever simultaneously. Stan now realized what this game was. He had his hand firmly grasped on the lever when the dot of light in the center of the screen flew upward and to the right, then bounced off the top of the screen and came down to the left. Stan pulled down on his lever and the line of lights on his side sunk down to his side of the screen. The bouncing ball of light struck the line of Stan's lights and ricocheted off toward Charlie's line as Charlie maneuvered it to return the ball toward Stan.

"You made Pong!" exclaimed Charlie in wonder as he scored his first point on Stan, and a light lit up the top of his side indicating that a point had been earned.

"That I did," replied the Mechanist. "I call it my Tennis Machine. Was absolute torture developing a point-tracking system, but I think I did all right. What say you guys?"

"This is awesome!" replied Stan.

"Yeah, I can't believe you figured all this out! Is there nothing you can't do?" asked Charlie.

"That is what I like to tell myself. Mostly for morale, but still," said the Mechanist with a smirk.

"Well, you're right," said Stan, devoting his last ounce of attention to the response before becoming totally engrossed in the game. It was a blowout. Charlie was exceptionally skilled at the game, which was, indeed, a perfect replica of Pong. After the first game, Kat took Stan's place, and she was much more closely matched to Charlie than Stan was. In fact, she was tied with him, and was about to score when a shout rang out from behind Stan.

"Hey, Kat! What're you doing?"

Kat whipped around to face G, ignoring the fact that Charlie had scored on her and won the game. "G? What are you doing here?"

"Looking for you!" replied G. He sounded irritated. "You promised that you'd spend some time with me soon. And, well, it's your day off. Here I am." And he opened his arms in front of him. Charlie rolled his eyes as he gave up his spot on the machine to two pedestrians who asked for a turn to play the game.

"Wait a second. G, today isn't your day off. Why aren't you with the council?" Kat said.

"Oh, I changed it so that I could spend the entire day with you," said G with a grin. "Frankly, Jayden, Archie, and DZ seemed a little upset. But who cares? Spending time with you is more important than stupid political squabbles."

"G, those 'stupid political squabbles' are actually really important, if you haven't noticed! It's nice that you want to spend time with me, but you can't just ditch work because of it!" moaned Kat. She seemed legitimately upset.

"Whoa, Kat! I thought you'd be happy! Do you not want to see me or something? 'Cause if that's the case, then . . ."

"No, that's not the case, G! I do like spending time with you, but you have to admit that we have been seeing each other a lot lately, and to cut work so that you can see me more . . ."

And the two of them went on and on. Charlie simply looked amused, occasionally giving a sigh or an eye roll of amusement. Stan, on the other hand, was slowly coming to a realization.

Ever since the incident with the Noctem Alliance had been put to rest, the biggest issues that faced Stan today were Kat's overly clingy boyfriend and an argument starting about whose turn it was on the Tennis Machine. The Grand

Republic of Elementia was now on the threshold of the greatest period of peace and prosperity that DZ, Blackraven, and the other older players could remember. Just in the past week, Charlie had discovered an underground mine rich in diamonds, gold, and iron. The day afterward, the railway to Blackstone had been extended to reach the Southeastern Mountains, and a glut of coal from the region was inbound.

As all this recent success crashed into Stan like a wave, he allowed himself, for the first time that he could remember, to give himself credit. In truth, from the time he had joined Elementia, he had just done what seemed natural, and he had ended up as the leader of the whole server. However, it was just now that Stan realized he had done an exceedingly good job in creating a country that he himself would gladly be a citizen of, a country of justice. And it was all due to the efforts of him and his friends.

As Stan stepped forward to break up the argument among the players in line for the Tennis Machine, and Charlie did the same with Kat and G, he couldn't help but feel a sense of pride. He looked around the sunny courtyard with a pleasantly liberating feeling that all was well, and nothing could go wrong today.

Although Leonidas still wasn't sure what the point of the upcoming offensive was, at least he was finally comfortable.

The steamy, humid climate of the jungle was much more pleasing to him than the whipping frigid winds of Nocturia. Bushwhacking through the deep underbrush with an iron sword, followed by five men trooping behind him in unison, Leonidas felt more at home than he had in a long, long time.

Leonidas glanced at the redstone compass in his hand, and he rubbed the condensation off the glass face to see the red needle. The needle indicated that they were going the right way, and the sight he saw when he burst out of the bushes confirmed this.

Situated in a small valley, cleared of trees, was a little house made of wood, with a small farm at the back. Leonidas recognized this house. He had come here months before, back when his partners Geno and Becca were still alive. They had searched this very house for the player who had since become president of the Grand Republic of Elementia. Leonidas knew the house was full of booby traps, so looting it would be more trouble than it was worth.

Leonidas knew the house would be empty. Its owner had been killed in the same battle as Geno, Becca, and King Kev. And so Leonidas led his men past this house. He knew the house was situated on the most direct path between Nocturia and the Elementia Jungle Base, and indeed, they only had to walk for another ten minutes before the outpost came into view.

The Elementia Jungle Base was located within a jungle temple, an ancient naturally generated structure of mossy cobblestone and stone brick, on the side of a hill. The trees and the cliff face created a natural defense. Leonidas signaled to his men to halt as he noticed the Elementia soldiers standing on patrol atop the base, bows raised. Leonidas had anticipated this. He had listened to an entire strategy session by Caesar indicating the most efficient way to attack this base, as described by the spy within Element City.

He gestured to his two frontmost soldiers, two privates, to circle the outpost through the trees, to the left and right. The two fighters pulled off their black tunics and pulled on their green ones, expertly dyed the exact same color as the jungle leaves. They set off in opposite directions, preparing to sneak in close and fill the base with gas at Leonidas's command. Meanwhile, Leonidas led his remaining three men straight toward the front of the temple.

As the players approached the jungle temple, with another two circling to the sides, Leonidas's breath began to quicken, his blood began to pump faster and faster. All the moral and strategic objections that he had to this plan to take the Jungle Base seemed to diminish as he got closer and closer to the battle. From the time he was new on the server, this had been what he had lived for. Leonidas was a fighter—he always was, and he always would be.

He pulled out a shovel with sweaty hands and led his party tunneling the last bit of the way to the outpost. Reemerging in a blind spot pressed right up against the wall of the outpost, the guards could not see the soldiers pulling themselves out of the ground. The timing was precise. No sooner had the last of his men pulled themselves up out of the hole than a cloud of noxious gray gas burst from the open window above them.

Leonidas and his team acted almost robotically as they pulled the Potions of Swiftness from their inventories and downed them in a single gulp. Instantly, Leonidas's senses were charged to the highest level of acuteness, his muscles primed for the ultimate battling stature. This effect of the potion would make him and his men invulnerable to the effects of the toxic Potion of Slowness that now hung in the air within the base. His pulse beating in anticipation, Leonidas scurried up the vines on the side of the base and drew his glimmering bow. Immediately, he downed three of the guards with flaming arrows as his men followed him into the base.

As his men swarmed the temple, Leonidas noticed that each one of the dead men's spilled inventories contained a book, the same book. The covers showed that it was *The Constitution of the Republic of Elementia* by Bookbinder55. Leonidas sneered. How noble, he thought, that each of these men carried the constitution of their country with them on their scouting missions. What a pity that it did not help them in the least against the supreme power of the Noctem Alliance. Then, in disgust, Leonidas tossed one of the books into the air and shot it against the wall with another flaming arrow.

Leonidas had been conflicted about this attack before, but that was all gone now. He knew nothing but an all-consuming taste for war, as the potion erased all his inhibitions. And with that, Leonidas continued the slaughter, leaving his inner compassion as useless, pathetic, and forgotten as the burning constitution of Elementia pinned on the temple wall.

CHAPTER 6

ELEMENTIA DAY

The next morning, Stan looked up and gave a groggy glance out the window. When he saw the red and blue wool blocks decorating the tops of the courtyard wall, he immediately jumped out of bed—it was an important day. As he walked downstairs from his room to eat breakfast in the castle common room, Stan remembered that the previous night, the moon had been barely a sliver. It would be dark tonight.

The common room, with its paintings, a fire in the Netherrack fireplace, and chairs in a circle around the room, was also decorated with red and blue wool. This was probably Archie's work. He always did love Elementia Day more than anybody else, despite the fact that it had been Blackraven's idea to start the tradition almost immediately after the creation of the republic.

DZ and Charlie were already awake, and they were sitting by the refrigerator, eating today's breakfast (prepared by the Imperial Butlers), which turned out to be pumpkin pie.

"Ah, Stam! Hubba Erumendaduh, ol behee!" said DZ through a mouthful of pastry. "Surry," he added as he gave an enormous swallow. "I said, Ah, Stan! Happy Elementia Day, old buddy!"

"Thanks, DZ," said Stan with a smile. "I can't believe it's really been four months."

"Four months ago today," replied DZ, imitating Archie's deep announcing voice, which he would use at the ceremony in the park later that evening, "the moon was dark, as it is tonight. On that day, our beloved president, Stan2012, defeated the tyrannical King Kev in battle and created the Grand Republic of Elementia. Now, four new moons later, we celebrate that victory!"

"That's actually pretty good." Charlie laughed. "What kind of stuff does Archie have planned for this Elementia Day?"

"Well, there's the usual pig races, sparring tournament, and reenactment of the battle," said DZ, "but I think we all know that the highlight of today is gonna be the Mechanist's new Tennis Machine."

"Yeah, you're probably right, but I gotta say, I'm excited about the races too," said Charlie. "I put down a big bet against Kat saying that Bob is gonna win the race."

"Really? What about Zoey and Porky?" Stan asked, referring to an acclaimed racer and her pig.

"Yeah, that's a good point, Charlie," said DZ. "Those two've won that race every Elementia Day so far, and this is Bob's first time. What makes you think he's gonna win?"

"'Cause it's Bob!" replied Charlie. "He's got a stronger bond with Ivanhoe than any I've seen, and that includes Kat and Rex."

"To that note," replied Stan, "where is she, anyway?" Kat

was usually the first one up in the morning, and none of them had seen her yet today.

"I saw her leaving the castle really early this morning with G. I can't say she looked very happy about it. He looked hyped, though," answered DZ.

Charlie sighed. "Those two . . . they're just . . ."

"I know, man," DZ cut in, shaking his head. "Some people just don't have any class," he added wisely.

"DZ, you have pumpkin flesh dripping from your left nostril," Stan pointed out as he pressed the refrigerator button. A pumpkin pie popped out, which he caught in midair.

"I really don't think it's Kat's fault, though," said Charlie as DZ wiped the orange goo from his upper lip. "G is just overly clingy. I honestly don't get why she puts up with him."

"Well, I think she's just . . . ," started Stan, but he was cut off when Archie burst into the room, his chest heaving from lack of breath.

"Ah, Archie! All set for the big day, are we?" asked DZ as he wiped the pumpkin goo off his finger and onto his pants.

"Yeah, but that's not why I'm here," said Archie in one breath.

Stan suddenly stood up straight. He knew something was wrong. "Archie, what happened?" he asked.

"Ben just sent me a messenger. Apparently when he sent a scout to report to him on the condition at the Jungle Base last night, the scout came back and told him the base had been hijacked."

"WHAT?" Stan asked, dropping the rest of his pie on the ground. "What happened? Who took over the base?"

"Well, the scout said that when he approached the base, he was shot at by figures in black tunics and caps that were patrolling the watchtower on top."

The room was filled for a moment by a stunned silence. Then DZ threw his hands in the air and yelled, "Oh, come on!"

"Do you mean to tell me that our Jungle Base was taken over by the Noctem Alliance?" asked Charlie, his face reflecting his shell-shocked disbelief.

"It would seem so," replied Archie gravely. "It looks like not only is the Alliance still alive, but it's powerful."

"It's not possible!" cried Stan. His stomach had knotted up, and he was beginning to sweat as he started to think about what this information meant. "The Jungle Base is one of our most fortified! All twenty of the guards in there were skilled fighters with enough armor and gear to fight at maximum capacity!"

"That's not all," added Archie, the fear in his voice almost tangible. "One of the Noctem soldiers was Leonidas, Stan."

"What the what!" shouted DZ. "Leonidas is dead! Wasn't he killed at the battle along with the rest of RAT1? Right? Stan?"

But Stan was staring at Charlie in horror, who returned

with a stare of absolute astonishment. Their eyes locked, and it was clear that they were both thinking the same thing. The military had, after investigation, concluded that Leonidas had been killed in Becca's TNT trap at the Battle for Elementia. The police had determined the same thing. There was only one source in the kingdom who had stated that Leonidas was still alive, a source Charlie had talked Stan into disregarding.

"You weren't just hallucinating that night, were you, Stan," said Charlie. It was not a question. Even Stan, who had brushed off the nocturnal visit by Sally's voice as nothing but a delusion brought on by fatigue, now knew perfectly well that everything he had heard was indeed Sally trying to contact him from beyond the server.

"What are you talking about?" asked Archie, in a nervous, alarmed voice.

"Yeah, what are you talking about, Charlie?" asked DZ, his face taking on an uncharacteristically freaked-out look.

"Stan . . ."

Stan leaped up. That voice did not belong to Charlie. It did not belong to Archie or DZ, either. And, based on a quick look around the room, he was the only one to hear it.

"What?" Charlie asked, looking at Stan in panic. Stan paid no notice to any of them. He was already sprinting down the hallway, taking a sharp left, and bolting into his room. He needed this conversation to be private.

“Sally? Is that you?”

“Stan . . . I don’t . . . much . . . time . . .” Sally’s voice from nowhere was punctuated by bursts of static, and Stan could barely make out what she was saying. “Noctem . . . Alliance . . . alive . . .”

“I know Sally, I know!” cried Stan. “They just took over our Jungle Base!”

“I know . . . but . . . another . . . attack . . . inbound . . .” Her voice was barely audible over the now loud static. It was as if somebody was trying to jam her signal.

“Don’t . . . know . . . heard . . . fragments . . . tennis . . . danger . . . losing . . . I . . . contact . . . you . . . later . . .” There was a burst of static, and then a pop, and Sally was gone.

Stan’s head was spinning. The Noctem Alliance had attacked them, and another attack was incoming. And she had also said something about the Tennis Machine! What did that mean? Regardless, after the attack on the Jungle Base that apparently was led by Leonidas, Stan had no qualms about deciphering the information given to him by Sally, and acting on it.

“Stan, what happened?” Archie asked when Stan walked back into the common room. “Charlie told us that you’ve been in contact with Sally? How is that? She’s dead, Stan.”

“I know that, but somehow she’s found a way to partially hack her way back on to the server, and I can hear her voice," said Stan, ignoring the looks of skepticism on Archie's and DZ's faces. "She contacted me once before, and told me that Leonidas was alive, and that he and Caesar were raising some kind of force. I thought I was dreaming it at first, but then it turns out that a well-equipped force led by Leonidas just took over the Jungle Base! It can't just be a coincidence."

Archie and DZ were staring at Stan wide-eyed, knowing that he was telling the truth even though they weren't sure how it could be possible.

"Okay, we get that," said Charlie after a moment, "but what did she say to you just then? That is why you ran out, isn't it?"

"Yeah, it is," Stan replied. "She just told me an attack was incoming, and that the Tennis Machine was a danger."

There was a pause. Then . . .

"Are you losing your mind, Stan?" asked DZ.

"Stan, how can the Tennis Machine be a danger? It's just a recreation thing," reasoned Charlie.

"I don't know, I wasn't the one who said it!" yelled Stan.

"Okay, okay, let's disregard that for a second," said Archie. "What was that about an inbound attack?"

"I don't know," said Stan. "Her voice was cut off by static half the time."

"Stan, it'd be nice if your dead girlfriend could be a little less vague," said DZ with an exasperated chuckle.

"Well, seeing as we don't have any real idea what the upcoming attack is, or when it's coming, I say the only thing we can really do is prepare our military," said Charlie. "I'll alert the soldiers to do double duty in patrolling our walls, and I'll send messengers out to tell all our outposts to do the same. DZ, can you go and tell Ben to get the police to step it up, too?"

"Aye aye, Captain," replied DZ, and he stood up and crossed the room to the door that led to the stairwell with the courtyard at the bottom.

"What do you want me to do, Charlie?" asked Archie. Stan's eyebrow twitched. He almost resented that Archie asked for a command from Charlie rather than him. On the other hand, he did feel rather disgruntled at the moment, and it probably showed.

"I want you to go out and finish the preparations," said Charlie with a grin. "We've still got to have Elementia Day, don't we?"

"That we do," boomed Archie, and he swept out of the room after DZ.

"I'm gonna see what I can do to reconnect with Sally," said Stan. "Maybe she can tell us more about this attack."

"Good thinking, Stan," said Charlie as he stood up and went the way of Archie and DZ.

Stan walked out of the common room back to his

quarters, and he lay down on the bed. Stan focused all his being on Sally, hoping there was some iota of chance that she could reconnect with him.

But Sally didn't reconnect with him. Not in his bedroom, not when Archie told him it was time for the celebrations to begin, not during the pig race when Charlie won his bet against Kat that Bob would win, and not during the sparring tournament. Stan found it difficult to think of anything else. It was as if the players in the crowd were on a TV that Stan wasn't really watching.

Stan kept telling himself he wanted to contact Sally for the sake of intelligence on the impending attack. Really, though, the reason was that he wanted nothing more in the world than to hear her voice again. Perhaps, although it seemed impossible, they could discover some way that Sally might rejoin Elementia.

"And now, ladies and gentlemen," boomed Archie's deep voice, cutting through Stan's thoughts like a knife, "President Stan2012 will take the stage for the reenactment of the great battle between himself and the tyrannical King Kev."

Stan sighed. This was perhaps his least favorite part of the ceremonies, yet, for some reason, it tended to be one of the most popular. Although the people of the republic had been loud and rambunctious in the ceremonies all day, the loudest cacophony of cheers and praises rang out now, as Stan climbed the stairs up to the imitation bridge that had been constructed at the center of the park.

The reenactment had only been added last Elementia Day. Blackraven had suggested that it was fitting that the people of Elementia celebrate how their beloved republic came to be, and that Stan himself should play his own part in the play. Stan was still determined to give his people the show they loved, despite how uncomfortable it made him to relive the deaths of his friends.

He looked down the bridge at the actor dressed now as King Kev. It was a different actor this month, Stan noted. Although it was impossible to tell two players with the same skin apart at a glance, it was possible to tell by truly examining their eyes. Every player's eyes had a unique gleam to them.

Stan, who had earlier been adorned in diamond armor with two iron axes strapped to his back just as they had been the day he had challenged King Kev, drew one of these axes now. The king's eyebrow twitched, as scripted, and Stan charged down the stone bridge toward the King Kev doppelgänger. The king's sword was drawn, as was necessary, and, at the right point, Stan threw the axe at the actor's head. The actor dive-rolled to the side and was then supposed to raise his diamond sword to counter the downward blow from Stan's axe.

Instead, the actor thrust the sword upward into the handle of Stan's axe and gave it a sharp twist, sending Stan's weapon spiraling to the side, just as the Avery actor grabbed Stan from behind in a full nelson and raised his own diamond sword to Stan's throat.

There was a horrified silence in the crowd for a moment, before screams began to erupt. All throughout the crowd, figures were buttoning on black tunics and pulling on black caps. They held blue-gray Potions of Slowness in their hands. Stan, even with his limited movement, could see that the black figures had enough radius to neutralize the entire crowd of thousands if need be.

The King Kev actor picked up Stan's axe, attached it to his belt, and then picked up his own sword. The instant it touched his hand, the sword darkened to black to match the tunic and cap the actor had pulled on. The King Kev actor cleared his throat, and spoke. "My name is Emerick, corporal of the Noctem Alliance. My agents and I have captured and taken your president hostage. As such, I now claim this city in the name of the Noctem Alliance and its leader, Lord Tenebris."

And through the stunned silence of the crowd around the imitation bridge, all the black figures gave the same unanimous cry that had haunted Stan's nightmares.

"VIVA LA NOCTEM!"

PART

THE DEVILS WITHIN THE WALLS

CHAPTER 7
THE COUP

With the sword held against his neck, Stan could barely breathe, let alone turn his head to see the looks of terror on his citizens' faces. Stan willed himself not to panic. He knew this bold attack by the Noctem Alliance would ultimately be useless.

Even as Stan thought this, arrows flew from the plain-dressed guards Stan had positioned throughout the crowd, an added security measure suggested by Gobbleguy. Stan saw with a painful glance that several of the Noctem troopers who had been holding the crowd at bay with potions had already been felled by arrows, and the rest had disappeared in bursts of fire.

Stan felt the grip around his neck loosen, and he broke out of the Avery actor's chokehold. Spinning around, Stan found him dead on the ground, an arrow protruding from his forehead. Stan lunged sideways and scooped up the dead actor's sword.

"Pursue the attackers!" Stan bellowed at the guards in the crowd, who pocketed their bows and began chasing the remaining attackers, who were fleeing the scene. A small smile crossed Stan's face as he turned his attention to the Noctem corporal named Emerick who, inexplicably, was returning the expression.

This didn't sit well with Stan, and his own smile

vanished. "Why are you smiling?" Stan demanded. "Your troops are dead and your little hostile takeover lasted less than ten seconds. What part of this do you find amusing, exactly?"

Emerick's smile just grew, and in a matter of seconds a low, evil chuckle sounded from the Noctem corporal. Stan suddenly felt a surge of rage toward Emerick and the Noctem Alliance that he served. His attempt to seize power had failed, yet he still found something to be happy about? Was this some sort of trick?

Stan lunged forward, sword in hand, ready to sink it deep into Corporal Emerick, but the corporal feinted backward faster than Stan had ever seen a player move before, and with one jump, he launched himself high over the crowd. A series of black orbs, barely visible against the black sky, flew from Corporal Emerick's hand and hit the ground in a burst of fire. As he disappeared into the smoke from the fire charges, Stan barely made out the faint blue and orange smoke curling off his back.

No! Stan thought. *If he's using Potions of Swiftness and Fire Resistant, how am I gonna catch him?* Corporal Emerick was clearly the head of the operation, and Stan knew that bringing him to trial was imperative. Stan then noticed the possessions of the Avery actor laying on the ground behind him. After a moment of rummaging, Stan found what he was looking for. Wasting no time, he poured the two potions into his mouth, and leaped into the flames after the corporal.

Stan, having never drank the Potion of Swiftness, or QPO, before, was amazed by how lighthearted and free he felt. It was as if he could do no wrong, and he instantly felt that regaining the huge lead Corporal Emerick had taken would be nothing short of easy. Stan recognized the pleasant tickling sensation that came from running through the flames the fire charges had left on the ground.

As Stan burst from the smoke, he saw Corporal Emerick sprinting full speed down the main street, a trail of blue and orange fumes in his wake. Stan followed in pursuit, his own feet feeling like they weighed nothing under the effects of the potion. He soon realized he was not alone. Stan glanced behind him and saw DZ and Archie running alongside him, trailing blue wisps of smoke themselves.

"Hey, Stan!" said Archie, surprising Stan. He hadn't realized the potion enabled them to talk easily while running.

"Hey, Archie," said Stan with a grim smirk. "Sorry all your plans got ruined."

"Honestly, I'm just thankful we all got out alive," Archie replied.

"So nobody got hurt in the attack, then?" asked Stan.

"Nah, our snipers took 'em all down," said DZ. "I gotta say, if this is the Noctem Alliance's idea of an attack, then we really ain't got too much to worry about."

"I'm still getting over the fact that the organization still exists," said Stan, his face reflecting the worry boiling within him. "I gotta be honest, these Noctem guys have shown that they can be both really smart and really rash and dumb."

"That's a good point," said Archie, a frown crossing his skeleton face. "One day they override the redstone circuits of the courthouse, something we still haven't figured out, and the next, they pull something like this? I mean, this was, like, the worst-thought-out offensive of all time!"

"It scares me, to be honest," said Stan, speaking truthfully as they rounded a curve, following the corporal onto the main street of the government district. "When there are inconsistencies like this, it makes it hard to draw patterns. Are these guys from the Noctem Alliance smart or not? And, more important, are they a serious danger to the city?"

"Well, hopefully this little jerk'll give us some answers. Look where he went." DZ smirked, pointing as Emerick disappeared into the front doors of the Avery Memorial Courthouse.

Stan's heart roared in triumph. The courthouse walls were made of obsidian. Corporal Emerick had just trapped himself in the building.

As they ran up the front steps of the courthouse, DZ yelled out, "Here, Stan!" and Stan saw something blue and brown flying out of DZ's hand. Stan caught it and recognized it as his own diamond axe. He nodded a quick thanks to DZ, holding it in his hand as he pocketed the sword he had been carrying. DZ drew out two glowing diamond swords, and Archie drew his bow. The trio burst into the courthouse. Stan reached back without checking his speed and, in one movement, punched a painting off the wall near the door and pulled down the switch hidden behind it. The iron doors of the courthouse slammed shut behind them. Stan heard the mechanical whirrs of various other mechanisms within the building ensuring that escape would be impossible until Stan input the security code.

The effects of the potion were beginning to wear off. Stan, Archie, and DZ walked into the main courtroom immediately adjacent to the entrance hall, which was the only room in the building. The room sat stagnant as ever, the same rotunda of wooden seats around the main floor. Obsidian pillars stood looming in the middle of the rotunda seats. The Noctem leader could be hidden behind any of the seats, or any of the pillars, Stan realized.

Stan, Archie, and DZ looked at one another in silence. A series of eye and head gestures seemed to indicate that splitting up was in order. As DZ snuck around the pillars and Archie stood ready to shoot at a split second's notice, Stan crept through the seats, methodically and meticulously checking behind each and every row. However, the search yielded no results, and a quick shout down to DZ confirmed that his search had been equally unsuccessful.

Stan was stumped. Corporal Emerick was clearly somewhere within the room, but Stan had checked all the hiding places. From where he was standing, Stan could see the entire courtroom, including behind every single seat. He saw DZ and Archie checking around the pillars for a second time, and the looks of bewilderment on their faces were indicating that it was to no avail. Where was . . .

"AAAAUUUGH!"

Stan almost stumbled forward off the seats at the yell from DZ that echoed throughout the rotunda. A pained grimace had taken to DZ's face, and he was clutching at his arm, staring in surprise at the arrow that had just sunk into it. Stan whipped his head to the side, wildly thinking for a moment that Archie had betrayed them, but his skeletal face showed surprise to mirror DZ's and his own.

Stan heard a whizzing sound, and he turned in time to see an arrow flying out of the vacant seats toward his face. Stan lunged to the side, the arrow sinking into the wall behind him. Sheathing his axe and drawing his bow, he tried to distinguish the source of the arrow. As he stared intently at the place where the arrow had originated, utterly confused and terrified as to what was happening, he noticed something from the corner of his eye. An iron sword, having materialized in midair in the middle of the rotunda floor, was now flying across the room, on a collision course with Archie's back.

"Archie, hit the dirt!" Stan bellowed. Archie did so without hesitation, and the sword soared over him just as Stan sent an arrow toward the sword's point of origin. The arrow connected. Stan heard a grunt of pain as the arrow found its unseen mark. Stan saw Corporal Emerick flicker into visibility for an instant, with an aggrieved look on his face, before vanishing once again.

"Guys, he's there!" Stan yelled, directing DZ's and Archie's attention to the place where an arrow was being yanked out of the unseen player's shoulder and tossed to the ground. "You can't see him, but he's there!"

Recognition flashed across Archie's face. "He's using an Invisibility Potion!" he cried, sending an arrow toward the invisible corporal, which Emerick sidestepped. Now that Stan knew where Emerick was, he was certain he could see a slight shimmering, as if heat were rising off of pavement, wherever the invisible player was. Stan saw Emerick darting across the room. A visible diamond sword appeared from thin air in what Stan assumed was his hand, flying right toward Stan himself. Stan drew his own axe to engage the corporal in combat.

This was easily the most bizarre fight Stan had ever been in, and considering what he had endured on his campaign to overthrow King Kev, that was saying something. Stan could not determine any distinct part of the invisible enemy he was fighting. It was all Stan could do to raise his axe to counterattack the levitating diamond sword, which was making floating jabs and slices.

Stan felt his legs being swept out from under him, and he knew that Corporal Emerick had swept his invisible foot underneath Stan's own. Stan tumbled to the floor, barely raising his axe in time to block the sword that was coming down onto his neck. As Stan struggled to regain his upright footing, he felt an invisible foot pinning his chest to the ground. Stan felt he was being drained of all energy as his blood rushed from his heart in a wave.

Just as Stan was about to determine that it was too much, that he couldn't fight anymore, the pressure lifted the slightest bit. This gave Stan the opportunity to fling himself upward and onto his feet. The corporal tumbled down the rotunda seats, a shimmering marking his place as well as the arrow sticking from his shoulder blade.

Stan's vision on the rotunda floor refocused on DZ trying to mend the wound from the arrow he had pulled from his unarmored bicep, but he did not see Archie by DZ's side. Stan saw Archie firing arrow after arrow at the place he assumed the crumpled form of the corporal lay. A black tunic shielded the onslaught of arrows. As the floating tunic crept farther and farther backward toward the door, Archie advanced on him at a much faster pace.

Having the upper hand, however, had made Archie overconfident. Just as Corporal Emerick was backed up against the locked doors, a potion bottle came flying out of nowhere as the black tunic disappeared into a newly created plume of black smoke. The potion slammed into Archie's red-haired skeleton head and exploded into a cloud of blue-gray smoke. He keeled over to the ground, clutching his head in agony. DZ rushed in to help Archie, but Stan was staring in horror at a lever that he had never noticed before on the wall. This lever was in the On position.

Fear coursed through Stan. He had fought far too many players who utilized explosive traps in their surroundings to not know one when he saw one. He and his friends needed to evacuate the courthouse immediately. His shout of "RUN!" was deadened by the explosion in the center of the rotunda seats behind him.

Stan didn't even have time to look toward his two friends when the wave of fire slammed into his back. He was launched forward at breakneck speed through the two doorframes that had held iron doors seconds before. Stan felt himself tumbling wildly through space, only stopping when he was thrown down into a viscous substance. As he opened his eyes, he realized that he had landed in the bottommost pool of the Apothecary Memorial Fountain. Although it sat a distance from the doors of the courthouse, it still had one of its sides blasted away by the explosion. Stan let the current of the gushing fountain carry him down to the road. Everything ached at once from the sheer force of being caught in that blast. However, as Stan turned his head to the side, he saw something that rendered all his pain irrelevant.

He could see two shadowy figures sitting not far away from him in the darkness. One appeared to be shaking the other, who was limp and unresponsive. Stan's forehead immediately broke out in sweat, as did his palms. The horribly familiar feeling of dread bubbled up inside him, threatening to boil over as he ran to the two figures. He saw DZ, uncharacteristically shell-shocked, holding Archie's body in shaking hands, a ring of items lying around them haphazardly.

Four months ago, when Stan had stood in the tower of Element Castle alongside the Apothecary, King Kev had chosen to kill himself rather than die at the hands of Stan. The magnitude of the alarm that had struck Stan at that point could only be described in two words: *shock* and *awe*. Now, seeing DZ sobbing as he shook Archie's dead body, demanding that he wake up, another round of shock and awe whipped Stan across the face like a white-hot iron. Six hours ago, Stan had believed the Noctem Alliance no longer existed. Now, their leader had just killed one of his friends.

As Stan realized this, he became aware of a presence watching him. As the shock gave way to fury—pure, unfiltered hatred—Stan whipped his head upward to look into the smirking face of Corporal Emerick.

Stan's body acted on its own. His axe flew from his side and into his hand as he charged the Noctem corporal. He brought his axe down onto that hatefully smug face, hoping to put as much pain as possible into the strike, only to have Emerick sidestep the attack. His axe collided with the stone ground with enough force to snap the diamond blade from the handle.

As Stan spat in fury, Corporal Emerick calmly pulled a bloodred Potion of Harming from his inventory and raised it to his lips. Realizing what he was about to do, Stan shot his fist at the corporal's mouth, shattering the potion bottle and splattering the ground crimson. Stan was so absolutely insane with rage that the force of the punch sent him stumbling forward. He spun around on his heel to find that the corporal had already drawn another red potion and raised it to his mouth.

Stan's shout had barely left his mouth when the bottle tilted back and the potion entered the Noctem officer's mouth, just as a flurry of green bottles flew from the corporal's free hand. The effect was immediate. A ring of items burst from his navel, and Corporal Emerick fell forward onto his knees, and then onto his face. Stan bellowed in fury, distressed beyond comprehension, and in a rush he felt himself fall to the ground, vaguely aware of a cloud of green gas swirling around him before he saw black.

CHAPTER 8
TENSIONS

"Honestly, sir, you're being unreasonable!"

"Please, just go back, lie down! You've been through a lot these past few hours, and you're not thinking straight!"

Stan didn't hear them. He was completely deaf to the objections of his two aides as he marched down the corridor and away from the castle infirmary. It killed him to think that while he had been lying in a bed, being detoxed of the effects of Corporal Emerick's final poison attack, his friends had been sitting in a council room discussing what to do about the atrocities committed by the Noctem Alliance. In his desperation to get into the council room, he finally spun around to face the aides.

"Enough!" Stan bellowed, harsher than he had anticipated. The aides staggered backward with fear in their eyes as Stan's hand had instinctively glided to the axe handle by his side. He was too infuriated to give them the luxury of an apology. The Noctem Alliance had killed Archie, and the only thing he cared about at that moment was destroying the organization once and for all. The aides now did nothing to stop Stan as he jammed his fist into the button on the wall, opening the double doors and granting him access to the council room.

The depression hanging in the room was plain, and this was reflected on the faces of the seven players sitting around the table. DZ, Gobbleguy, the Mechanist, and Charlie sat next to one another in a row. Their expressions were forlorn, and seemed more weary than sad. To their left, however, was a totally different story. Jayden and G were Archie's best friends, and they did nothing to hide the fact that they had been crying over his death. Their eyes still red and puffy, they exuded an aura of grief and anger. Stan felt the terrible sensation of likening their emotions to his own when he had learned of Sally's death.

Only when Stan's eyes lingered on Kat, however, did he stop for a moment. She seemed filled with the same depressed exhaustion that Charlie and DZ were giving off, but there was a distinct note of discomfort on her face as well. As Stan pondered what it could be that was causing this, he noticed that she was shooting a stream of uneasy glances in the direction of G, who was sitting next to her. All of Stan's curiosity vanished in an instant, to be replaced with irritation. Kat merely had a problem with G. Worrying about such things at a time like this was unthinkable.

"Hey, Stan," said DZ, his voice devoid of its usual cheery, upbeat quality. "They let you out of the hospital early?"

"I checked myself out," Stan mumbled in reply. "They say I should still be there, but I feel fine." Nobody was foolish enough to disagree with him.

As Stan walked over and took his seat between Charlie and Kat, he looked up and a sob erupted from his throat without warning. Sitting directly across from his seat at the table was the chair normally occupied by Archie—empty. It was at that moment that it hit Stan like a wrecking ball: Archie was gone, and he could never again return to Elementia. Grief welled up within Stan yet again, only to be immediately replaced with more rage at the Noctem Alliance. The reason he was there flooded into Stan, and he turned to Charlie, a gleam of fire in his eye.

"Is the city secure?" he asked.

"Yes," replied Charlie. He sounded beat. "Bill, Ben, and Bob have the city on lockdown. There are patrols on all the walls, and nobody's allowed in or out of the gates until we say so. They also have officers searching the entire city, making arrests and interrogating anybody who may be linked to the attack. So far"—Charlie let out a sigh—"they haven't found anybody. Eleven fighters were part of the attack, including Corporal Emerick. All of them died rather than be captured."

Stan's heart sank. He hadn't really been expecting anything else, but it still infuriated him that he had no way of capturing these players and interrogating them. Stan was just about to make a remark to that effect when the door flew open behind him. He spun around to see Blackraven marching into the room, a book in his hand and a triumphant smile on his face.

The effect of his arrival on the rest of the room was immediate. Stan felt all those sitting nearest him on the table immediately tense up, shooting a dirty glance in Blackraven's direction. Across from them, Jayden and G also snapped upright in their seats, but their anger seemed to be more directed at their fellow councilmen around the table than at Blackraven. Stan realized with a start that he must have missed something in the days he had spent recovering. After all, this was a closed council meeting, and Blackraven was not on the council. Something serious must have happened.

"Here it is, it is right here, Charlie!" said Blackraven, barely suppressed joy in his voice, and brandishing his finger to a page in the open book. "Even you can't deny what is written in the ultimate law of the land!"

"For the last time, Blackraven, it is *not* happening," whispered Charlie harshly, a vein twitching in his temple. Stan was alarmed to see Charlie's quiet fury. "There is absolutely no reason to do something that extreme now that the crisis is over."

"Excuse me," cut in Stan, "but what's going on here? Blackraven, what are you doing here? This is a private council meeting!"

"I am well aware of that, Stan," replied Blackraven, plopping himself down squarely into Archie's vacant seat, "and so I figure that I had best be here for it, considering that I am now a part of the council."

"Get out of his chair!" barked Charlie. Kat gave a little squeak of horror at the outburst, and Gobbleguy broke into tears. "You are not a part of this council, Blackraven, and to try to suggest it would make you a traitor!"

"You are accusing me of treachery, Charlie?" bellowed Blackraven, standing up to stare Charlie down from across the table. "I only want what is best for Elementia, and I would like to see action taken against our enemies quickly, without wandering through the political swamp of your bureaucratic elections!"

"Are you aware, Blackraven," responded Charlie, kicking back his seat to stare the bird-man in the eye, "that those elections are the only thing keeping Elementia from turning into a dictatorship, like the one that we fought to take down just four months ago?"

"ENOUGH!" screamed Stan. Without thinking, he pulled the ceremonial golden axe from its sheath and brought it down into the table between Charlie and Blackraven. The golden blade snapped from the handle and fell onto the table with a loud clang. Stan didn't care. He wasn't even sure what they were arguing about, but he knew that if they were to deal with the Noctem Alliance, they could not be fighting with each other. The room fell silent. All were staring at Stan with humbled looks on their faces. He was the president, and it was his turn to speak.

"No more yelling!" said Stan, speaking in such a way that he was breaking his own rule. "We are the ones in charge of running Elementia, and right now we have to deal with the fallout of this attack. Anything that we need to discuss, we can discuss it like responsible people." Stan turned his head to Blackraven. "Now, Blackraven, why do you think that you're on the council? Council members don't just join, they're elected by the people."

"Thank you, Stan! You see, that's what I'm—" started Charlie, but Stan raised a hand to cut him off.

"Yes, I'm well aware of that, Stan," replied Blackraven, smirking at Charlie. "But this is a special case. It says so, right here in the Constitution." And he held up his book so that Stan could see the words *The Constitution of the Republic of Elementia*, by Bookbinder55, on the front cover. Blackraven pointed to a spot on the open page and began to read.

"'All members of the Council of Eight, a group of eight players whose job it is to run Element City and the rest of Elementia, shall be elected by conducting a vote among the entire population of the server, UNLESS . . . ,'" he said with emphasis, as Charlie had opened his mouth to interject, "'the server of Elementia is in a state of emergency. In that case, the council may appoint a temporary member until the emergency is resolved.'"

"Dude, we keep telling you, we ain't in a state of emergency anymore!" said DZ, his eyes wide with frustration. "The police've got the city secure, and the Alliance is gone for now! Why is there still an emergency?"

"I'm sorry, are you serious?" asked Jayden, speaking for the first time and with a dark note in his voice. "Do you not realize that Archie is dead?" He hesitated for a moment, trying to keep his composure. "G and I have known him since we first started playing this game. We thought that . . . when we lost Sally . . ." Jayden's jaw was trembling, and tears were slowly leaking from his eyes, but he pressed on, "that we would never have to go through that again. But . . ."

"But now Archie is gone too," continued G as Jayden became too distraught to continue. "The Noctem Alliance took Archie from us, just like King Kev took Sally. And now you expect us to just sit here and go through an election while the people who killed our friend are still out there?"

"Jayden, G, I understand what you're saying," said Stan evenly, trying to hide his alarm that the two of them were taking Blackraven's side. "But you know, you're not the only ones who're upset that Archie's gone, and the fact that he is doesn't mean . . ."

"Oh, please, don't even try, Stan!" cried Jayden, whose red face was now knitted in anger. "You don't care that he's dead as much as we do, don't even pretend that you do! If you did, you'd agree with us without even thinking about it!"

"That's out of line, Jayden!" seethed the Mechanist, jumping to Stan's defense. "Stan is devastated, as we all are, that Archie is dead! He's just keeping a level head and trying to preserve the values of our country instead of acting out of rash hatred!"

"But we deserve the right to act out of rash hatred!" bellowed Jayden, his face contorted. "The Noctem Alliance killed Archie, and we want justice to be served!"

"What you're speaking of is not justice, Jayden!" the Mechanist countered. "You are thinking of nothing but revenge! Justice is keeping a level head and determining the best course of action to ensure that no further tragedies occur. The revenge you speak of, however, is taking action blindly, without sight of future consequences, thinking only of what is best for you!"

"Do you even hear yourselves?" shouted Blackraven. "It's not like I'm asking for anything crazy or over the top! All that I ask is that, in recognition of the fact that the Alliance is dangerous and must be disposed of, I am appointed to the council . . . temporarily, of course . . . so that we can take immediate action against them, instead of having to wait for days as we organize elections."

Charlie, Jayden, and the Mechanist all opened their mouths to respond to this, but Stan cut in first. "Enough talk," he said firmly. "Let's put it to a vote. We'll go around the table, and each take a vote as to whether we should allow Blackraven to become an unelected councilman for the time being, or to abide by the constitution and set up an election tomorrow for a new council member to replace Archie. A majority of five votes will decide."

In his mind, Stan knew that he would never be comfortable with Blackraven joining the council unelected. As he looked around the table, though, he was quite confident that, out of the nine of them, only Blackraven, G, and Jayden would vote in favor of it.

"Let me start off by casting my vote," began Stan, "which is for Pro-Constitution. The country of Elementia was founded on our constitution, and the present situation is not bad enough that we should start ignoring it." Stan turned to the person sitting to his right, Charlie.

"I also vote for Pro-Constitution," said Charlie, his voice steely as he shot a quick dirty glance at Blackraven. Thankfully, it went unnoticed.

"My vote is for Pro-Constitution as well," added the Mechanist, glancing at Stan and giving him a warm smile, which Stan returned. As tired, depressed, and angry as he was,

Stan couldn't help but take a moment to notice how very wise and kind a person the old Mechanist was.

"I vote for Pro-Emergency Powers."

That voice caught Stan off guard. He tore his glance away from the Mechanist and looked, to his horror, to see Gobbleguy, sitting in his chair, looking timid and afraid.

"What?" Stan couldn't help bursting out. "Why? Why would you support emergency powers?"

"Shut up, Stan!" yelled G. "He doesn't have to justify anything to you, it's his vote, not yours!"

Stan closed his eyes and took a deep breath, furious with himself for his outburst, but he now felt incredibly uneasy. He had completely forgotten about Gobbleguy, the former mayor of Blackstone, who had remained completely silent throughout the debate. Why would he of all people want to support the emergency powers?

"Well, I, for one, am all in favor of keeping Elementia true to what the country was founded on. Pro-Constitution all the way, man!" yelled DZ, a little louder than he ought to, but it made Stan feel a little better. Just one more vote and they would have a majority, and the entire issue would be resolved.

The feeling did not last, however, as one by one, Blackraven, Jayden, and G all cast their votes for the Pro-Emergency Powers. The votes were now tied, four to four, and the final vote would decide. All eyes at the table were now fixed on the last council member.

In his entire life, from the minute he had first met her, Stan had never seen Kat look as uncomfortable as she did at that moment. Her reluctance to enter the NPC village during their trek through the desert months ago seemed like nothing compared to the girl that Stan saw now. Kat was squirming in her seat, trying to shake the feeling that all the power was now in her hands.

"What's your vote, Kat?" asked Stan carefully, after the silence and staring had gone on for well over a minute.

"Well I . . . um . . . I think that they both have their positives and negatives," Kat stammered. Stan couldn't believe it. She was still undecided? Now was his chance to ensure that the constitution was upheld.

"Kat, why are you even debating this?" he asked. "The state of emergency is over, this deserves to be done right!"

"Don't listen to him, Kat!" replied Jayden. "Having an election now would be stupid! It would only allow time for the Noctem Alliance to regroup, which would lead to another attack, and more people being killed!"

"Kat, you were with me and Stan the entire time we were on the journey to take down King Kev," said Charlie, a note of pleading in his voice. "We fought so hard so that we could have a constitution. Do you really want to ignore it now?"

"You're not ignoring it, Kat!" said Blackraven. "You'd be doing the best thing for our safety, and everyone else in Elementia, by getting this done as quickly as possible!"

"Archie wouldn't have wanted us to ignore the constitution, Kat!" shouted DZ.

"But he can't say that for himself, because the Noctem Alliance killed him!" cried G, grabbing Kat's shoulders and turning her to look him straight in the eye. "Think about it, Kat," he said softly. "What if that was you who'd died? I don't think that I could bear it."

"Enough, all of you!" cried the Mechanist, wiping a bead of sweat from his brow. "Kat is more than capable of making her own decision, so everybody, stop talking! Kat, what is your vote?"

Kat had not said a word throughout the entire debate, but as she detached herself from G, she now looked more lost for words than ever. She looked slowly around the table, eyebrows knitted in confusion, sweat rolling down her forehead. Her eyes passed over the faces of all her fellows before finally resting on G, who raised his eyebrows expectantly. Kat opened her mouth, and it hung open for a moment, before . . .

"I vote . . . Pro-Emergency Powers," she muttered in a resigned, uncomfortable voice.

A ripple of shock emanated from Kat and made its way

across the room. Stan felt as if he had just been slapped across the face. Kat, one of his best friends, who had fought long and hard alongside him to instate the constitution of Elementia, was now voting against it. He glared at her, and caught her eye for a moment. She seemed embarrassed and tense, and soon broke the connection to hug G, which did not seem to ease her tension or embarrassment at all. Stan gave a subtle scowl, and shot a determinedly neutral look at Blackraven as he lowered himself into Archie's chair, a faint air of smugness about him.

Stan was hardly listening as Blackraven dived straight into his ideas for hunting down the Noctem Alliance. After all, Stan trusted Blackraven as a strategist, and he knew that together with DZ and Charlie, the other two gifted strategists, they would figure out the best way to hunt down the remaining members of the Noctem Alliance.

It was undoubted, however, that something had changed within the council. The nine of them had always gotten along as friends, ever since the rebellion against King Kev. They had had their minor issues, sure, but they were always on the same side. This had been the way the council was, and it had served Elementia very well.

Now, as Stan looked around the table at the Council of Eight, he saw a divided group. As Blackraven spoke on, Charlie was huddled in deep conversation with the Mechanist, while Jayden and G did the same. The two groups kept shooting dirty looks at each other. DZ glared down at the table, a brooding expression on his face, while Gobbleguy looked straight-up terrified at all that had gone down. And Stan was sure Kat was feeling a lot of things at that point, but no feeling was as evident as the discomfort reflected on her face as G hugged her in thanks for her support.

Even Stan himself felt like he had been torn apart from half the group. He could never see eye to eye with G, Jayden, and Blackraven, and he would have a hard time forgiving Gobbleguy too. And Kat . . . what Kat had done was outright betrayal, and he had no idea where they were going to go next.

As Stan looked around and saw all his friends arguing, it scared him more than a little bit. They were in the midst of fighting a war against an evil terrorist organization that had killed one of their own, and if they couldn't even cooperate with one another to take their common enemy down, then how was the Republic of Elementia possibly going to survive?

CHAPTER 9
THE BATTLE OF THE BASE

"I just don't understand!" cried Leonidas. "Since I came out here, nothin' you've had me do has made any sense!"

"The decisions are not mine, Leonidas," replied Caesar, a note of irritation in his voice as he paced the main floor of the Jungle Base. "Lord Tenebris has assured me that he has a plan that will make complete sense in retrospect, but will only succeed if you, Minotaurus, and I follow his instructions to the letter!"

"Are ya tellin' me he hasn't told ya stuff? Ya know, ya being his right-hand man and all?" asked Leonidas.

"I never said that," replied Caesar coolly. "As the apprentice of Lord Tenebris, I naturally have access to more information than either you or Minotaurus."

"So why can't ya tell me?" asked Leonidas, exasperation ripe in his voice. "I've done all this stuff that seems ridiculous to me! Takin' over this base, sendin' half my guys into Element City just to kill themselves. And now you're takin' even more of my guys back with ya?" For that was the reason Caesar had made the journey out to the Jungle Base. He was to collect half the men remaining there with Leonidas for use in a separate mission of his own.

"Now see here, Leonidas—" started Caesar, but Leonidas cut in.

"NO!" he bellowed, his anger over running around the server on blind instructions finally bursting forward. "I will *not* see here! The three of us went into this as equals, ya know! There is no reason why ya should get to be best pals with Lord Tenebris while I go around and do your dirty work!"

"Enough!" yelled Caesar aggressively, whipping his glowing diamond sword from its sheath and driving it forward into Leonidas's leather armor, pinning him against the wall. Leonidas was dumbstruck. He had not expected the conversation to turn hostile.

"Leonidas, when we joined this organization," spoke Caesar, a fearsome power radiating from him, "we pledged that we would do whatever it took to return Elementia to its former glory, and to subjugate all the lower-level scum! Your role in the plan of Lord Tenebris is to be a field commander, while mine is to be an adviser and an apprentice. If you take issue with that, then you are a threat to the Alliance, and you know how I deal with threats to the Alliance," he finished with a growl, punctuating each word with another poke of the sword into Leonidas's armor.

Leonidas's and Caesar's eyes were locked, neither player willing to back down. Leonidas was conflicted. He was not scared of Caesar. He was positive that, if the need arose, he himself would win in a fight. That being said, he was terrified of Lord Tenebris, having heard rumors of his limitless powers from his first days in Minecraft. As much as he hated to admit it, Leonidas realized that he had locked himself into a position of no escape. To contradict Caesar was to contradict the Noctem Alliance, and by extension Lord Tenebris himself. If he did that, he would die, plain and simple.

Recognizing defeat, Leonidas lowered his eyes. "Fine," he mumbled, humility forced into his voice. "Take half my men. Go do whatever ya have to do."

Caesar smiled, and slowly drew back his sword, returning it to the sheath at his side. "Now that is what I like to hear."

Leonidas refused to give Caesar the satisfaction of a response to the quip. That, at least, was still in his power. Instead he asked a question: "So what does Lord Tenebris want me to do?"

"He wants you to stay here at the base," replied Caesar simply. "The army of Element City will be here soon enough, as soon as they've recovered from the offensive on Elementia Day. When they arrive, let them take the base. Put up a fight, take as many of them down as you can . . . but let them win."

Leonidas looked up. This was far too ludicrous for him not to question. "So, what? Ya want us all to die for no reason? Ya just want to give them this base back? Why? What is the point of that?"

"Oh, so silly of me! I forgot to mention one thing." Caesar's upper-class accent was prominent in the statement, and he followed it up with an amused chuckle. "All who remain at the base must die . . . except for you, my friend. When the attack comes, lead your defenses, but when you are beginning to fall behind, use Ender Pearls to escape from the base, and then make your way back to Nocturia as soon as possible."

Leonidas opened his mouth, his face showing utter disbelief. But then he closed it again. There was no point in questioning this. If Lord Tenebris wanted something done, Leonidas would have to do it, or be killed. He had to keep reminding himself of that.

"Okay," he said slowly. "So wait for Elementia to attack us, and when they do, we let them win, but I escape and head back to the capital?"

Caesar smiled. "Now you're catching on, my friend. All right, I'd best be off." And with that, he walked over to a hole in the stone floor and descended the wooden ladder to the hillside. Leonidas watched out the window as Caesar and five men walked down the hill into the dense jungle, continuing on until the opaque foliage finally blocked them from sight.

Leonidas sighed. Not for the first time, he sat down on the floor, his back against the temple wall, and told himself to think. This was something that seemed to happen a lot these days, as he was sitting around the Jungle Base with nothing to do.

Why was he, Leonidas, part of the Noctem Alliance? Because he had agreed to join it alongside Caesar and Minotaurus. Why did he agree to join? Because he had just lost everything in the Battle for Elementia, including his partners, Geno and Becca, and his ruler, King Kev. Why did he lose those players? Because of Stan, a piece of lower-level scum who had driven the inferior lower-level players to rebel against their masters. Why did Stan do that? Because he believed that the lower-level players deserved all the rights that the upper-level players had. And why don't they? Because they were inferior. And why were they inferior?

Leonidas faltered for a moment. He had always accepted, without question, from the moment that he had joined RAT1, that the lower-level players were inferior. But . . . why? Leonidas shook his head. He didn't need justification for that, it was simply nature, it was the reason he was now going through all this trouble to take down Stan. It was just the way it should be. But then . . . why was it that whenever he went to kill a lower-level player, who he vastly outclassed in combat skills . . . why did killing those players never fail to make him uneasy? Even if, in the heat of combat, Leonidas had no inhibitions, they would inevitably come back to haunt him after the fact.

Leonidas looked up and realized that all his remaining five men were gathered in front of him. He had apparently been lost in his thoughts for a while. Leonidas shook the fog from his head. There was no time to be thinking about reason. An attack from Element City was inbound, and they had to be prepared for it when it came.

"Prepare for battle, men!" Leonidas yelled, pulling himself to his feet. "Man the defensive positions, and prepare yourselves! Stan and his guys are comin' and we're gonna make our last stand, right here, right now!" Leonidas whipped out his bow and brandished it above his head, flourishing it up and down as he led a round of cheers at the proclamation. He felt a knot in his gut as he realized that within the day, all five of these players would be dead and he would still be alive, fleeing the scene.

Leonidas shook his head again. *Don't think*, Leonidas told himself. *Just defend. Just defend the base until they make their way in, and then ya can run.* Leonidas climbed the ladder to the top floor of the base, which stood open to the sky and offered a gorgeous view of the setting sun.

As Leonidas took his position atop the tower, arrow nocked into his bow, he did not allow himself to think, lest he convince himself to do something against his orders. No, instead he forced himself to repeat over and over in his head the creed that had become his entire life.

Viva la Noctem, Viva la Noctem, Viva la Noctem, Viva la Noctem . . .

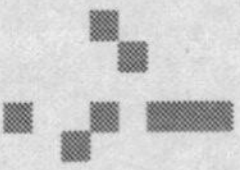

Stan was on edge as he marched through the jungle, geared up with a diamond axe in hand, hacking his way through the bush alongside Kat and Charlie. The council's decision to take back the Jungle Base had taken way too long. Even more irritating was the fact that Stan had had to fight tooth and nail to even be a part of the raid. To top it all off, Kat still refused to apologize for her vote against him.

Had Blackraven not been on the council, Stan was sure that the eight of them would have put a plan together in minutes. But what should have been a simple assignment turned into a gigantic snowball of arguments over the most insignificant, pointless details. Stan now led Kat, Charlie, and ten other soldiers to the base, irritated that the decision had taken up so much precious time.

Stan was convinced the council was just angry and wanted to argue about something. Indeed, all the discussion about the offensive had been a battle with Stan, Charlie, and DZ on one side, and Blackraven, G, and Jayden on the other. The Mechanist had tried to stay moderate, but had ending up agreeing with Stan on almost everything. Gobbleguy and Kat had just stayed out of the debates, which Stan saw as cowardice. This did not elevate Stan's feelings for Kat as they bushwhacked their way through the jungle together.

Stan remembered the good old days, when the three of them had traveled across the entire land of Elementia together, all with a common goal. It had been one of the best times of his life, despite all the dangers. It was amazing how the pressures of running a country had turned them, once three inseparable friends, into a divided group, barely willing to look one another in the eye. And thus it was in uncomfortable silence that the three of them led their soldiers through the jungle and toward the outpost.

He was so sick of all the stupid talking his job as president entailed, and he was looking forward to a straight fight. At the moment, the only thing Stan wanted was to do something directly against the Noctem Alliance, instead of debating about it in a council room. He was looking forward to his assignment on the mission. While Kat's and Charlie's job was to apprehend as many of the Noctem forces in the base as possible, Stan's job was simple: find and capture Leonidas.

Stan was still a little thrown off by the fact that Leonidas was alive. Until two days ago, he had been convinced that Leonidas was dead, blown to bits in a crater during the Battle for Elementia alongside his partner Becca. Yet somehow he had survived, and he had joined the Noctem Alliance. This told Stan that the Alliance was made up not just of random prejudiced players, but the remnants of King Kev's army as well. The last time Stan had seen Leonidas up close, they had been in the Ender Desert, and Leonidas had hit him with a Potion of Slowness and stomped on his chest before Stan had gotten the upper hand, and Leonidas fled. Taking him down would be the most satisfying thing Stan had done in a long time.

After almost a half day of walking, the setting sun cast a cloak of darkness over the land. Not too long afterward, the glowing torchlight of the Elementia Jungle Base came into view. Stan knew the outpost was actually a jungle temple, a ruin of a structure that was generated there, and not built by players.

At the foot of the hill, Stan glanced back at Kat and Charlie. Now that they were on the brink of battle, all thoughts of disagreements in the council room were gone. All they were now were three warriors, ready to lead a charge on an evil organization that needed to be taken down.

As they had planned, Stan pulled a pale blue potion from his inventory. He downed the potion in one gulp, with the other twelve following his lead. Stan knew that the effect of the Potion of Swiftness would be countered by the Potions of Slowness that the Noctems were bound to be using in combat, but the rush of adrenaline was nice while it lasted.

Now that they were ready and enriched with the potion, Stan ordered the charge. Silently, the first of the soldiers climbed the vines that stretched up the side of the hill, reached the top, and burst into the base with a savage yell. Stan heard yells of surprise followed by the metallic clangs of swords, and before long, a wave of dark gray gas rolled out the windows of the base. As the last soldier ascended the vines, Stan offered one last encouraging look at Kat as he pulled himself up the vines, kicked off the hill face, and dive-rolled into the jungle temple.

The gray Potion of Slowness in the air immediately made him feel like his normal self again, but his normal self was still full of adrenaline. All around him, his soldiers were locked in combat with four figures clad in black leather armor, surrounded by potion clouds of all colors and swords colliding. *This is where I belong*, thought Stan as Charlie and Kat appeared behind him.

"Okay, you know what to do!" yelled Stan. His friends nodded and ran to join the fray, Kat with her diamond sword already whistling forward to meet a Noctem soldier in combat, and Charlie with a diamond pickaxe ready in hand. Stan glanced around. No Leonidas. He noticed a ladder on the side of the stone wall that seemed to lead to an upper level. Wasting no time, Stan gripped his diamond axe firmly in hand and pulled himself up the ladder in no time flat.

Standing atop the roof, Stan looked up, only to find an arrow flying toward him. Stan dive-rolled to the side and saw this arrow did not come from Leonidas. Although Leonidas was indeed standing there on the roof, clad in black armor, a grim look on his face, it was a Noctem trooper attacking. The soldier rushed Stan with a diamond sword in hand. The fight was over before it began. One quick sidestep and Stan's axe had cut the soldier's black leather armor in two, knocking him to the ground with a decent-size gash across his exposed chest.

As if programmed, the fallen soldier pulled a bottle from his inventory containing bloodred liquid. Alarm bells sounded in Stan's head. Determined to keep the soldier alive for questioning, he dived forward to knock the bottle out of the soldier's hand. As he moved, however, Stan felt a dull pain in his chest, and he flew backward as three arrows glanced off his diamond armor, leaving a distinct crack in the center of the chestplate. Stan jumped back up to his feet. He saw Leonidas pulling out another arrow and the soldier on the ground, his inventory scattered about him, an empty potion bottle in his hand.

Angered but determined to stay focused on his mission, Stan sheathed his axe, whipped out a bow and arrow, and notched the arrow, pointing it directly at Leonidas's heart, just as Leonidas did the same. The two players held their weapons up, staring each other in the eye. They were at a stalemate. Both of them were waiting for the other to make the first move.

"Hello, Stan," said Leonidas evenly, his bow still raised.

Slightly taken aback, Stan felt somehow compelled to respond. "Hello, Leonidas."

"Fancy meetin' ya up here," Leonidas continued.

"Yeah," said Stan. *This is really eerie*, he thought uneasily. "It is. . . ."

"I gotta admit, Stan," continued Leonidas politely, as if the two of them were just old friends catching up, "I'm kind of surprised that ya came here yourself. I was honestly expectin' ya to just send a couple of your lackeys to come and do your dirty work for ya."

Stan's eyebrow twitched in disgust. "They're not my lackeys, they're my friends. Not that I'd expect you to understand about that." Now it was Leonidas's turn for an eyebrow twitch. "Charlie and Kat are downstairs with some of my guys, and they're gonna overpower your guys pretty fast."

"Is that so?" said Leonidas, with almost an amused quality in his voice, which was ominous in comparison to the bow he was still pointing at Stan.

"Yeah, it is," replied Stan, with the same portentous amusement. "And as soon as they're done mopping the floor with your men, they're gonna be up here. So if you want to fight me before they get here, I'd suggest firing that arrow." Despite the fact that he was playing mind games with Leonidas, Stan was scared out of his wits, and just wanted the first shot to be fired so they could stop the banter and let the weapons do the talking.

Leonidas smiled. "I'm an honorable guy, Stan. I never fire unless someone fires at me or my allies first."

Stan returned the smirk. "Oh, you're an honorable guy? Well, you've done a fantastic job of showing it so far. Let's see, first you worked for King Kev, then you join this Noctem gang, and, oh yeah, you've devoted your life to terrorizing people who can't defend themselves. Yes, bullying is a very *honorable* thing to do. . . ."

Stan sidestepped the arrow that came flying from Leonidas's bow, then proceeded to let his own arrow fly and whip out his axe. Leonidas ducked the arrow and let five of his own fly in rapid succession, all of which were deflected by expert blocks with Stan's axe.

"Attack me all ya want with your weapons, Stan," boomed Leonidas, a terrible look on his face, "but don't ya go insultin' my honor! Ya don't know what it's been like for me ever since the king fell!" Another spray of arrows flew from the bow, which Stan, again, deflected.

"Yeah, you joined the Noctem Alliance, which is . . . news flash, Leonidas . . . *exactly the same* as being part of King Kev's army!" yelled Stan, resentment clear in his voice.

"I didn't have a choice, Stan!" cried Leonidas. "If I hadn't joined the Alliance, what woulda happened? Ya'd have found and killed me, no questions asked! Did it ever occur to ya that I might not want to be part of this Alliance? That I didn't choose the Alliance, but the Alliance chose me?"

Another arrow followed this statement, but as Stan blocked it without effort, he stared at Leonidas as the archer loaded yet another arrow. Stan recognized something in Leonidas's voice that he was utterly unprepared for: sincerity. Suddenly, he was seeing the ruthless, emotionless killing machine who had stalked him across Elementia with new eyes. What if Leonidas was telling the truth?

"Leonidas . . . ," started Stan, but before he could get out any words, a voice from below Stan caught him off guard.

"Stan! Watch out, he's loaded!"

An arrow flew from the trapdoor behind Stan toward Leonidas, who rolled out of the way before landing on one knee and sending his own arrow back in the direction of the sender. Stan followed the path of Leonidas's arrow just in time to see it find a chink in Charlie's armor and sink deep into his chest.

The split second of pity that Stan had had for Leonidas was gone. All pretense of peace between the two of them had just gone out the window. Stan knew Charlie was down by Leonidas's hand, and he himself wanted to cause the archer as much pain as possible. Stan charged Leonidas, barely noticing the look of horror on his face as he brought his axe down on top of Leonidas. The archer reacted at the last second. He kicked off the roof of the outpost and launched into the air. As Stan pulled his axe out of the cavity it had made in the stone, he saw that Leonidas had grabbed on to some vines hanging from a nearby tree and was dangling from them, desperately trying to notch an arrow.

Kat burst up through the door, a warrior's glare on her face. "Don't worry," she said, "I've got two guys down there healing Charlie, and all the other Noctems are down. Where's Leonidas?"

"He's out in that tree," responded Stan, drawing his bow as Kat did the same. Within ten seconds, the remaining eight members of the team were on the roof alongside them, their bows drawn and aimed at Leonidas.

Although Leonidas attempted to return fire a few times, it was futile. Firing a bow and arrow while hanging from vines was hard enough, but doing it while avoiding the rain of arrows from ten archers was impossible. Stan watched in fury as Leonidas pulled a blue-green orb out of his pocket and, without hesitation, flung it as far as he could into the dense jungle in the distance.

The split second it took Leonidas to do this cost him, however, as an arrow sunk into his right shoulder blade. With an audible cry of anguish, Leonidas released his grip on the vines and started to fall to the ground below. Stan's soldiers managed to sink two more arrows into Leonidas on the way down; Stan couldn't tell where they had hit. Stan was counting on Leonidas hitting the ground before the Ender Pearl took effect, but Leonidas disappeared into a puff of purple smoke an instant before he would have made impact.

Stan did not have time to be infuriated at that moment. He bounded over to the trapdoor and dropped to the floor below. Ignoring the slight pain in his legs, he trained his eyes on Charlie. The soldiers had removed his diamond chestplate, but the arrow was still stuck deep in his chest, as Charlie heaved and coughed from the intense pain.

"Why haven't you healed him yet?" yelled Stan, frantically pulling his own red Potion of Healing from his inventory and applying it to the arrow.

"We're out of potion," replied one of the soldiers, as the potion took effect, popping out the arrow and leaving just a small red hole in Charlie's chest that was in definite need of more potions. "We used it all healing ourselves after the Noctem soldiers killed themselves in a potion attack."

Stan hardly cared that, once again, they had taken no prisoners from the raid. He was far too desperate to keep Charlie alive. "So what is there to do?"

"We have to get him medical attention," replied Kat, pulling a potion of deeper red from her inventory. "You three," she said, gesturing to the soldiers closest to her, "run back to

Element City, tell them to send a medic out here as quickly as possible. We can't leave here until Charlie's healed."

"Good thinking, Kat," replied Stan. Then he remembered something. "And the rest of you, take your weapons. Head out into the jungle and hunt down Leonidas. He's probably gone, but if there's a chance he isn't, then it's worth it to try to capture him, dead or alive. Leave all your potions with us."

The soldiers all nodded, dropped their potion bottles into a pile, and headed down the ladders to carry out their respective assignments.

"Okay, Stan, I need you to sort out the Potions of Strength from the other ones in that pile," said Kat, already using her own Potion of Strength on Charlie. "They're not healing, but they should keep him alive until real help gets here."

There were a few moments of silence while Kat used her own potions to try to stabilize Charlie, and Stan sorted out the rest of them for her use. As soon as he was done, he looked up at her.

"Wow, Kat, you've gotten pretty good at this. Where did you learn so much about medicine?"

"G taught me," Kat replied, still not taking her eyes off Charlie's wound. Then, after a moment, she afforded him a small smile. "To be completely honest, it's one of the few good things that's come out of my relationship with him."

Stan faltered. He was aware that Kat wasn't exactly in

a perfect relationship, but he wasn't aware she was that unhappy. Furthermore, it occurred to him that, despite the fact that they were fighting for Charlie's life at the moment, he felt something he hadn't felt since before Elementia Day: he cared about Kat's happiness.

"Well," he responded slowly, taking a shot in the dark, "if you're unhappy, then why don't you just break it off?"

Kat glanced up at him. "Well, to paraphrase Leon Livingston . . . 'I began on a whim, continued because I loved the life, and now continue because I'm not sure how to stop.'"

Stan's heart skipped a beat. He flashed back to just moments before, when he was talking with Leonidas atop the base. Something he had said came back to Stan. *Did it ever occur to you that I might not want to be part of this Alliance? That I didn't choose the Alliance, but the Alliance chose me?*

Of course, that was right before he had shot Charlie in the chest.

Stan banished the incident from his mind. Finding Leonidas again was a task for tomorrow, and as of now, another thought had come into Stan's mind. He looked at Kat as the two of them were fighting hard to keep Charlie alive and realized something.

Despite any differences the three of them might have in terms of their views, despite any disagreements they may have on the council room floor, Kat and Charlie were Stan's best friends in all of Elementia. No matter what, he wasn't going to let politics or debates get in the way of his friendships ever again.

Stan looked at Kat one more time, caught her eye, and gave her a smile. And as she returned the smile before requesting another Potion of Strength, it was somehow clear to Stan that the feeling was mutual.

CHAPTER 10
THE VILLAGER'S VISIT

"So Leonidas got away?" Charlie asked in a raspy tone.

"Yeah." Stan sighed. He sat himself down on a chair beside Charlie's hospital bed. "We sent our guys out to try to find him after he ran, but he had Ender Pearls. We had no chance."

"Trust me, Charlie," added Kat, plopping down on the bed next to him, "we really did try to find him. I mean, beyond the fact that he's part of the Alliance, what he did to you was just . . ."

"Don't worry, Kat," interrupted Charlie with a chuckle. "I'm sure you did all you could. We'll get him eventually."

Kat didn't say anything; she merely looked down at the wooden floor of the infirmary and absentmindedly stroked Rex's head between the ears.

Kat had been unusually apologetic toward Stan and Charlie for most everything over the past few days. She and Stan had spent most of their time since the attack in the hospital with Charlie as he recovered from the arrow wound, and during that time Kat had made it very clear that she deeply regretted her vote on the council, and that she hoped they would forgive her.

"I mean, what was I thinking?" she had said as she and Stan followed Charlie's medical escort back to Element City from the Jungle Base yesterday. "Why did I think that ignoring the law was a good idea? It was G—I swear that was it. He made me feel guilty about going against him."

Stan had assured her it was okay, that he forgave her and that, even if they had set up an election, Blackraven probably would have been elected to the council by the people anyway. Nonetheless, in the single council meeting Stan had attended since the fight at the base, Blackraven's presence on the council stuck out to him like a sore thumb.

"So anyway, has the council actually decided anything yet?" asked Charlie, although he was sure he knew the answer.

"Nope," said Stan, shaking his head grimly. "I've talked to Bill, Ben, and Bob about it, and they say the police and army are more than ready to launch a strike against the Noctem Alliance, but the council is still too divided to decide anything."

"It's the same thing that happened with the vote," Kat added glumly. "Jayden, G, and Blackraven are pushing for us to lower our defenses in the city and to go out into the server to hunt down the Alliance, while the rest of us are saying that we can't just drop all our defenses in the city, because if we do, they'll attack us again."

Charlie sighed. "I'll be completely honest, guys, I've been

giving it a lot of thought while I've been lying in here, and I've realized that the way the Noctem Alliance is fighting is actually ingenious."

Kat and Stan looked up at him in surprise. "What makes you say that?" Kat asked.

"It's called psychological warfare," said Charlie, a shadow crossing his face. "They're attacking us in a different way every time they strike, so we never know what to expect. Because we don't know what to expect, we're terrified. And that fear is driving us apart from the inside. It's making us fight with ourselves more than we're fighting them."

"Wow," said Stan, realizing the truth in the statement. It made a lot of sense, actually. The Noctem Alliance struck from out of nowhere, and they were willing to die for their cause. This was a type of fighting that none of them had ever seen before, and it wasn't nearly as straightforward as their quest to take down King Kev had been. Stan was about to make a remark to that effect when the door to the hospital room swung open.

Through the door stepped someone Stan had not seen for a long time. Stan's eyes widened in surprise before his face broke into a wide grin at the sight of Oob, the NPC villager, walking through the doorframe. His brown robes were more worn and torn up than Stan had remembered, but the huge smile on his giant-nosed face was unmistakable.

"Oob!" cried Stan. Kat burst up off the bed, ecstatic, to give him a hug.

"It's good to see ya, buddy!" Stan grinned as he threw his arms around Oob as well, causing the villager to tumble back awkwardly a few steps.

"It is good to see you as well, my friends," replied Oob jovially, struggling to keep his balance. "Now, will you please do a favor for me and let go of me? I am happy to see you but if you do not let go of me then I will fall over and get Charlie's present all dirty."

"Aw, Oob old pal! You got a present for me?" asked Charlie, smiling as he sat upright in his bed, looking happier than Stan had seen him in a long time.

"Yes, I have a present for you," said Oob as Kat and Stan released him. "I did hear from a traveling player that you, Charlie, had been wounded while fighting the bad men who tried to make me dead during the battle at the big castle. So I decided that I would come from the village with a gift to make you feel not bad anymore."

Stan couldn't help but stifle a chuckle. Just hearing Oob's slow yet sincere speech pattern was enough to brighten his day.

"Thanks, Oob! You're the best!" replied Charlie. He looked thrilled. "So whadja get me?"

"Behold!" said Oob, plunging his hands into his brown

robe and pulling out something pink. Stan examined it more closely and saw that it was a raw pork chop that appeared to be oozing a little bit of blood. Oob's face was glowing with pride at the humble piece of meat, and Charlie gladly humored him.

"Thanks, Oob!" said Charlie, with an amused look. "Where did you get this?"

"Well, it is a funny story, actually," said Oob, creasing his brow as he thought. "I had originally decided that I would bring two carrots from my village to give to Charlie. I took the carrots and immediately began to walk along the railroad tracks toward the city. As I walked through the big trees that have the yellow cats living in them . . ."

"The jungle," interjected Kat, her face just as sincerely happy as Stan's and Charlie's.

"Thank you," Oob replied with a smile. "As I walked through the jungle, a pig began to walk behind me. It was a very cute pig, and so I let it follow me. Then, I sat down under a big tree to rest, and when I put my two carrots that were to be a present to Charlie on the ground, Mr. Piggy-Oink-Oink . . ."

"Mr. Piggy-Oink-Oink?" asked Stan with a grin as Charlie laughed.

"Yes, that is the name of the cute pig that was following me," said Oob in an almost exasperated tone, as if this should have been obvious as day. “Anyway, Mr. Piggy-Oink-Oink put both of the carrots into his mouth and ate them! I was very mad at Mr. Piggy-Oink-Oink for doing that, and so I hit him with my hand. This must have made Mr. Piggy-Oink-Oink scared, because he ran away from me and right off the side of a cliff.

“I looked down over the cliff, and at the bottom, I saw this!” replied Oob, holding up the pork chop with a smile. “But I did not see Mr. Piggy-Oink-Oink anywhere. I was very confused, but then I figured out what must have happened. Mr. Piggy-Oink-Oink was embarrassed that he had eaten my carrots, and so, after he ran off the cliff, he left this . . . thing”—he gestured with the pork chop again—“to say that he was sorry, and ran away. I don’t think that Mr. Piggy-Oink-Oink was very polite for not saying sorry. But it is okay, because now I have a new present to give to Charlie!

“And now, Charlie,” said Oob, his chest swelling with pride, “I give you, the gift from Mr. Piggy-Oink-Oink!” Oob held the raw pork chop out and dropped it into Charlie’s outstretched hand, an expectant smile on his face.

“Thanks, Oob! This is a fantastic gift!” said Charlie, biting his lower lip to hold in the laughter. Oob beamed.

“Do you think we should tell him?” Kat asked Stan under her breath, a smirk on her face.

“Don’t you dare!” replied Stan, giving Kat a lighthearted

punch in the shoulder.

"So, Oob," said Charlie, storing the oozing pork chop in his inventory, "how's stuff in the village going?"

"Life in the village has been quite well," replied Oob, kneeling down to pet Rex, who had been circling Oob's feet since his arrival, almost as interested in the villager as in the piece of meat he had been holding. "Ever since the almighty Notch bestowed our Iron Golem, Plat, upon us, life in our village has been very safe. As long as the villagers retreat to our dwellings at nightfall, Plat will battle the evil mobs all throughout the night."

And with that, Oob's eyes slid out of focus, and he began to wander around the room in a confused manner, as if unsure how he had gotten there in the first place. Charlie chuckled.

"I'm glad to hear that, Oob," said Stan, standing up and turning Oob around to face them again. "So your family's doing okay?" he continued, prompting the refocused villager along.

"Oh, my family is very happy indeed," replied Oob with a smile. "My father, Blerge, and my mother, Mella, were very happy when I returned to the village after I had taken part in the large fight at the big castle. In the village, my family and I are seen as heroes because we helped you players. My younger brother wishes to be like me one day."

"Ah yes, your younger brother!" exclaimed Charlie as he pulled a watermelon slice out of his inventory to eat. "How's he doing, what's he been up to? Does he know the story of how he saved your village just by being born?"

While Stan, Kat, and Charlie traveled across Elementia on their campaign against King Kev, they had been in Oob's village for the birth of his younger brother, Stull. In fact, it was Stull's birth that had made the village population large enough for Plat the Iron Golem to spawn and help the players defend the village from a siege of hostile mobs.

"My younger brother, Stull, is doing very well. He does, indeed, know that his birth was the reason that the almighty Notch bestowed Plat the Iron Golem upon us. This fact makes our family even more famous in the village. Stull does not like the attention. He much prefers to play with Plat, and with his friend Sequi, the daughter of Ohsow, the village butcher. In fact, the two of them are going to be married when they are old enough."

"Wait, what?" spat out Kat, caught off guard. Stan's eyes widened in surprise, and Charlie gagged on his watermelon.

"I said, my younger brother, Stull, is going to be married to the butcher's daughter Sequi," said Oob, again sounding as if this were obvious fact, before proceeding to slip out of focus and wandering around the room again.

Once they had wrangled a very confused Oob back over

to the conversation, Stan asked, "How does that work, Oob?"

"It is simply the way that we NPC villagers discover our mates," replied Oob. "If a boy and girl are best friends as children, then they are to be married when they are old enough. Is this different from the way that players mate?"

Kat gave a dark chuckle. "Trust me, bub, it's not nearly as simple as that." Oob nodded, a disinterested look on his face.

"So wait a second," said Charlie, something dawning on him. "Does that mean that you're arranged to be married to someone in the village too, Oob?"

Stan's ears perked up. "Yeah, were you ever good friends with a girl villager growing up?"

"I never was," replied Oob, no discernible emotions in his voice. "You must understand, players, that I was the last child that was born before the Sacred One left our village to protect us from the bad players. After the Sacred One left, there was a time of Great Sadness in our village, during which no children were born. The Great Sadness lasted until you players arrived and killed the Spider Jockey. During the Great Sadness, the only child born was Sequi. She was born not too long before you players arrived, so she was far too young to be my wife."

The three players looked at one another uncomfortably. They hadn't realized just how bad life for the villagers had been before they arrived. The Great Sadness must have been unspeakably terrible, if they had stopped having children during it. Nobody was entirely sure what to say to Oob, who was looking around at all their faces.

"You look sorry for me, players," said Oob. They all stared at him. He was rarely able to read players' emotions accurately. "Do not be sorry for me, players. Personally, I have never been very interested in having a wife and starting a family. I was never sure what I wanted to do with my life until I met you players. Then I knew I wanted to help you protect other players and other villagers.

"And besides, ever since you good players have controlled the world, the Great Sadness has been over. New players travel through our village all the time. We have been able to trade with them, and all the members of my village are happy again. They have begun to have children once more. Our village is happier than we have been in a very long time, now that you good players are in control. We are more safe, too. In fact, there are now some players who have come to the village for the sole purpose of protecting us!"

"Those are members of the Elementia army, Oob," replied Stan. It was true. After the Noctem Alliance had attacked Elementia during the Elementia Day festival, Stan had determined that it would be wise to give the NPC village a little extra protection. He had sent out three of his men to protect the village from any Noctem Alliance troops who should cross paths with them.

Oob's eyes widened. "Is that true? You have used your own resources to keep my people safe? Thank you very much, my good friend Stan!" Oob exclaimed with a huge grin.

Stan was touched, and he, not for the first time, allowed himself a moment to congratulate himself for the job he and his friends had done here in Elementia. They had managed to touch the lives of the villagers, far away from Element City. It seemed, though, that Oob had finished talking, and there was one thing Oob had neglected to mention that Stan knew he had to discuss with the villager.

"Well, I'm glad that you and your people are happy, Oob," replied Stan, giving the villager yet another warm smile before his face became serious. "But there is something I need to ask you. You say that players pass through your village all the time now. Have you ever heard of a group called the Noctem Alliance?"

Stan saw Kat and Charlie flinch out of the corner of his eye. They, too, knew that it was necessary to discuss the Alliance with Oob, but it was still painful to talk about something like that in the midst of all his joy.

Oob's unibrow creased on his forehead, and his giant nose scrunched up a little bit. "The Noctem Alliance? I have never heard of anything called the Noctem Alliance. What is it?"

He took a deep breath, and thought for a moment about

how to explain the situation to Oob without revealing to him the very real possibility that another great war was on the horizon. He opened his mouth, but before he could get a word out, the door to the infirmary flew open with a bang. The three players and villager looked up with a start to see Ben, completely out of breath, sweat running through his sleek black hair. Rex barked at his sudden entrance.

"Stan . . . I came as . . . as soon as I could," he panted, bending over and out of breath. "I have . . . new report for you . . . couldn't believe it . . ."

"What happened, Ben?" Stan asked, his stomach already tightening. Surely the Noctem Alliance couldn't have counterattacked already!

"We just . . . got a messenger from the Noctem Alliance," replied Ben, standing up straight as he regained his breath. His face showed alarm and confusion. "He came here under a white flag, and he delivered a message to the police to give to you, Stan."

Stan was floored. The Noctem Alliance had sent a message out to them?

"And . . . what was the message?" Stan asked. The tension in his voice was palpable. He wasn't sure he wanted to know the answer. Kat and Charlie looked equally panicked. Oob looked around, terrified and perplexed at what was happening.

Ben took a deep breath. "I'd think you'd better hear it yourself." And with that, he pulled the door open. In marched five players. Four of them were in Elementia police uniforms, holding out diamond swords pointed at the one player standing between them. This player was dressed in a dusk-gray jumpsuit with a black sash and a wrapping concealing his face.

"Give President Stan your message," Ben ordered gravely.

From behind his face wrap, the player spoke. He had an unexpectedly oily and devious-sounding voice, but Stan didn't notice this. It was what the player said that hit Stan with a feeling of being punched in the gut.

"I am here to tell you, President Stan, that the great and powerful Lord Tenebris, founder of the Noctem Alliance, has founded his own city in the Southern Tundra Biome, which he has named Nocturia. Lord Tenebris has claimed the city, and the land surrounding it, as his own. He has declared independence from the Grand Republic of Elementia. He has called his new country the Nation of the Noctem Alliance, and it will forever be a haven for those upper-level players who have been wronged by your tyranny, President Stan. Long live Lord Tenebris! And long live the Noctem Alliance! Viva la Noctem!"

And Stan could see from the look in the player's eyes that, had his face not been concealed, his features would have broken out into a wicked grin.

CHAPTER 11
HOME AGAIN

Leonidas was in agony. With every step he took, immense pain shot through his entire body. He had used his two potions of healing to cure the arrow wounds in his legs. However, when the potion ran out, he was forced to grit his teeth and endure the pain in his shoulder and arm.

Leonidas glanced back at the jungle disappearing in the distance behind him, wincing in pain as he did so. He tried not to think about the fact that he was in the middle of the Ender Desert, only halfway back to the tundra that held Nocturia. He would love nothing more than to use his remaining Ender Pearls to teleport great distances in one throw, cutting the travel time in half. However, each Ender Pearl that he used took a toll on his legs, and seeing as they were the only part of his body that didn't feel like they were on fire, he thought better of it.

Leonidas's thoughts drifted to Caesar, and quickly turned bitter. He imagined Caesar was with Lord Tenebris now, plotting the details of their next attack against the Republic of Elementia. Leonidas knew Lord Tenebris was planning to found his own country out in the tundra around Nocturia. He wondered if the plan had gone into effect yet.

This thought was fleeting and vague, however.

Leonidas found it hard to focus on anything else besides how much he resented Caesar. Why was it that Caesar got to sit around in a comfortable throne room, commanding Leonidas to go around on errands like a grandmaster maneuvering an expendable chess piece? There were four players who had started the Alliance on Spawnpoint Hill all those months ago, and somehow he, Leonidas, had ended up in a far worse position than any of the other three. Caesar had been in a nice, completed building the entire time. He had never been forced to run dangers like Leonidas had. Leonidas had no idea what Minotaurus or the Noctem spy within Stan's government were doing, but he found it hard to imagine they were much worse off than he was.

A wave of anger crashed over Leonidas as these thoughts spiraled around him like a vortex. He had braved the cold of the tundra, constructed the whole of Nocturia with insufficient manpower, fought to take the Jungle Base, and then abandoned that same base the second Stan tried to take it back, getting seriously hurt in the process. And for what? Why was it that he, Leonidas, was still part of the Alliance? It had done nothing for him.

Leonidas looked back on that night atop the Jungle Base with painful recollection. He had spoken his mind to Stan that night . . . he really didn't feel like he had chosen to join the Noctem Alliance, he had simply latched on because there was no other choice. Leonidas had never had any problems with lower-level players, or any players at all for that matter. He had never wanted to join King Kev's army to begin with. The only reason he had was to save his family.

Suddenly, a rush of comprehension slammed into Leonidas full force, as he realized where he was. His mind began to race. Was there any possibility that they were still out here? Did the community that contained Leonidas's family still exist out here in the Ender Desert after all this time? Leonidas didn't have to think twice about it. He had to find out. Whatever Caesar had for him to do back in Nocturia, well, he could just get up out of his comfortable little safe room and do it himself.

Leonidas glanced up at the sun. It was early afternoon, so the sun was just past its apex and starting to tilt toward the west. Leonidas still knew where the village was by heart, and so he turned to face northeast and walked out into the barren stretches of desert. He did all he could to ignore the wounds that hurt exponentially more the faster he walked, instead focusing on the thought of seeing his family for the first time since he had joined King Kev's army all those months ago.

As Leonidas trekked on for hours, the pain became harder and harder to ignore. The sun swung farther and farther toward the horizon, each minute bringing Leonidas closer to being trapped in the middle of the desert with evil mobs and roaming gangs of nomads. He had dealt with both of these dangers before, and had no intention of doing so again. Finally, when the sun was nearing the horizon and the sky was starting to turn pink, Leonidas saw it—the outline of buildings against the fading light of the sky.

Adrenaline and excitement surged through Leonidas as he soldiered on, the pain suddenly seeming trivial. As he got closer and closer to the village, more details came into view despite the fading light. The wooden houses, the gravel pathway, the rings of wood blocks containing water and wheat farms. Leonidas was overwhelmed by a feeling of joy to be back here, among his family once again. He saw farms of carrots and potatoes next to the wheat farms. It was good to see that the villagers had expanded their produce. They must have been doing pretty well for themselves.

As Leonidas walked down the pathway and toward the main well, he saw them for the first time. They looked exactly as he remembered them—brown robes, dark brown shoes, and odd faces with creased unibrows and noses that would give Squidward a run for his money. He looked at one of the NPC villagers that he knew to be called Libroru. The villager gave him a polite smile before continuing down the path. Leonidas wondered for a moment why Libroru didn't acknowledge him, before remembering that he had changed his skin since the last time he had been to the village all that time ago.

Leonidas knew who he had to see. He knew for a fact that there was one resident of the NPC village who didn't recognize players by their outward appearance, but instead by their eyes, which retained some unexplainable quality of individuality even when skins were changed. Leonidas was about to head down the path when he paused for a moment.

All of a sudden, he was overcome with a tremendous amount of anxiety. It was just now occurring to him that these villagers had not seen him for dozens of months. How would they react to him? Would they even remember him at all? Was it worth finding out?

Leonidas hesitated for a moment, before collecting himself. *Yes, it's worth it*, he told himself firmly. *You're here*, he thought, *and you're goin' to at least try.* Not allowing himself to be nervous, Leonidas marched down the gravel pathway, coming to a halt outside the church. The cobblestone building was tall and imposing, standing high above the rest of the buildings of the village. Taking a deep breath, Leonidas knocked on the door.

Moments later, the door swung open. Leonidas was now standing face-to-face with a villager clad in purple. Leonidas knew that this particular villager was wiser than the others, and it was difficult to catch her off guard. However, as

Moganga stared into his eyes and realized who he was, her eyes widened and her mouth dropped open, and she actually tumbled backward a few steps in shock, as if she were seeing a ghost.

"Oh, great Notch above!" she moaned, struggling to comprehend the player who stood before her. "Is it truly . . . could it really be . . . ?"

Leonidas smiled. "Yeah, Moganga, it's me. Did ya miss me?"

Moganga clutched her chest and sunk to the ground, overwhelmed that this player who she believed to have gone forever from the village had returned and was standing before her. Leonidas was elated, and offered her a hand up, which she accepted tentatively. Even when he let her hand go, she still stared at it, in a state of complete disbelief.

"Do ya think ya could call a village meetin' in here, Moganga? I wanna say hi to everyone."

There was no hesitation. Leonidas stepped to the side as Moganga nodded fervently and moved to the doorstep. She took a deep breath and proceeded to emit from her mouth a ghostly wailing noise, as if a spirit were trying to contact the living. The effect of the wail was immediate. Every single door in the village flew open as the villagers filed into the streets, recognizing that a town meeting had been called in the church. Leonidas watched the villagers enter, his heart racing in excitement.

Although none of the villagers paid a second glance to Leonidas standing next to the church entrance, he recognized some of them as they assembled. Some that stood out were Ohsow, the village butcher, adorned in a white apron, a confused look on his face, as well as Mella and Blerge, two villagers in the typical brown robes who stood very close to each other, with a very young villager holding his mother's hand.

Leonidas was a little surprised that their older son wasn't with them, and a resurgence of anxiety knotted in Leonidas's stomach. As the last of the villagers filed in, it occurred to him that there were far less of them than he remembered. He could only assume there had been a lot of death in the village since he had last been there.

"Please, come in," said a voice from the doorway, jolting Leonidas from his thoughts. It was Moganga, the look on her face nothing less than ecstatic. Leonidas forced himself to suppress his anxiety. It wasn't his place now to worry about the dead villagers, but to reunite with those still here.

As Leonidas walked down the middle aisle of the church behind Moganga, the villagers stared at him inquisitively, chatting among themselves in bemused voices. They were baffled as to why their leader had called them to a meeting just to see this alien player. When the two stood before the altar of the church, Moganga turned around and raised her hands. Instantly, the congregation fell silent.

“My dear brothers and sisters,” boomed Moganga, her voice containing some indefinable quality of mysticism. “I doubt that any of you here will be able to recognize this player standing beside me at a glance. He has changed greatly in appearance since the last time he was in our village, which was long ago.”

The villagers murmured in confusion. A player from long ago? They had never had players visit the village until very recently. What player could this possibly be, if he was from long ago?

“I ask you now, my brethren, look into the eyes of this player!” wailed Moganga, exuding power. “Do any of you recognize this player by his eyes, the trait that remains consistent no matter how appearances may change over time?”

Leonidas felt twenty pairs of eyes trained on him. Most of the villagers simply looked even more perplexed than before. However, there was one villager who stood up from his stone seat. His eyes were wide, and his face showed a look of disbelief that mirrored Moganga’s from moments before.

Blerge staggered down the middle aisle, a shaky hand outstretched toward Leonidas, a look of sheer blissful incredulity in his features. There was a long pause, during which the teary-eyed villager seemed unable to speak. Then, finally, his mouth opened.

"Is that . . . could it be . . . ," he stammered, tears of joy streaming down his face. "Is it . . . truly you, Leo-nidas?"

The moment the name left his lips, the face of every single villager in the assembly showed shock, followed by a type of joy powered by an almost religious fervor. Even the youngest of the villager children recognized this name, as they had been taught from birth about the story of a brave player, a player who had lived in their village in a time before the Great Sadness. When the evil King Kev had risen to power, this player had sacrificed himself to the king so that the villagers may live in peace. The villagers had hailed the player as their savior, and vowed never to speak the player's name again except in the most important of ceremonies, until the day that he would return to their village.

This was the player who stood before them now. Leonidas watched in awe as every single villager sunk down to their knees in reverence. As Moganga sunk down beside him, she enunciated the words clearly, unfazed by the tears streaming down her face.

"At last, the savior of our village has returned! All hail, Leo-nidas! All hail the Sacred One!"

"All hail the Sacred One! All hail the Sacred One!" the bowed villagers repeated in a unified chant.

Leonidas watched in awe, amazed as he realized what was going on. He had remembered back in the old days when the villagers would perform this ritual. It was a sacred ritual to them, performed only to hail Notch, their creator. And now they were performing it for him! Tears welled up in Leonidas's eyes, and he was about to pour out his heart to the villagers, telling how much he had missed them, when the door slammed open.

In the doorway of the church stood three players who were silhouetted against the setting sun behind them. They stepped inside. Leonidas was horror-struck. He knew the villagers took their religious customs very seriously, and it was an offense of the highest degree to interrupt them. Moganga seemed to recognize this. She stared at the three players, appalled. The other villagers didn't even seem to notice the three players, as they were too focused on worshiping Leonidas.

As the three players stepped into the torch-lit room, Leonidas could make out their features. One of them looked like the standard Minecraft skin, but he was decked out in a full brown beard, with holsters and sheaths for twin swords covering his body. Another one resembled Master Chief, but his armor was indigo instead of green, which gave a sleek contrast to his orange visor. Standing in front of these two was a player with a simple tunic skin, but the look on his face could only be described as the embodiment of menace. A bow was slung over his back. All three of these players had one thing in common: a badge on the left of their chest that designated them as part of the Grand Elementia Army.

Leonidas was instantly struck into panic as the eyes of all three soldiers locked on him. How had the army tracked him out here? And why did they have to find him here, when he had finally reconnected with the only real family he'd ever had? Despite his growing angst, Leonidas refused to pull his bow. He refused to kill any player in front of these villagers. He would rather be captured.

Leonidas swore to himself that he would go down with honor, and not give the players the satisfaction of making him show pain. It was all Leonidas could do to stop from wincing as the player opened his mouth, surely about to call out his arrest.

"Villager! Why have you not paid tribute today? It's almost sunset!"

Leonidas did a double take. He couldn't believe what was happening. The player had looked straight past him to Moganga. She looked outraged for a moment before her face suddenly looked mortified, as if she were the one who had interrupted their ritual.

"Oh, I am very sorry! I have forgotten to organize the collection today," said Moganga meekly. Leonidas was flabbergasted. He had never seen Moganga look submissive toward a player before in his life! Who were these guys?

"Well, then," replied the one in the tunic, "I suggest you

round that up quickly, villager. That silly little song you were doing can wait." His voice was calm, collected, and cool, yet menacing and chilling to the core.

Leonidas realized the players didn't recognize him. He supposed the soldiers must be here for some other reason. Come to think of it, he did vaguely recall that Caesar had, some time ago, shared intelligence with him that Stan had sent troops to protect the NPC villages. He recalled that Caesar had been quite upset about it, too, stating that the villagers were integral to a later phase in Lord Tenebris's plan.

As soon as he realized this, he was livid. What audacity he had to address Moganga, the leader of the villagers, with such disrespect! It was bad enough for an average player to insult the villagers, but what if these soldiers really were here to protect the villagers and they were still insulting them? Leonidas was about to open his mouth to defend Moganga, but out of the corner of his eye, he caught her giving an almost imperceptible shake of the head. Leonidas was confused, but he bit his tongue nonetheless.

"I will organize them now," replied Moganga with great humility. "You shall receive your tribute as quickly as possible, sir."

Sir? She was callin' him sir? Leonidas had never heard Moganga address a player as her superior in his life. *What was goin' on here?*

No more was said for a while, as Moganga ordered the villagers to go and collect their tribute, whatever it was, and bring it to the church. The villagers obeyed without question, and they all filed out of the church. Leonidas watched in shock as slowly but surely, every villager returned to the church with a good stock of supplies in hand. Mella and Blerge returned with armfuls of wheat and carrots and dropped them at the feet of the players before quietly returning to their seats.

The other villagers soon followed. Libroru brought a whole mess of arrows to the pile, Ohsow the butcher added a large number of cooked chickens, and Leonidas's eyes popped as Leol the blacksmith dropped a significant number of uncrafted diamonds and iron ingots onto the heap. Even more startling was when Moganga herself dropped some of her own personal supply of glowstone dust, which Leonidas knew she guarded jealously, onto the pile. As the size of the pile increased with each villager, so too did the size of the ecstatic grins on the faces of the three players.

"Your contribution to the army is much appreciated," said the lead soldier with the tunic and chilling voice as the three of them covetously stuffed their inventories with the villagers' supplies. "As usual, we'll expect another payment in three days' time. Go back to whatever you were doing, villager," he said, with a condescending look at Moganga, before he led the other two out the door, slamming it behind him.

The instant the door slammed shut, the villagers broke out into a cacophonous cheer that caught Leonidas off guard. They all swarmed around him, greeting him, exalting him, staring at him to be sure he was real. As excited as he was to be with the villagers again, he couldn't properly enjoy it until he figured out what had just happened.

"Excuse me, everyone," said Leonidas, and instantly, the congregation fell quiet.

"Yes, dear Sacred One, Leo-nidas?" asked Moganga reverently. Leonidas had to suppress a chuckle. He had almost forgotten the disjointed way that the villagers pronounced his name.

"I'm so glad to be back here, ya have no idea," said Leonidas. "Right now, though, I'm pretty tired from hikin' all the way out here. How about I just take a rest tonight and I can catch up with you all tomorrow?"

"Your wish is our command, dear Leo-nidas," replied Moganga. She turned to her people. "People of the village, nightfall is nearly upon us. All villagers are to return to their homes immediately. The Sacred One Leo-nidas shall stay in the church for the night. All people of the village shall meet in the church when the sun next rises, at which point we shall proceed to speak with Leo-nidas. Now, off you go!" she said firmly.

Leonidas was always impressed by how readily the villagers followed Moganga's commands. Not five seconds after her mandate was finished, the church was completely deserted save for Moganga and himself.

"I have noticed that you have suffered from wounds, Leo-nidas," said Moganga, gesturing to the arrow marks in his shoulder and arm. "I shall mend your wounds hastily, and then, I too shall respect your wishes and leave you to sleep in peace." And with that, Moganga, in an almost businesslike manner, reached into the folds of her purple robes and pulled out the same type of glowstone dust that she had just given to the soldiers. Leonidas climbed onto the altar and lay down on his stomach, allowing Moganga's magic-enhanced hands to treat the wound on his shoulder. Leonidas allowed himself one sigh of relief as the pain began to ease, before he started talking.

"Hey, Moganga, I have a couple questions," he said slowly.

"If I am able to answer your questions, Leo-nidas, I most certainly will," replied Moganga kindly.

"Well . . . they're about those guys that just came in. First of all, who are they?"

"Oh, those players are members of the army of a very brave player named Stan2012," she replied. "He is the new ruler of the players of this world, and he believes that the villages should have protection in case bad players come into our village. We are all very happy regarding their presence here."

Leonidas nearly fell off the altar. "What? You guys are happy that the soldiers are takin' your stuff?"

"It is a small price to pay for the protection," replied Moganga. "The soldiers explained to us when they first came to our village that they would require resources to protect us. Therefore, every third day, we villagers offer tribute to them, giving them all the goods that we can."

"And you guys are all okay with that? It doesn't make life harder for ya to give these guys so much of your stuff?"

"Oh, certain aspects of our life have become more difficult," replied Moganga as she shifted the focus of her healing to the puncture wound on his arm. "Many of us now go to bed hungry each night because our farmers are giving so much of their crop to the soldiers. It is a small price to pay so that we are protected from dangers."

Leonidas's stomach clenched. He did not like the sound of what was going on. "What about an Iron Golem? You guys have a pretty big village here, don't ya have an Iron Golem to protect ya?"

"Oh yes, we do," replied Moganga. "However, the Iron Golem is more adept at fighting the evil monsters that threaten our village at night. The players have told us that they are specially trained to combat bad players who might come into our village and attempt to do us harm."

Leonidas had nothing to say to this. He knew what he had to do next; however, it might not be prudent to do it with Moganga's knowledge. He simply let her finish her job healing his arm. When she was finished, she simply walked over to the ladder at the back of the church and climbed to her quarters without so much as a good night.

Leonidas smirked. The NPC villagers certainly were quirky little buggers, but he loved them like family. He couldn't bear to see them abused for their naiveté like this, and he determined that he had to put an end to it immediately.

A few minutes after Moganga had entered the loft, Leonidas prepared himself for what he was about to do. He pulled on his leather armor and slung his bow over his back, praying that he wouldn't have to use it, but prepared to do so if the necessity arose. A quiver of arrows at his right hip and an iron sword at his left, Leonidas silently opened the front door of the church, stepped outside, and closed the wooden door behind him with a faint creak.

CHAPTER 12 CLASH OF THE SAVIORS

Leonidas glanced at the sky. The moon was almost a complete square in the star-speckled black velvet sky. He remembered the old days, fighting off massive waves of mobs each full moon during the siege on the village, always failing to kill the elusive Spider Jockey. The village was safe tonight, but within a few days, the three players would have to fight off the largest horde of evil mobs they had ever seen. *Even more of a reason*, he thought, *for gettin' these soldiers to leave the village.*

The village had an eerie, ominous feeling, in the light of the moon, slightly extenuated by the wavering torchlight. The roads were silent, save the distant sound of evil mobs crying in agony, punctuated by splats. This, he supposed, was the Iron Golem doing its work. Besides this, Leonidas's ears caught the faint sound of joyous, raucous laughter and conversation.

Leonidas traced the sounds to a house at the far end of the gravel road, near the outer border of the village. He dashed up to about ten blocks away and then silently snuck up to the back window. He began listening to the conversation within, hoping for any more information about these mysterious soldiers.

"Can you believe this? This is like, twice as many diamonds as last time!" one of the players exclaimed, his voice deep and with a slightly Russian accent. There was the clinking sound of the player sifting his blocky hands through a pile of diamonds.

"I know, man, I know! And I can't believe this chicken!" This player had an upper-class accent, and sounded as if he were talking through a mouthful of food. "Honestly, what does the villager thing put in this stuff? It's delicious! When I go home, I'm taking one of those villager things with me so it can be my personal chef!"

"Oh, come on! The chicken, seriously? That's what impresses you? Not the stack of hundreds of diamonds and gold and iron ingots?"

"We could mine our own diamonds if we wanted to, man, but I don't think that any player alive could make chicken this good!"

"I can't believe you, man." The Russian guy sighed in exasperation. "You'd choose a chicken buffet over a diamond buffet? I mean, just think about it! How hard is it to get a chicken, and how hard is it to get a diamond?"

"It's not about how hard it is, it's about how good it tastes!" This player seemed irritated now. "The meat is just so succulent."

"Aw, why am I even bothering with you?" the Russian player scoffed. "You don't get what I'm saying, you've never mined a diamond in your life!"

"Well, I've tried a few times, but it's so hard! You have to fight off a ton of monsters down there, it's all claustrophobic and everything, half the time you can't even find . . ."

"I *know*! I've actually done it before, unlike you! So I actually understand that it's really nice to have these villager things do all the work!"

"Hey, it's not my fault my dad gives me all the diamonds I want!"

"How did I get stuck with you as a partner? You're a total brat, you know that?"

"I didn't ask to get drafted; don't yell at me!"

"Would you two shut up!" a third voice bellowed, and Leonidas almost fell out of his crouch in surprise. He recognized this voice as the one who had ordered Moganga around in the church. "I might as well be working with two of the villagers. You two are so insufferably idiotic!"

"Hey, sorry, Boss, but I just like chicken, don't yell at me!" the upper-class player replied snootily.

"That's enough of you," the boss said in his cool, collected, yet terrifying way. "Why haven't you two started to craft the diamond armor yet?"

"Why would we need diamond armor?" the Russian player asked. "We're not actually going to protect the villager things, are we?"

"Of course not!" the boss scoffed. "These villagers are

unintelligent animals. I don't even understand why President Stan wants the things safe. What are they doing for him? We should just count ourselves lucky that we got assigned out here, where we can just sit around, do nothing and let the . . . ah . . . taxes pile up!"

The player laughed as Leonidas was fighting to keep himself from vomiting with rage.

"So . . . er . . . what's the point of crafting the armor again?" the upper-class player asked.

"What? Oh, right," the boss replied as if being awakened from a daydream. "We need to look like we're doing something if President Stan sends someone out here to take a report on us. The diamond armor makes it seem like we're actually trying."

"So . . . we're not actually going to be fighting anything?" the upper-class players asked.

"Of course not!" the boss laughed. "I certainly don't care about the villagers! They're just mindless NPCs, right?"

"Well, of course I agree . . . "

"Then we're not gonna be fighting anything!" said the boss in an airy voice, clearly amused at how slow his soldier was being. "And even if we were doing anything, it's not like there's anything out here that's an actual threat!"

"That's where you're wrong," snarled Leonidas under his breath as, unable to contain his indignation any longer, he sprinted to the front of the house and slammed the door open.

The three players whipped their heads up in shock. Leonidas was taken aback for a moment by the sheer amount of materials that he could see in the house. The players were gathered around chests spilling over with chicken, cookies, wheat, carrots, potatoes, diamonds, gold, iron, and dozens of other things that the villagers handled in their professions.

The player with futuristic blue armor and the one with the tunic, who was clearly the boss, were sitting atop two wood blocks on the ground. The bearded player knelt next to a crafting table and was in the process of crafting a diamond chestplate. All of them wore an identical look of outrage on their faces.

"What do you think you're doing?" the one with the blue armor asked in his upper-class accent.

"I'm demandin' that ya leave this village. Right now," said Leonidas firmly, eyebrows creased and voice shaking in fury. He drew his bow and loaded it, much to the alarm of the three players. "And you're to leave all the materials that you've taken from the villagers here."

"Who do you think you are?" the boss asked in a voice of composed fury, keeping his cool, but obviously flabbergasted nonetheless.

"Wait a minute . . . ," said the bearded one in his Russian

accent. "You're . . . You were that player who was in the church with the villagers when we collected our taxes today!"

"Ya weren't collectin' taxes," seethed Leonidas, pulling the string of the bow back even farther. "Ya were abusin' the villagers. Ya knew that they weren't smart enough to see that ya were takin' advantage of 'em. Ya three don't deserve to call yourselves members of Stan's army. You're just a bunch of thugs."

"How dare you!" cried the boss, slamming his fist onto the crafting table in rage. "You have the audacity to speak to a ranking officer of the army of . . ."

He stopped in midsentence as the arrow left Leonidas's bow and flew directly toward him. The boss's eyes followed the arrow as it passed within an inch of his neck before embedding in the wall behind him. He spun back around to look at Leonidas, outraged.

"Yeah, I do," replied Leonidas, loading another arrow, no trace of mercy in his face. "As much as I despise the three of ya, though, I don't wanna kill ya. Don't make me. I'll spare the three of ya if ya leave this village, don't take anythin' with ya, and never come back. It's your choice."

There was a moment of tense silence. Then, slowly, the boss smiled, and, quick as a flash, he whipped a diamond pickaxe out of his inventory. The other two followed his lead, the armored one drawing a bow of his own and the bearded one pulling out a diamond sword.

"Very well then, stranger," the boss replied. "If you'd like to fight, then we will gladly oblige you. We are members of the army of Stan2012, the greatest armed forces in Minecraft. There are three of us and only one of you, so if you're man enough, fire the first shot." A sinister grin broke on his face at these words.

That was all the invitation Leonidas needed. Leonidas jerked the bow downward, rapidly changing aim from the boss's head to his stomach, and fired. With equal swiftness, the boss flicked his pickaxe downward and deflected the arrow with a rapid spin, laughing and waving his free hand forward. The bearded player rushed Leonidas with his sword drawn, while the armored player shot an arrow at Leonidas from afar.

Leonidas ducked the arrow and short-hopped backward to dodge the powerful downward strike from the bearded player's sword. This initial strike shifted the gears of Leonidas's mind into tactics mode. The armored one clearly wasn't a great shot, and the bearded one's overpowered initial strike told Leonidas that he wasn't great with a sword either. That left the boss as the only true threat, as he had moved surprisingly fast with that pickaxe.

Leonidas sprinted into the street, followed in hot pursuit by the bearded one, while the armored one fired more shots.

Leonidas reloaded his bow as he ran, and in an instant he spun around, took aim, and shot an arrow straight at the bearded one's chest. He managed to deflect the first arrow, but the next two sunk directly into the bearded player's heart, causing him to keel over sideways, a ring of items bursting about him.

For some reason, Leonidas felt uneasy. Although the rage he felt at these players' maltreatment of the villagers could not be expressed in words, Leonidas still felt a twinge of uncomfortable guilt as he saw the lifeless body of this player whose name he didn't even know. Despite this, he also couldn't help but think: *one down, two to go.*

The next kill was even more effortless. Leonidas's skill with a bow was equal to the skill of the armored one tenfold. While none of his opponent's shots had come close to touching Leonidas, it only took one arrow from Leonidas's bow to send the armored player the same way as his bearded comrade.

There, again, came the twinge of guilt, now even more than before as he realized the implications of what he had just done. This player hadn't even wanted to join Stan's army, he had been drafted.

But Leonidas shook away the feeling, for the time being at least, when he heard a voice from behind him.

"Very impressive, my friend. Clearly, you are more skilled than you look."

Leonidas spun around and locked eyes with the boss, still standing in the doorway of the house containing the villagers' loot. He smiled that unnerving, merciless smile, holding up a loaded bow. There was no hint of anger in his voice, no hint of any concern that Leonidas had just killed his two comrades. The only emotion present was coldhearted amusement. Leonidas's temple twitched with vehemence, and he knew he would feel no remorse at all for ending this life.

The two arrows flew at the same time. Leonidas dive-rolled to the side, and then looked up to see that the boss had done the same. Leonidas shot off three more arrows, which the boss evaded by sprawling onto the ground and tunneling with his pickaxe into the sand.

Leonidas knew what the boss was trying. Leonidas stepped up onto the wooden ring encircling the nearest wheat farm and, with a running dash, leaped and grabbed on to the edge of the roof of the nearest house, loading his bow and waiting for the boss to come up from the ground.

Leonidas waited, but the only sounds he could discern came from the Iron Golem's distant massacre. He began to become a little unnerved. Where was this guy? Shouldn't he have resurfaced by now?

Leonidas heard the sound of a string being stretched just as he thought this. He barely turned in time to see that the boss had silently resurfaced behind him, and an arrow was flying straight toward him. *Very clever*, thought Leonidas bitterly as he dodged the arrow, losing his balance and tumbling off the roof of the house.

He landed on the ground with a sickly thud, and he felt pain course through his leg. Through gritted teeth, Leonidas glanced up to see that his bow had fallen on the ground a good ten blocks away. At the same time, he became aware that the boss had rounded the corner of the house and was charging at him at full speed, diamond pickaxe drawn.

Leonidas quickly formulated a plan. He reached for the bow before allowing himself to fall face-down on the ground, pretending to be completely out of energy. The boss gave a devious grin, and he was upon Leonidas in moments. He raised his diamond pickaxe, and right as the killing blow was about to fall, Leonidas sent the iron sword he had been concealing swinging up toward the boss in an almighty thrust.

The sword struck the boss across the arm, opening a gaping gash in his right shoulder. As he clutched his arm in pain, he was in no position to stop Leonidas from scampering over to his bow and sending four arrows into his chest in the space of less than two seconds.

Leonidas watched in satisfaction as the boss staggered backward toward the house, seconds away from death. That satisfaction turned to horror in an instant, however, as the boss haphazardly tossed a block of TNT onto the ground and touched it with a redstone torch before finally collapsing.

Leonidas could only hobble as fast as he could on his crippled leg toward the house outside of which the TNT block sat hissing. As soon as he realized whose house it was, he bellowed in desperation, "LIBRORU! Get out of there, quickly!"

The front door flew open seconds later, and the groggy-eyed head of Libroru poked out.

"What is happening out—" the villager began to ask, before he was cut off by the explosion.

Leonidas, who had desperately and senselessly been limping toward the house, was knocked back by the force of the blast and felt the heat scorch his arms as he tumbled across the gravel road. As his disorientation faded, and his world slowly fell back into place, Leonidas felt a terrible pain coursing through both his legs. He forced himself to glance up at the scene around him. What he saw made his stomach dissolve.

The face of Libroru's house had been completely blown apart. Scattered blocks were lying all over the ground, and there was a crater where the stairs had been. Despite his every instinct to look away, to avoid seeing the horror before him, Leonidas's eyes traveled downward to the lifeless body of Libroru, lying in the street in front of the crater beside the corpse of the boss. Most alarming, however, was the Iron

Golem that had walked around the side of the house and was staring at the scene before it.

Leonidas's stomach clenched. His grief over Libroru's death was completely washed away by his immediate fear of the giant metal behemoth standing before him. The Golem's head shifted from side to side with a series of ominous creaks, surveying the scene around him. Leonidas realized how the scene looked—a blown-out house surrounded by the body of a villager and the three players tasked to defend the village, with Leonidas as the only one still alive.

Leonidas could not fight the Iron Golem. He had heard far too many stories of players challenging these iron monsters to try something that foolish. The Golems were faster than the players, making escape a non-option, and Leonidas's arrows would simply bounce straight off a Golem's solid iron body. The only attacks strong enough to damage an Iron Golem were TNT or an exceptionally powerful strike from a diamond sword, neither of which were available to Leonidas.

But what was he thinking? He didn't want to kill the Iron Golem at all. The Golem was the only thing truly protecting the villagers from the evils of the Minecraft world, and if it were to fall, then the village would be in serious trouble. He only had two options, both of which seemed equally impossible: either convince the Golem that he was not a threat to the village, or escape.

Leonidas slowly pulled himself up, ignoring the screaming pain in his legs, and forced himself to quell the anguish of Libroru's death. He remembered Libroru from the old days, when the villager would give Leonidas a free cookie every day and would laugh hysterically at Leonidas's terrible jokes. Regardless of how much he wanted to grieve, Leonidas looked the Iron Golem in the eye, forcing himself to focus on the metal beast in front of him.

"I am not responsible for this," he choked out, painstakingly staring into the Golem's emotionless red eyes. "The players that said they were protectin' the villagers were actually just bullyin' them. I tried to stop them, so they killed Libroru, and tried to kill me. I promise, I meant no harm to any of ya. Please, just let me be."

A moment of silence, in which the Golem stared Leonidas down, and he stared back, nervousness ripe on his face. Then, in an instant, the Golem took off, moving faster than Leonidas had seen any mob move, and launched itself into the air, its giant iron arm headed straight toward Leonidas.

Leonidas barely managed to roll to the side in time to dodge the giant fist, terror tripling his crippled speed. The Golem wasted no time in continuing to attack, wildly flinging its giant iron arms. Leonidas fell backward, the giant iron hand coming within inches of his face. Leonidas looked around wildly, desperate for anything he could use to buy an escape.

His eyes stopped on a diamond sword lying on the ground. Although the bodies of all four of the dead had vanished, the sword of the bearded player still remained. Leonidas snatched it just as the Iron Golem threw another punch toward him. Leonidas kicked off not an instant too soon, scooting himself through the giant's legs. Leonidas swung his sword across the back of the Golem's knees, and the iron behemoth toppled to the ground with an almighty clang.

Leonidas jumped to his feet and gave an audible scream of pain. With his survival instincts upped to the maximum, he had forgotten about the spiking pains in his legs, and his knees buckled. He glanced over his shoulder as he fell. The Iron Golem was back on its feet, and it was turning around to ready another charge at Leonidas. He got back to his feet and sprinted as fast as his crippled legs could carry him, aware of an omnipresent metallic clanging growing louder and louder behind him at an alarming rate.

Leonidas cut a sharp right-hand turn at the corner of a house and ducked into an alleyway, instantly feeling a rush of wind behind him as the Iron Golem sprinted past. He heard the scrabble of gravel on iron as the Golem attempted to reorient itself, and realized this was his chance to escape. He eyed the open desert in front of him. If he could just make it out into the dune sea, he could return tomorrow and explain his predicament to the villagers, who would tell the Iron Golem to calm down. . . .

His thought was cut off as he stumbled over a small sand pit, tumbled through the air for a moment, and face-planted. The diamond sword flew from his hand and clattered across the blocks. Leonidas gave another shout of pain. He had landed on a rock-solid surface of sandstone. The ground hit Leonidas's body like a giant smack. The pain in his body was suddenly universal, no longer confined to just his legs.

Leonidas managed to flop over onto his back, just in time to see the Iron Golem staring at him from the top of the sand ledge. Leonidas only held the gaze of the beast for a moment before it swung its arms backward, and with an almighty leap, flew through the air, fist outstretched and headed straight for Leonidas. The reaction was instinctive. In the space of a second, he sought a way to protect himself. His eyes fell on the sword. He snatched it up and was just spinning it into a defensive block as the iron body made contact.

Though his eyes were closed, Leonidas could hear the earsplitting metal clang that reverberated around him, piercing his ears, but he could not feel the impact. He supposed that this was what happened when you died. Finally delivered from all pain, you couldn't feel the impact that killed you. As Leonidas opened his eyes to see what being dead looked like, he was confused. The world wasn't all black. It wasn't all white either. All that Leonidas could see was what looked like a giant mass of iron covered in vines, sitting inches away from his face.

Bewildered and a little frightened as to what exactly was going on, Leonidas reached out to touch the iron wall. He winced. His arm still throbbed from the impact against the ground. But . . . hold on . . . if his arm still hurt, then . . . that meant that he wasn't dead! How was he not dead?

Leonidas gritted his teeth as he raised both of his arms, preparing his psyche for the mental and physical strain of moving this iron mass off of him. He was caught totally off guard, however, when the iron mass moved quite easily at the slightest touch. One good push later and the metal body rolled over onto its side. Leonidas struggled into a sitting position and looked to see exactly what the iron mass was. What he saw knocked the wind out of him.

The Iron Golem lay on the ground beside him. The beast was unmoving, eyes closed, completely unscathed except for its chest. On the left side of its chest, right where its heart would be, a diamond sword stuck out, driven deep into the Iron Golem. Only a remarkably powerful force could drive a sword that deep into an Iron Golem. As Leonidas realized the truth, that the Iron Golem had impaled itself on the diamond sword as it attacked him, a feeling of dread washed over him.

The sensation doubled an instant later as the giant Iron

Golem's body faded into nothingness, leaving only two iron ingots and a red rose in its wake. *This was a peaceful monster,* thought Leonidas as tears welled up in his eyes, *devoted only to protectin' the village and the villagers within. And now it's dead, and the villagers have nothin' to protect them from the dangers of the night.*

"My God," said Leonidas in horror.

"Leo-nidas?"

Leonidas spun around, and the pain in his body from the sudden movement was nothing compared to the pain that gripped his stomach, heart, and lungs as he saw the entire population of the NPC village, Moganga at the forefront, staring down into the pit at him. All the villagers had a mix of horror, bewilderment, and fear on their faces as they looked at Leonidas, sitting alongside a diamond sword and the pitiful remains of their great defender. Only Moganga's face showed the emotion that pierced the armor of Leonidas's soul: unspeakable sadness.

"Leo-nidas, did you kill Plat, the Iron Golem?" Moganga asked.

Leonidas started to panic. He had no intention of lying to Moganga, and knew that she would be able to tell if he did. He only prayed that she'd be willing to listen to his reasoning.

"Yes, Moganga, I did, but—"

"And you also killed the three men protecting us from

outside dangers to the village," she interjected with equal gravity, the seeds of anger present as well.

"Yes, I did," said Leonidas, his voice cracking and the tears started to run. "But Moganga, I swear I only did it to—"

"It does not matter, Leo-nidas," replied Moganga, looking intimidating and furious against the blazing red and pink of the rising sun at her back. "Murder is not allowed in this village. You are to leave now."

"No, please, Moganga," wailed Leonidas as he sunk to his knees, hands pressed together before him, pleading for mercy. "I didn't mean to do anythin' to hurt ya, I only wanted to help you guys!" Sobs were interspersed with the words now as Leonidas spilled his heart out, begging his only true friends in the world to forgive him. "Don't ya remember? I'm the Sacred One, I gave my life away to save you guys! Do ya remember? I love y'all, you're my family!"

Leonidas glanced up at Moganga pleadingly. Only pitiless eyes shown down on him. Then the villager priest spoke five words that hurt Leonidas more than any weapon ever could:

"There is no Sacred One."

Leonidas felt nothing but horrified shock, not willing to believe what he had just heard. He looked at the faces of the other villagers. The child villagers silently wept, burying their faces into the hems of their parents' robes. All the grown villagers now wore expressions identical to that of Moganga.

Their leader had spoken, and the subjects had followed without question. Even Blerge and Mella, though there were still visible tearstains on their faces, now showed only contempt for Leonidas. The villagers were all united under their leader, ready to stand against any threat to their village. And now Leonidas was one of those threats.

Leonidas turned. He could not look at the villagers any longer. He wasn't crying anymore, either. His grief was beyond tears. He was dead to his family. The last memories of joy and happiness that he had in Elementia were now corrupted in his mind. So, with his back to the villagers, Leonidas walked toward the desert, headed for Nocturia, ready to return to the only thing he was really good at: destroying.

CHAPTER 13
THE NATION OF THE NOCTEM ALLIANCE

"This meeting of the Council of Eight has come to order," read Stan hastily, desperate to get through all the formalities of the meeting as quickly as possible so they could discuss the problem at hand. "Do I need to take a roll call? No, I don't, I can see that everyone's here, so let's talk about this."

"I've gotta say, Stan," said Jayden arrogantly, "for somebody who claims to care so much about doing exactly what the law says, you certainly rushed through that opening."

"Eh, shut up, Jay!" snapped DZ in exasperation. "That part of the opening ceremony is stupid anyway, I don't even know why we put it in there. And he's right, we can't waste time now. We have to figure out how to deal with the Noctem Alliance's country, and we're gonna have to figure it out fast."

"Sounds pretty hypocritical to me," replied G, who seemed to be enjoying the quickly mounting tension way too much. "So you're saying that when Archie died, you still wanted to do everything totally to the letter, not skipping anything, but now that the Noctems have their own country, that's a real emergency where we can't waste time?"

"Now see here—" started Charlie.

"Stop it, arguing is just wasting more time," said

Stan, not loudly but sternly. Charlie stopped talking, while G and Blackraven, who had both opened their mouths to respond, closed them again.

"As you all know, the Noctem Alliance has founded their own country out in the tundra, which they call the Nation of the Noctem Alliance. Obviously, we've gotta do something about it. And honestly," said Stan, "I'm really not sure what we should do. Ideas, anyone?"

"Well, I put forward the idea of marching out there and burning it to the ground," said Jayden, almost disinterested, as if this were the most obvious solution in the world.

"I second that," said Blackraven, raising his hand.

"Third," added G, doing the same.

"Are you serious?" exclaimed DZ. "You guys do realize that now that the Noctem Alliance has their own country, everything is different, right?"

"I don't follow," replied G, a blank look on his face.

"DZ's right," said the Mechanist wisely. "Now that the Noctem Alliance has founded their own country, it means they're organized, and more important, we know where to find them. This opens up the doors to talking to the Noctem Alliance, and solving our problems peacefully instead of fighting."

"Are you serious?" said Blackraven in disbelief. "These people have been waging open warfare on us for the past few weeks! And now that we finally know where they are, you don't want to wipe them out?"

"That's just the thing," said Charlie. "They aren't trying to hide it. If they're gonna keep attacking us, then why would they willingly tell us where their base is? And they aren't trying to keep it from us either. I mean, that messenger willingly told us the exact location of the base when we asked."

"So what? That doesn't change the fact that they've attacked us before!" G pointed out.

"You know, the Noctem Alliance isn't just attacking us for the sake of it," replied Charlie. "We're only really fighting them because they're still prejudiced against lower-level players. And you know, while that view is obviously wrong and misguided, maybe for now, it's not a bad idea to give the prejudiced people a place to go where they can be away from everyone else."

"You're endorsing them!" yelled Jayden in shock. "You want to give the bigots their own country and not do anything about it! That's just handing them power! If they have their own country, they'll be able to get their own resources, and then they'll declare war on us!"

"And that's better than what's happening right now?" Kat shot back. G's head spun around and looked at her in shock. Clearly, he had not expected Kat to speak. "Right now, the Noctem Alliance is fighting a war that we're not prepared to fight. If we let them have their own country, then yes, they'll be stronger, but at least we'll know how to deal with them, instead of this game of whack-a-mole we seem to be playing right now."

"And think about it," continued DZ. "We're the Grand Republic of Elementia! We've got all the resources in the world at our fingertips, while they're stuck in the middle of the tundra. If we end up fighting a regular war, then we're gonna win."

"Enough talk," said Stan, now sure of what he had to do, and praying that the others would agree. "Here's what I propose. I'll go out to the capital of the NNA, and I'll . . ."

"The NNA?" asked Blackraven skeptically.

"The Nation of the Noctem Alliance," Stan responded offhandedly. "Anyway, I'll go out to the capital of the NNA, and I'll take Bill, Ben, and Bob with me for protection. I'll talk to the leader of the NNA, and I'll try to open up peace talks with the country. All in favor?"

Stan raised his hand into the air. Charlie, DZ, and Kat thrust their hands up with a sense of determined purpose. The Mechanist raised his hand calmly.

"And all those in favor of burning Nocturia to the ground?" said Stan with a smile, well aware that he already had a majority.

Jayden and G thrust their hands up just like Charlie, Kat,

and DZ had done, as if to show just how much they believed in their votes, even if they didn't count for anything. Blackraven raised his hand slowly, still with purpose, but not with the same vivacity as the younger players.

Gobbleguy was the only one who didn't raise his hand, and just looked timidly around at both sides, seemingly unable to decide. Stan sighed. He was getting really sick of Gobbleguy's indecision every time they had to make a choice. Stan was going to have to stage an intervention with him some time, because he had no business being a councilman. He had only been elected for his role in the rebellion against King Kev, not for his leadership. Stan put the thought aside for now. He had other, more urgent matters to attend to.

"Okay then, I'll talk to Bill, Ben, and Bob. We'll leave tomorrow morning and probably be back by tomorrow night," Stan said as he stood up.

"Oh, and by the way, probably not a good idea to mention this to the general population," Blackraven said, a little bit of resentment from the vote lingering in his voice. "I don't think the citizens will agree with us talking to the NNA instead of fighting them." This was met by general nods all around the table.

Stan began to head for the door, but he was stopped by Kat's voice. "Hold up, did you say tomorrow night?" she asked.

"Yeah. Why, is that a problem?" Stan replied.

"Well, kind of," she said, looking concerned. "Tomorrow is the semifinals of the Spleef tournament."

"So?" Stan asked.

"So, Ben is on the team," DZ added as the realization spread across his face.

"What does it matter?" Stan asked, bewildered that this was even coming up. "We're in the middle of a war, you guys are just gonna have to forfeit the tournament!"

"Are you crazy?" shot out of Kat's mouth as "No way!" flew out of DZ's.

"We can't forfeit, these are the semifinals of the most popular competition in Elementia!" exclaimed Kat. "What would all the fans think?"

"Are you telling me," Stan said in a rage, not believing what he was hearing, "that you're willing to blow an opportunity to end all this fighting just because you don't want to disappoint your fans?"

"Stan, may I say something, please?" the Mechanist said before DZ could respond.

"Go ahead!" exclaimed Stan, ready for the Mechanist to talk some sense into Kat and DZ.

"I think they should compete in the tournament," the Mechanist responded coolly.

"Wait, what?" Stan yelled, shocked that the oldest and

probably wisest of the council was taking their side.

"Stan, think about it. You may be fighting a war, but you're also president of a country, and it is your job to keep the people happy. They've elected us to lead them because they trust us to take care of their problems, and they don't want to be affected by the problems themselves."

"What does that have to do with anything?" Stan asked.

"If you take Ben with you and force the Zombies to forfeit, then it would cause a huge upset among the people . . . the people that you pledged to keep happy, Stan. If that was the only option, then it would be a different story entirely, but in this case, you could easily bring someone else in Ben's place."

"I'll volunteer," said Charlie. "I'll go out to Nocturia with you, Stan."

Stan considered this for a moment, then nodded and said, "Okay, good point. Charlie, you, Bill, and Bob can come with me. We'll leave tomorrow morning."

"Okay then," said Charlie, nodding.

"And guys," added Stan, looking over at DZ and Kat, who were looking excited, as the Spleef match was the only thing on their minds. "Try to win tomorrow. And take Oob to the match, won't you? He's gotta be really confused by all this, and the little guy could use a good time." He smiled.

"Yes, sir," they replied in unison, huge grins on their faces.

"Okay, everybody, move out!" declared Charlie, and all of them filed out at various speeds, ready to make preparations for the events of the following day. However, the last three players to leave the room had dark thoughts running through their heads.

Jayden was left completely staggered by the entire ordeal. Since Stan, Kat, Charlie, DZ, and the Mechanist were always in agreement over everything, they had five out of nine votes on the council. That was more than half the votes, which meant that the five of them could pass any law or action they wanted, regardless of what he, G, or Blackraven thought. Jayden felt so powerless, and there was nothing he could do about it. Fuming, Jayden stormed out of the council room, wondering how to make things right.

G sat for a moment, still dumbfounded by the fact that Kat had voted against him. They had been so happy back during the campaign against King Kev, when they had gotten together on a whim and had always been on the same page. It all changed once they won. Kat had been drifting further and further from him ever since they joined the council, despite his best efforts to keep her happy, going so far as to ditch work to meet up with her. G left the council room in confusion, thinking about how to get the old Kat back.

At last, there was only one remaining councilman at the table. Blackraven's face showed no emotion, though it was clear that gears were turning in his head. After a little while, he smiled. He didn't know exactly how, and he didn't know precisely when, but as Blackraven slowly walked out of the council chamber, he had faith that everything would turn out for the best.

Stan was shivering terribly. He had no idea that Minecraft could get so cold. He had been through forests, jungles, deserts, and mountains since he had joined Elementia, but he had never been to a snow biome before, and he was totally unprepared for it. Charlie felt the same way, but the two of them were absolutely on cloud nine in comparison to Bill and Bob, who had spent a good deal of their time in Elementia marooned in the Nether, the dimension of lava and fire. Stan remembered Bill once saying that the desert was pleasantly cool to them, and the forest was downright cold. Now, they were in a biome that was below freezing. Although they appeared to be holding up pretty well, Stan knew they were truly dying inside. In fact, the only one of the group who seemed truly unfazed by the winter environment was Ivanhoe the pig.

Stan had been amazed when the four of them had taken the train ride through the Ender Desert and seen the very rigid boundary where the desert ended and the tundra began. Stan had assumed that there would have been at least some type of divider between the hottest and the coldest of the biomes, but no, the desert and tundra literally bordered each other, with one block being hot and sandy and the one to the right of it being cold and snowy. Maybe they'd make biome generation a little less abrupt in future updates, Stan thought.

Although Charlie had overseen the construction of a network of railroads spanning the entire Ender Desert in the past months, he had not yet expanded into the tundra. Therefore, the four of them had to walk the rest of the way to the NNA. It seemed like they had been trekking in the same direction for hours before finally, Stan could make out the faint glow of lights in the distance. Stan's body tensed as he became aware that they were finally about to meet Lord Tenebris.

In terms of the members of the Noctem Alliance, Stan knew next to nothing. He knew it was composed mainly of prejudiced upper-level players and that one of the leaders was Leonidas, but that was all. Stan felt he could safely assume that Caesar and Minotaurus, as the only other surviving commanders of King Kev's army, were likely to be involved too.

Of the three of them, Caesar had been the highest-ranked, and so for now, Stan was assuming that Caesar had taken the title of Lord Tenebris, which, he had been told by Blackraven, had roots in Latin and meant something like Lord of the Night. Then again, there was always the possibility that Lord Tenebris was another person entirely, one Stan didn't know about. He guessed he would find out soon enough.

Through the never-ending snowstorm, a massive shape loomed out of the darkness. Stan squinted and saw that he was looking at a lengthy, lofty cobblestone wall. It looked ominous, bringing about a feeling of despair, as the majority of the wall was shrouded in blackness. The only sources of light came from the top of the wall, torches flickering in the howling blizzard but never going out, illuminating figures staring down at Stan and his friends with bows in hand. These players, despite being lit by the only visible light for miles, still seemed somehow shrouded in shadows.

Charlie was trying to keep his cool, and Stan could hear his friend's deep breaths, also visible through steam ejected from his mouth into the frigid air. Bill and Bob did not speak, nor did they look particularly scared from what Stan could see, just serious, in preparation for whatever should be behind that wall.

As Stan approached the wall, there was a whirring and clicking sound. An opening appeared, two blocks high and a block wide, just large enough for a player to fit through. The players exchanged final glances, knowing they were entering the point of no return. Then, with a deep breath, the four players entered the Noctem capital.

Stan looked around. He was surprised at how depressing the inside of the walls looked. If possible, it seemed even more devoid of hope than the outside. There was light, but just barely. A good area in front of Stan contained nothing but basic dirt shacks, all in a grid pattern, save one stretch of flat, snowy ground free of structure that Stan supposed functioned as a main road. There was torchlight shining out of some of the shacks, sure, but the light was greatly suppressed by the eternal darkness created by the swirling snowfall.

There was really only one impressive building in the entire capital, and it was the only true source of light in the complex. It came from a centrally located ornate building, made mainly of stone brick with accents of mineral blocks, with multiple floors. It was quite impressive, and Stan imagined that it had taken some time to build.

As Stan, Charlie, Bill, Bob, and Ivanhoe marched down the main road, a feeling of uneasiness mounted. They were in enemy territory, willingly walking into the complex of the organization that had been actively trying to kill them for weeks. Shouldn't they have encountered some players by now?

No sooner had Stan thought this when a door below the balcony of the building opened. Two soldiers stepped out, fully clad in black leather armor, black swords in hand. Only their eyes showed, and neither of their faces had any distinct characteristics. The two stared down Stan and his friends.

"I am Stan2012, president of the Grand Republic of

Elementia, and these are my associates," said Stan, gesturing to his three friends, who all nodded in turn. "I've come to seek an audience with the leader of the Nation of the Noctem Alliance."

"Very well," said one of the soldiers in an unreadable voice. "Follow us inside. The chancellor is expecting you."

"He is?" Charlie blurted out, and despite getting death glares thrown at him by the other three, he blabbered on. "How did he know we were coming?" Charlie demanded.

"The Noctem Alliance knows many things," came the foreboding response from the other soldier, and with that, the soldiers spun around and marched through the iron door, both in perfect unison. Stan felt a unanimous shudder behind him, and he knew why. It was unnerving, what with the dead, emotionless delivery of words and the fact that the two soldiers were perfectly in sync.

Stan took a deep breath, tried to quell the butterflies in his stomach, and entered the building. As they passed through the doors, he leaned back and hissed to Charlie, "Shut up and let me do the talking!" to which Charlie sheepishly nodded.

The inside of the building was much the same style as the outside, with stone brick walls and ornate details here and there created with mineral blocks. Stone pillars towered to the high ceiling from the floor, and all light was provided by fireplaces in the wall that Stan could only assume were burning on Netherrack. The entire setup of Nocturia matched Stan's general opinion of the Alliance: stone cold and dark, with a flare of grandeur, and any light within it flickering and casting ominous shadows. And it made him extremely uneasy.

At the end of the hallway sat a wooden door, which they were led through. Stan took note of this detail. Should they be forced to flee from the scene, these doors would provide much less of an obstacle than their iron counterparts. Stan looked around the room they had entered. It was styled in a strikingly similar manner to the rotunda of the courthouse of Element City. Stan was actually unnerved by how similar it was. It was as if someone in the Alliance had seen it and copied it perfectly. The only difference was, where the judgment panel should have been, instead sat three thrones, only one of which was occupied.

The rotunda surrounding the middle of the stone floor was full of probably fifty forms clad in black. Stan could hardly make out any distinguishing features, as they all looked identical save a thin strip of exposed flesh containing the eyes. The single throne that was occupied held a familiar face. The last time Stan had seen it was on the battlefield.

Stan felt Bill and Bob tense up behind him, especially Bob. He shot an offhand glance backward and saw that the two police chiefs were keeping straight faces, but just barely.

It wasn't hard to imagine why. The player sitting on the throne before them was the reason Bob had had to ride into Nocturia on the back of a pig. He only hoped the two of them would manage to hold their tongues.

"Welcome to our capital, President Stan," said Caesar, sounding more hospitable than Stan had expected.

"Thank you," replied Stan, trying to sound like the president he was. "Are you the leader of this city, Caesar?"

"No, Stan, I am not," replied Caesar. There was a moment of silence as Stan expected Caesar to continue, before Stan decided to help him along.

"So . . . who is?"

"The leader of the Noctem Alliance is the all-powerful Lord Tenebris, the greatest being in the history of Minecraft," replied Caesar, an almost bored tone to his voice. "He, unfortunately, is otherwise occupied, having matters to attend to in other parts of the server. Until he returns, however, I have been made interim Chancellor of the Noctem Alliance. So, as of now, you may refer to me as the Head of the Noctem Alliance."

Stan felt that the aura in the room was deadly ominous. He couldn't shake the feeling that there was something very wrong about the setup. "What about Leonidas? I know he's with you guys too, I fought him at the Jungle Base. And what about Minotaurus?"

"Well, those two are also my allies in the Noctem Alliance, and right now they're out in the server, doing various tasks to help the Noctem Alliance grow," replied Caesar. A tiny smirk spread over his face, and maybe it was the all-around unpleasant and threatening aura that radiated from Nocturia, but Stan found it extremely off-putting. He was about to ask what kind of tasks when, to his dismay, another voice rang out behind him.

"What do you mean, tasks out in the server?" asked Charlie savagely. "You Noctem guys have your own country now, and we don't intend to take it from you. So why do you still have to be doing stuff out in the server?"

Stan sighed in exasperation, and hoped that Caesar wouldn't take issue with Charlie's outburst. In a room full of fifty Noctem soldiers, keeping Caesar happy had to be a priority. Rather than be offended, however, Caesar's smile grew. Frankly, seeing the maniacal grin on his face, Stan would have preferred if Caesar had yelled at them.

"Ah yes, Stan, you brought an entourage with you," Caesar said in an oily voice. "Charlie, how have you been doing lately? Has your NPC friend recovered from the giant gaping hole in his chest yet?" He asked this with disturbing mock concern in his voice, and Charlie gave an almost imperceptible growl of fury.

"Ah, and Element City's esteemed chiefs of police. I

haven't seen you in a while," continued Caesar. Stan felt them tense up behind him, and he did the same, seeing where this was going.

"I thought there were three of you. Did one of you bite the dust? Well, I wouldn't be surprised. Frankly, Bob, dismembering you was laughably easy, and if your strength is any indication of your brothers', it wouldn't take an exceptionally talented player to take one of you down." He chuckled, and Bill and Bob began quivering, emitting audible snorts of rage.

"Stop it, Caesar," said Stan, trying hard to focus on getting information. "Just tell me what exactly it is you're trying to accomplish by founding your own country out here."

"Well, Stan, what you have to realize is," replied Caesar, his blocky hands pressed together in front of him in an almost businesslike manner, "the Alliance has many long-term goals, not just one. But while you're here, you may be interested to know that the Alliance fully intends to extend its walls and city to encompass the entirety of the tundra biome, and eventually expand well into other biomes."

"Well, that's not gonna happen," said Stan slowly, wondering what kind of a statement that was. "You're not gonna extend into Elementia territory, Caesar. My armies will stop you if you extend your borders anywhere beyond what you have now."

Caesar shrugged. "Well, your armies are only going to do

that if you command them to, Stan, and . . . well . . ." Caesar's eyes flicked downward and he tapped his hands together a few times, as if he were on the brink of revealing awkward information. "As it turns out, you're about to die."

Caesar moved his arm off the armrest of the chair, revealing a lever behind it, and before Stan could react, he pulled it.

CHAPTER 14
THE SPLEEF SEMIFINALS

"Are we there yet, are we there yet, are we there yet, are we there yet, are we—?"

"Oob, for the third time, yes, we're almost there. You can see the building, it's right in front of us!"

"Oh. I am sorry, Kat, I forgot to look and see if we were there yet before I asked if we were there yet."

"It's okay, Oob," Kat replied with a chuckle. "Everybody makes mistakes."

"I still cannot believe that I am here!" said Oob, awe permeating his voice as he stared up at the goliath building that was the Spleef arena. "It is the most beautiful building that I have ever seen in my life, I think!"

"I think so too, Oob. And I promise you," said Kat, smiling kindly at him, "you're gonna have the best seat in the whole house. Nobody has ever gotten to visit the preparations room with me, Ben, and DZ before. You're the first one!"

Kat expected another gushing response from this, but when none came, she looked around. Oob had wandered off again, and now seemed to be examining a topiary bush that resembled a pig made of leaf blocks. He was poking at it, apparently checking to see if the animal was real. Kat shook her head with a laugh, and grabbed Oob by the collar, saying "Come on" in a playful voice. She lead Oob into the arena, where the semifinal round of the Spleef tournament was about to begin.

Kat took a side door out of the decorated main entry hall of the arena. She walked down the cobblestone corridors, toward the room where DZ and Ben were waiting. As she rounded a corner, she came face-to-face with a player clad in full white leather armor and red lips that took up half her pale face.

"Oh, Kat, darling, how are you? It's been so long! Still in the tournament, eh?"

Kat's jaw clenched. She knew this player, and she couldn't stand her. Cassandrix was the captain of the Skeletons, and Kat's least favorite person in the Spleef tournament. She came fully equipped with a snooty upper-class accent and a level of vanity that would put G's level of neediness to shame.

"I'm doing pretty good," she replied, trying pointedly to keep her voice pleasant. "About to go up there and play against the Ocelots."

"Oh, the Ocelots? Well, I wish I were in your place, dear. I've been simply dying to face a team that would allow me to kill a . . . cat, so to speak." Cassandrix chortled irritatingly as she looked Kat directly in the eyes. That last word struck a nerve with Kat.

"Well, if you were to try that, I'm sure the cat would fight back," Kat retorted with a smirk. "And I'm sure that this hypothetical cat would be more than happy to take on your entire team. And she'd win, too." Kat looked around. "Where is the rest of your team, anyway?"

"Oh, they're just reveling in the affections of the crowd," responded Cassandrix. "After all, we did just win our match and advance to the World Finals."

Kat's stomach clenched. Yeah, that was another thing about Cassandrix. Although Kat couldn't stand her, she and her team were, admittedly, excellent.

"Well, congratulations," Kat mumbled back. "Now if you'll excuse me," she said, her full voice now harsh, "I'd like to get up there"—she jerked her blocky thumb toward the stairs—"and win my match."

"Oh, my dear, I know that you'll *try*." And with a light pat on Kat's head, Cassandrix strutted down the hallway.

For a moment, Kat seriously considered reporting her to a tournament official. Cassandrix had patted her head, and members of opposing teams weren't allowed to touch each other outside the arena or they would be disqualified. But Kat dismissed the thought from her mind. She wanted to beat Cassandrix's sorry face fairly, not win by default.

"Excuse me . . . Kat?"

Kat spun around. She had completely forgotten that Oob was there, and he now looked confused.

"What was all that about?"

"Oh, nothing," Kat replied. "Just a . . . friend of mine. Anyway, Oob, do you want to go up to the room now?"

"That is something that I would enjoy very much!" exclaimed Oob happily. Kat lead him up the stairs, and she saw a man in diamond armor standing outside the iron door. Kat knew the drill. She waited patiently while the player examined her, before he nodded, stepped aside, and opened the door. Oob followed her inside, looking curious.

"What did that player just do to you, Kat?"

"Oh, he just frisked me. You know, he checked to make sure that I wasn't carrying any items in here."

"Why can you not bring items into this room?"

"'Cause they don't want us to cheat," replied Ben, who had just finished pulling on his dark green armor and walked over to greet them. Kat let the two of them talk, and she hustled over to the chest, yanking out her armor and sitting down next to DZ, who was still struggling to pull his armor on.

"I swear, I'm never gonna get used to this," he grunted to himself. He turned to Kat. "So what took you so long?"

"Well, I promised Stan I'd bring Oob along, but he kept getting distracted on the way over here and I had to run off and find him. Especially when we walked past the park plaza, that was the worst. You know that emerald statue of Avery over there? Well, Oob became obsessed with it. Oh, and also, I ran into Cassandrix on the way up here."

"Ah, Cassandrix," mumbled DZ in disgust. "I remember her from back in the old days. She was a snob back then too."

"I didn't know that Cassandrix played back in the old days," said Kat in surprise.

"Oh, yeah, she was there," DZ replied. "Most people don't remember her, her team wasn't very good back then. She was, though, and still is. She's more famous now than she ever was back in the day, and she's desperate to beat me, because, as you know, I'm the cream of the crop when it comes to Spleef. And also everything else," DZ said as he flashed a white smile.

Kat punched him in the shoulder as she laughed, and then focused on getting her armor on. As she sat there, with only the sound of Ben explaining to Oob what the purpose of the shovel was in combat, she felt nervous. It wasn't because of the match, though. The thought of entering the Spleef arena again gave Kat a rush of adrenaline, not fear.

No, her nerves stemmed from the thought of Stan, Charlie, and the police chiefs, who had no doubt entered the territory claimed by the Noctem Alliance by now. Kat was, to be frank, terrified of the Noctem Alliance. When she had been fighting alongside Stan and Charlie to take down King Kev, Kat had never once doubted that they would win in the end. Now, though . . . Kat had no idea what to expect from the Noctem Alliance.

She had learned to control her recklessness during her travels, but the Noctem Alliance was now toying with Kat's instincts. She knew she couldn't be careless and endanger her friends and country, but at the same time . . . well, she had to do *something*! Kat was well aware that none of them truly knew what would come next, and she only hoped her friends would be on their guard for any traps that the Noctem Alliance had in store for them. Also, it killed her that she had to stay here while the others got to go on a dangerous mission.

"You okay, Kat?" DZ asked.

"What?" Kat asked, slipping out of her train of thought. "Oh, yeah, sure, I'm okay."

"Whatcha thinking about? Beating Cassandrix over the head with a shovel and knocking her off a cliff? Don't be embarrassed, Kat, those are perfectly normal daydreams for a teenage girl."

"Oh, shut up, it's not that," said Kat, laughing for a moment before her face tensed up once again. "It's just . . . Stan and Charlie. I'm worried about them. And honestly, I'm kinda ticked that I didn't get to go with them."

"Oh, come on, Kat, you know that's nothing personal," said DZ nonchalantly, waving his hand. "You know, me and Ben wanted to go too."

Kat nodded and shrugged. This didn't surprise her.

"But we've gotta keep the people of the city happy," said DZ. "They shouldn't have to worry about problems, that's the council's job. And come on, the people are content just watching us try to kill each other! They have the shortest attention span ever! Well, except for maybe Oob," he said thoughtfully. Kat glanced over and saw that Ben, needing to get ready for the match, had distracted Oob by giving him his compass. Oob stared at it in fascination and tried to tap the little red needle to get it to move.

Kat chuckled. "Yeah, I guess you're right. Alrighty then. If these people want a show, then let's give 'em a show."

DZ's face exploded into a grin. "Oh yeah! Let's go!" And with that, he started leaping around the cobblestone room, having spontaneously burst into song.

You know you're headed for trouble,
When I hit you in the head with a shovel!
Zombies! Zombies! We're the best!
Zombies! Zombies! Uh . . . Don't go into
cardiopulmonary arrest!

Kat and Ben halted in their preparations and stared at him. "What was that?" Ben asked in bewilderment.

"Oh, you mean the ending?" DZ shrugged. "I don't know,

it was the first word that came into my head that rhymed with 'best.'"

"Of course it was," mumbled Kat under her breath before saying, "Well, that was just wonderful, DZ. In fact, maybe you should just be our cheerleader and let Oob be the third member of our team."

Well, she instantly regretted saying it. . . . When Oob heard that, he became convinced that he really should be a member of the team. It took the three of them five minutes to convince Oob that he may not be the best suited to playing Spleef. They had just managed to talk Oob out of his last argument —"What does it matter that I cannot hold a shovel or snowballs properly? I can help . . . I was able to knock Mr. A into the lava pit, do you remember?"—when the mechanical door clicked open.

"Okay, let's go, team!" cried DZ as he picked up his shovel and darted out the open door with Kat in hot pursuit. Ben bid Oob a quick good-bye, and reminded him to stay put and watch the match, before following his teammates into the open arena. The door creaked shut behind them, one last cry of "Go, players!" escaping from Oob before it slammed.

The team surveyed the field around them in the ten seconds they were given before the match started. Unlike the last arena, this one was completely flat, the ground made entirely out of snow blocks, which was the standard block for making up a Spleef arena. The arena, however, was not the conventional flat surface. The ground was filled with two-block-by-two-block holes that punctuated the field, creating the illusion that the entire arena was a giant chessboard of snow and emptiness. Across the arena, the players got a glimpse of three players clad in yellow—the Ocelots, their opponents.

The team blocked out the cheers of the crowd and their villager friend, and focused on the match.

"Let them move first," mumbled DZ, and Kat and Ben obliged, scrutinizing the Ocelots and waiting to see what their strategy would be. The Ocelots took the bait. As soon as the door shut, they were dashing down the center of the arena, sticking together and ready to meet the Zombies as a single unit.

In a series of rapid hand gestures, DZ signaled his team, and without hesitation they sprung into action. DZ sprinted head on toward the Ocelots, leaping over the holes in the field like a gazelle. Kat did the same, while veering slightly to the right and away from the players. Neither of them took notice of where Ben was. He knew his job, and he would help soon enough.

Right as the Ocelot team was about to converge on DZ, he dived to the left over an open gap and swung his shovel into one of the hovering squares of snow, slicing it in two just as the Ocelots were about to land on it. Two of them continued their forward momentum and were able to land on the remaining half square before jumping onward. The third one cut a sharp left, right into a mighty swing of Kat's shovel. The Ocelot landed on the half square, the wind knocked out of him, in the perfect position for DZ to jump in the air and kick the Ocelot into the watery depths below.

Just as DZ landed, however, he found the remaining two Ocelots rounding on him, swinging their shovels. DZ fought back as hard as he could, and was about ready to succumb when Ben flew in from out of nowhere. Ben drove his shovel into the snow square they were all standing on. This gave DZ the relief that he needed and he was able to jump backward onto another snow square just as the two Ocelots did the same. As one of the Ocelots flew through the air, his shovel flew out at a random angle, catching Ben totally off guard. The diamond blade slammed into the side of Ben's head, knocking him to the ground. The crowd roared with a collective "Ooooh!"

One of the Ocelots engaged DZ in shovel combat, and the other one spun around toward Ben. He was just about to bring his shovel down onto the square Ben was on when a snowball hit him squarely in the side of the head and he tumbled backward. He looked around in bewilderment to see Kat rushing in, snowballs flying from her hands like a machine gun. The projectiles hit the Ocelot one after another, knocking him away while he mitigated the knockback with his shovel. This gave Ben enough time to pull himself back to his feet as the two of them charged the Ocelot.

This Ocelot was clearly the strongest Spleef player of the team. Wasting no time, he performed a flying kick at Ben in one direction and shot a snowball at Kat from the other. Kat managed to duck under the snowball in a very near miss, but the kick connected with a thud as Ben went skidding along the snow squares, somehow avoiding falling into the holes as he tumbled. Kat sprinted after him. This player was far too powerful to face by herself. She had to get Ben back onto his feet, and fast.

Ben came to rest hanging over the edge of a snow square, while his lower half hung down toward the water below. Kat fell to her knees and grasped Ben's wrist, flinging him up onto the snow blocks above with an almighty swing of her arm. Suddenly, though, Kat felt nothing but air beneath her feet. She glanced up and saw the Ocelot drawing back his shovel, getting smaller and smaller as she plunged downward, finally landing with a splash in the pool below.

Kat resurfaced a few seconds later, cursing herself for going down so easily, before looking up at the bottom of the arena above her. Before long, a chunk of it burst apart and a player fell down from the top with a yell, landing in the pool with a splash. Kat glanced at the water, waiting for the Ocelot to resurface. She was shocked, however, to see Ben's face emerging from under the water.

"Ben!" Kat shouted, appalled that they were now down two to one. "What happened?"

"I tried . . . to fight him . . . ," Ben gasped, panting heavily, "but I just . . . couldn't . . . keep fighting . . ."

"Deep breaths, Ben," said Kat, swimming to the edge of the pool with Ben in tow. As she helped him out of the water, Kat looked up at the bottom of the arena in anxiety. It was two on one! Kat knew that DZ was perfectly capable of handling a two-on-one Spleef game, but this was obviously an exceptional team. How was he going to . . .

And then Kat watched in dismay as yet another hole opened in the arena above, and the blurry form of DZ tumbled downward and hit the water with a splash. He surfaced a few seconds later, exhaustion and frustration in his face as the stadium above them exploded with a cacophony of cheers, boos, and shouts of surprise.

"And it's over, folks!" the announcer cried, sounding shocked. "In a stunning upset, the Ocelots have beaten the Zombies in the semifinal round, with two players left standing! They will now advance to the Spleef World Finals against the Skeletons! Wow, I don't think anybody saw that one coming! This will certainly shift the odds on the Ocelots!"

DZ paddled over to the side of the pool and looked up at Ben and Kat. There were no words to describe the look of blank shock on his face.

"It's over," Kat said, sounding almost confused, still not completely comprehending what she was saying.

As the one Ocelot in the water celebrated by pumping his fists up and down, the Zombies heard a scuffling on the ladder behind them, which lead back up to their room. Oob stepped off the ladder and turned to face the players, looking crestfallen.

"Players," said Oob quietly. "You . . . did not win?"

"No, Oob," responded Ben, his voice quiet and disgusted. "We didn't."

"It's all my fault," spat DZ, still in the water, staring down at the stone ledge he was grabbing on to.

"No, it's not," responded Kat and Ben in unison, the response coming out automatically.

"Yeah, it is!" spat DZ angrily. "I shoulda scheduled more practices! Ever since the Noctem Alliance thing, I've been slacking in getting our team ready for this tournament. How many practices have we had since the last match? Like, two? I shoulda been pushing us harder!" DZ slapped his hand to his head in angst.

"Dude, you can't blame yourself for that!" said Ben. "We're fighting the Noctem Alliance. Spleef hasn't been the first thing on any of our minds! Besides, there's always next year."

"Assuming that there even is a tournament next year," a snarky voice came from their left.

The group turned and saw Cassandrix, clad in white armor, strutting up to them with her two teammates lumbering behind her.

"What are you doing down here, Cassandrix?" snapped DZ, pulling himself up onto the ledge.

"Oh, I just wanted to have a little talk with you all. Well, you specifically, Kat," replied Cassandrix brazenly.

"Just go away," mumbled Kat through clenched teeth, doing all she could to stay calm, but Cassandrix continued anyway.

"First of all, I just want to thank you for taking my advice earlier," she said with a chuckle. "You clearly wanted me to face the Ocelots too. I mean, that's the only reason I can come up with for your team playing even worse than usual, which frankly I didn't think was possible."

"Shut up!" cried Ben as Kat began to shake with fury and DZ gnashed his teeth. "We lost, we get it! Now shut up about it and go away, I don't want to see you again till we beat your sorry face next year!"

"Oh, but didn't you hear me, Ben?" simpered Cassandrix in reply. "I don't think that there's going to be a tournament next year. Well, not if the NNA is still around, anyway."

Those three letters hit the three Zombies like a shock wave, knocking the air out of their lungs. After a moment of shell shock, Kat spoke. “How do you know about the Noctem Alliance’s country?” she asked. “That’s supposed to be confidential.”

“Oh, is it?” replied Cassandrix with a smug grin. “Well, I certainly wouldn’t have guessed that. After all, it’s all everyone’s been talking about for the past afternoon.”

“Wait . . . hold on a sec . . . you’re serious?” asked DZ.

“Of course I am, darling,” said Cassandrix with a ditzy laugh. “And I don’t think there will be a tournament next year if the NNA continues to exist. They’re certain to go to war with us, aren’t they? And yet, for some reason, the council of this city saw fit to negotiate with them, rather than wiping their country off the server.” Cassandrix’s grin was wide now, and Kat thought it looked almost evil. “Needless to say, the population of the city is not very happy with you three, or your friends, right now.”

Oob was looking around in horror. He couldn’t comprehend what was going on, but he had enough common sense to know that it was very, very bad.

“How do you know all this?” Ben demanded.

“Well, through the leak, of course,” replied Cassandrix in surprise. “Do you three really not know? Well, I knew the council was dysfunctional, but not *that* dysfunctional.”

“Cut to the chase!” shouted Kat, shoving her face right up into Cassandrix’s until their noses were almost touching. “What leak are you talking about?”

“Well, that’s just the question, isn’t it,” replied Cassandrix, smiling as she gently pushed Kat away from her. “Nobody really knows where it started. All there is to know is that somebody in the castle leaked your plans for dealing with the Noctem Alliance’s new country. Oh, and one more thing, you three,” she said, and all of a sudden her voice became dark, steely, and menacing.

“I, for one, think the Noctem Alliance is a menace and needs to be wiped out immediately, not given a firm talking-to. And the rest of the citizens seem to agree with me. I’ve heard a lot of nasty things being said about you and your president since the leak came out. Why weren’t we told that the Noctem Alliance is a country now, why did we have to find out through a leak? And why aren’t you destroying them now that you have a chance?

“I came down here because I wanted to tell you this: the council isn’t doing its job properly. Make it work, or the people, myself included, will take matters into their own hands.”

And with that, Cassandrix turned on her heel, walked over to the ladder, and climbed away, followed by her two teammates, leaving Kat, DZ, Ben, and Oob to stand speechless, reeling at what they had just heard.

CHAPTER 15
THE LABYRINTH

Stan suddenly found that there was no floor beneath his feet. The view of Caesar smirking down at him grew farther and farther away as suddenly all Stan could see was blackness whizzing by around him. Stan finally landed face-first on the ground. Dazed, he looked around and saw nothing but darkness, and before long three more thuds hit the ground around him, followed by a sharp squeal.

Stan had no idea what had happened, and he could not see a thing. He was about to panic when a light flickered to life. Stan glanced at the torch Bill had just placed on the wall.

"I never leave home without emergency supplies," he said brusquely.

"Well, that's very resourceful of you," a sadistic voice rang out from above. "A Boy Scout is always prepared, yes?"

Stan looked up and saw Caesar grinning down at them into the pit. His look of glee made Stan want to swing his axe right into that stupid face of his.

"What do you think you're doing, Caesar?" bellowed Charlie, who had stood up beside Stan and Bill.

"Oh, just thought we'd have a little fun with you before you all die," replied Caesar.

What does he mean by that? thought Stan in alarm,

and he was about to ask when Caesar yelled out. "Oh, Minotaurus!"

"*What*?" came the baritone reply, and Stan's heart skipped as he heard that it did not come from up above, but from somewhere around him. Stan glanced around the newly torchlit room and saw that there were entranceways all over the place, three blocks high by three blocks wide.

"They're down there, Minotaurus! Have at them!"

"Does that mean I get to kill them now?"

Caesar sighed. "Yes, Minotaurus, you get to kill them now. Just do it. And count yourself lucky that I'm letting you do it rather than doing it myself."

"Oh, okay. Thank you, Caesar."

Caesar sighed again, before looking down into the pit at his captives one last time. "Enjoy my labyrinth, boys. It'll be the last thing you ever see." And with that, Stan heard a faint click, and the trapdoors swung shut above them.

Stan was just about to tell everybody to keep calm and not panic, when he heard a faint moan. He looked down, and his heart dropped. Bob lay sprawled out on the floor, his bad leg stuck out at an odd angle. Ivanhoe lay on his side next to Bob, giving faint squeals of pain.

Bill followed Stan's gaze, and his eyes widened in alarm. He hastily knelt down next to his brother. "Bob, are you okay?"

"Ugh . . . yeah, I'm fine," he grunted. "I just got the wind knocked out of me. What about Ivanhoe? I can't see him, he broke my fall. Is he okay?"

Charlie ran over to check on the pig. Ivanhoe brushed his snout up against Charlie's hand, and Charlie helped the pig onto its feet. Though Ivanhoe was capable of standing, he was clearly shaking with effort.

Bob pulled a carrot on a stick out of his inventory. He held it up above his head and whistled. "Come here, Ivanhoe. Come here, boy! Come get the carrot!"

Stan, Charlie, and Bill watched as Ivanhoe limped over toward his master, his front left leg clearly damaged. The pig licked Bob's face, and he gave an appreciative smile, before twisting around to look up at the others. "I couldn't see him walk, is he okay?"

"I think he'll be fine, but he's hurt, bro," replied Bob sadly. "I don't think you're gonna be able to ride him."

"Well, that's just fantastic." Bob sighed, glancing at the ground before looking up at his friends again. "Guys, you're gonna have to leave me here. I can't walk on my own, and Minotaurus is gonna be here any minute."

"You're kidding, right?" replied Bill, already stooping down to get his arm under his brother's shoulder. "What's the first thing we learned at the academy, bro?"

Bob sighed again. "Yeah, yeah, I know, 'leave no man

behind.' But guys, in this situation . . ."

"You know he's right," replied Stan, almost laughing that Bob was still fighting them. "No way we're leaving without you."

"But guys, I'm just gonna hinder—"

"Look, Bob, there are four of us! Even if one of us is helping you, there's no way that Minotaurus could take on two of us at once," said Charlie, sounding like he was trying to convince himself more than Bob. Stan felt the same way. None of them had ever actually locked blades with Minotaurus. Stan remembered seeing both G and Archie fighting Minotaurus during the Battle for Elementia. Even with all their rage over Sally's death, he still managed to hold them off and escape. This memory fueled Stan's drive to get out of the maze as soon as possible.

"Stop arguing, Bob, we've gotta move, and you're coming with us," ordered Stan, cutting off Bob's response. Bob resigned himself as Bill hoisted him into a standing position, his arm around his brother's shoulder.

"Here, this might help us get out," said Bill, using his free hand to grab a map from his inventory and handing it to Charlie. As he held the map, a small white dot appeared on it, marking Charlie's position. The dot was right under a gray square that marked the location of Nocturia on the map, surrounded on all sides by the white of the tundra.

"Charlie, use the map to lead us through this maze until we're not under Nocturia anymore. Then, we can tunnel our way out."

"How are we gonna tunnel out?" Bob asked in dismay, eyeing the black walls. "The walls are made of obsidian, they'll take ages to punch through!"

"Don't worry, I've got a diamond pickaxe, remember?" replied Charlie, flashing it from his inventory before looking at the map again.

"Hurry up, Charlie!" whispered Stan urgently. The ground had begun to vibrate, indicating that something very large was prowling the corridors, and getting closer to them. Almost immediately after he said this, a deep voice rang out from seemingly everywhere, the echoes ricocheting off the chamber walls.

"Fee! Fie! Foe! Fum! I smell the blood of a . . . um, I mean, the blood of four . . . uh . . . players! Oh, and also a pig! I smell the blood of four players and a pig!"

"This way," said Charlie urgently, and he rushed down the left corridor, followed by the limping duo of Bill and Bob, the latter of whom was enticing Ivanhoe the pig to follow with a carrot. Stan took up the rear.

The group scuttled around the corners like mice, desperately searching for a way out of the black, twisted deathtrap. The footsteps of Minotaurus were omnipresent. He clearly knew the maze and was able to follow where they were going, for although the footsteps would occasionally fade, they were always right back to their loud booms within the minute.

Not helping matters were the mobs. It was entirely dark in the maze, and with Charlie putting up the torches that Bill and Bob were feeding him, Stan took the duty of killing the mobs that had spawned in the darkness. The Zombies, Skeletons, and Spiders were easy pickings for Stan's well-trained bow and diamond axe, but he was totally caught off guard when they turned the corner and found themselves face to face with a Creeper. Stan only just managed to sink his axe into its head before the swelling creature would have blown them all sky-high. The body of the Creeper fell down next to Ivanhoe, who gave it a derisive snort before it despawned.

"You know, I read that pigs and Creepers are related," said Charlie offhandedly.

"Is that a fact?" replied Stan, his heart rate too high for him to think to question it.

"Yeah, look it up. The model for the Creeper was created when Notch was trying to make a model for a pig and screwed it up pretty badly. He decided to turn the messed-up model into a monster, and the Creeper was born."

The other three players glanced at him for a second.

"And . . . what does that have to do with anything?" asked Bob.

Charlie shrugged. “I dunno,” he replied, and with no further discussion of the subject, the four players continued trekking through the maze.

Stan was getting seriously alarmed now. The footsteps were now unnervingly loud and constant. Minotaurus knew where they were and would be on them at any second. Soon, they hit a long corridor that ended in a dead end. Charlie glanced down at the map. The white dot was now a good deal outside the border of the gray city.

“This is it,” replied Charlie, and he whipped out his diamond pickaxe and began hacking away at the black wall of the dead end. Stan sighed in relief, turned around, and gave a gasp.

There, standing in the middle of the corridor, silhouetted against the torchlight, stood the largest player Stan had ever seen. His body twisted through modding and hacking, Minotaurus stood a whopping two and a half blocks tall, and a block and a half wide. His legs were about the size of a normal player’s, covered in brown leather trousers, but his bare chest was huge and muscular, with the horned head of a bull topping it. In his hand, Minotaurus held a two-block-long wooden pole, on both ends of which sat glinting diamond axe blades.

“Hello,” said Minotaurus in his deep voice, a smile on his face. The other three players spun around, and Charlie gave a squeal of fright.

"I see that you four are trying to escape. Well, that's not gonna happen, 'cause I'm gonna kill ya!" And with that, Minotaurus began to walk forward.

As Stan watched this behemoth of a player rapidly approach, something stirred within him, building in his stomach like a fire, racing through his veins, searing his heart and mind. This was the player who had killed Sally. There was no way both of them would leave alive. Stan promised himself this.

"Keep mining," Stan whispered to Charlie, who nodded and continued hacking at the wall, a frantic air about him now. Stan drew his diamond axe and stepped forward with no fear. He was eagerly anticipating the forthcoming battle and for the first time in his life, wanted his axe in his hand not to defend, not to wound, but to kill. He locked eyes with Minotaurus's arrogant grin, and he returned the smile with equal gritty determination before sinking into a fighting stance. Stan became aware of another presence beside him. He turned and saw Bill standing, fishing pole in his hand.

"What're you gonna do with that?" Stan hissed out of the side of his mouth, and Bill hissed back, "I've got a few tricks up my sleeve."

Minotaurus was just ten blocks away, and he raised his axe and began spinning it around, like a vertical helicopter rotor. As the diamond blades flew faster and faster, Stan was forced to step backward, panicking as Minotaurus forced him toward the wall. Just as Stan was about to back into Charlie and Bob, a white blur flew toward Minotaurus. The bobber of the fishing rod tangled in the rotating blades, binding the diamond axe awkwardly to Minotaurus's hand in an instant.

The bull-man looked confused, which gave Stan just enough time to bring his diamond axe over his head and toward Minotaurus's chest. Minotaurus raised the tangled axe awkwardly in front of him and managed to block the powerful blow and stumbled backward, snapping the fishing line from the rod.

Unfazed, Bill drew another rod from his inventory as Stan went in for the attack. Minotaurus got to his knees and managed to break the fishing line with one flex of his muscles, snatching his axe just in time to block Stan's attacks. Stan held nothing back, sending one powerful swing after another at Minotaurus, hoping to get under his guard. It was apparent, though, that Minotaurus was not just a mindless grunt with brawn and no brains. He was a skilled axe fighter, capably blocking all Stan's attacks. Stan judged him to be not nearly as skilled as himself, but a worthy opponent nonetheless, and with far more brute strength.

After one strike, Minotaurus leaped backward away from Stan with surprising agility, and swung his blade forward right toward Stan's head. Stan ducked under the swing and rolled in between Minotaurus's legs. Wasting no time, Minotaurus spun around and raised his axe, bringing it down just as Stan raised his own.

The two blades clashed, and Stan felt himself becoming quickly overpowered as Minotaurus drove his weapon down into Stan. Suddenly, the burden lightened. Stan glanced up and saw that Bill had hooked his line on the blade of Minotaurus's axe, and was pulling as hard as he could to lighten Stan's load. Even with two players fighting him, though, Minotaurus was still stronger, and he slowly managed to push his axe farther down, soon crushing Stan into the floor. Stan began to choke as the axe pressed into his neck, and was just about to panic when he heard a clinking sound.

An arrow had bounced off of Minotaurus's horn. The bull-man whipped around and immediately bellowed in agony as another arrow sunk into his muscular chest. Stan pulled himself to his feet and looked back to where the arrow had come from. Bob was sitting on the ground, positioning another arrow. Stan also saw Charlie break through the second obsidian block, creating an opening large enough for them to fit through. Stan saw that there was dirt behind the blocks. *Excellent*, he thought. They had an escape.

Escaping was the least of their worries at the moment, though. Minotaurus was now rearing up, and he began to barrel down the hallway headfirst. Charlie rolled to the side, but Minotaurus wasn't aiming for him. Bob, who was unable to move, watched in horror as the giant player charged toward him like a freight train.

When Minotaurus was just ten blocks away from Bob, a fishing line snagged Bob by the pant leg. He managed to grab Ivanhoe around the torso just as Bill's fishing rod yanked the two of them out of harm's way, and Minotaurus barreled headfirst into the wall. A giant crash came from the wall and a cloud of dust rose from the scene of impact. The cloud rolled over the four players and the pig, and they could hear the howl of wind. When the dust cleared, Stan looked up to survey the scene.

Minotaurus was lying facedown in the tunnel of dirt that had been created by his reckless charge. His eyes were closed, he wasn't moving, and there was a sizable lump on his forehead. He was clearly unconscious. Snow fell on him, as Minotaurus had managed to crash straight through the dirt and into the blizzard. Stan was amazed. How was this possible? They were underground!

Stan stepped outside the hole and saw that they were in the very lowest point of a valley, at the ridge of which stood one of the outer walls of Nocturia. Now fully aware that their escape would be a simple matter, Stan looked down at Minotaurus and, with no hesitation, raised his axe.

As he held the diamond blade above his head, staring

with mortal hatred at the unconscious monster on the ground before him, Stan once again felt a feeling sweep over him. It was the same feeling that had overtaken him when he had had the opportunity to kill King Kev in the Battle for Elementia all those months ago. Minotaurus was just as weak, unarmed, and vulnerable as King Kev had been then. Stan knew he could not deliver the death blow. It was not in his nature to harm the defenseless. Stan lowered the weapon to his side. He knew that, in time, he would face Minotaurus again, and when that time came, he could finish the job on equal terms.

Stan turned around and was about to walk away when he saw a bottle containing bright red liquid latched on to Minotaurus's belt. He pocketed it, and then headed back into the tunnel, where Bill was checking over the others for injuries. Stan explained the situation to them.

"So we're right outside the walls of Nocturia?" Bill asked. Stan nodded.

"Well, I say that we keep tunneling for a little while, and when we're far enough from Nocturia so they won't be able to see us, we'll dig to the surface and make our way back to Element City," said Charlie.

"I still can't believe they attacked us like that," said Bob as Bill helped him onto Ivanhoe's back, having healed the pig's leg with Minotaurus's potion. "What are they trying to accomplish? Even if they had killed us, Elementia would have declared war on them anyway. Why didn't they just kill us outright if they wanted us dead? None of this makes any sense."

"It's because we're not dealing with anything that we know," replied Charlie as he began tunneling away from Nocturia. "The Noctem Alliance isn't a real country. I don't know what it is, and neither does anybody else. The only people who know how to play their game are their members, and the only way we can beat them is if we know how to play the game ourselves."

"So you're saying . . . ," said Stan.

"Yes," replied Charlie. "Catching a member of the Noctem Alliance alive has got to be our next step."

"Well, then what are we tunneling away for?" asked Bob incredulously, stopping in his tracks and forcing Stan and Bill behind him to do the same. "We've got a while until they figure out that Minotaurus didn't kill us. Why don't we use that time to sneak into Nocturia and kidnap one of their members?"

"You know, that's not a bad . . . ," Bill started to say.

"That's not necessary," replied Charlie quickly.

"Why not, Charlie? You scared or something?" asked Stan, annoyed.

"Yes, I am. Just the thought of the Noctem Alliance makes

me almost poop myself, but that's not the reason why it's not necessary."

"And what is the reason, then?" asked Stan.

"'Cause we already have a Noctem Alliance member captive," Charlie replied with a shrug. "You remember that messenger they sent us? Well, Kat had him locked up in Brimstone for just such an occasion."

"Okay, that's a good reason," said Bill fairly. "All right, Charlie, I think we're far enough away now. Why don't you tunnel up?"

Charlie nodded, and aimed his pickaxe upward. After going diagonally up for a couple of minutes, Charlie's pick-axe struck air, and he stepped up into the raging snowstorm, followed immediately by the other four players.

Charlie pulled out a map and had to squint to see it through the dark blizzard. "Okay, so it looks like Element City is . . . that way!" Charlie exclaimed, pointing in a west-erly direction. "Let's go."

"Oh, how rude of you! We host you in our city, and you leave without saying good-bye?"

All four players whipped around and found themselves face-to-face with Caesar, standing ten blocks behind them, no weapon in his hand. The reaction was immediate. Stan whipped out his axe, Charlie held up his pickaxe, Bob notched an arrow in his bow, and Bill threw his fishing line forward and snared Caesar in the line. Bob was about to let the arrow fly when Caesar, wearing a sly smile, spoke.

"Now, now, boys. Are you sure you want to do that?"

Stan sensed movement, and his jaw dropped in terror as, from all sides of them, no less than fifty players clad in black emerged from the snowstorm, all holding Potions of Harming and aiming right at the four players.

"If you value your lives, you will all lower your weapons, and you, Bill, will let me go right now."

He said this very calmly, and with equal calmness, Bill placed the fishing rod on the ground. He kicked it over toward Caesar, and stood with his hands in the air and a defeated look on his face. He was mirrored by the other four players as they lowered their weapons.

"It humors me that you four honestly thought escaping from Nocturia was an option," said Caesar as he shrugged off the coils of string and stepped out of the tangled mess at his feet. "In fact, it humors me so much that I think that I'm going to let you get away with it." He snapped his blocky fingers, and instantly, the black figures at the easternmost section of the circle stepped to the side, creating a gap.

Stan stared at Caesar. He was obviously dealing with a lunatic here. "What are you trying to do, Caesar?"

"Well, presently, I'm trying to let you go, Stan," said Caesar obviously, gesturing to the gap. "I just said that."

"But why the . . ."

"Does it really matter *why*, Charlie?" asked Caesar whimsically. "I'm giving you a gift. Accept it."

"But it doesn't . . . ," responded Bill.

Caesar snapped his fingers again, and the black figures drew back their throwing arms. Positive that Bill's last outburst had just cost them their lives, Stan flinched, preparing himself to be doused with the maroon gasses that would spell the end for all of them. Instead, he watched in awe as the men in black flicked their wrists, sending their potions backward. The bottles shattered on the ground far away from the circle, staining the snow crimson.

"Those could have been flying toward you, remember that," said Caesar, irritation in his voice now. "Lord Tenebris ordered me to set the trap in Nocturia for you, and told me that if you managed to beat Minotaurus, you would be allowed to live another day for your resourcefulness. Personally, I would love to see you all dead, so I suggest you hurry up and scurry back to that hovel you call Element City before I change my mind and disobey my master!"

There was a moment of silence following Caesar's outburst, then Stan hastily walked through the gap of Noctem soldiers, closely tailed by his friends. As they walked through the tundra, away from Caesar and his men and back toward the city, Stan's mind was so confused that it felt like it was going to burst.

"The sooner we understand the game these psychopaths are playing, the better," mumbled Stan to nobody in particular, yet he still got three mumbles of concurrence.

CHAPTER 16 THE LEAK

Caesar was pacing the floor in the common room impatiently. Oh boy, was he going to kill Minotaurus! How could Minotaurus possibly have been defeated by those players? Caesar was just thinking of what exactly he was going to say when there was a knock on the door.

"What?" he barked.

The door opened, and one of his soldiers, clad in black, walked in. "Chancellor Caesar, I think it might be pertinent for you to know that General Leonidas has just arrived."

A fresh wave of rage swept over Caesar. "Tell him to get up here right now!" Caesar responded loudly, and the soldier hastily left the room.

In his rage at Minotaurus, Caesar had forgotten his anger at Leonidas from earlier. Leonidas was supposed to return to Nocturia immediately after the fight with Stan at the Jungle Base, and he had had Ender Pearls to expedite the journey. It was a day's travel at most, but now they were entering their fourth night after the battle!

The door swung open once more, and Minotaurus lumbered into the room, his hulking form having to duck in order to avoid cracking his head on the doorframe. He flopped down in one of the chairs next to the fire and began to rub the crest of his head. Caesar hadn't even opened his mouth to speak when Leonidas limped through the door, looking absolutely terrible. Caesar had no sympathy for Leonidas. He had some serious explaining to do. He allowed Leonidas to retrieve a potion from the chest in the corner, mend his leg, and sit in a chair next to Minotaurus. Caesar walked in front of them, his back to the fireplace.

"You've disappointed me," said Caesar simply.

Leonidas look outraged. "I disappointed ya, did I? What the—"

"I'll get to you in a minute," Caesar cut in, his voice quiet with fury and his blocky finger jabbed at Leonidas. "You, Minotaurus," said Caesar, and the giant bull-man raised his head and looked tiredly at Caesar. "Would you care to explain to me why you let those impudent players live?"

"I tried to kill them, just like you said," Minotaurus said deeply, sounding exhausted. "Stan is very good with an axe, Caesar, you know that."

"Yes, I do know that," replied Caesar indignantly. "I also happen to know that you know that you're not allowed to kill Stan anyway! Even if Lord Tenebris wants to kill Stan himself, it does not excuse you from letting the other three go!"

"Caesar, I—"

"There is no excuse! One of them is a cripple riding a pig!" bellowed Caesar. "One of them was hacking away at a wall during the entire fight! And the other one fights with a fishing rod! FISHING ROD, MINOTAURUS!" screamed Caesar, now standing over Minotaurus and bellowing in his face. "How much more incompetent could you possibly get?"

"Caesar, lay off him!" yelled Leonidas, his eyebrows knitted in anger, as Minotaurus's eyes began to tear up with fear. "Maybe he could've managed to take 'em down if ya were down there helpin' him!"

Caesar spun around and glared down at Leonidas. "Oh, so you want yours now, do you? Fine, then! What took you so long to get back here?"

"I got hurt, 'kay?" barked Leonidas hostilely, jumping up from the chair to look Caesar in the eye. "Believe it or not, when I fought Stan, he actually hurt me. Ya know, he's actually a pretty good fighter. Oh yeah! That's right! Ya don't know cause all ya do all day is sit up on your high horse, makin' Minotaurus 'n' me do your dirty work!"

Caesar raised his hand and struck Leonidas hard across the face, sending him toppling to the floor. Leonidas clutched his face in pain. The strike was sure to leave a mark. He struggled to open his eyes, and when he finally did, he was staring up the length of a diamond sword held by Caesar, whose face looked almost inhuman with rage.

"Don't you dare speak to me like that ever again!" Caesar howled. "I have my job in the running of this Alliance, and you have yours! And unless you want Lord Tenebris to answer to, you will obey me without question! Do you understand, Leonidas?!"

So much hatred was packed into those last four syllables that Leonidas found himself stymied. He pulled his legs in, gently pushed the diamond sword to the side, and stood himself up to full height. He looked Caesar directly in the eye. The two were exactly the same height, the same height as every other Minecraft player besides Minotaurus, who was presently watching the unfolding scene with terror in his eyes.

As the two locked eyes, both full of resentment, Caesar sheathed his sword, never lowering his gaze. "I am going to the war room," said Caesar quietly. "I have to finalize our plans for the next attack on Element City. You are going to go and check on the troops. I expect a report by nightfall."

And with that, Caesar turned and walked out of the room, gently closing the door behind him, leaving Leonidas to look with passionate disgust at the place where his chancellor had just been standing.

"Oh, man, it's good to be home," said Stan as the train picked up speed.

"Sshh, be quiet, man, I wanna just enjoy the ride!" replied Bob, sitting in the minecart behind Stan, Ivanhoe sitting in a cart behind him. Stan didn't blame Bob. Of all of the things the Mechanist had designed, the connection of the transcontinental railroad to the monorail system was one of his favorites too.

The engineer behind them scampered to each of the powered minecarts in the back, stuffing more coal into them so the train could gather enough speed to climb the grade. Stan saw the sharp incline coming, and he felt the rush of being launched straight upward from the forest floor, over the wall, and down onto the monorail system of Element City.

Stan had used this monorail system numerous times before, but he never got over how cool it was to be traveling at breakneck pace high over the heads of the citizens of the city. Everything looked smaller from up here, and Stan could see all the houses and stores in the city. The train eventually slowed down as they neared the gargantuan castle. Stan noticed a large assembly of players in the courtyard, and vaguely wondered what was going on. They departed the main track and the engineer switched off the powered minecarts, now using a special golden powered rail that accelerated their train around the castle wall and into the royal train room.

"Okay, *now* it's good to be home," said Stan as the minecart screeched to a stop on powered rails that were turned off, doubling as brake pads. He stepped out of the minecart and stretched his legs.

"Ditto to that," said Bill as he lifted Ivanhoe out of his minecart and helped his brother mount the pig.

"Alrighty then," said Charlie, joining the others. "Bill and Bob, you guys should probably check in at the police station, and get a group ready to visit Brimstone Prison. Stan and I will come with you after we talk to the council."

"Excellent!" cried Bob. "Back to the Nether!" Ivanhoe snorted in agreement. Since the newest update, animals could travel through Nether portals, and Ivanhoe seemed to share his owner's affinity toward the fire dimension.

"Okay, thank you, SourDog, you can go now," said Stan, gesturing to the engineer of the train, SourDog50, who caught the diamond Stan flipped to him as a tip. SourDog then hopped back into the train and pressed a button on the wall. The powered rails flashed on, sending the train flying back onto the main monorail lines.

"Hey, DarthTater, please announce a council meeting," Stan ordered one of the head Imperial Butlers, who wore a Darth Vader mask on his head with the rest of his body resembling a potato. DarthTater nodded curtly before disappearing to make the announcement.

Stan and Charlie made their way up to the council room and sat down in their respective chairs around the table. As they sat there waiting for the other council members to arrive, Stan gave a little chuckle.

"What is it?" asked Charlie.

"It's just weird," said Stan, smiling. "We have all these butlers waiting on us hand and foot, doing everything for us, and yet somehow we're still probably the most stressed-out people in Elementia."

Now it was Charlie's turn to chuckle. "Yeah, well, we've got a lot of people to keep happy. I think we probably deserve a little special treatment for doing our jobs right."

Stan nodded in agreement just as the door clicked open and the council members filed in. Stan immediately sensed something was wrong. All the council members wore looks of exhaustion and stress, and particularly between Kat and G there seemed to be a lot of tension hanging in the air. Stan guessed something was in jeopardy other than their relationship this time.

Stan got out the paper and did the formalities to open the meeting, completing them this time. He was sick of dealing with Jayden's and G's arguments, and he figured it was easier to appease them than to fight them. When he was finished, he asked, "Okay, so you guys are all clearly worried about something. What happened now?"

A lot of uncomfortable glances were exchanged around the table.

"Erm . . . do you think we should tell him, or show him?" Gobbleguy asked.

"What do you mean?" Charlie asked, alarmed. "What is there to show us?"

"Well, um . . . just, come on," said Kat, standing up and walking toward the door. Stan and Charlie followed her through the castle until they were standing on the castle bridge, looking down into the courtyard. What Stan saw made his stomach drop.

The assembly that he had seen coming into the castle was nothing less than an angry rabble, clustering around the castle gates with soldiers standing outside, keeping the peace by forming a blockade of raised swords. The crowd was screaming and yelling, and there was an unmistakable tone of anger to the noise.

"Look, there he is up on the bridge! President Stan!" a voice yelled out from the crowd.

Immediately, the crowd exploded into a new level of frenzy, screaming and bellowing louder than any noise Stan had ever heard before. As he listened and watched in horror, he caught screams of "Your conspiracy will fail, Stan!" and "Stand and fight for us, you coward!" and "Maybe we should burn both of your castles to the ground!"

Stan ducked his head down, afraid that somebody might throw or shoot something at him. He and Charlie turned to Kat.

"Kat, what happened? Why is everybody so mad?"

"Our plans for dealing with the Noctem Alliance were leaked," replied Kat gravely.

"What do you mean?" asked Charlie, eyes wide, sweat trickling down his forehead.

"I mean somebody in the castle or the military told the general public that the Noctem Alliance founded their own country," replied Kat. "And that you went to try to talk to them instead of attacking them. By the way, how did that go? If it went well, then we might still be able to avert a crisis."

"Well, it was a fiasco. I'll tell you more about it when we're back in the council room," answered Charlie.

Kat shook her head in despair. "That may have been our last chance."

"Our last chance at what?" Stan asked, confused and feeling sick with worry. "What are they so upset about?"

"Well, a couple things," said Kat hastily, beginning to walk back to the council room. "For one, they didn't like that we didn't tell them about something so important. Also, they don't like what we did. Most of them seem to think after everything that the Noctem Alliance has done to us, it would have just been smarter to destroy their city."

"Okay, hold up, you said *most*," Charlie pointed out. "Does that mean there are still people who think we did the right thing by taking the peaceful approach?"

"Oh, you bet," replied Kat solemnly, looking even more

upset for some reason. "I'd say about half the people think that. Also, there are some people who think we were right for keeping the mission a secret. They say it's our job to deal with it and they don't want to know about it."

"And that's not a good thing because . . . ?" asked Charlie, confused as to why Kat still looked extremely gloomy about this.

"Everybody in the city is divided now!" cried Kat. "They're all fighting with each other over what was the right thing to do, and who's right about this whole stupid thing! It's the same thing that happened to our council, but now it's happening to everybody!"

There was dead silence as they continued walking, and they eventually wound up in the council room with the others. Stan didn't really want to speak. His head hurt from this latest development, but he and Charlie gave the council the full run-down of what had happened during their trip to Nocturia.

"Are you telling me you didn't negotiate with Caesar at all?" cried Jayden.

"Weren't you numbskulls listening?" responded DZ, jumping to their defense. "Caesar dumped them into a pit before they could say anything. He was never going to negotiate with them!"

"So we were right!" announced G triumphantly. "Talking

our problems out with them was pointless, and it would've been better if we'd just attacked them!"

"This isn't about who's wrong and who's right!" the Mechanist cut in. "Maybe trying to talk to them was worth a shot, maybe it wasn't, but that is not the issue at hand. We have an entire city's rage to quell, we can't be arguing about who was wrong or right about something that's over now."

"Even though it was us . . . ," mumbled G.

"Yeah, when the Nether freezes over," Charlie snapped back under his breath.

"STOP IT!" bellowed Blackraven, slamming his fist down on the table. "The Mechanist is right, the matter isn't important now. Maybe we can discuss it further later, but right now, we have more important issues to attend to."

"What we need to determine," continued the Mechanist, "is who leaked that information. That person needs to be jailed for exposing classified council secrets."

"I agree," replied Charlie. "That's not our business to figure out, though."

"What are you talking about!" yelled G. "Of course it's *our* business! Whoever's been leaking our information is a traitor to the council and needs to be put away! Without a trial!"

"Oh, come on, do you ever think anything through?" snapped Kat. "First taking a day off to see me, now this. G, if you put them away without a trial, then you get the people who're rioting on the lawn outside even more mad! I bet as soon as somebody takes credit for all this, half the city will probably call them a hero for exposing what we were hiding from them! And then if we jail that guy, and especially if we don't give him a trial, then what will they think of us?"

"Sounds like you've put a lot of thought into this, Kat," replied Jayden suspiciously as G stared at her in disbelief. "Is it possible that you know more about this than the rest of us?"

"Oh, shut up, Jayden, we've all put a lot of thought into this!" Kat retorted. "Excuse me if I like to think about the consequences of my actions before ordering in Operation Bomb-the-Crap-Out-of-Everything and Project Jail-People-Without-Trial!"

"Oh, yeah, and your ideas are pure diamond!" Jayden shot back. "Yeah, your plan for dealing with the NNA went over perfectly, didn't it?"

Kat stood up in her place, sending her chair toppling over. "Why, you little . . ."

Gooooooooonnnngggg!

The sound of the note block rang loud and clear throughout the room, courtesy of the wooden button under the table that Stan had just mashed. He had hit the button so hard that it cracked, but he didn't care. Stan was beyond fury now. He was actually getting to the point where he hated these council meetings, which he used to enjoy.

"The next person," said Stan, his voice shaking with rage, "who throws an insult at someone else at this table is going to be kicked off the council! Permanently!"

"What?" exclaimed Jayden in shock.

"You can't just make empty threats like that!" said DZ, startled.

"As a matter of fact, I can!" said Stan, whipping out a copy of the constitution from under the table and flipping it open to a page he had had bookmarked for some time. "It says right here that I can nominate anybody to be kicked off the council if at least three other council members vote to support me! And I don't know if you've noticed, guys, but you're divided in two, and both sides have at least three people!"

There was a moment of silence as the truth behind this statement hit the council. Everybody sat there, mulling it over, until finally Charlie spoke. "What I was saying before," he said, almost timidly, "is that it's not our duty to search out the person who leaked that information. That's the police's job. I'll talk to Bill, Ben, and Bob about organizing an investigation."

"Okay, thank you, Charlie," replied Stan. He was glad that was taken care of. He had other orders of business to attend to. "Mechanist, I need you to do me a favor."

The old player nodded. "Name it."

"You're pretty good at explaining things. I need you to make an announcement to the people explaining to them why we kept the information about the attack from them, and why we need any leads about who leaked the information. Can you do that?"

"I'll do my best, Stan," the Mechanist replied in his Texas drawl.

Stan nodded. "All right, then. In the meantime, the rest of us need to stop worrying about the leak, and worry about our biggest problem: the Noctem Alliance. Let's be honest with ourselves, people. We know absolutely nothing about them, how they work, and what their game plan is. The only way we're gonna figure that out is by interrogating one of them."

Jayden snorted. "Oh yeah." He laughed sarcastically. "'Cause we definitely have a captive Noctem soldier just sitting around."

"Yeah, we do," replied Kat, a hint of arrogance in her voice. "I ordered the messenger that told us about the NNA to be put in a high-security cell in Brimstone."

Jayden paused. "Oh," he replied sheepishly after a moment.

Stan ignored Kat's smug smirk and spoke on. "I'm gonna visit Brimstone myself to interrogate him. Charlie, Kat, and

DZ, do you guys wanna come with me?"

Charlie and Kat nodded, and DZ pumped his fist up and down. "Sweet!" he exclaimed. "It'll be just like old times! Except instead of slaying a dragon, we're gonna do a political interrogation! Swiggity swag!"

Stan couldn't help himself. He grinned. "Okay!" Stan announced, clapping his hands together. "Meeting adjourned!" And with that, he put the constitution back under the table and walked out the door.

In the hallway, Stan turned back to close a door DZ had left open. He was about to walk to his room when he heard some noises coming from a side hall near Kat's room.

". . . go away, G, I don't want to talk to you right now."

"Come on, Kat, it'll just take a second."

There was a moment of silence. Stan put his back to the wall and edged closer to the hallway. As much as he knew it wasn't any of his business, he had to know what was going on between G and Kat.

"G, I don't have time for . . ."

"Why don't you wanna talk to me, huh?" G's voice simpered back. "We haven't spent any time together, just the two of us, since Elementia Day."

Kat snorted. "Yeah, that was the day Archie got killed, and we've all been working nonstop since then to take down the guys responsible."

"But I miss you, Kat."

"Oh, get over it, G! It's been five days, that's not that long! And honestly, given everything that's hit the fan since then, our relationship has been the last thing on my mind."

G gave a cynical grunt. "Huh, yeah, sure . . . since then . . ."

"What's that supposed to mean?"

"Come on, Kat, ditch the others, don't go to that prison. Stay here with me instead."

"How can you even say that?" Kat sounded appalled.

"There's still three of them going; they don't really need you."

"I want to go, G! This is important, and I want to be a part of it!"

"If you really like me, then you'll stay, Kat."

"Oh, come on, G, you know I like you, that's not fair!"

"No, I'll tell you what's not fair!" cried G. He sounded enraged now. "Back in the old days you were different, you were committed to me, and I really liked you then! But now, what happens? I ditch work to try to come see you, and I'm so nice to you! And how do you repay me?"

There was a moment of silence. Stan's body tensed, and his hand instinctively moved to his axe. He had a premonition that he was going to have to intervene here.

"I'll tell you how. You tell me to get back to my job, and

you spend more time with your friends than with me!" Every syllable G spoke now was punctuated with contempt.

"G, I . . ."

"And you vote against me and my friends on the council! Why would my own girlfriend betray me like that? Tell me that, Kat. *Why*?" roared G.

There was a moment of silence, punctuated only by G's snorts of rage. Then, all of a sudden, G spoke, and he suddenly sounded different, gentle and kind. The sudden shift in tone sent shivers down Stan's spine.

"Hey, Kat, there's no reason to look so upset," said G, with something resembling sympathy, which Stan found even more disturbing to hear.

"Yes, there is," Kat spat. G pretended she hadn't said anything and kept talking.

"It's okay, Kat, I'll forgive you. Even if you're not perfect, I still really like you, and I'm perfectly willing to keep you if we could just go back to the way we were. You know, happy. What do you say?"

There was a pause during which Stan held his breath. When a voice spoke again it was G's, not Kat's.

"Tell you what, Kat. You stay with me instead of going to check on that prison, and we'll have a nice day out, away from all these political debates and war talk."

There was more silence.

"Come on, Kat, give me a hug."

"I don't want to give you a hug, G," said Kat, finally speaking again, her voice furious now.

"Come on, Kat, I'm trying to work with you here! Just give me one hug and I'll let you . . ."

"No, G, you won't let me do anything!" cried Kat. "You don't own me, and you don't get to decide what I can and can't do!"

"I'm just asking for a hug. It's not hard."

"I said *no*, G!" Kat yelled.

G gave a shout of frustration, his voice ripe with anger now. "You are the worst girlfriend ever, you know that? I'm still willing to keep you, even after everything you've put me through, and you won't give me one stupid hug?"

Stan had heard enough. He bolted out from around the corner and stood in the middle of the hallway, his eyes widened with concern as Kat and G stood screaming into each other's faces.

"Is there a problem here?" Stan asked.

G's head spun around to face Stan, and Kat used his distraction to shove G away from her, causing him to stagger backward into the wall.

"For heaven's sake, Kat, I just want a hug!" cried G. "Stan, is that too much to ask? To get a hug from my girlfriend? That's all I want!" He spun back toward Kat, his eyes blazing. "What's your problem?"

"I'm not the one with the problem here, you are!" Kat shot G a look of disgust before turning to Stan. "He won't listen to me, and he's trying to force me away from you guys. How long were you standing behind that wall?"

"Long enough," Stan answered solemnly.

Kat eyed G with contempt. "G, I'm telling you right now that if you try to hug me without my permission, I will fight back, and I'll win, too."

"And you'd better not ever talk to her like that again," said Stan coldly.

"Or what?" spat G.

"Or I'll have you removed from the council and kicked out of this castle," Stan retorted.

There was a moment of charged silence. G looked bewildered, glancing back and forth from Kat to Stan, both of them holding him in their eye lock with contempt. After a moment, G's body loosened up. He looked at Stan.

"Fine," he said in a defeated voice, but when he turned to face Kat, resentment dripped from his voice. "Well, I hope you have fun by yourself, Kat, because we're done."

"You took the words right out of my mouth," Kat replied, matching his level of scorn.

G opened his mouth as if he were about to speak, then closed it again. Finally, with one last look toward Kat that said more than any insult ever could, G turned around and sulked down the hallway. Stan and Kat watched him as he took a left at the far end and entered his room, leaving Stan and Kat standing alone in the hallway.

There was an awkward silence. Stan knew that he should say something. "Uh, Kat?" he asked after a moment. "Are you . . . I mean, are you gonna be . . ."

"Yeah, I'll be fine." Kat sighed, looking at the ground. "I've been meaning to end it for a while now. Thanks for backing me up, Stan," said Kat, looking at him with something that Stan hadn't seen in Kat's eyes in far too long: genuine happiness. "You're a good friend."

Kat gave him an earnest smile. Stan returned it, trying to express without words that no matter what happened, he knew they would always be there for each other. Suddenly, Kat spoke in a loud, excited voice that caught Stan off guard. "Now come on, Stan! That Noctem prisoner ain't gonna interrogate himself!"

CHAPTER 17: THE PRISONER OF BRIMSTONE

Considering that Kat was about to enter a dimension that housed the most dangerous living criminals in the history of Elementia, Stan was amazed at how giddy she was. He sat next to her now, alongside Charlie and DZ, as they waited for their escorts to arrive and take them through the portal to Brimstone Prison.

"So, Kat, DZ, how did the Spleef semis go?" asked Stan.

"Oh, yeah, I had forgotten about that!" Charlie exclaimed. "Tell us all about it!"

As Stan and Charlie looked on expectantly, DZ suddenly looked downcast, and all the happiness that had been building in Kat's face vanished in the blink of an eye.

"What's the matter, guys?" asked Charlie with concern.

"You did . . . I mean, you did win the match, didn't you?" asked Stan.

"Well, of course they won!" said Charlie, as if this should be obvious. "All the stats and leader boards said the Ocelots stood no chance. . . ."

"No, Charlie." DZ sighed. "We lost."

"Shut up, no you didn't." Charlie laughed. "You guys are way better than that other team, the leader boards had you at first place in the tournament, there's no way you could lose to a team as average as the Ocelots."

"Thank you, Charlie," snapped Kat bitterly. "It's not like that's all we've been hearing every time we've talked to anyone, and it's not like Cassandrix has already rubbed our noses in it, no, we haven't heard that at *all*, Charlie, thank you for pointing it out!"

"Whoa, okay there," said Charlie, raising his hands. "Back off, I just can't believe it. You guys actually lost?"

"Yerp," replied DZ, sighing. "Well, I guess there's always next year."

"Or there's always this year!" a thrilled voice came from behind them.

The four players looked at the doorway and saw Ben enter. He was waving a piece of paper in his hand and looked elated.

"What are you talking about, Ben?" Kat asked, looking bewildered.

"We're back in the tournament, guys!" he exclaimed.

"Wait, what?" Kat asked, so surprised that she tumbled backward off her chair in the midst of pulling on her iron boots.

"Are you serious, man?" asked DZ as he ran over to look at the paper, quickly followed by Kat after she regained her footing. "How the Herobrine did that happen?"

"Read for yourself," replied Ben with a grin as he flourished the paper forward for his teammates to see. Kat read it aloud.

"'Attention members of the Zombie Spleef Team. The Ocelots Spleef Team, which was due to compete in the upcoming Spleef World Finals, has been disqualified from the tournament for unsportsmanlike conduct. As a result, you, the runner-up to the disqualified team, are now slotted to take their place in the Spleef World Finals'!" Kat finished, and she gave a scream of joy before jumping into the air and landing in a group hug with her teammates.

"The Ocelots got disqualified?" asked DZ in awe. "What did they do?"

"You guys haven't heard yet? It's all anyone's been talking about," Ben answered. "People are talking about it even more than they're talking about the leak. Apparently, the Ocelots were at a victory party when Cassandrix and the other Skeletons came up to them and started trash talking them. They got the leader so worked up that he punched one of Cassandrix's teammates. People who were there say that it was hardly anything at all, that it shouldn't leave any lasting damage, but Cassandrix is making a big deal out of it, making it out like her teammate took an arrow to the heart or something."

"Yeah, that sounds like Cassandrix," said Kat with

disdain, "milking it for all it's worth."

Ben nodded gravely before continuing on with equal vivacity as before. "Anyway, the incident may have gotten overblown, but the good news is, when the league found out, they disqualified the Ocelots and now we're back in! We get a second chance!"

The three Zombies danced around, making victory noises and acting insane with happiness. Charlie and Stan watched in amusement with huge smiles on their faces.

"Okay," DZ said. "So now that we're back in, we're gonna have to practice our butts off every day until the finals. They're in just a couple weeks, so we're gonna have to push ourselves harder than we've ever done before as soon as we get back from Brimstone."

"Are you guys sure that you still want to go to Brimstone?" Charlie asked. "I'm pretty sure that Stan and I could do the interrogation ourselves, and you guys have training to do." Stan nodded in agreement.

"Are you kidding me?" DZ laughed. "Job first, sports later. We're not gonna miss the interrogation of this guy just so we can practice! I mean, come on, we may finally figure out what the Noctem Alliance is planning!" Kat backed him up with a swift nod of the head.

"Okay, then, you guys go on with the investigation," said Ben as the entourage of guards began to enter the room.

"I gotta say, it's a shame we can't go with you guys. Bob seemed particularly upset about it, but my brothers and I are setting up an investigation into the cause of the leaks, so I'd better get back to that." Stan nodded, and the scarlet-clad police chief left the room.

As he did so, the four guards dressed in army uniforms who would serve as their escort to Brimstone Prison formed a square pattern around the four council members. Stan sighed. He disliked traveling with guards and longed for the days when he could go anywhere he wanted unattended. However, since the attacks by the Noctems had started, the citizens had wanted to keep their president safe, so Stan had instated the guards for protection on the journey to the perilous dimension.

The eight players marched through the purple glowing portal two by two. As Stan entered the mysterious purple mist, he felt the agonizing squeezing sensation that he had been dreading, where it felt like he had a black hole in his stomach. Then, as suddenly as it had started, the sensation stopped. Stan inhaled the warm, arid air around him as he looked around the Nether.

Stan hadn't been to the Nether since the official opening of the Brimstone Prison back before the last major update, but it looked largely unchanged. The Netherrack cave was as ominous as ever. The lava sea was as majestic as he had remembered, and the Nether Fortress looming in the background looked just as imposing.

The Nether Fortress was made primarily of cobblestone now, and resembled an ancient bastille more than a hellish fortress of nightmares. Months ago, Stan had been cornered in that fortress by RAT1, King Kev's assassin team that consisted of Leonidas and two of his now-dead accomplices. Charlie had managed to get Stan, Kat, and the Nether Boys out right before RAT1 had blown up the majority of the fortress. After the battle, a place was needed to hold the dangerous war prisoners. The bits of Nether brick that had been blown apart were then rebuilt with cobblestone, and it had become Brimstone Prison.

That was when Stan had last seen it, during the renaming. He knew now, though, that many changes had taken place within the fortress. While he originally had teams of guards watching the prisoners within the fortress, he received a message one day that his guards in the fortress had all been slaughtered. Stan sent a scout to see what happened, and they had discovered that Brimstone Prison was now home to giant black Skeletons known as Wither Skeletons. Research had told them that these monsters had appeared in the prison during the latest update to Minecraft, and they could fatally poison a player with one swipe of their gigantic stone swords.

Stan gave a lot of credit to Blackraven for figuring out

a way around that problem. It was he who discovered that the Wither Skeletons were much more intelligent than the other evil mobs in the game. He had managed to reason with them, and convinced the Wither Skeletons to become the guards of Brimstone Prison. The mobs were a sadistic race, gaining joy from the aura of the anguished prisoners. They were happy to provide their services to the prison, provided that there was a constant supply of new prisoners to add to the cesspool of misery from which they drank.

As they began to walk down the cobblestone bridge that led to the entrance to the prison, Stan felt Charlie shaking beside him.

"How are you shivering?" asked Stan, wiping the sweat from his brow. "It's gotta be at least a hundred degrees in here!"

"Nah, it's not that," Charlie stammered. "It's those . . . those . . . things, in there . . . they creep me out. . . ."

"What, the Wither Skeletons?" Kat butted in. Charlie nodded.

"Dude, don't worry, they're on our side. They're not gonna attack us, I promise," said Stan. As much as he might disagree with Blackraven, Stan did trust him to do his job right.

"I know they're on our side, I believe that, it's just . . . I don't feel right getting help from a monster that feeds off pain and uses poison to attack."

"It's actually called the Wither Effect, not poisoning," corrected Kat, looking at him in surprise. "Come on, Charlie, you're the bookworm, you're supposed to know all this stuff."

"Well, what's the difference?" Charlie asked.

"Oh, they're the exact same thing, except the Wither Effect can actually kill you, whereas poisoning can just make you incredibly weak."

Charlie was about to respond when he gave a shout of surprise at something behind the other players. Rising above the cobblestone viaduct were no less than three giant, cubic Jellyfish, all of which had blazing red eyes and fireballs flying out of their mouths. Three of the guards leaped forward to take the hits for the players, but Stan, Kat, and DZ had already notched and fired three arrows at the projectiles, hitting them dead-on, knocking them into the distance.

As the guards got to their feet, they could only watch in awe as the four elite players rained a wave of arrows onto the Ghasts. At one point a fourth Ghast rose up behind them, but before the fireball could make contact, DZ whipped around and swung his diamond sword into the fireball, sending it careening back into its sender. The Ghast fell a little before regaining its balance, giving DZ the time to leap in the air and send an arrow flying into the Ghast's forehead. The giant white beast plummeted downward and landed with a whooshing noise on a Netherrack island in the middle of the lava sea before vanishing.

DZ turned around to see that his comrades had just downed the other three Ghasts. The four players looked at one another, saw that nobody was hurt, and gave a quick sigh of relief. Then they looked over at the guards, who were staring at them with jaws dropped. Only now, it seemed, did the guards realize that their job was pointless. The four players they had been mandated to guard were heroes, who had built their reputation by traveling Elementia and ridding it of some of Minecraft's greatest threats.

"Um . . . ," one of the guards with a bushy moustache said. "Should we . . ."

Stan chuckled with amusement. "Go," he said, and with that, the guards scurried back down the cobblestone bridge toward the Nether portal. All four council members laughed to themselves a little before they continued toward the imposing Brimstone Prison.

As they neared the front gate, Stan saw, for the first time in his life, the Wither Skeletons that now had the run of the prison. They were terrifying. Standing almost as tall as an Enderman with bones bleached black and gray, these undead monsters lugged giant stone swords on the ground behind them. A single player dressed in an army uniform stood between them.

As they approached, the two Skeletons guarding the door leered menacingly at the players. The guard stepped forward and asked in a gruff, emotionless voice, "State your business."

"Presidential Request to interrogate prisoner number 02892," said DZ, having memorized the prisoner's ID number.

The guard took one glance at Stan and nodded, before turning to look at one of the Wither Skeletons. The four players watched in curiosity as the guard made a series of clicks and vocations with his mouth, which were echoed by the Wither Skeleton in some form of conversation. After a minute of this, the guard turned to DZ and gave him the directions to the prisoner's chamber. DZ nodded his thanks and walked into the prison. The other three players hustled to catch up to him.

"What just happened, DZ?" Kat asked, wonder in her voice.

"Oh, Blackraven had that guy learn how to speak the language of the Wither Skeletons," he replied.

"Where would he learn how to do that?" Stan asked.

"The internet," DZ replied nonchalantly.

"What?" exclaimed Kat skeptically. "Where on the internet did he find something like that?"

DZ slowly turned around to look at her, and replied, "Kat,

the internet is a strange place . . . so don't question it." And with no further discussion, the four players continued into the fortress.

Ominous didn't begin to describe the feeling of walking through the prison. The ceiling was made of cobblestone, but patches of the floor still had the original Nether brick blocks of the fortress, giving the impression in the dim light that the floor was scattered with pools of blood. The light was faint. Stan knew that Wither Skeletons, like normal Skeletons, were dark-dwelling mobs. There were no torches, with the only light coming from the lava sea and glowstone stalactites on the roof of the Netherrack cave.

As the four players walked down the corridor, all ill at ease, Stan caught glimpses into a few of the cells through the windows of the iron doors. What he saw made him feel a stir of pity. The players were curled up on the floor, hopeless, with nothing left to live for. However, Stan only had to remind himself that these were former members of King Kev's army, and had they not been captured, they would surely be fighting for the Noctem Alliance by now. That ebbed his sympathy instantaneously.

There was one particular cell that caught Stan's attention, and he fell behind the others because he had to take a look inside. Stan glanced in abhorrence at the player sitting up, back against the cobblestone wall, looking back at him.

This player had a black ski mask, a bare muscular chest, and black pants. The first time Stan had seen this player, Jayden's brother Crazy Steve had been shot. The second time, Jayden had gotten his revenge. It never occurred to Stan that the Griefer would have ended up here. It took a yell from Kat to get Stan to rip his fascinated gaze away from this player.

At last, the players reached the end of the corridor, and Stan could tell just by looking at the door that they had made it to the highest-security vault. Stan had passed a few Wither Skeletons patrolling the hallways, but here, four of them stood guard before the iron doors. DZ walked up and pressed a stone button on the wall. The iron door clicked open, but only revealed a second door. The four players walked past it, and the door slammed shut behind them.

"Now we just wait for the redstone circuit to turn over and the door to open. Then we'll finally get to face this guy," stated DZ.

They waited for about half a minute. In that time, Stan took deep breaths. He couldn't put his finger on it, but something seemed off about the whole situation. He knew that it was very possible that the spooky old building was just playing games with his mind, but something about the idea of interrogating this Noctem messenger in general made him feel uneasy, and he had no idea why. At last the door swung open, and the four players drew their weapons and entered the room. *The quicker that we can get this interrogation over with*, thought Stan as he perspired from the heat and his discomfort, *the better.*

This room was lit by torches, presumably to keep mobs from spawning, but the room was still black inside, being ringed in obsidian. At the exact center of the small room, a player sat with his back to Stan and the others. Stan recognized the gray jumpsuit, black shawl, and hood as, indeed, the Noctem messenger who had first told them about the NNA.

The second door slammed shut behind him, and Stan knew that the time for interrogation had begun. Stan took a step toward the player, but before he could open his mouth, a voice sounded from the player, echoing ominously around the room.

"I know why you are here."

Stan glanced at his friends. DZ was the first to speak.

"Is that a fact?" he sneered.

"Yes," the messenger replied. "You wish to question me, and hope that by doing so you may find out more about the inner workings of the Noctem Alliance, which you know so little about."

"Well, someone catches on pretty quick," replied Kat, her brows knitted and her hand gripped tight on her sword. "So here's the first question: Are you going to cooperate with us, or are we gonna have to make you? It's your choice."

"Have you ever stopped to value the beauty of the night?"

The players glanced at one another again for a minute, eyebrows raised, before Stan responded, "Answer her!"

"The night is a fascinating thing. By day, the light of the sun shines upon us from above. We cannot avoid it, and it exposes all of us for who we truly are. At night, however, that light takes rest. Darkness and mystery rule the world. You can be whatever you want to be, and from all eyes, you are hidden from sight. And judgment is nothing more than the petty twin of sight."

"Stop talking in riddles, or we're gonna tranquilize you!" cried DZ, whipping a bottle of blue-gray liquid from his inventory.

"Black is the color of night, a time of haven from the omnipresent judgments of the world, which calls itself civilized. Black is also the color of the Noctem Alliance, a place of haven from the ever-present constitution of Elementia, which calls itself just, yet still forces us to share our world with the lower-level scum that does not deserve it."

"Okay, guys, let's sedate him," ordered Stan, and all four players now whipped out their potions as the player spoke on.

"The black of the Alliance has saved me before. And the color black shall now deliver me from here!" And from the player's hands, two black blurs flew, hitting the ground in bursts of fire and enveloping the prisoner in a plume of dark smoke.

"Attack!" bellowed Stan. Four potions flew into the smoke, shattering with loud clinking noises. Stan was dumbfounded. All players in the prison were stripped of all their items before they were brought to the Nether! How could this have happened?

As the smoke died down, a second ripple of fear struck Stan, tightening his chest. Somehow, the messenger had managed to box himself in a cube of obsidian that he had pulled out of nowhere. Stan reeled in confusion. What was this guy playing at? And where was he getting all these materials?

As Charlie began to hack away at the black box with his pickaxe, a series of black blurs flew out of a hole in the front of the box. As they hit the door, the fire charges ruptured into bursts of searing flame.

Stan sprinted to the hole in the front of the box, adrenaline coursing through his veins and a Potion of Slowness held in his hand. He was immediately forced to leap backward, narrowly missing the block of TNT that flew out of the hole. It was all Stan could do to watch in awe as the block hit the iron door. The door, weakened from the heat, fell apart as the TNT landed in the obsidian corridor. An instant later, the TNT block exploded with the force of a Creeper, sending a shock wave over the players. Stan had to raise his axe in a block to stay safe. By the time they had lowered their defensive stances, the messenger had pitched an Ender Pearl through the blown-out doorframes and into the hallway. He then disappeared into a puff of purple smoke.

The entire escape happened in the space of less than ten seconds.

Stan, Kat, Charlie, and DZ stared at one another for a moment. Stan was completely dumbfounded. It took him a moment before his brain could fully process what had just happened. Then, all at once, the realization came to him. This was the Noctem Alliance playing another game with them. There was only one way to determine how the Noctem messenger had gotten so many materials in the prison. They had to capture him.

“Come on!” Stan yelled, and with that, his friends seemed to snap out of their stupefied states. They followed him, leaping over the burning door and sprinting into the hall.

The messenger was leaping and rolling around the room like a rabbit, but always with the slashes of the Wither Skeleton’s stone swords right on his tail. A wall of the tall dark mobs blocked the entrance to the prison, and Stan could barely make out the form of the guard from the front entrance, who was trying to comprehend the madness breaking loose within the fortress. Stan stared at him.

"Go get backup!" Stan yelled to the guard. After the guard looked around, saw Stan, and processed what he had said, he nodded and sprinted down the cobblestone bridge toward the Nether portal.

Stan's heart, which felt as though it were being clenched in a giant fist, loosened slightly, but immediately tightened twofold when he saw that the messenger had reached the entrance. There was no time to waste. If they hurried, they could still catch up to him. They had Ender Pearls on hand, but there was no room to warp. There was a crowd of Wither Skeletons in front of them. Stan pushed and shoved his way through the throng of idle monsters.

Wait a second, thought Stan, the realization dawning on him as he pushed nearer and nearer to the exit. If a highly dangerous criminal was in the process of escaping . . . and the Wither Skeletons were there to guard the prison . . . then why were they just standing there idly as the highest-security prisoner escaped? Why had they stopped fighting? As Stan finally made his way to the front of the crowd, he saw the reason, and he staggered in shock.

The Wither Skeletons were standing, transfixed, as the Noctem messenger stood at the base of the fortress stairs, clicking and making sounds that Stan recognized as the language of the Skeletons. He barely had time to be caught off guard by the messenger speaking the language of these monsters when the messenger jabbed a finger directly at Stan and his friends, and gave what sounded like a powerful command in the clicking language.

Stan's instincts kicked in and he feinted backward, down the stairs, as no less than three giant stone swords swung toward him. Stan managed to duck the attacks, but he lost his balance and fell down the stairs, landing painfully on his back on the cobblestone bridge. Stan looked up and saw all the black Skeletons converging on his flabbergasted friends, except for one, which sprinted down the steps and prepared for another swing at him. Stan clambered for his axe, which had fallen on the ground beside him, but before he could reach it, the giant Skeleton fell apart, courtesy of the sword that the guard of the fortress had stuck into its side. He reached down toward Stan.

"Are you hurt, President Stan?" the guard asked, pulling Stan to his feet.

"No, I'm fine," replied Stan gruffly as he brushed himself off. He looked back toward the fortress. His friends were gradually fighting their way out, past the giant black Skeletons.

"What happened in there?" the guard asked urgently.

"I . . . I really don't know," replied Stan, trying to recall the insanity that was the last sixty seconds. His thoughts landed on the messenger, conversing with the idle Wither Skeletons. “Listen,” Stan asked hastily, whipping around to face the guard. “Did you hear what he said, the guy who escaped, to the Skeletons?”

“Yeah,” the guard replied, looking confused. “He said something like, ‘The time is now, my friends, fight the tyrants and rejoin your master,’ but I still don’t understand how he managed to—”

“Listen, we can explain later, we’ve got to catch that guy!” exclaimed Kat, huffing and puffing as she ran over to join Stan, the others close on her tail.

“Where did he go?” panted DZ as he reached the others as well.

“There he is, over there!” shouted Charlie, pointing down the bridge. The messenger was already a third of the way down the cobblestone bridge, headed toward the Nether portal.

“Oh, no you don’t!” bellowed Kat as she flung an Ender Pearl down the bridge toward the messenger.

“You,” said Stan, turning to face the guard as Kat disappeared in a puff of purple smoke, and Charlie and DZ threw their Pearls in the same direction. “Lock down the fortress, and see if you can get them to settle down.” He gestured to the Wither Skeletons, who were falling back into the fortress for reasons Stan had no time to care about. Stan didn’t even wait for a response before he flung his Ender Pearl down the bridge and an instant later felt the rush of air all around him as he warped into the air and landed feetfirst on solid brick.

It was pandemonium around him. Kat and DZ had drawn their swords and Charlie his pickaxe, and were stabbing and slashing away, hoping to land one single hit on the Noctem messenger, hoping to do anything at all to pin him down. It seemed in vain, however, as the messenger ducked, weaved, and bobbed his way through every attack with the ease and grace of a bird surfing an air current. Curls of light blue smoke rose from his back. He wasn't trying to counterattack, didn't even have a weapon drawn. It seemed that, yet again, this agent of the Noctem Alliance was simply toying with them.

Stan knew better than to try to pull his axe, which would do nothing to help in the fight. An opponent like this required precision to take down. Stan drew his bow and arrow, pulled back the string, and looked down the shaft of the arrow, constantly shifting his aim as the messenger swerved and bounced around like a jumping bean. Finally, after the messenger dodged a particularly close swing of DZ's sword, Stan saw his shot, and fired.

The arrow came within an inch of the messenger's shoulder before he sensed it coming and leaped to the side, right into the path of a powerful swing of Charlie's pickaxe. The hit connected, and the messenger staggered backward, colliding with the side guardrail of the bridge and tumbling over it, beginning a free fall toward the lava sea hundreds of blocks below.

Stan sprinted to the edge of the bridge and saw a Netherrack island protruding from the lava. Stan knew he couldn't let the Noctem officer die from the fall—there was far too much precious information riding on it. An insane idea coming into his head, Stan leaped over the edge of the bridge after the messenger.

Stan was too focused on putting his extremely dicey plan into action to be terrified at his increasing rate of free fall. He drew two Ender Pearls from his inventory and pitched one toward the messenger. As the Ender Pearl made contact with the messenger and cracked open, Stan felt himself fly at the speed of sound, appearing next to the messenger in a puff of purple smoke. The messenger's eyes flew open in shock, and before he could react, Stan pulled him into a bear hug and pitched the second Ender Pearl at the fast-approaching Netherrack island.

The effect was immediate. Right as the duo was about to slam into the ground at terminal velocity, the Pearl shattered on the ground and took effect. Both players were dumped on the ground in a puff of purple smoke, a slight stinging in the legs as the only memento of the fall.

Stan kicked the still stunned messenger off him and

leaped to his feet, pulling his bow and arrow out of his inventory and training it on the messenger. The messenger shook his head clear of the shock and sprinted toward the edge of the island. He was about to jump off the edge when Charlie materialized on the ground in front of him in a puff of purple smoke, bow raised. The messenger cut a sharp left and was about to dive off in that direction when DZ suddenly appeared in his way, followed by Kat opposite him, both with bows drawn. The messenger was surrounded.

The messenger glanced around at the four players before finally chuckling and throwing his hands up in the air.

"All right," he said, sounding amused. "You caught me, good job, you four. Well, you obviously want me really bad for something or other. What is it?"

"We want answers," said Stan gruffly, pulling the bowstring back a little bit tauter.

"Yeah, and you'd better not lie!" shouted DZ.

"Oh, give me some credit, DZ." The messenger chuckled, and four pairs of eyebrows raised at the use of his name. "The Noctem Alliance is a great many things, but it is not dishonorable, and as an agent of the grand organization, neither am I. You four have rightfully bested me, Count Drake, in combat. I, therefore, will provide you with any answers that I am permitted to give. I shall not, of course, lie. That wouldn't be very honorable at all now, would it?"

"I don't see what it is you're so amused about," said Kat, the cheery tone of Count Drake's voice clearly getting under her skin. "But whatever. How did you get the materials to break out of Brimstone?"

"Why, they were given to me, of course," Drake replied, as if this should have been obvious.

"By who?" Kat demanded.

"Why, you don't know? Oh my, I knew that your council was dysfunctional, but I didn't know it was that dysfunctional."

"Shut up!" seethed Kat, a small growl escaping her mouth as her nostrils flared with rage. "What are you talking about?"

"The spy, my dear Kat," Drake replied with a chuckle. "The spy in your midst slipped in the materials necessary for my escape, along with my daily lunch."

"You're saying that you guys've got a spy in Elementia?" gasped DZ.

"Oh, dear, I really do have to spell this out for you, don't I," replied Drake in mock exasperation. "Yes, there is a spy within the command of Element City. The spy has lived in your city since the inception of the Noctem Alliance. In fact, along with Chancellor Caesar and Generals Minotaurus and Leonidas, the spy was one of the very first followers of the great Lord Tenebris."

"Who is this Lord Tenebris, anyway?" asked Charlie before Stan could reply. "Even after everything you guys have put us through, we still have no idea who the guy is. What, is he afraid to show himself?"

"Charlie, stay focused!" hissed Kat, who, like Stan, couldn't believe that Charlie could think about anything else after they had just heard a claim that there was a spy in Elementia.

"Oh, Kat, don't fret," replied Drake in a voice of mock concern. "There will be plenty of time for all questions to be answered. And besides, I will never grow tired of praising our great leader, Lord Tenebris."

"Okay then, spill! Who is he?" asked Charlie.

"Lord Tenebris," Drake said, "is the most powerful entity who has ever inhabited Minecraft. To call him a mere player would be an insult. He has experimented, pushed the limits of the game of Minecraft. In doing so, Lord Tenebris has become more powerful than the mind can imagine, far surpassing any limits of the average player, or even those of a player with operating powers. There are reasons he has not yet revealed himself, and those reasons are not mine to tell you. However, rest assured, my esteemed captors, that when the great Lord Tenebris does show himself, it shall be a dark day for the disgusting ideals you claim as justice." And with that, Count Drake leered an evil grin and licked his lip threateningly.

Up until that point, Stan had taken care to appear just as powerful and confident as he really was, so that he could intimidate this Noctem agent and discourage him from lying. But as Stan listened to Drake talk about his leader for the first time, a wave of fear swept over him. There was a flame, a passion in Drake's voice as he talked, a passion that made Stan wonder for a moment what exactly they were dealing with in the leader of the Noctem Alliance. After a moment, Stan snapped out of it. There was plenty of time to worry about that later. They had more pressing matters at hand.

"Whatever," shot back Stan, trying to keep his voice steady. "Now, back to the spy. Who is it?"

Drake's grin faded a bit, but a hint of smile still remained as he turned to face Stan.

"Stan, I swore to you that I would be honest with you," replied the count. "And I will not lie to you now. However, just like the plans of the great Lord Tenebris, there is some information that I am not at liberty to share. The identity of the spy in your walls falls under that category."

Stan's eyebrow twitched, and his grip on the bow tightened further still as Charlie exploded at Count Drake. "Enough of your double talk, Drake! Tell us who it is, or things are gonna get ugly!"

Drake's full smile returned. "Oh, by all means, go ahead and shoot me. I've given you all the information I'm authorized to give you. I'm of no use to you now. The Noctem Alliance will not negotiate with you if you take me hostage—I am of no significance in the grand scheme of things. And besides, I . . ."

His speech was cut off by a gagging noise as Kat leaped out, quicker than a striking rattlesnake, and knocked the butt of her sword against Drake's chest. She was quick to follow up by pinning him to the ground under her knee, sword drawn. She had passed the normal levels of rage long ago. Her face was so contorted in fury that she looked inhuman.

"Well, then, if that's the case, let's see if a little pain will get you talking!" snarled Kat, and she began slowly lowering the point of her sword toward Drake's face.

"Kat, no!" bellowed DZ, and he leaped forward to knock the sword to the side. Count Drake beat him to the punch, and in one motion he knocked the sword to the side with his hand, pushed off the ground with it, and propelled his body onto his feet. He then proceeded to do a backflip between Kat and DZ, plummeting to the lava sea below. Stan's eyes followed him down toward the expanse of orange magma, and as the body entered the molten liquid, Stan saw a distinctive trail of orange smoke above the lava.

"He survived, guys." Stan sighed. "He had a Potion of Fire Resistance." But as he looked up, Stan realized that nobody was listening to him. Instead, Charlie and DZ were fixated on

Kat with pointed concern. She was still seething with rage, but there was another element in her eyes, too, as if she were about to cry. Stan had seen it before. Long ago, in the Ender Desert, as Stan had watched Kat on the verge of killing an unarmed soldier of King Kev, she had had the exact same look on her face.

"Kat, what . . . what was that?" DZ asked, looking at Kat in a way that he never had before.

"I'm . . . I'm sorry . . . ," panted Kat, heaving fast and hard. "I'm just . . . so sick of the Noctem Alliance and their mind games. . . . This isn't my kind of fight. I'll take anyone on in a sword fight but this . . . this . . . this whatever-it-is . . ." Kat's breathing had calmed, but Stan was shocked to see the utterly defeated look on her face. "I can't do this anymore."

"I agree with you, Kat," said Charlie fervently. "I don't think any of us can deal with these mind games for too much longer. But you can't go around torturing people for information. We may be playing a different game than they are, but if our values are going to survive, we have to hold fast to them. You understand, don't you?"

"Oh yeah, for sure," replied Kat hastily, trying to get any shred of doubt out of the air as soon as possible. "I'm sorry, I just lost myself for a second."

DZ and Charlie sighed in relief, but Stan gave a solemn glance down at the lava sea that Drake had disappeared into just moments before. The time he had feared for so long had finally arrived. The Noctem Alliance had pushed one of them past the breaking point. Stan had known Kat back in a time where she would kill without remorse to get what she wanted. However, even back then, Stan knew that it would never even cross her mind to torture a player for information.

The Noctem Alliance had corrupted her. Sure, it may have only been for one moment, and she definitely had the most troubled past out of all them, but the tension that the Alliance's omnipresence had placed upon Kat had broken her in that one moment. And if the Noctem Alliance had caused one of them to betray their ideals, it was only a matter of time before the others began to follow.

In fact, hadn't they begun to fall already? It dawned on Stan that Jayden and G had already begun to turn their backs on justice, being ready to do anything and everything to destroy the Alliance that had killed their best friend. Wanting to burn Nocturia to the ground with no second thoughts, appointing council members without election, torturing prisoners for information—it was all the same, wasn't it? All those things went against the principles of democracy and fair treatment to all. They were only thinking like that because the Noctem Alliance was putting them under such pressure.

Although, Stan had to admit, Caesar was never going to negotiate with him, he was sure of it, so perhaps it might have been better to burn Nocturia to the ground. And perhaps a little bit of pain would have convinced Count Drake to share that so-called classified information.

Stan shook his head, catching himself. *Look at me!* he thought. *Here I am, thinking that betraying my ideals just to take down the Alliance faster is a good idea! Obviously that way of thinking is wrong, right? Isn't it?*

However confused Stan was about what was right and what was wrong, there was one thing he knew for sure: the situation had become critical. Despite having next to no information to go on, it was crucial that the Noctem Alliance go down very soon. The Alliance had already begun to rot away at the core of justice in Elementia. They had to dispose of it before the core finally rotted through.

CHAPTER 18
THE WARNINGS

As the earthshaking footsteps of Minotaurus grew closer and closer, Leonidas cringed. Dirt particles fell from the roof of his foxhole outside Element City with every step Minotaurus took.

Leonidas brushed the dirt off his black leather armor in disgust. It was bad enough that he had to share a tiny dirt hole with six other players, one of whom was modded to double size. Even though the stuffiness and perpetual perspiration were inevitable, Leonidas was determined to keep the sweat on his brow from turning to mud.

"Ouch!" came a bellow from the entrance to the hole, and two dirt blocks broke loose from the roof of the doorway and tumbled to the ground, bouncing off something invisible as they fell.

"Shut up!" hissed Leonidas. "Ya want the entire kingdom to know we're here, ya idiot bull? And put those dirt blocks back!"

"I am sorry, Leonidas," replied Minotaurus in a glum voice as the blocks of dirt levitated up and fixated themselves back onto the cave wall. Leonidas shuddered. He still wasn't used to the effects of the Potion of Invisibility. It kind of freaked him out.

"And drink your milk when you're done with that," Leonidas reminded Minotaurus.

"What? Oh, right." And with that, a bucket of milk materialized in midair, and began pouring itself, disappearing into thin air. Moments later, the milk nullified the effects of the potion, and the giant, muscled form of Minotaurus became visible in the hole. Three other buckets appeared behind him, and within a few seconds, three Noctem troopers materialized.

"Did ya get it all set up?" Leonidas asked, trying to keep his overwhelming boredom out of his voice.

"Yes, we did," replied Minotaurus. "The explosives have been completely wired. As soon as the next person uses the machine, it will go ka-boom!"

"And the note?" asked Leonidas in a disinterested voice.

"Taken care of," replied Spyro, the private standing closest to Minotaurus. "We set it up perfectly. When they scan the wreckage of the machine, they'll find the message. Then, it's all up to Chancellor Caesar what happens after that."

"Yes, I know," replied Leonidas through gritted teeth. "It's all Chancellor Caesar's decision what we do next."

"Yep," replied Spyro, sounding irritatingly peppy. "All right, back to Nocturia we go!"

"Not yet." Leonidas sighed.

"Why not?" Spyro asked, tilting his head to the side like a confused puppy.

"Accordin' to the great Chancellor Caesar, we have to wait for it to go off."

"And . . . why is . . ."

"I dunno, kid, all right?" barked Leonidas. "It must be the same reason Caesar had us dig this stupid, tiny foxhole to stay in instead of settin' up a normal-size hideout like any normal Minecrafter would do!"

"But," cut in Minotaurus, "Chancellor Caesar said that we needed a small hideout so that we would be less constipated!"

"The word is 'conspicuous,' Minotaurus, not 'constipated.'" Leonidas sighed, putting his palm to his forehead. *I'm surrounded by idiots*, he thought as the other soldiers snickered.

"Let's just get as comfortable as we can in here," mumbled Leonidas. "We'll head to Nocturia as soon as possible."

As the six troopers settled into place around the walls of the hole, Leonidas pulled an arrow out of his inventory. He held it like a pencil in his hand, doodled a sloppy stick figure in the dirt, and stabbed it through the heart, imagining Caesar's face on it. Leonidas was surprised to find that this actually relieved some of his stress. As he pondered what exactly that meant, he leaned back against the cave wall and closed his eyes, hoping to get some sleep before the bomb went off.

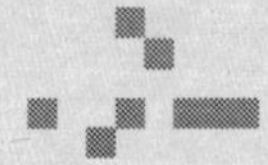

"Are you serious, Charlie?" asked Blackraven in alarm.

"Would I joke about something like that?" replied Charlie gravely. "We're still waiting on the official report from Bill, Ben, and Bob about the situation. All we know for sure is that the Wither Skeletons have joined the Noctem Alliance, and they helped Count Drake escape from Blackstone."

"Oh, well that's just wonderful," spat Jayden in disgust. "You know, maybe G and I should handle the interrogations and stuff from now on. It seems like every time you do it, we somehow manage to wind up worse than we already were!"

"Well, maybe I should point out," shot back DZ, "that you guys handled getting the Wither Skeletons on our side, and they turned on us pretty fast! It's almost like they were ready to turn on us from the start or something."

"Do not blame Jayden and Goldman for my mistake!" boomed Blackraven, his voice loud and echoing around the council chamber. "I was the one who attempted to reason with those monsters, I am the one who should take the blame for their betrayal!"

"It's not your fault, Blackraven! Think about what the guard heard Drake say. 'The time is now, fight the tyrants, rejoin your master,'" pointed out the Mechanist reasonably. "He must have spoken to the Skeletons while he was imprisoned, and convinced them to join the Noctem Alliance. What he said to convince them, though, I can only guess. . . ."

"Well, it's not hard to imagine," said Charlie. "The Skeletons gain strength from the misery of players, and the Noctem Alliance is a terrorist organization. . . . I can't imagine that misery would be something they're lacking in."

A five-note chime rang out as Charlie finished speaking, and Bill walked in. The look on his face set off alarm bells in Stan's head. He looked utterly distressed.

"What's the word, Bill?" Stan asked, almost hesitantly.

"Nothing good, Stan, nothing good," Bill replied gravely, and Stan's stomach dropped, continuing to plummet as Bill gave his report. "We sent a team in to secure the Nether Fortress, and it turns out that Drake was very busy in the ten minutes it took us to get in there. The entire prison was empty. He let all the prisoners in Brimstone escape. I'm assuming that he also managed to convince all of them to join the Noctem Alliance, 'cause as soon as we sent out search parties, we came under heavy arrow fire from sources we couldn't see. Stupid Invisibility Potions. And so," Bill concluded with a heavy sigh, "we'll fight for it for all it's worth, but as of now, the Noctem Alliance has control over the Nether.

"And what's worse," continued Bill darkly, "is that as long as the Noctems have the Nether, they'll be able to fast-travel."

"What does that mean?" Kat asked apprehensively.

"For every block that you walk in the Nether, you move eight blocks in that direction in the Overworld. When you consider the fact that the Noctems can use Invisibility Potions to stay safe from the Ghasts, they can now use portals to warp across the entire Overworld in a matter of minutes."

Eight mouths around the tables dropped open at this statement, but before anybody had a chance to respond, the doors flew open yet again, this time spitting Ben, Bob, and Ivanhoe into the courtroom. The pig skidded to a stop. Stan felt the beginnings of a migraine coming on as he realized that both of the other chiefs had looks on their faces identical to Bill's.

"What happened now?" Stan said, not sure how much more bad news he could take.

"The Noctem Alliance bombed the Tennis Machine," Bob stated solemnly.

"*What*?" Stan, Kat, DZ, and Jayden burst out simultaneously.

"What did they do?" breathed the Mechanist, reeling in shock.

"The Tennis Machine blew up while people were in the middle of playing it. When the police got to the wreckage, we found a book inside that was titled *The Demands of Lord Tenebris*. We haven't read it yet, it's in evidence right now. The bomb went off about twenty minutes ago. Eleven people were killed in the blast, and the citizen population is freaking out. We had to order a military quarantine and force people back into their houses. They're there now, waiting for orders."

There was a moment of silence as the sheer gravity of what was going on sunk in. The Noctem Alliance had just gained about fifty members who had escaped from the Element City prison. They now had control over the entirety of the Nether. Using that dimension, they could warp across the entire world in no time flat. And now, the same players had detonated a bomb in the heart of Element City and killed its citizens. *This is the last straw*, thought Stan. The Noctem Alliance had killed Elementian citizens. It was time to go on the offensive.

"We've come here to ask your official permission to instate a draft, Stan," said Bill tiredly. "Our normal army isn't going to have enough manpower to do all the stuff that we have to do now that they've killed our citizens. We've got to use about half our normal forces to fight the Noctems in the Nether, and it'll take a lot more men to take back Brimstone from the Wither Skeletons."

"And that's just in that dimension," Bob continued. "In the Overworld, we have to send even more forces into the city to patrol for hostile activity, secure our walls, and investigate how the bombers got in. The most soldiers of all, though, have got to go into the invasion of Nocturia. All we need is the council to officially declare war on the NNA, and then we'll march into Nocturia with two hundred men and destroy the Alliance once and for all."

"Well, I think the council will definitely be behind you in declaring war at this point," replied Stan, and there were grim murmurs of assent behind him. "But there's another thing I'm gonna have to ask you to add to your agenda."

"Stan, it's gonna be impossible to do all this at once," grunted Bob. "We're fighting a war here in the Nether and in Nocturia all at the same time. Our forces are going to be stretched paper-thin as it is. Whatever it is you need us to do, it had better be really important."

"Trust me, it is," said DZ. "There's a spy in our government. Drake told us, and trust me, he wasn't lying."

"Stan, can you hear me?"

Stan's eyes widened and his ears perked up. That voice. The voice that he had almost forgotten about over the past week, echoing from somewhere far beyond the server. Sally.

He jumped up from his seat. The others were still reeling from the announcement that there was a spy in their midst, but Stan trusted Charlie, Kat, and DZ to address the issue completely and tell the chiefs what Drake had told them. Right now, he had to concentrate on not letting Sally's voice slip from his mind again.

"Sally is contacting me, guys, I'll be back in a few," Stan

exclaimed, and not waiting for a response, he ran out of the council room and straight to his room. He pulled the lever to close the iron door and sat on his bed, concentrating.

"Sally, can you hear me?"

"Yeah, I hear you, Stan," the response came back, and Stan sighed in relief.

"It's good to hear from you, Sal."

"Yeah, ditto to that, noob. I've been warping in and out of different places all around Elementia, and by listening to people, I've gotten a pretty good idea of what's happened there since the last time we talked. A lot has gone down since then, huh."

Stan faltered for a moment. So much had happened over the past week that Stan was having trouble remembering when he had last talked to Sally. In fact, since Elementia Day, he couldn't remember even thinking about her once, let alone remembering what she had said. Then it came to him. The afternoon of Elementia Day, punctuated by static, Sally's voice had come through to him. She had warned him about the incoming attack on the city. . . . And she had also said . . .

"Sally!" Stan exclaimed, remembering the conversation clearly now. "How did you know the Noctems were going to bomb the Tennis Machine?"

"Oh, did it happen?" she responded glumly. "Hold on . . . Stan, how did that happen? I told you it was going to happen . . . so why did you not, like, put extra security measures around the machine or anything?"

"Well, the others didn't believe you at first," replied Stan. "And I was going to try to convince them to at least take precautions. but then the attack happened, and . . . You know what happened to Archie, right?"

"Yeah," Sally said. "I heard some people in the city talking about it. It's a real shame. Archie was a good guy, I knew him for a long time."

"Well, anyway," continued Stan. "That happened, and then after that, stuff wouldn't stop happening, so I kind of got distracted."

"Understandable," said Sally reasonably. "In any case, I know that you must realize the Noctem Alliance is becoming more powerful by the day, but I don't think you realize just how powerful they're becoming. Stan, you're not gonna like hearing this, but they've started to work against me too."

"What? How is that possible?" Stan asked, bewildered. "You're not even in Elementia anymore, how can the Noctems be going against you?"

"Your guess is as good as mine," said Sally grimly. "But haven't you wondered why my voice has been all static-y every time we've talked?"

"Well, yeah, but I just assumed it was because the blacklist is hard to get around, and it's causing you interference."

"Well, that is part of it, but trust me, Stan, I'm a pretty good hacker. If this were just a normal blacklist, I would have bypassed it and been able to rejoin Elementia by now. Somehow, somebody in the Noctem Alliance is putting up more firewalls and other security measures, to make hacking back into Elementia almost impossible. And that's not all. As I try to bypass the new security, I find messages coded into it, and they're all saying that attempting to hack into Elementia is futile and that I'm just making things worse for the players of Elementia. The messages are signed in the name of Lord Tenebris."

"So . . . that means . . . ," Stan said slowly, putting the puzzle pieces together in his head.

"That's right, Stan. The Noctem Alliance has a tech-savvy of their own, and whoever it is, they're countering all my hacking."

Stan sighed. "Does that mean you're not going to be able to spy in on their conversations anymore?"

"No, I don't think so. In fact, I have reason to believe that now they know when I'm spying on them."

"What makes you say that?"

"Because they caught me in the act once. Just yesterday, I was thrilled when I accidentally warped right into Nocturia, in the middle of Caesar briefing his men on their upcoming plans. He revealed some pretty interesting information, but then a messenger came in and told Caesar that he was being spied on by an Elementia-backed hacker, and so they moved their conversation away. Honestly, who else could they have been talking about?"

"That is really unfortunate," said Stan. "Did you at least hear a lot of their plans before they caught you?"

"Yeah, I did, Stan, and that's actually what I need to tell you about. Basically, Caesar was briefing new recruits to the Noctem Alliance. I managed to get a glimpse of the recruits themselves, and there were hundreds of them. I guess that recruitment for the Alliance must have gone way up in the past week. If I had to guess, most of the new members are players that have always hated the lower-levels, but up until now they thought the Alliance was too weak to risk joining."

Stan cringed. He hadn't realized that he very well may have been losing his own citizens to the Noctem Alliance this entire time, with more and more bigoted players defecting as they grew confident in the Alliance's strength.

"What were the plans, Sally?" Stan asked finally.

"Well, as it turns out, the Noctems know that after the takeover at Brimstone and the Tennis Machine bombing they had planned, Elementia would have no choice but to declare full-out war on them. And the Alliance is preparing to fight too. They're sending a lot of troops into the Nether to secure that dimension, I assume mainly so that they can fast-travel.

And they also have an entire army prepared to fight on the home front in the Overworld."

"Is that it?" Stan demanded. This was nothing that he hadn't already expected.

"No, it's not, Stan. There's one more critical piece of information that Caesar revealed."

"Well, spit it out!" pressed Stan.

"Basically," said Sally, her voice becoming slightly hastier and more urgent for reasons that Stan could only imagine, "the Noctem Alliance knows that you're going to assume that the leaders of the Alliance will be commanding the troops from their castle in Nocturia. They also know that the leaders of Elementia are going to be fighting out on the battlefield instead of commanding from far away. Their basic plan is to lure you into the castle in Nocturia, and then capture and kill you in there."

"Well, isn't that worth it, then?" Stan asked. "I mean, I'm sure that we can take on their leaders in combat and win. And if we get trapped in Nocturia, I'm sure we'll be able to fight our way out of any traps they set for us."

"That's the thing, Stan. The leaders won't be in Nocturia. They've converted the entire building into a gigantic bomb, and the Noctem troops fighting around Nocturia are going to lure you deep into the heart of the castle and then blow you sky-high. That's the biggest thing that you need to know, Stan. The leaders of the Noctem Alliance will not be in Nocturia during this war. They're going to be somewhere else."

"Where?" Stan asked, appalled by the cruel trick the Noctem Alliance was planning to play.

"Well, I don't know where it is. Caesar only referred to it as the 'Specialty Base,' a Noctem outpost far away, where the leaders of the Noctem Alliance can safely wait out the war. Also, I'm not positive, but he implied that that may be where Lord Tenebris has been hiding out this entire time. Stan, if you want to destroy the Noctem Alliance, you need to locate and attack the Specialty Base."

"Okay," Stan said slowly, trying to process all this new, vital information, with two main questions surfacing in his head. "I have a couple of questions. First, if the Noctem leaders are hiding away in the Specialty Base, then who's going to be commanding the troops?"

"Caesar told his men that while he himself and the other important Noctem leaders are away, the army will be under the command of General Leonidas and Count Drake, whoever that is."

Stan shuddered, remembering the devious Count Drake and knowing exactly the kind of underhanded tactics he would use in war. As for Leonidas, Stan was a little bit surprised that Leonidas didn't qualify as one of the important

Noctem leaders who would be safe in the Specialty Base. Then, Stan shook his head in revulsion as he realized that Leonidas had probably volunteered for the task, preferring the rage of war over a safe house, being the ruthless killer that he was.

"Okay, one more question, Sal: you said Caesar was aware that you had been listening in. Do you think they might change their plans because of that?"

"Honestly, I don't think so. As they walked away, the messenger told Caesar that I had only been there for a short time listening. And immediately afterward, I was thrown out of the server by the most impressive set of firewalls yet. It took me all day to get around them and contact you. And besides, the plans the Alliance put together were very complex, what with converting their entire capital into a bomb and constructing a foreign base just to capture you. I seriously doubt they would abort their plan just because of the possibility that someone might know what's going on. For all they know, I wasn't even able to get the information to you because of the firewalls. They'll probably just go along with the original plan."

"Okay, thank you, Sally," said Stan, the gears already spinning in his head. "I'll make sure to have the military send some scouts out into the server to try to locate this Specialty Base. Although I don't know how they're going to spare the manpower—we already have to fight a war on two fronts."

"Don't worry, I'm sure you'll find a . . . wait . . . ooooh boy . . ."

"What is it, Sally?" Stan asked, startled by her sudden change in tone.

"The Alliance just put up some more new firewalls. Really nasty ones too. I'm gonna lose contact with you in a few minutes, Stan. How about you go and start planning with the others now? I've told you all that I need to, and if I log out now, maybe I can get rid of the new security before it really takes hold."

"Okay, do what you have to do, Sal," replied Stan. He knew very little of hacking and computers, and trusted that what Sally recommended was for the best.

"Right. Later, noob." And with a pop, Sally's voice, and the slight static undertones that denoted its presence, disappeared.

Stan wasted no time. He sprinted down the hallway back to the council room.

". . . necessary it is to investigate this, Charlie," Bill exclaimed in exasperation, staring across the table at Charlie, "but I just don't understand how we're going to do this! I mean, even with a draft in place, we're not going to have enough players to do all this at once!"

"Ah, Stan, you're back," the Mechanist greeted him, and

with that, all eyes in the room turned to him.

"Hey, Stan," said Kat. "Did Sally tell you anything important?"

"Yeah, she told me a ton," replied Stan, and wasting no time, he recounted to the council and police chiefs everything Sally had told him.

"She wants us to send out scouts?" Bill yelled in angst when Stan had finished. "I'm sorry, but it's just not possible!"

"I don't care if it's not possible, Bill," replied Stan in vexation, "it still has to be done! Take troops away from the front lines if you have to, but we have to find this Specialty Base if we ever stand a chance of ridding ourselves of the Noctem Alliance!"

"Do you even hear yourself?" Bob shouted. "Without at least a hundred men on the front line, we won't be able to stop the Alliance from marching up to our front doors. Especially if what you say is true, and they really do have hundreds of new recruits incoming!"

"Personally, I really only see one course of action," said Blackraven calmly.

"Then spit it out," cried Charlie, to fervent nods. At this point, any course of action was a good one.

"We have to instate the Double Draft," Blackraven replied simply.

Dead silence reverberated around the room. Blackraven

had just touched the land mine that nobody had wanted to step on.

"No," said DZ firmly.

"There is no other way," replied Blackraven.

"Well, I'm not doing that," said DZ again, an edge to his voice now. "It'd be tyranny if we did that now, especially at the start of the war. If we were losing the war, then it might be a different story, but . . ."

"I think Blackraven may be right," cut in Gobbleguy, and everybody's eyes shot over to him in surprise.

"Do you really think so?" Blackraven asked. Even he seemed caught off guard.

"Yes, I do," replied Gobbleguy. "The city needs to be kept safe at all costs. Having double the number of soldiers than a normal draft would provide would allow us to fulfill all the tasks required to defend Elementia, with no shortages in any area."

"Are you kidding me?" shouted Kat with a mean laugh. "The first time you ever have an opinion about anything, and you're supporting the most desperate measure we have?"

"Shut up, Kat!" yelled G. "It's not your decision, it's his! Jeez, do you ever think rationally about anything?"

"What's that supposed to mean?" demanded Kat.

"Oh, I don't know," retorted G, his voice dripping with sarcasm. "Wanting to risk going into a war with too few soldiers when having more than enough is just a vote away. Thinking that a guy giving up his time to spend it with you is desperate, not sweet. I don't know, after all these ignorant opinions, you start to notice trends."

"That's enough, you two!" the Mechanist intervened as G snickered and Kat snarled in hostility. "You can deal with your personal problems outside the council room. Now, as for the matter at hand, I believe we should put it to a vote."

"Good idea," said Stan, confident that the idea would be shot down with ease. At least he and his friends were smart enough to realize that drafting half the population of the city into the army (through the power of the Double Draft) would do nothing more than make the citizens angrier with the council than they already were. Even if the number of players added to the army by the regular draft looked a little bit low now, Stan was sure they would still be able to manage. If things got desperate in the future, then they could instate the Double Draft.

"All in favor of a Double Draft?" asked Stan with the hint of a smirk. He looked around the table and watched the hands go up one by one. Blackraven . . . G . . . Jayden . . . Gobbleguy . . . the Mechanist . . . haha, as Stan suspected, they had only gotten five votes . . . wait . . . five votes? The Double Draft had gotten five votes? It had passed?

"Well . . . okay then . . . ," came a voice. Stan jumped.

He had forgotten that the police chiefs were still in the room. Bob spoke on. "If you guys really think the Double Draft is the best idea, I'll go make the announcement to the citizens." And with that, Bob directed Ivanhoe out the door, followed by Bill and Ben. They all had distressed looks on their faces.

"What are you thinking?" cried Charlie, wheeling around to the Mechanist.

"Yeah, why would you support the Double Draft? It's overkill, is what it is!" agreed DZ.

"In an ordinary situation, I would say that you are right," replied the Mechanist coolly. "In a regular war, calling half our citizen population to fight would be too much. However, this is the Noctem Alliance we are dealing with. They have proven to us on multiple occasions that they are not afraid to use sly and dishonorable tactics to fight. Therefore, if we want to maintain our integrity, we must fight them using all the raw force we can muster."

The council room was quiet for a moment. Stan sighed. Why'd he have to go and say something logical like that?

"Well, how about the citizens, huh?" demanded Kat. "What's your response to that? The citizens already think we're doing a terrible job running the server, especially with the leak and all these attacks by the Noctem Alliance . . . they hardly even trust us anymore. How are we gonna tell them that one in every two people in this city is going to be drafted into the army against their will?"

"The key is happiness," replied Blackraven wisely. "If we are going to keep the citizen population from despising us, or even turning on us, we must keep them distracted from the war going on, and we must keep them happy. While the army is fulfilling all of their duties, it must be our jobs to think of and execute ways to keep the citizens still in the city content."

"How about this?" Stan exclaimed, a brilliant idea popping into this head. "The Spleef finals are coming up in just a couple weeks. How about we hype that up, and get everybody all excited about that?"

The room fell silent. The silence had a certain weight to it, and Stan could tell he had just said something wrong.

"What is it?" he asked cautiously.

"Stan . . . while you were in there, talking to Sally, a soldier came in with another message," said Charlie slowly.

Stan gulped. What else could possibly have happened in such a short time?

"You know how they found a book in the bombed-out Tennis Machine?" Charlie continued. "Well, they finally got their hands on it, and it was a threat from Lord Tenebris. I actually have the book here." And with that, Charlie pulled a book out of his inventory and tossed it over to Stan. The leather cover was charred, but Stan could still read the title and author: *The Demands of Lord Tenebris* by Caesar894. With trembling hands, Stan opened the book and flipped through it. It was entirely blank, except for the first page. Stan read it.

This is a message for the Council of Eight and the president of Element City.

If you are reading this, then it means the bomb we have planted in your recreational machine has gone off. The resulting explosion has more than likely killed at least one, possibly more, of your citizens. However, it has caused nothing compared to the destruction and suffering that will occur should you fail to comply with the demands of the Noctem Alliance.

The demands are as follows: you shall not stage the World Finals of the Spleef Tournament in the Element City Spleef Arena. You shall not stage any sort of replacement event in any other venue. Furthermore, you will ban the practice of Spleef in your country for as long as Elementia shall stand. Failure to comply with any of these demands will result in terror beyond comprehension.

I sign this message in the name of the glorious Lord Tenebris, founder and Supreme Commander of the Noctem Alliance.

Cordially signed,

Chancellor Caesar894

As Stan finished reading, he put the book down and looked up at his friends.

"Why would the Noctem Alliance care about us playing Spleef?" he asked, flabbergasted.

"I'll tell you why," replied the Mechanist gravely. "Because this Lord Tenebris, whoever he is, is far more brilliant than we thought. He knows our current situation just as well, if not better, than we ourselves do. He knows that we are going to have to use excessive amounts of players and resources to fight this war, which will make our citizens angrier at us than they already are. And now he's put us in an even more difficult position.

"If we ban Spleef, then the citizens will despise us for taking it away from them, and they will have nothing to distract them from the atrocities of the war. If we ignore the demands, then the citizens will be outraged that we put them at risk just for the sake of a sports tournament. We could ignore the demands and not tell the citizens, but if we do that, then the plan will get leaked to the public, and they will loathe us for withholding more information from them. No matter what we do next, we lose."

Stan was stunned. He couldn't think for a moment, but then the truth of what the Mechanist had said soaked into him like a sponge. He was right. The Noctem Alliance had put them into a checkmate. There was no way out. No way that they could win. Except . . .

"Well, some of our military is still going to be patrolling the city for our security," said Stan. "Why don't we just use some of those guys to defend the Spleef arena during the event?"

There was quiet for a moment as everybody pondered the idea. Finally the Mechanist said, "You know, Stan, I supposed that could work. We will have a few extra forces in the city now that the Double Draft has been instated, I supposed we could use some of them to defend the Spleef arena."

"Okay then," said DZ. "Here's the plan: we announce to everybody that we're doing the Double Draft so that we can go to war with the Noctem Alliance. Then we tell them that they've threatened the Spleef arena, but we're not afraid of them, so the finals will go on, just under military supervision."

"Okay," replied Charlie. "All in favor of the plan?"

And, for the first time in as long as Stan could remember, all nine hands on the council raised up into the air.

CHAPTER 19
THE SPLEEF WORLD FINALS

The two weeks between the bombing of the Tennis Machine and the Spleef World Finals were two of the most stressful weeks in Stan's life, rivaling all that had happened since Elementia Day.

As soon as the council meeting had officially concluded, Stan had ordered a Proclamation Day and made DZ's announcement to the people of Elementia. He told everybody about the declaration of war on the NNA, the Double Draft, the Noctem threat against the Spleef arena, and that the match would go on anyway. However, long gone were the days when any announcement that Stan made was greeted with thunderous applause. The crowd was loud, but now it was a mixture of shouts of admiration, screams of outrage, and everything in between. Not one person was silent. Each person had their own opinion, and the need to express it loudly.

Multiple protests against the Double Draft, as well as the war altogether, erupted throughout Element City over the two weeks after the bombing. One of these protests turned violent, and the new troops were given their first foray into action as they shut the protest down. The violent protesters who were arrested had to go into jails throughout Element City, because Bill had yet to take back Brimstone Prison from the Wither Skeletons.

Bill and Bob had used their new troops from the draft to launch massive offensives on both of the Noctem Alliance's footholds. Bill was the leader of the Hot Front, which was the code name for the invasion of the Nether. Bob was in charge of the Cold Front, or the attack on Nocturia. The Cold Front wasn't entirely in the cold of the tundra, since the Noctem Alliance had managed to force Bob's troops back as they approached Nocturia. Some of the Elementia soldiers had been forced all the way into the Ender Desert. The Cold Front now consisted of various strong posts surrounding Nocturia in the tundra and the desert, with both sides fighting sporadically and not gaining any distance.

While his brothers were out fighting on the fronts, Ben, as the last remaining chief of police, oversaw all the operations that needed to be done away from the war zone, including in Element City itself. It made Stan's heart heavy to see troops patrolling the streets of his city, launching interrogations off tips, and putting fear on the faces of his people.

By far, the most stressed-out department of the military were the detectives, who were in over their heads with major investigations. The most important of these was identifying the spy within Element City. All the employees of the castle, as well as visitors and even the council members were subject to interrogation. Stan was surprised one day when a detective told him that it was his turn for interrogation. Needless to say, Stan complied and answered all the cop's questions truthfully, and it was determined that Stan was innocent of the crime. Unfortunately, so were all the other questioned players, and so the investigation went on.

A lot of time also went into investigating the cause of the leaks, which were still to be resolved, as well as trying to figure out how the bombing of the Tennis Machine had happened. It was quickly determined that they were both likely linked to the spy, but the detectives weren't about to assume anything.

Ben was also in charge of sending scouts out into the server, trying to locate the Specialty Base. These scouts swept over huge areas of land, trying to locate any clues as to where the Specialty Base might be. Over the two weeks, no news surfaced. Ben reported this to Stan, who insisted that the search continue.

All the council members were kept busy, all day every day, for the whole two weeks. Most of them spent their time volunteering with the military and doing whatever they could using their talents. The Mechanist told Stan how he had set up and activated a complex wiring trap to blow up a desert temple that had been turned into a base by the Noctem Alliance. Jayden told Stan about his visit to fight on the Hot Front, and showed Stan the burn wound on his arm from where an invisible Noctem soldier had hit him with a splash of Potion of Harming.

Kat spent most of her time down at the headquarters of the police, constantly training new troops. For the first time since Elementia Day, Kat brought Rex with her everywhere she went. She had loaned him to the police department while she had been sitting on council meetings and making voyages into the Nether. During that time, he had met another wolf named Diamond, and the two of them had become very close. This had given Kat an idea. Using the police department's store of rotten flesh, she had coaxed Rex and Diamond into having a litter of puppies. After being fed some rotten flesh, the puppies grew up into fully fledged wolves. The new recruits were able to use the store of bones to tame the adult wolves, thus gaining a companion to accompany them into battle and beyond. When she wasn't helping with the wolves, Kat spent every spare second she had training with DZ and Ben for the Spleef World Finals.

Charlie did his volunteer work around the city, preparing people for the finals. As he did so, he was surprised to find that many players were almost more angry with the finals going on than they would have been had they been cancelled. It didn't even have anything to do with the looming threat of the Noctem Alliance. Rather, many citizens were under the belief that the Skeletons should be declared the champions automatically, since the Zombies had already lost once and were only reentered into the tournament on a technicality.

Determined to keep the spirits in the city high, Charlie took advantage of this discontent and formed two clubs, one of which supported the Zombies and the other the Skeletons. Both clubs had nightly meetings. Charlie used the rivalry between the supporters to rally the city into high spirits all the way up until the match.

Stan spent his time doing a variety of things. Whenever he received word from Kat that a new shipment of drafted recruits had come in, he would personally go over to the police station and thank them for their service to their country before they went off to war. Stan was surprised to see that it really did boost their morale to have their president personally address them.

He also spent a good portion of his time trying to contact Sally, but this proved to be in vain. Somebody in the Noctem Alliance clearly knew their way around a computer, because although Stan managed to hear his name erupt through the static of space a few times, he wasn't able to have a full conversation with her.

Most of Stan's free time, however, was spent with Oob. After Stan had announced to the public that Elementia had declared war on Nocturia, Oob was terrified and told Stan that he wanted to go home. Oob's village was all the way across the Ender Desert, which had become a war zone on the Cold Front. Stan knew it would be far too dangerous to bring Oob through the desert now. The trains that passed through the desert were for the transport of military personnel and materials only, and even they had to travel in convoys with armed soldiers. Stan still had his three men positioned in the village to defend it from the hostile mobs, but it seemed extremely unlikely that the Noctems would attack it. Stan had made sure to tell the rest of his men to stay away from NPC villages at all costs, to keep them from becoming targets.

Because he couldn't go home, Oob tagged along with Stan most of the time, occasionally visiting with Kat, Charlie, and DZ. When he was with Stan, the question that wouldn't stop bursting from his mouth was "How long must I wait until the Spleef World Finals?" Stan became so fed up with this that as payback, when the day finally arrived, he didn't tell Oob until they were on their way to the stadium to watch the match.

After two of the hardest weeks in the history of Element City, the day of the Spleef World Finals finally arrived.

Since he was a member of the team, Ben had put a member of his police force in charge of the defense of the Spleef arena. Before the match, the entire building had been searched, with every last possible hiding place for explosives or Noctem agents checked. Though they found nothing, the police continued to prowl about the arena, on the lookout for anything suspicious. The match was at night, but fans began to flood the Spleef arena at midday, and every single player who entered the arena was frisked by a police officer, looking for explosives or weapons.

Kat was on her way to the arena. Her time helping out with the wolves at the police station had run a bit late, and so Kat slipped into the side door of the Spleef arena hastily. She sprinted up a plain corridor made of cobblestone that led up to where DZ and Ben were waiting for her. She took the second left turn toward the stairs, and as she rounded the corner she saw a figure leaning against the wall next to the door to her room. The full white leather armor and red lips that took up half the player's pale face filled Kat's stomach with acid.

"Well, hello there, Kat, darling," simpered Cassandrix, a smug grin on her face.

"Shouldn't you be over in your room on the other side?" Kat grunted.

"Oh, don't worry, my darling." The words slid out of Cassandrix's mouth. Her upper-class accent was particularly irritating tonight, Kat noticed bitterly. "They won't start the match without me, I'm rather important, you know. Unlike some people, I actually earned my spot in this match, it wasn't handed to me by default."

"Well, seeing as you were the one who handed it to me," seethed Kat, infuriated that she couldn't say that Cassandrix was wrong, "I would shut up about it if you know what's good for you."

"Well, dear, I'm sorry that you lost the semifinals, but really, are you surprised? Correct me if I'm wrong, but you only practiced three times between the quarterfinals and semifinals, yes? Well, if you really think that's putting your best foot forward . . ."

"Okay, you obnoxious little snob, listen up," snarled Kat, stepping right up and pushing her face into Cassandrix, who was still grinning widely. "First of all, we've been practicing all day every day for the past two weeks, so let's see how smart that mouth of yours is after you've fought us in top form. And second of all, the only reason that we could only practice three times between the last two matches is because we were all busy defending your sorry butt from the Noctem Alliance!"

"Oh, yes, and you've done swimmingly in that department," Cassandrix said, chuckling. "Yes, fighting a war on two fronts and taking people against their will to do it . . . very noble, Kat, that's defending the cause of justice."

Kat couldn't control herself. Her rage had broken the

limit. She pulled her fist back and was preparing herself to sink it as hard as she could into Cassandrix's face when an unseen force pulled her back from behind. Kat struggled to get free, but before she knew it, she had been dragged into the preparation room. The iron door had shut behind her, closing out Cassandrix's manic laughter. She seethed at Ben, who had pulled her back, preventing her from throwing what would have been an extremely satisfying punch.

"I am going to *kill her*!" snarled Kat.

"Calm down, Kat," said Ben steadily. "She's just trying to get under your skin and unhinge your focus. The best way to get back at her is to show her up in the Spleef arena."

Kat took deep breaths, trying to tell herself that Ben was right, but all she could think of was Cassandrix's face and how she wanted to cause her as much pain as possible. She hardly noticed when DZ gave her a cheerful hello, only returning it with a solemn grunt. She threw her armor on haphazardly, not realizing that her helmet was on backward until DZ pointed it out.

When the iron doors finally swung open, indicating that the match had begun, Kat snatched up her diamond shovel and burst out onto the snow. She drew in strength from the roar of the crowd, and then shut everything out of her mind except for her teammates, the flat arena of snow blocks, and the white-clad figures standing across the expanse.

"Okay, guys, this is it," said DZ, no hint of cheeriness in his voice now. It was game time. "Engage Operation Hero's Flank K."

Kat and Ben nodded and took off alongside DZ. Ben cut softly to the left, while DZ did the same to the right and Kat charged down the middle. The K in the name indicated that Kat was to be the center of the Hero's Flank Operation. Kat smirked. DZ must have been aware of her animosity toward the other team, and decided to let her tackle them head-on. Well, she wasn't going to disappoint him.

The Skeletons were sticking together in a group as they sprinted forward. Kat knew that they were going to adopt their signature strategy: stay back to back and lash out as a team toward anybody who comes close to them. Kat smiled even larger. They had been planning for this, and had adopted the Hero's Flank strategy specifically to counter them.

Just as Kat was about to reach the Skeletons, she hopped back and swung her shovel down, cutting a wide ditch in the snow. The Skeletons cut their sprint short to avoid tumbling into the ditch, having no space available to jump it. This allowed Kat, through a series of fancy footwork and quick shovel swings, to arc two smaller ditches into the snow, creating a curve that connected to the two other ditches created by DZ and Ben, who had been circling around. The Skeletons spun around in shock as Ben's and DZ's shovels connected, completing the ring of nothingness around the Skeletons. The three Spleef players were now standing in the middle of a snow block island, surrounded by a ring that led to a fall into the watery pit below.

Okay, thought Kat, picking up a snowball from the ground as the Skeletons urgently whispered in one anothers' ears. *Let's get this party started!* And with that, she pitched a snowball right at Cassandrix.

The unidentifiable power that the snowballs of Minecraft hold took effect, and Cassandrix was knocked backward off her feet, flying through the air and right into a shovel swung by Ben. The blow connected with her chest, and she tumbled backward into the hole. She would have fallen into the pit, too, had her teammate not sprawled to the ground and grabbed her hand. Ben lunged forward to knock them both into the pit, but Cassandrix swung herself up onto the outside ledge, kicking Ben in the stomach as she did so.

Ben tumbled backward onto the ground, and Cassandrix pursued him, shovel raised. One of her goons jumped over the ledge to assist her, but he was caught across the stomach by a shovel blow from Kat. Kat was astonished when he didn't fall backward into the pit. Rather, he caught onto the edge with his hand and propelled himself into the air, his foot hitting Kat's hand and knocking her shovel far into the distance.

Man! thought Kat. *These guys are good!* Kat sprinted over to pick up her shovel, her opponent choosing to double team DZ with his teammate rather than pursue her. Desperate to assist him, Kat was about to sprint over to DZ when she saw it.

A figure, clad entirely in black, standing on the uppermost bleacher of the Spleef arena . . . a bow raised in his hand, an arrow, flying through the sky, toward the two players closest to her.

"Look out!" screamed Kat as she launched herself toward Ben and Cassandrix, engaged in shovel combat. They barely had time to look before Kat slammed into them, knocking the three of them to the ground, the arrow grazing Kat's shoulder and sticking point-first into the snowy ground.

Kat twisted her neck around, becoming aware of the screams ringing out around the arena as she looked over at the others. One of Cassandrix's goons fell face-first to the ground, an arrow sticking through the back of his leather helmet. An instant later, two more arrows sunk into the ground next to Kat's head, and immediately afterward two more found the heart of the other Skeleton, sending him to the ground. An arrow sunk into DZ's arm, and the force of the attack sent him backward and through a hole in the ground.

"Get off me!" growled Cassandrix, pushing Kat to the ground. "What are you playing at?"

Kat regained her footing. She sensed an incoming danger, and ducked just as something whizzed over her head. She heard a screech of pain as the arrow pierced Cassandrix's leg. The white-clad player flew backward and into a hole in the ground.

Kat was unable to help Cassandrix, or even think about her. She was only able to think about the black figure who had appeared in the middle of the Spleef arena in a burst of purple smoke. The Noctem agent pitched fire charges to the ground, using them to burn a circle in the snow blocks around himself until he was suspended on a single snow block in midair. Down below, DZ and Cassandrix could be seen struggling, trying to cure their wounds and stay afloat at the same time. The figure was far from the edges of the snowfield. There was no way to get to him.

As the black-clad figure pulled off his helmet, Kat noticed a black shawl draped over his shoulders, and when his face came into view, Kat saw, with a twinge of fear, that it was Count Drake standing in the midst of the arena. As he spoke, his voice, oily and snakelike, seemed magnified. "You had your chance to listen, people of Elementia," the voice boomed through the air. "We warned you not to toy with the Noctem Alliance, and now it is time for you to pay for your impudence. I call upon the great power of the Noctem Alliance now, to summon the punishment of the people of Element

City! VIVA LA NOCTEM! Bring on the fire!"

And with that, Count Drake pulled a blue-green orb and pitched it far into the distance. All Kat could do was watch in helpless horror as Count Drake turned around, caught her eye, grinned an evil smile, and disappeared in a puff of violet smoke.

Then, all at once, the Spleef arena erupted into a radiant light, immediately followed by screams of terror. From the tops of the bleachers of the arena, molten lava was pouring from some unseen source. As Kat stared at the liquid fire in shock, she realized it was pouring out of the dispensers that usually shot off fireworks during a victory.

Standing in the middle of the arena, so far away from everybody else and armed with nothing but a shovel, there was nothing Ben or Kat could do but stare as the massive wall of molten fire rolled down the stands and toward the center of the arena. The wave of lava was preceded by a wave of players, sprinting down the stands, over the bleachers, and over one another, trying to escape the fiery death that chased them. They saw some players trip and immediately be trampled under the wild herd of players. Others fell behind, and the lava caught them, drowning them in magma.

As the last of the players drained out the doors of the arena, Kat and Ben were speechless. They thought they had been prepared, maybe not to foresee everything the Noctem

Alliance would do to them, but certainly to handle it. But this . . . nothing in the world could have prepared them for this.

The lava was flowing from source blocks, and the once-proud bleachers of the Spleef arena had turned into a never-ending lava flow, which had started to pour over the railings and into the pit below. The snow blocks at the edge of the arena had started to melt, but Kat, shell-shocked as she was, knew that they were in no danger. They were standing at the center of the arena now, their snow blocks would be too far from the lava to melt. The only players who would need to worry now would be any players who were somehow still . . .

The realization slammed into Kat like a train, and she grabbed Ben by the shoulders and shook him. "Ben!" she bellowed. "We've got to help DZ and Cassandrix, they're still down there!"

Comprehension rushed into Ben's face, and the two of them raced to the edge of the hole to look down into it. Sure enough, the lava had poured down the arena walls and was now beginning to intrude on the edges of the water lake. The water turned to stone on contact with the lava, but immediately afterward, new lava rolled over it, creating more stone. And right at the center of the shrinking square of water swam DZ and Cassandrix, the latter of whom was freaking out and being calmed by DZ.

Ben and Kat had the same idea simultaneously. Using their diamond shovels, they struck two blocks of snow and compressed the four resulting snowballs back together into a block. With the blocks in hand, they sprinted to the edge of the remaining snow blocks.

"Up here!" Kat screamed, and tossed the snow block down as Ben did the same. The two players looked up. Realizing what was happening, they caught the blocks and placed them on the ground, hopping on top of them.

It was a mad race. The lava was closing in on the two players in the hole, and Kat and Ben sprinted as fast as they could to get the snow blocks down to the two players. Ben tossed his blocks down to Cassandrix, while Kat tossed hers to DZ. By the time the towers of snow blocks were three blocks high, the lava had completely surrounded the base of the towers. By the time the fourth block of the tower had been placed, the bottommost one had melted into nothing.

Upon seeing this, Kat and Ben became even more frantic, throwing blocks of snow down as fast as humanly possible. It wasn't looking good. For every two blocks the two players placed on their stacks, the bottom three blocks would melt from the intense heat. By the time DZ and Cassandrix were just five blocks below Ben and Kat, their towers were just two blocks high and still melting.

"Forget the blocks, there's no time!" yelled Ben. "Just help me pull them up!"

Kat and Ben sprawled out on the ground and reached down to the nearest player, who happened to be Cassandrix. She bent her knees and propelled herself upward, latching on to Kat's hand. The two top players gave an almighty pull, and Cassandrix came flying out of the hole, landing in a pile on the surface of the arena.

Wasting no time, they sprawled down again, seeing in horror that DZ's tower was down to its last block. DZ jumped just as the block melted from beneath his foot. His outstretched hand came up and just missed Kat's fingertips before he fell downward to the lava pit below.

A cry of "NO!!!" left Kat's mouth before, without thinking, she dived down into the hole, latching on to DZ's arm. She felt his hand gripping her arm back, just as she realized what she had done. She felt herself falling down the hole, the heat from the lava becoming more pronounced by the second. Then, all of a sudden, the falling stopped. Kat twisted her head backward to see Ben clutching her leg as if his life depended on it. Slowly, though, he too was being dragged into the pit by the combined weight of DZ and Kat. Just as the three Zombies were about to be pulled down into the pit together, Kat, in the midst of squinting her eyes shut in preparation, saw a pair of white hands that undeniably belonged to

Cassandrix latch around Ben's torso.

Kat didn't open her eyes again for half a minute. She was vaguely aware that the heat of the lava was growing fainter and fainter. She released DZ's hand once she had pulled him up to safety, though she hardly remembered doing so. Kat finally opened her eyes when she felt the soft coolness of the snow block on her face, and when she did, she saw DZ, Ben, and Cassandrix all lying on top of one another in a pile, exhausted.

Kat pulled herself to a sitting position and looked around. The announcer's box, the president's box, and all the other protrusions from the stadium bleachers had gone up in flames. As Kat rotated around, seeing the cascade of fire and death that was her beloved Spleef arena, a single tear rolled down her cheek, hitting the snow below her silently. The gravity and terror of the situation finally registered, and Kat's mind refused to take in any more—she passed out on the ground beside her three fellow Spleef players.

NIGHTFALL

CHAPTER 20
AN EMERGENCY MEETING

There was a knock on the wooden door. Leonidas glanced up at it, his train of thought broken.

"Enter," he said.

The door swung open, spraying Leonidas's face with an icy blast of wind. Through his squinted eyes, Leonidas saw Private Spyro struggling to get the door shut against the howling winds of the snowstorm. When it finally shut, Spyro, wasting no time, jumped to full salute.

"I have your dinner, General," he announced respectfully.

Leonidas gave a faint chuckle. "Private, how many times do I have to tell ya? I'm perfectly capable of gettin' my own dinner on my own time." Nonetheless, Leonidas did realize just how hungry he was, and graciously accepted two cooked chickens from Spyro's inventory.

"I'm aware, sir," replied Spyro. "I just thought I'd bring it out to you, seeing as I was coming out here anyway. Corporal Tess sent me to deliver a message to you."

"And what is it?" asked Leonidas, bracing himself. Leonidas, as well as the other troops, had retired from the battlefields surrounding Nocturia for the night, and so Leonidas knew this was not a message related to fighting. There was only one other message that this could be and, truth be told, Leonidas didn't really want to hear it.

"Lieutenant Drake has just returned from Element City. He announced to us that the attack on the Spleef Arena has gone off without a hitch. Everything went exactly according to plan."

Great, thought Leonidas bitterly. He figured he might as well ask about it now, and hear it in Spyro's official, military voice rather than hearing Drake brag about it. "And what were the casualties?" he asked tiredly, not really wanting to know.

"The lieutenant said he sent a scout into the city, and he overheard the high-ranking council members discussing it. None of the high-ranking officials of Elementia were killed. Two of the Spleef players were killed by our snipers, and the lava trap managed to kill fifty-nine civilians."

Leonidas shuddered at the last word. It was incomprehensible to him how Caesar could think that organizing an attack like that on players who weren't harming anybody was honorable, just, or anything besides malevolent. Nonetheless, Leonidas knew what he had to do, and he knew what the consequences would be if he failed to do it.

"Tell Lieutenant Drake," responded Leonidas slowly, "to assemble our troops in front of the headquarters, so that I can give him an official congratulation and promote him to the rank of captain."

"Yes, sir," responded Spyro. He turned on his heel and marched out the door, once again struggling to close it against the frigid gusts. Leonidas spat in disgust as the cold caused him to break out in chills and huddle closer to the fire. Even now, when he was the interim commander of the Noctem Army, he was forced to stay in a tiny stone hut alongside all the other enclosures belonging to the soldiers.

Leonidas was very close to his breaking point with Caesar. The player had, after all, basically stated that he saw Leonidas as his inferior by a vast degree. What other reason could there be for Caesar ordering Leonidas to stay out in the war zone while Caesar himself went safely to the Specialty Base with Lord Tenebris? Leonidas knew Caesar didn't want him in Nocturia for the sake of leadership. Caesar had had nothing but glowing praise for Count Drake, stating that he was capable of commanding the army by himself, promoting him to lieutenant, and ordering Leonidas to promote him again if he pulled off the attack on the Spleef arena. With that in mind, Leonidas could think of no reason why he should not be at the Specialty Base with the others.

However, Leonidas's anger with Caesar cut even deeper than that, because not only had he commanded Leonidas to stay and fight, but Caesar had brought Minotaurus with him. The claim had been that it was for defense, so that two of the Noctem Alliance's strongest fighters were there to protect Lord Tenebris should Stan's forces discover the base. However, Leonidas knew that Caesar was well aware that Leonidas was the more powerful fighter of the two. After all, Leonidas had managed to escape from Stan, Kat, and eight of their soldiers at the Jungle Base, while Minotaurus had lost what was essentially a two-on-one fight in Nocturia, only surviving because of Stan's mercy. Even comparing their fighting styles, it made no sense; Minotaurus's giant battle-axe and manic fighting style were the perfect fit for a large-scale war, while Leonidas's precise and deadly arrows were ideal for a bodyguard.

Clearly, there were other forces at play here. The choices Caesar had made, beyond enraging Leonidas with their unfairness, made no sense in the long run. There must have been some other reason that Caesar had commanded Leonidas to stay in Nocturia. And as Leonidas pulled on his ceremonial armor for the rank advancement ceremony of Count Drake, he was sure that the reason, whatever it was, was nothing good.

"The role call has been completed, and I hereby call this Council Meeting of the Grand Republic of Elementia to order," said Stan, ending the ceremonial introduction to the meeting, which he was only doing for the sake of Jayden, G, and Blackraven. As he finished, though, Stan realized there would be very little arguing during this meeting. The table was charged with silence, and it was clear that they were all in a very similar mind-set. DZ seemed especially electric. His arm still bore the wound of the attack on the Spleef arena.

"My friends," said Stan, the power of his voice filling the entire room. "The day that we have feared for so long is upon us. The Noctem Alliance has launched a large-scale terrorist attack on our city. They destroyed one of our proudest buildings and killed fifty-nine of our citizens. This is a crime we cannot forgive. Atrocities committed on the battlefield are one thing. Atrocities committed toward civilians are a different story altogether. Clearly, we have to do something."

"I agree with you, Stan," said Jayden. "I think a few members of the council can agree with me when I say I've had my disagreements with you and some of your closer friends in the past. But after this, I think we're all on the same page now."

"Let's not classify ourselves into friends and closer friends," the Mechanist's old voice came, tired and weary. "If we are to stand any chance of taking down the machine of evil that is the Noctem Alliance, we must all stand united, no barriers between us of any kind."

There were murmurs of assent around the table.

"I think it is clear this action can't go unpunished," continued Stan, grateful for the input of the players, but determined to swiftly agree on a course of action. "Does anybody have any ideas of what we can do?"

"Well, I don't have an idea," said Kat, "but I do have some information that I feel I should share."

"Go ahead," replied Stan.

"As I was on my way up here for the meeting, I ran into a messenger from Ben," Kat announced. "He said that their spies have determined a possible lead to the location of the Specialty Base."

"Really?" cried DZ. "That's fantastic!" He pumped his fist up and down in triumph, only to cringe and wince in pain as he did so. He had clearly forgotten the arrow wound in his arm.

"Yeah, it is," continued Kat, her face still serious. "He said the police just got word back from a scout who was sweeping over the Far Western Desert. Apparently, he was trekking along the border to the ocean, when he saw a boat being driven by a player in full black. He watched the player travel northeast until he couldn't see him anymore."

"That means the Specialty Base is probably located on an island in the Northwestern Ocean!" exclaimed Jayden.

"How many islands are there in that ocean?" asked Stan, being unfamiliar with the region.

"Tons of them," said G. "Back when Jay and I worked for Adoria, she would send us out there to map the islands and occasionally to go on missions. It's not a very well-known area. I don't think players had ever mapped them before we did, and nobody ever goes out there except to visit the resorts on the Lesser Mushroom Island."

"In other words," cut in DZ, "it's the perfect hiding place for the Noctem Alliance."

"Okay then," replied Stan. "That's where we should concentrate our searches. Blackraven, you go down to the police headquarters and talk tactics with Ben. Have him recall his scouts and send them out into the ocean to scout out the islands."

Blackraven gave a grunt and a nod before getting up and leaving the room.

"If that's all there is to say, then I hereby adjourn this meeting. Any final words?" Nobody had any, and the eight remaining players, one by one, got up and exited the room.

Stan walked down the hallway, not particularly aiming for anywhere, and ended up in the common room. The Netherrack fire blazed as brightly as ever, and Stan sat down in front of it, lost in deep thought. One by one, he felt others join him. After the third, Stan looked up to see Charlie, DZ, and Kat all sitting in chairs beside him. Rex was curled up sleeping next to the fire.

"It's infuriating, isn't it?"

Stan looked over and saw Kat looking at him. DZ and

Charlie looked up too.

"You talkin' about anything specific, Kat? 'Cause frankly, I'm infuriated at a lot of stuff right now," grumbled DZ, massaging his arrow wound.

"It's just . . . I don't know . . . the Noctem Alliance just stepped so far over the line by attacking the arena. And what have we done in response?"

"You know what we're doing, Kat!" exclaimed Charlie in surprise. "We're focusing our search for them in the islands region, and Ben has promised me that the military is going to double its numbers of raids and searches."

Kat sighed. "I know that, but that's playing by the rules! When the Noctem Alliance attacked our Spleef arena, they took a sledgehammer to the rules of war! Isn't one of those rules that you're not supposed to directly attack civilians?"

Now it was Charlie's turn to sigh. "That is true, Kat, but the fact that we're willing to play by the rules is what makes us different from the Noctem Alliance. We're fighting an honest fight against them, and you know that justice will always prevail in the end."

"That's just it, though!" yelled Kat. She was irritated now. "I know we're doing the right thing by fighting an honest fight, but here's the thing . . . the honest fight isn't working! Where have we gotten since the beginning of this war? Absolutely nowhere! And where has the Noctem Alliance gotten? They've killed dozens of our innocent people in their attacks!"

"Kat," said DZ reasonably, "I want you to ask yourself this: When we win this war, do you want to have won it honestly and with integrity, or do you want to have won it by committing atrocities like they have?"

Kat turned around and looked DZ squarely in the eye. "You said when we win the war, DZ. And to be honest, I don't think we're going to win if we keep fighting the way we are."

Stan almost fell forward out of his chair in shock. "How could you even . . ."

"Stan, answer this question for me," said Kat firmly, turning to look him in the face now. "What's better: winning a war fought unfairly or losing a war fought honestly?"

Stan found himself unable to speak, and when he glanced at Charlie and DZ he saw that they, too, were lost for words. They were spared the need to respond, however, when the door flew open. Into the room marched a soldier, who stood at attention upon seeing Stan, and was followed, to Stan's surprise, by Oob, who looked bewildered.

"I've come with a message for President Stan," the soldier said officially.

"The mean man in the uniform ran into me while I was on the stair, and now he will not tell me what the message is!" wailed Oob.

"Mister . . . um . . . Oob," said the soldier in discomfort, "please wait outside while I deliver the message to the president and his council members."

"Oob, buddy, wait outside, okay?" said DZ.

"No!" cried Oob, stamping his foot on the ground. "I want to hear the message too!"

"Come on, Oob," said Charlie grimly. "Go outside. These messages are usually about pretty ugly stuff going on during the war, you don't want to hear about it."

"But I would like to help!" said Oob in exasperation. "I can fight just like you can! Do you not remember that I defeated the Griefer Mr. A over the lava pit?!"

Stan sighed. "Oob, it's the messenger's job to deliver the message to the people it was meant for, and nobody else. If you just go out the door and wait there, then I might tell you the message after we hear it."

Oob opened his mouth to protest, but then closed it again. He scrunched his eyebrows together tightly, as if he were thinking very hard, and then his face relaxed. "Okay, Stan," he finally said. "I will wait outside." And with that, Oob turned around and walked out the wooden door, closing it behind him.

DZ spun around to face Stan. "Why'd you lie to him!?" he shouted accusatorily.

"I wasn't lying," responded Stan with a sigh. "Whatever

the message is, I'm sure we can tell him . . . you know, if we tone it down to a G rating for him."

The messenger looked extremely uncomfortable now, and said, "Uh, Mr. President . . . I don't think you're going to be able to tone this message down for him."

Stan's chest flooded with dread. Clearly, something exceptionally terrible had happened.

"The Noctem Alliance launched an attack on a target in the Ender Desert," the messenger said.

Stan waited expectantly for more. This wasn't breaking news, it happened quite often. "And . . . ," he finally said.

The messenger took a deep breath, and then continued. "The attack wasn't on a military target, Mr. President. It was on the NPC village."

Stan's throat dropped into his stomach, and he was unable to think. He was vaguely aware that his three fellows shared equal expressions of horrified, all-encompassing shock. Then, without warning, the wooden door flew open, and in stepped Oob. The villager had clearly been listening at the door. Oob's mouth hung open, his eyebrows raised, his hands limp, and his eyes terrified with dismay.

CHAPTER 21 RETURN TO THE VILLAGE

The sun was high in the sky as Captain Drake scanned the horizon. He knew that she would be returning soon. Her target was not far off from the Noctem outpost where Drake was. It wouldn't be a long walk for her. A makeshift wall of sandstone ringed the dirt shacks hastily built on top of the sand hill, and it was on top of this wall that Drake was now perched.

As Drake waited for his compatriot to return, he smiled as he thought about his new title. Captain Drake. It felt good just to hear it in his mind. *Captain Drake*. Perhaps he would drop the Count title altogether and just go by the name of Captain.

As Drake looked out into the desert plains, he could see the Elementia camp in the distance, with little dots scurrying around it. He supposed they must be doing some sort of training drill or something. Well, Drake was sure that, whatever they were doing, it was of no concern to him. His job was simply to counterattack anything the Elementia army threw at him, and occasionally to pick a fight if things got too quiet here on the Cold Front, as Element City liked to call it.

Finally, on the horizon, he saw a black dot approaching the hill. As it got closer and closer, Drake made out the pink face of Corporal Tess approaching the gates.

Excited to hear how the operation had gone, Drake climbed down off the wall and walked through the rows of makeshift huts to meet her at the gate.

"Well, if it isn't the big bad Captain Drake," she said with a smirk as she walked in the door.

"Doesn't it sound good?" he said. "That's the kind of name people remember . . . Captain Drake, hero of the Noctem Alliance . . ."

"Oh, for sure." Tess laughed, punching Drake in the shoulder to snap him out of his daydream. "You realize we have to win the war before the whole world starts praising you, right, Captain Bonehead?"

"True, true," said Drake.

"Anyway," continued Tess, "I suppose you want to hear about the attack on the village now, right?"

"Of course," replied Drake with a smile.

"Well, you'll be surprised to hear that there actually weren't any soldiers in the village. There wasn't an Iron Golem either."

"Huh?" asked Drake, caught off guard. "But I thought President Stan sent . . ."

"Yeah, me too." Tess shrugged. "I didn't even need the Invisibility Potion to finish the job. I just blew up the fronts of their houses, climbed onto one of their roofs, and let the full moon do the rest."

"Excellent," replied Drake with a grin. "And did any of the villagers . . . well, you know . . ."

"I don't know yet," replied Tess. "I've got Private Spyro stationed out there in case any of them turn, and if none of them do, well, I guess we could always find another village."

"True," said Drake, nodding his head. "Okay then, the village has been attacked. . . . do me a favor, Tess, and send out a messenger to General Leonidas back in Nocturia. Let him know what a success the attack was."

As Tess nodded and ran to send off the message, Drake smiled a huge smile to himself. *Fantastic! Chancellor Caesar's plan has worked perfectly! I can't wait until General Leonidas finds out about how well the attack on the NPC village went . . . he'll be so proud. . . .*

Stan had been conflicted about letting Oob come with him, Kat, Charlie, and DZ on the train ride out to the NPC village. On one hand, it was his village, and Stan knew that Oob would have hated all of them if they had kept him from going there in its hour of need. On the other hand, Stan knew full well what they were going to see when they arrived at the village. He himself was taking deep breaths, preparing himself to keep from completely breaking down. The thought of Oob's reaction to what they were about to see was unimaginable.

Whatever aversions he had had, the four players now sat alongside Oob, as an engineer shuttled the five of them down the railroad tracks, across the Ender Desert. The setting sun cast brilliant pastel colors into the sky. It was a shame that none of the passengers on the train could appreciate it. They were too occupied with what they were about to see.

After far too short a time, the silhouettes of the houses of the NPC village became apparent against the gorgeous sunset. The convoy of minecarts slowed down before finally screeching to a halt. Rex appeared out of nowhere next to Kat's car. As Stan and his friends climbed out of the carts, it occurred to Stan that the village looked largely unchanged from a distance. However, Stan's stomach sank lower and lower as he walked toward the village and more and more details came into view.

The once-smooth gravel street was pockmarked with craters, arrows stuck out from everywhere, and, most horrifying of all, the fronts of each and every house had been blown out by some massive explosion. There was not a villager to be seen anywhere.

Desperate, frenzied footprints were scattered all over the gravel and sand, and they all seemed to lead straight toward the church. And yet, despite all the evidence of carnage that surrounded them on all sides, only deafening silence rang out as the players walked slowly toward the church. Rex sniffed around the footprints, and he whimpered, his ears and tail drooping in despair.

"Where are all the bodies?" whispered Kat in a shaky voice.

"They must've despawned already . . . or else they escaped," came DZ's reply, a catch in his throat.

"No," came Charlie's hollow reply. "Villagers aren't like players and mobs anymore. I read that their bodies don't despawn nearly as fast for some reason since the last update."

Oob stepped forward. Since he had entered the village, tears had silently streamed down his face. His mouth hung open as he tried to take in the travesty that was the destruction of his home. Now, though, Oob walked up to the door of the church.

"Oob," said Stan, his voice incredibly warbly as tears streamed down his face, and he struggled to keep composure. He took a step forward and put his hand on the villager's shoulder. "I wouldn't open that door, Oob. You don't want to see what's inside."

There was a moment of nothing but the sound of Charlie and DZ choking back sobs as Kat and Stan stood white with consternation, looking at Oob. Then, Oob turned to face the players. His face was streaked with tears, but there was no catch in his voice now.

"No," he whispered. "I must know."

And with that, Oob turned around and opened the door to the church.

"AURAUUURRGH!!!"

Oob screamed in terror as the Zombie lurched out of the door, arms outstretched and flailing through the air. In his alarm, Oob tumbled backward onto the ground, and the Zombie knelt down to prey on its target. It never got a chance, though. DZ's sword stuck through the back of the Zombie, pinning it to the ground and killing it with one final choking noise. Rex began barking frantically. As DZ resheathed his sword, the four players became aware of a sobbing sound. They looked at the ground and saw Oob, kneeling and sobbing his eyes out, transfixed on what he could see through the open door. Stan turned around and peered through the door, and was instantly seized by an ice-cold fist clenching his heart.

There were villagers in the church, sprawled out across the seats and littering the floor. All of them had sought refuge inside the church during the attack, but to no avail. Stan walked forward hesitantly, and could do nothing but stare at the terrible carnage before him. Stan felt a dull blow to his stomach as he recognized Ohsow, the butcher, and Leol, the blacksmith. He fought the almost irrepressible urge to vomit when he saw Moganga, the priest and leader of the village, leaning back against the altar, eyes peacefully closed, two arrows protruding from her heart. And beside her, covered in various monster wounds—Mella, Oob's mother; Blerge, Oob's father; and Stull, Oob's little brother.

Then, as Stan was staring down at Oob sobbing over the bodies of his dead family, wondering how he could possibly say anything to his villager friend, Mella's unibrow twitched.

"Oob!" cried Stan in surprise. "She moved!"

"What?" Oob sobbed, taking his tearstained face and reddened eyes out of the palms of his hands.

"Your mom, she just moved! And your younger brother too!"

For Stull, too, had just twitched his arm. As Stan watched in amazement, Stull and Mella began to stir.

"Guys, come in here quick!" yelled Stan. The other three players, who had been looking in on the situation with dismay, sprinted over to him. Kat commanded Rex to stay as she did so, and he obeyed, looking extremely uncomfortable.

"What is it?" demanded Charlie, whipping out his pickaxe.

"They're still alive!" cried Stan, pointing down to Mella and Stull, who were recovering from their position as Oob's face shined with sudden-onset elation.

The other's faces showed signs of pleasant confusion, when suddenly, in an instant, Charlie's face morphed into horror. "Oob!" he bellowed, lurching forward as Oob bent down to hug his family. “Get away from . . .”

But it was too late. In a flash, little Stull’s face flew upward, his face a sickly green, and his eyes shining bright red as he launched himself forward, his teeth latching onto Oob’s chest. The four players stood immobile with shock and horror as Oob cried out in pain, spasmed for a moment, and then sunk lifeless to the ground.

Almost in a trance, Stan drew his axe. He had no idea what was going on. To be honest, his brain was having a problem processing anything at the moment. All he knew was that those creatures were not Oob’s family. They were obviously some new type of monster, and they were hurting Oob. Stan raised his axe, his sights set on what he had thought was Mella.

“No, Stan!” cried Charlie, panic in his voice as he knocked Stan’s axe to the side. “You’ll kill Oob’s family!”

“Those things aren’t Oob’s family!” Stan gasped in horror as Oob’s skin began to transform from pale to a disgusting slime green.

“Yes, they are, Stan. They’ve been infected!” cried Charlie, trying to calm himself down. “It’s something that was added on the last update. If a Zombie bites a villager, then they have a chance of turning into a Zombie themselves!”

“S-so are you telling me . . . ,” stammered Stan as the three zombified villagers pulled themselves to their feet, "that Oob and his family . . . are gonna be monsters forever?"

"No, they won't . . . ," said Charlie, backing away from the Zombie villagers as the others did the same. "They can be cured. . . . I don't know how, but I can find out."

"So how long are they gonna stay like this if we can't find it?" demanded Kat as they backed out the door to the church.

"They'll stay like that until someone cures them. Or, you know, until they get killed somehow," replied Charlie as the Zombies followed them out of the church, their arms outstretched toward the players now. Rex began to bark like crazy at them, only to back down at Kat's command.

"And what are we gonna do with them until then?" squealed DZ, the terror in his voice almost palpable as the family of three Zombie villagers advanced slowly toward him.

"They'll come with me," came a voice from besides them.

The four players tore their attention away from the zombified Oob, Mella, and Stull to see a player standing in the gravel road, at the edge of a crater. He was dressed entirely in black and had a bow drawn, an arrow positioned in it.

Without hesitation, the four players drew their bows and arrows, aiming them toward the Noctem agent. Stan felt an intense surge of hatred toward this player. This was clearly one of the soldiers who had attacked the village. He was the reason that these villagers, helpless to help themselves, who had shown Stan and his friends so much hospitality, now lay dead and zombified around them. Stan was about to let the arrow fly, already planning out the following axe strikes in his mind, when the player spoke.

"Drop your weapons or your villager friends get killed."

Stan didn't have to think twice. His weapon clattered to the ground, alongside the three others. Stan knew that, though the villagers may be Zombies now, they were still villagers. As long as they could be cured, Stan still had a personal duty to protect them.

The Noctem soldier smiled. "Now, don't speak either, or they die."

As the Noctem soldier said this, the three Zombie villagers became aware of his presence. Their eyes shifted to the bow in his hands, and aware that he was threatening them, they shifted their attention to the soldier. Little Stull seemed to be significantly faster than his mother and brother, sprinting toward the soldier at top speed.

The soldier smiled. "Now," he said conversationally to the Zombies, "would you really kill me when I can help you get more flesh than you could eat?"

The three Zombies screeched to a halt. They looked at the player for a moment with poignant curiosity. Then, Zombie Oob's mouth opened.

"You . . . give . . . us . . . flesh?" The voice that came from his mouth was like rusty nails dragged on a chalkboard.

Stan was flabbergasted. He couldn't have moved or spoken even if he had been able to, he was so caught off guard. Did that Zombie just speak?

"Yes, I can give you flesh. My name is Private Spyro, and I belong to an organization called the Noctem Alliance. If you join the Noctem Alliance, then you will be able to get all the flesh that you want."

The Zombies were silent for a moment. Then Zombie Mella slowly asked in her gravelly Zombie voice, "Where . . . you . . . get . . . flesh?"

"The Noctem Alliance," replied Spyro calmly, as if he were having a conversation with any old player, "is currently at war with a country called Elementia. During the war, we will capture many prisoners. Any prisoners that we capture are yours to eat."

Stan's mouth dropped open in repulsion, but before any sound could escape, Spyro's bow flipped to face him for a moment, and all the air vanished from his lungs.

"Play-ers . . . no . . . kill . . . us?" asked Zombie Oob slowly.

"The Noctem Alliance will not kill you if you agree to join us," said Spyro, his bow still pointed toward Zombie Oob's forehead. "The prisoners that we give you to eat will not try to kill you either. We will knock them unconscious before you feast on them."

Stan heard a sound to his left, and out of the corner of his eye saw DZ puking. Spyro ignored this.

The three Zombies looked at one another, and let out a series of moans and groans. Stan watched in horror. How could this be happening? The Noctem Alliance was recruiting Zombie villagers right in front of them, and there was nothing they could do about it!

After the groaning had ceased, Zombie Mella turned to face Spyro and, to Stan's utter distress, managed to get out, "We . . . join . . . you . . . Noc-tem . . . Li-ance."

Spyro grinned. "Good," he said. "And you realize that means you must obey every command I give you?"

"We . . . o-bey . . . you," replied Zombie Oob.

"Excellent," replied Spyro jubilantly. He glanced over his shoulder to the west. The sun had finally set behind the desert skyline. He was not the first to notice this. Stan had been, for the past half a minute, glancing around the desert, and noticed with growing unease that monsters were spawning all around them. There were the regular Zombies, the bow-wielding Skeletons, the scuttling Spiders, the menacing Creepers, and even a few tall, black, ominous Endermen, with whom Stan was careful to avoid eye contact.

"What are your names?" Spyro asked.

"Mel . . . la," Mella croaked out.

"Oob," Oob followed.

"Stull!" spat the tiny Zombie child.

Stan was shocked. Even through the zombification process, they somehow all remembered their names. He realized, with a terrified jolt of his heart, that this confirmed to him that, in fact, the three villagers still existed within the undead monsters.

"Okay then. Mella, I want you to order all the hostile mobs in the area into the vicinity. Tell them to hold their attacks, though," replied Spyro, his bow still raised at Oob's head.

Stan watched in sheer fright as Mella obliged, opening her mouth and letting out a terrifying roar, an aggressive Zombie moan of massive proportions. As she did, the eyes of all the hostile mobs in the area looked to her. A series of shorter moans later, and all the monsters in the area began to walk toward the players and Zombie villagers. Stan began to shake uncontrollably as the circle of mobs closed in, getting closer and closer. He closed his eyes, unable to bear the tension, when suddenly, Mella gave another moan, and Stan heard the footsteps of the monsters stop. He opened his eyes and saw a rabble of hostile monsters surrounding the five players and three Zombie villagers.

Private Spyro, his bow still trained on Oob, spoke out. "I am giving you this one chance to leave unharmed, President Stan. For reasons that I cannot disclose, Lord Tenebris does not want you or your fellows dead yet. Just know this, however. The Noctem Alliance now has control over the armies of hostile mobs. If you'd like to take control of the mob armies away from us, you are going to have to kill all three of your villager friends. Keep in mind, President Stan—they may be Zombies now, but there's always the possibility that they could be saved."

He turned to the Zombie villagers. "Stull," he ordered, "tell the monsters to allow these four players to pass without harm. Do not pursue them. If they speak, or attempt to arm themselves with weapons, kill them immediately."

And with that, little Stull gave a series of high-pitched wails, and some of the evil mobs stepped to the side, creating a pathway back toward the train line. Not wanting to spend a second more in the forsaken village, Stan turned on his heel and silently marched through the horde of monsters. As he approached the train, the gears were whirring in his head at top speed. He hardly felt any grief at all now; rather, two feelings were struggling for control over his mind.

One of these feelings was terror. The Noctem Alliance had managed to gain the allegiance of intelligent monsters in the Overworld. This gave them total control over all the monsters in the world of Minecraft. He had no idea how they were going to be able to combat the literally infinite amount of monsters that the armies of the undead would be able to produce.

The second feeling was that of conflict. The armies of the night were incredibly dangerous, and they could be taken from the Noctem Alliance in an instant if they could only kill Oob, Mella, and Stull. But therein was the problem. How could they possibly kill Oob, Mella, and Stull?

CHAPTER 22
THE DECISIONS

Not for the first time, a soldier came to the door of Leonidas's hut to check on where he was, and once again, Leonidas turned him away through the tears. Although the bawling had subsided, Leonidas still felt the occasional fit of sobs rack his body. He just couldn't believe it when Captain Drake had delivered the message to him. Every member of the NPC village . . . Ohsow, Mella and Blerge, and even Moganga . . . all dead. . . .

It was his fault, Leonidas thought through the tears, the guilt of it threatening to strangle him. He had been the one to kill the Iron Golem, leaving his family vulnerable to attack. And he had also killed Stan's soldiers, who, as horrible as they were, surely would have defended at least their own lives in the case of a Noctem attack.

As Leonidas thought this, he realized with a start that this was not random. He had been so overwhelmed in his grief over the attack on the NPC village that he had not realized it had been just that: an attack. And it had been committed by the Noctem Alliance, the organization that he, Leonidas had pledged his life to. His organization had just launched the attack that had killed his family.

Memories came flooding back to Leonidas,

threatening to drown him. The massacre of the prisoners' village. The bomb in the Tennis Machine. The attack on the Spleef arena. And now the NPC village, too. All of these attacks were committed by the Noctem Alliance. All of them had been committed for no good reason. And all of them had been committed against innocent beings who were unprepared to defend themselves. *And this*, thought Leonidas, *this was the last straw.*

All at once, Leonidas made a decision. It was not the first time he had thought about making this decision. Indeed, it had been growing in his mind for a while now, slowly sprouting into a full-blown plan over the weeks. Leonidas had always had too many hesitations to go through with it, but now he knew the time had come to put his plan into action.

Leonidas pulled a map out of his inventory and looked down at it. The nearest encampment of Elementia troops was massed a good distance away from Nocturia. Leonidas would order Captain Drake to take all his men and launch a full-out assault on the encampment. Leonidas knew Drake would not question the plan. The armies he had in Nocturia were more than capable of taking the encampment. And, most important, an encampment that size was sure to put up a good fight. With any luck, the offensive would distract Drake long enough for Leonidas to put his plan into action.

The gears spinning in his head, Leonidas walked out of

his shack and into the blizzard, looking for a messenger to tell Drake to attack the encampment. As he did this, he scrutinized the plan in his mind, looking for any way it could possibly go wrong. After all, he thought, it was essential that the plan be executed flawlessly on the first try.

"Stan! Kat, Charlie, DZ! Thank goodness you're back!" cried Ben, leaping up from his seat in the castle train station as the minecart train pulled in. "Quickly, you need to join the council meeting going on. There's been a startling new development in the war!"

"Let me guess," spat Kat bitterly, and Ben was surprised to see her sullenness reflected on the faces of the three other players. "Up until now, the Elementia army and the Noctem Alliance have called ceasefires at night so that they wouldn't have to deal with the hostile mobs on the battlefield. Since we've been gone, though, the Noctem Alliance has started to fight at night and the hostile mobs have been helping them."

Ben was flabbergasted. "How . . . what the . . . how the . . . ," he stammered before finally getting out, "How could you possibly know that?" As he said this, and took in the crestfallen expressions on their faces, he realized what was off. One of them was missing.

"Wait a second . . . ," he said slowly. "Guys . . . where's Oob?"

Stan sighed. "The Noctem Alliance got him," he responded, sounding disgusted.

"What?" Ben gasped, his face morphing to dread. "Do you mean he's . . . I mean, do you mean that they . . ."

"No," spat DZ, "he ain't dead. He's worse than dead. He's working for the Noctem Alliance now."

Ben heard, but he didn't understand, and couldn't believe. "But . . ."

"He got infected and turned into a Zombie," explained Charlie, a catch in his throat and tears in his eyes. "That was the reason the Noctem Alliance attacked the NPC village. They must've weakened the village, and then stayed there during a full moon and let the Zombies attack all the villagers, infecting them. The Zombie villagers can communicate with players, so the Alliance recruited them into their army so the Zombie villagers can be a link of command between the Noctem Alliance and the hostile mobs."

"Come on, we'll explain it more in the council room," Kat said, and she ordered Rex to sit before she walked down the hallway, followed by the other four players, with Ben still sputtering in confusion.

As Stan followed Kat into the council room, he saw the eyes of four council members sitting at the table shift to them. Stan realized one of them was missing. A quick head count told him that it was Blackraven who was absent. He didn't really care why.

"Good, you're back!" exclaimed G, his face stressed, as the four players sat around the table. "You four were supposed to go out and investigate the attack on the village. What did you find?"

The four players looked at one another uncomfortably, their gazes eventually settling on Charlie. He opened his mouth to speak, but before he could, another sob escaped, and he broke down crying, laying his head in his hands on the table.

"Pull yourself together, Charlie!" grunted G harshly. "What did you find in that village?"

"Give him a moment, for heaven's sake!" the Mechanist cried out, his eyes widening with anxiety. "He's clearly upset about what they found there! Stan," he said gravely, turning toward him. "Is it what I feared?"

Stan nodded his head, glancing down. "Worse, actually," he replied. To this the Mechanist gave an exclamation of surprise and clutched his heart, terrified of what could possibly have happened.

Before Jayden, G, or any of the other players could ask, Kat jumped in and began to explain everything that they had seen and been through in the NPC village. The faces of the other players fell when they heard of the tragic demise of all the villagers, and then mutated to shock when they heard that Oob had been turned into a Zombie.

"The good news," said Stan at the end of Kat's speech, trying to sound optimistic but failing miserably, "is that the Zombie villagers can be turned back to normal somehow, and once we find out how, we'll be able to turn Oob and his family back and take control of the hostile mobs away from the Noctem Alliance."

"Okay, so I have a couple of questions," said G slowly, following a moment of dead silence. "First of all, you said that Oob and his brother and mom were turned into Zombies . . . What about his dad, didn't Oob have a dad too?"

"He didn't turn," croaked Charlie, speaking his first words since they had entered the council room. His eyes were red and puffy, and his words were pained. "Not all of those villagers were killed by Zombies. Some of them were killed by Skeletons, Spiders, and Endermen too. Even if the Zombie villagers can be cured, the other villagers . . . can . . . never . . ." And once again, Charlie broke down.

Stan stood up, walked over, and patted his friend's shoulder, while Kat did the same. Obviously, all the friends were devastated that the NPC villagers had fallen prey to the Noctem Alliance. Stan was doing all he could to keep his composure, knowing that the only way to avenge them was through the decisions made here at this council meeting. But Charlie . . . Charlie had been the closest to the NPCs.

Stan remembered the time they had spent in that village. While Stan and Kat had been planning out their invasion of the End, Charlie had been out in the village with DZ, joking and spending time with Oob and his brethren. Even after the quest was over, it was those two who had gone out to visit the village by far the most out of anybody. Stan could only imagine how traumatic this was for him personally.

"Anyway," said G awkwardly. "So this latest development means the Noctem Alliance has three Zombie villagers under their command that give them control over the evil mobs?"

"Exactly," replied Stan grimly.

"They need to go down."

Seven members of the council spun around. The eyes of all fell on DZ, and Stan was shocked to see the look on his face. His eyes had a darkness to them now, and he exuded an aura of malice that Stan had never sensed from him before. In fact, he had never sensed anything like it before. The dark power DZ was exerting frightened him, especially when DZ continued.

"They need to go down now. The Noctem Alliance took it a step too far this time. As terrible as their attacks on us were, it was because they disagree with our ideals. As awful as the bombing of the Tennis Machine was, it was because we were openly fighting with them. As horrible as the attack on the Spleef arena was, it was because we ignored their warning. But this . . . nothing in the world could ever justify what we saw in that village."

"DZ . . . ," Jayden started, but DZ wasn't done yet.

"The NPC villagers never did anything wrong. They were peaceful. They minded their own business. The villagers and the Noctem Alliance had never crossed paths before this. But now, all those people, all the village people that I knew, that I joked with, that I was friends with . . . they're all dead for no reason other than a way to make it easier for the Alliance to win this stupid war!"

DZ spun around to look at Ben, who had been standing in the corner, quietly observing the council meeting. "Ben," he seethed, "you need to do something against the Noctem Alliance. Launch some sort of military operation against them. Something big that'll make them pay for what they've done."

Ben blinked twice, staggered. "But DZ, I . . . I mean, we're already using more resources than we're supposed to, doing what we're doing."

"I don't care!" bellowed DZ, his face almost inhuman with rage. "Draft more people if you have to! The Noctem Alliance has got to pay! They can't commit this atrocity without retribution! We've got to stick it to them!"

"Calm yourself, DZ," said the Mechanist, himself taking deep breaths to remain calm. "I understand that you feel a need to do something drastic, and to do it right now. . . .

Believe me, we all feel terrible about this tragic turn of events . . ."

"Not like me!" bellowed DZ, veins pulsating in his forehead. "Not like Charlie!" and he jabbed his pointer finger toward Charlie, still sobbing with Stan and Kat comforting him.

"That's a fair statement," replied the Mechanist. DZ felt as though he had been slapped across the face. He had been expecting the Mechanist to disagree with him in his claim so much that when he agreed, DZ felt the need to listen to what he had to say.

"You and Charlie were undeniably the closest to the NPC villagers, and it is therefore you who feel the pain of their demise the most poignantly. However, it is for precisely that reason that I ask you two to refrain from suggesting rash actions. The Noctem Alliance will fall. In order to expedite their demise, however, we must act through logic, not through the need for revenge."

There was a pause, during which nobody spoke.

"Fine," replied DZ, his breathing deep and exaggerated. "It makes sense I guess . . . but honestly," he said, looking over at Ben with huge, meaningful eyes, "you're telling me that there's absolutely nothing more in any of our power that we can do against the Noctem Alliance?"

"How does cutting off the Alliance's head sound?"

All nine players in the room spun, once again, to face the

door as Blackraven burst in, an air of excitement surrounding him. As he almost jogged to his seat at the council table, a soldier walked in behind him, looking very proud of herself.

"What do you mean by that, Blackraven?" the Mechanist asked.

"I mean we have the opportunity now to destroy the Noctem Alliance by taking its leaders out of the equation," he replied with a huge grin.

Stan's eyes widened as he realized what Blackraven was implying. "Wait . . . Blackraven, are you saying . . ."

"Yes, Stan," replied Blackraven triumphantly. "We've located the Specialty Base."

Immediately, everybody around the table burst into cheers and applause. Even Charlie managed a little smile of hope, and DZ's scowl vanished in the blink of an eye.

"It was actually this brave soldier here," continued Blackraven, gesturing to the soldier, who stepped forward, humble as she realized just who it was she was being presented to. "This is Corporal Elaine of the Army of Elementia. She was one of the naval scouts sent out to patrol the Northwestern Islands."

"Where is the Specialty Base, then, Corporal?" asked Stan, walking away from Charlie and sitting down in his own seat. "And how did you locate it?"

"They attacked me, Mr. President," Corporal Elaine

responded, respectfully yet proudly. "My commander had told me to patrol the seas to the south of the Mushroom Islands to check the southern coastlines for any signs of enemy activities. I steered my boat in close to the shore, and I came under arrow fire. I saw Noctem soldiers, all in boats, firing at me, and coming at me from the direction of the islands.

"I knew I couldn't take all three of them on at once, and I didn't have any backup with me on that particular day, so I fled the scene. I led them to the east. If they had followed me, they would have run into the heavily armed armada massing at the Elementia Sea Base. I looked back and saw that they had turned back and were headed for the strait between the two Mushroom Islands. The cliff blocked my view, so I couldn't see which of the two islands the boat returned to. I would have gone back and investigated the islands myself, but I didn't want to take the chance of walking into an ambush. Immediately after, I reported all that I had seen to my commander."

"The commander of the Sea Base," continued Blackraven, "sent out two more armed scouts to inspect the Mushroom Islands further. They were able to confirm that there is Noctem activity in the waters surrounding the Mushroom Islands. As a reward for her discovery and her bravery, the commander then promoted Elaine to the rank of corporal."

"Well, I offer you my thanks, Corporal Elaine," responded

Stan. "This information is imperative for winning the war, and we're in your debt. You are dismissed now."

Elaine bowed her head. "Thank you, Mr. President," she responded, before turning on her heel and marching out the door.

"The commander of the Sea Base assured me that we have the right spot," continued Blackraven to the council. "He also has a blockade around the islands. The army is putting together an operation to stake out a network of old mining tunnels under the islands, making escaping by digging underground impossible. The commander's just not sure what to do now. The obvious next step would be to organize a naval invasion of the island. However, we have to approach the situation carefully. After all, this is the Mushroom Islands we're dealing with."

Charlie, DZ, and the Mechanist all nodded wisely, but Stan, Kat, Jayden, and G were all confused.

"Why can't we launch a strike on the islands?" Jayden asked.

"Yeah, if we know the Noctem Alliance is there, then what are we waiting for?" asked Kat as Stan and Charlie nodded in agreement. Personally, Stan had no knowledge of the Mushroom Islands, or any islands in the Northwestern Ocean, for that matter. But if the Noctem Alliance was on the islands, then it didn't really matter to him what was on them.

They would have to be invaded.

Blackraven sighed in exasperation. "Weren't any of you there when we drafted the section of the constitution that dealt with the Mushroom Islands?"

Stan faltered. Honestly, he had forgotten about that part of the constitution. When they had been writing all the laws regarding the Mushroom Islands, the others had started talking about some pretty high-end political stuff, and he had just let them handle it, feeling in over his head. Clearly, Kat, G, and Jayden had all done the same. He didn't respond to Blackraven, though. He knew Blackraven would explain himself anyway.

"Because of some agreements that we made with some people back when we first drafted the constitution, we're not allowed to perform any military operations on the islands regardless of the situation."

"It makes perfect sense that the Noctem Alliance would hide there, if you think about it," said Charlie sullenly. "What better place to hide than somewhere we can't bring our military?"

"There's a loophole in that law," responded the Mechanist shrewdly. "As president, Stan has the right to carry a small force of guards with him wherever he goes. He also has the right to inspect any part of Elementia at any time. Stan could go to the islands and say he's just there on a visit, but use that as a secret cover to search the islands for the Noctem Alliance."

"So what you're saying is," said Stan slowly, trying to piece together what was being said, "you want me to use an inspection as an excuse to get onto the islands, and use my bodyguards as a way to get soldiers onto the island with me?"

"Exactly," replied the Mechanist with a smile. "And we use an armed convoy of soldiers as your bodyguards."

"I'll be in your convoy, Stan," said Charlie, wiping the last of the tears from his cheeks. "I've read tons of books on the Mushroom Islands, and I know their geography too."

"Count me in too," added DZ, his terrifying rage gone, but a definite fire lingering in his eyes. "There's no way we plan a mission to destroy the Noctem Alliance once and for all and I'm not a part of it!"

Kat opened her mouth, her face showing her clear excitement to join the other three, but before she could speak, Blackraven cut in.

"I think it would be best if only those two went along with Stan," he said.

"Why's that?" Kat demanded, looking outraged.

"If we're going to take the Noctem Alliance down, we should attack them from all angles at the same time. The council members should lead the troops in a massive attack to take back the Hot Front and the Cold Front at the same time. We need to do it simultaneously with the attack on the Specialty Base. If we time it right, then all parts of the Alliance will be hit at once, and the organization will collapse."

"That's good thinking, Blackraven," replied the Mechanist, nodding his head as Kat did the same. "Stan, Charlie, and DZ, you sail out from Diamond Bay to the Mushroom Islands, locate the Specialty Base and assassinate the Noctem leaders. Jayden and G can go out and lead the charge on the Hot Front, while Ben and Kat do the same on the Cold Front. Gobbleguy and Blackraven, you stay here with me and run the council while the others are gone."

"That sounds like a plan to me," replied Stan. "We'll leave at daybreak tomorrow morning. Does anybody have any objections?"

There was silence around the table.

"Okay then!" exclaimed DZ, punching his fist in the air. "Let's do this thing!"

As the ten players in the room scattered, the only feeling apparent in the air was that of charged excitement. Gone were the days when they stood on guard, waiting for the Noctem Alliance to strike and praying that they would be able to counter them. They were on the offensive now; at long last, the Grand Republic of Elementia had a plan of attack to take the Noctem Alliance down, once and for all.

CHAPTER 23

THE BATTLE OF THE ARCHIPELAGO

Stan rubbed his eyes and yawned, a bit of annoyance clouding his mind. He knew he had ordered that they leave on their missions at the break of dawn, but he was still irritated that the Mechanist had woken him up literally at the instant the sun had broken the skyline. Stan sighed. Why do old people have to wake up so early?

As tired as he was, Stan knew it was for the best that they had gotten such an early start. The night before, he, Charlie, and DZ had equipped themselves with all the gear they would need for their trip. After they had finished the early morning preparations, they made the long hike to the Diamond Bay Naval Harbor.

Element City was situated on a plain, and Element Castle sat at the edge of the plain farthest from the forest. Directly behind Element Castle, a sheer cliff dropped down to the ground below. Stan, Charlie, and DZ had taken a path down this cliff face, taking each step down the precarious pathway slowly and carefully until, finally, they reached sea level. At the bottom of the cliff was a swamp biome. They had to trek through it for a good distance before they finally got to the naval harbor. Thankfully, their early start allowed them to reach their destination around noon.

This was the first time Stan had personally been

down to inspect the Diamond Bay Naval Harbor, and he was very impressed by it. The jagged coastline where the swampland met the ocean had been filled in by cobblestone blocks, making a giant, flat surface of rock that sat at sea level. On top of this flat surface sat tall warehouses, which Stan assumed were full of military supplies.

Where the cobblestone surface met the ocean, wooden docks extended out into the seemingly endless water, and lined up next to these docks were hundreds of single-man boats, more than Stan cared to count. As Stan glanced down the rows of docks, he could see shelters, around which soldiers were already moving. Stan subconsciously nodded his head in approval. He knew that, as hard as the war may be on land, the military of Elementia was well prepared for an attack by sea. Stan looked over the bunkers of the troops until, before long, a soldier came jogging up to him from the army barracks, dressed in full iron armor with a brown face visible.

"Good morning, Mr. President," the soldier said, standing at a full salute. "Our forces have just finished preparing your escort of ships. We'll take you as far as the Elementia Sea Base, which is about three quarters of the way to the Lesser Mushroom Island. There, you can plan out your visit with the commander of the base."

"Thank you, soldier," replied Stan, nodding his head.

The use of the word "visit" by the soldier was not lost on

Stan. He reminded himself that they would have to be careful as they undertook their raid on the Noctem base. The word had been given out to the soldiers that Stan, Charlie, and DZ were on a presidential visit to the Mushroom Islands, just to inspect them. Only the commander of the Sea Base and the Elementia ambassador who lived on the Lesser Mushroom Island were told that the visit was actually just a facade to locate and conduct a raid on a Noctem base.

Although Stan still wasn't entirely sure why all this secrecy was necessary, the Mechanist had reminded him how crucial it was to keep up the front. He reminded DZ and Charlie of this need for secrecy as they boarded their one-man boats.

"Are you kidding me, Stan?" exclaimed DZ as Charlie nodded his head in understanding. "When have I ever spilled the beans about anything?"

"Well, there was that time you swore you wouldn't tell Kat that I changed the color of Rex's collar on April Fools' Day, but you told her anyway," said Charlie, raising one eyebrow in accusation.

"Oh, come on, you should have been happy to take credit for that!" said DZ, as though this should be obvious. "It was the best prank ever! Rex looks so generic that Kat couldn't tell him apart from literally any of the other dogs with green collars!"

"And there was that time you told Oob his real name

after we convinced him it was actually 'Testificate.'"

"Come on, guys, that was cruel and you know it, the poor little guy was beginning to question whether or not everything in his life was a lie after that!"

"And there was the time you told Gobbleguy where we had stored the castle's anvil collection, even though we specifically told you . . ."

"Hey!" DZ cut in. "He wouldn't stop bugging me about it, and I thought, 'Hey, what's the worst that could happen?' And that was the Mechanist's fault. Who designs a room so that the lever that retracts the shelves holding the anvils is next to the light switch?"

Charlie was about to come up with another example (he could think of dozens just off the top of his head) when a soldier came up to them and told them it was time to depart.

"We will finish this conversation later." Charlie smirked back at DZ as the two of them pulled out in front of Stan and into the harbor.

Stan was a bit hesitant to pilot the boat. He had never driven a boat in real life before, let alone in Minecraft. The soldier had explained to Stan that the way to pilot the boat was to use his mind to give commands. He hoped it would work. The rest of the fleet had already moved out, and Stan saw no oars, sails, motor, or any other means of propulsion on his boat.

Tentatively, Stan thought, *Forward*, and immediately, the boat gave a sudden lurch out toward the sea, sending Stan reeling backward, nearly tumbling off the stern. After he recovered, amazed at what he had just done, Stan tried again, and tried to think about the word with a little bit more finesse. After a little bit of experimenting, Stan was able to fully control his boat with his mind, including accelerating, braking, and turning.

Contented with his mastery of the controls, Stan then gunned it at high speed to catch up with the approximately fifty boats that formed his military escort to the Sea Base. Thankfully, the escort was waiting for him at the mouth to Diamond Bay. As he joined them, the soldier at the head of the fleet addressed them all.

"Okay, we're all ready to move out to the Elementia Sea Base. We're going to have to make a slight roundabout to avoid the ice around the Taiga Archipelago, but it's a straight shot after that. Expect to be at the Sea Base by nightfall. Just match my speed and we'll get there quickly and without incident."

And with that, the soldier headed out of the mouth of the bay and into the vast expanse of water that was the Northwestern Ocean. Stan looked back over his shoulder like a curious child seeing the world for the first time as, slowly, the shorelines of Elementia grew farther and farther away. Stan was soon treated to the brilliant spectacle of Element Castle, reaching into the sky from atop the cliff that overlooked the swamp and sea. As the convoy of ships traveled farther and farther into the endless flat expanse of blue, an eerie feeling came over Stan. As he looked over his shoulder at his castle, which was now disappearing into the far-off render fog, Stan was captivated by the ominous feeling that he would never see Element City again.

Stan was jolted out of this feeling just as soon as it came on, because DZ's wooden craft came careening toward him, ramming his boat to the side on impact and nearly knocking Stan into the ocean.

"What was that for?" demanded Stan as he steadied himself in his boat.

"Shots fired, man! What're you gonna do about it?" asked DZ slyly, a devious smirk on his face.

Realizing what DZ had done, Stan returned the expression on his own face, and willed his boat to swerve back toward DZ's, knocking him sideways.

"Oh, it's on now, Stan! BOO-YAH!" bellowed DZ as he made to smash back into Stan's boat just as Stan did the same, sending them both spinning randomly away from each other, laughing wildly. Stan was having the time of his life. In all the intensity of the war, all the stress he had felt over the Noctem Alliance, and all his grief over the fate of the

NPC villagers, Stan had forgotten just how good it felt to have fun every now and then.

"Hey," said Stan in a soft voice, a brilliant plan coming into his mind as he saw DZ readying another assault.

"What?" DZ asked, halting his preparations.

"Let's do a sneak attack on Charlie," replied Stan, barely able to keep in his excited laughter as he gestured to Charlie, who was calmly poring over his papers, blind to the world as he sailed peacefully in front of them.

DZ gasped. "YES!" he exclaimed as his face lit up. "Stan, are you familiar with Operation Gravel Trap? You know, the Spleef technique that I made up back in the day?"

"Not at all," replied Stan.

"Excellent! Let's try it!" said DZ in elation as he quickly pulled his boat away from Stan. DZ maneuvered directly to the back right of Charlie, before glancing meaningfully at Stan and giving him a series of hand motions. Stan had no idea what he was doing, and decided on a whim to circle around to Charlie's back left side. DZ nodded his approval, indicating that Stan had clearly done something right.

Stan glanced tentatively in front of him and saw that, to his amusement, Charlie still had not noticed them closing in, being far too devoted to poring over information on the islands that they were about to visit. *Well*, Stan thought with a grin, *it's about time for Charlie to take a break and have some fun.* He saw DZ wave his hand forward toward Charlie and, as it was obvious what this signal meant, the two players willed their boats forward at top speeds and rammed Charlie's vessel from behind.

Charlie's boat burst apart. The tiny wooden dinghy erupted into a puff of white smoke and ceased to exist, spewing three wooden blocks and two sticks into the air. They fell back down and sunk, presumably to the seafloor (Stan, as alarmed as he was, found this odd; he assumed that the wooden materials would have floated). Charlie fell into the water with a splash, his papers flying haphazardly into the air.

There was a moment of stunned silence as DZ and Stan realized what had happened. Then, with incredible agility, DZ whipped out his sword and, with the extended range, managed to skewer all of Charlie's papers on the point before they could fall into the water, where Charlie now flailed, disoriented.

Stan steered his boat over to Charlie, ready to reach into the water to help him out and apologize for the accident. However, before he got a chance, an arrow sunk into Charlie's leather armor, and he slowly slipped below the surface.

Stan was thunderstruck for a moment. Then, as his brain connected what had happened, he needed no time for further thinking. Stan heard the sounds of arrows whizzing through the air and the soldiers beginning to shout in alarm as he jumped out of his boat and into the water.

Stan took a moment to let his eyes adjust to the dark, blurred world of the underwater seascape of dirt and sand below him, with cerulean water turning everything blue. And in the midst of this foreboding setting, Charlie was sinking fast, bubbles spewing from his mouth. Stan was relieved to find that it was much easier to hold his breath underwater in Minecraft than in real life. As such, he managed to dive down and reach Charlie relatively quickly, just as Charlie settled on the ocean floor, dangerously close to a deep abyss.

Stan put his arms underneath Charlie's, trying to regulate his air supply as he did so. It would be a long swim back up to the surface, swimming with just his legs and carrying the weight of an extra player. Stan looked skyward, preparing to swim, but was forced to drop Charlie when he saw what was overhead. Stan barely managed to lunge sideway to dodge the swing of the sword from above him.

As Stan found his footing on the seafloor and Charlie sank yet again, Stan could see a player, all features obscured by his black leather armor and a pumpkin on his head. The figure had a diamond sword drawn and was once again swimming toward Stan. Trying not to panic, Stan drew his diamond axe and engaged the player in combat.

The water all around them bent this fight in ways that

Stan had never experienced before. This player was clearly practiced in underwater fighting, as he swam gracefully through the water and delivered strikes with his sword in equal precision. Regardless, Stan, disoriented as he was, managed to block all the attacks, the force of each one sending both players reeling backward through the omnipresent liquid.

As the fight went on, Stan felt the strain of continuously holding his breath. After one particularly hard strike of the sword, Stan went flailing downward, landing squarely on his back on the gravel seabed. All the remaining air he had been rationing so carefully burst out of his mouth in a colossal bubble, and Stan felt his mouth fill with salty brine.

Dazed and delirious, Stan looked up at his assailant. The pumpkin helmet on his head was clearly helping him breathe in some way. As the dark form came closer and closer, Stan willed his failing nervous system to react, to raise his diamond axe over his chest and at least attempt to defend himself.

Then, out of the corner of his eye, Stan noticed something. A jet of bubbles, streaming rapidly down from the surface, approaching the trio of players. The Noctem attacker looked over his shoulder a split second before DZ's diamond sword, outstretched in his hand, impaled the attacker through the back. Stan noticed a faint purple tint on DZ's blade, almost imperceptible in the water, before the Knockback enchantment took effect, sending the Noctem soldier careening deep into the nearby trench, disappearing into the darkness almost instantly.

Stan could barely feel anything through his delirium now, and he was only vaguely aware of DZ snatching Charlie under one arm and him under the other. Then, all of a sudden, Stan was shooting upward like a rocket, breaking the surface in a matter of seconds. Stan spewed up water like a hose for about half a minute, during which the sounds of warfare became more and more apparent. Stan finally gained the strength to open his eyes and look down below them. The three players were sitting draped over a boat. DZ must have set it up underwater and let the buoyancy of the boat propel them to the surface. Then, Stan looked at the source of the fighting.

Far off to the right of the fleet of boats a chain of small islands sat, surrounded by an expanse of ice blocks that extended into the ocean. The islands themselves were covered in snow and patches of spruce trees, matching the descriptions Stan had heard of the Taiga Archipelago. Standing on the expanse of ice around the island were five Noctem soldiers, all shooting arrows at the naval brigade, which was returning fire.

Stan saw that six of their ships now sat vacant, drifting in the sea with the contents of their pilots' inventories scattered about them. However, they had fared no worse than the Noctem Alliance, whose icy shore was positively littered with items from their fallen combatants. As Stan looked around the islands, he could have sworn that the foremost of the Noctem soldiers looked him in the eye for a moment before raising his hand, signaling to his men to stop firing.

The lead soldier of the naval contingent raised his hand as well, and the Elementia troopers stopped firing. There was a moment of silence. Then . . .

"Leaders and soldiers of the Kingdom of Elementia," the foremost soldier announced, his voice echoing across the empty stretch of sea. "What you have just experienced was absolute child's play compared to the terror that awaits you should you continue on your journey. The Noctem Alliance's Specialty Base is impregnable, and should you be foolish enough to attempt to attack it, we will unleash terror and destruction beyond comprehension upon you."

"We're not gonna attack this base of yours!" cried Stan's lead soldier. For all the soldier knew, what he was saying was true. "We're escorting high-ranking members of the Council of Eight on a diplomatic mission."

"Be that as it may, the Nation of the Noctem Alliance has seized many islands in the Northwestern Ocean during this time of warfare. If you should cross us again, we will not hesitate to retaliate."

And with that, the head of the Noctem troops waved his hand backward, and the remaining Noctem soldiers sprinted back over the ice and into the thick grove of spruce trees on the nearest island. As they did so, the head soldier of the Elementia convoy looked back at Stan. "Would you like to conduct a raid on the islands to capture those soldiers, President Stan?"

Stan looked around. Many of his soldiers looked beaten and were nursing arrow wounds, while those few empty boats drifted away through the volition of the sea. Charlie was stirring, regaining consciousness, and DZ looked exhausted. Stan himself still felt the effects of nearly drowning. He shook his head.

"No," he said, still breathing heavily. "The faster we can get to the Sea Base, the better."

The head soldier nodded. Five minutes and dozens of Potions of Healing later, all the soldiers, including Charlie, were recovered and ready to head out. As the ships began to steadily chug forward again, Stan turned to face DZ. "Hey, DZ?" he said, getting a turn of the head in response.

"I just want to thank you. You know, for saving my life down there."

DZ waved his hand and shook his head humbly. "Aw, don't worry about it. It was actually pretty fun. It was trippy, fighting underwater like that."

Stan smirked. "Yeah, *la vida loca* is being lived," he replied, which merited a weak laugh from DZ before they joined Charlie at the back of the convoy.

The day from that point onward was quite uneventful. Stan slowly recovered from the illness that accompanied his near-death experience, and he found the gentle back-and-forth sway of the boat to be quite relaxing. The same could not be said for Charlie, however. He looked almost as sick as the time he had accidentally eaten a piece of rotten flesh.

The day went by slowly. None of the players were in particularly good moods, and Stan and DZ didn't dare think about pranking Charlie again after the events of that morning. So, as it was, Stan had nothing to do for the remainder of the day but will himself forward, keeping pace with the others, and worrying about the Noctem Alliance. As the hours ticked away, the square of the sun traveled into the highest point of the sky, before sinking down into the west. The sky gradually shifted from a bright blue to a brilliant pink, before chromatically shifting further into oranges, reds, and violets.

Just after the sun had dipped under the horizon, bringing the majestic dark of night to the vast ocean, Stan heard a commotion in front of him and looked up. His eyes were immediately drawn to a large, glowing form in the distance, just appearing out of the render fog and sitting atop the water.

"Hey!" Stan yelled up to the soldier leading the crew, "You'd better cut a wide circle around that island. If the Noctem Alliance is in this area, we don't want to fight them now. It's getting late, they'd have the advantage at night."

The soldier turned around and looked Stan squarely in the eye.

"That's no island," he replied. "It's the Sea Base."

CHAPTER 24
THE ELEMENTIA SEA BASE

Even in the fading daylight, Stan was blown away by the Elementia Sea Base. Much like Brimstone Prison and the Diamond Bay Naval Harbor, Stan was just now becoming aware that while he and his friends were stuck in their council room deciding what to do with Elementia, their minions had been building some pretty awesome things.

The Sea Base itself was a pretty standard complex. It was a square platform on top of the ocean, which supported dozens of gray buildings and a series of docks stretching into the sea. Glowstone blocks lit up the complex, making it shimmer in the night, but it was the water that really caught Stan's eye. Light came beaming up from beneath the surface, and Stan realized that glowstone blocks were actually levitating under the water surrounding the base. From their light, he could see that there was no land underneath the Sea Base itself.

The entire base was floating on an artificial cobblestone island on the ocean. Stan knew what this meant. The builders would have had to make pillars that stretched from the bottom of the ocean to the surface, building the glowstone blocks underwater and the complex on top of them, and then going back to the seafloor and destroying them. It must have taken a marvelous feat of engineering to pull that off.

As the fleet of ships drew closer and closer to the Sea Base, Stan grew more and more fascinated. The buildings were made of stone brick blocks, the same material that his castle was made of. Troops marched around the complex, bows flung over their backs. Stan wasn't sure who the commander of this particular base was, but he was clearly preparing for war.

Stan followed the other ships in his fleet to the docks, and when he had safely steered his ship to his space next to the dock, he disembarked. Stan reached up and cracked his back. It felt good to finally be standing on solid ground again after a day at sea. He saw Charlie and DZ a little farther down the dock, and walked over to join them.

"Hey, Stan, old buddy old pal!" exclaimed DZ, turning to look at Stan.

"Hey, DZ," replied Stan, smiling as he rotated his arm in a circle. "Man, it feels good to be out of that boat."

"Sure does," said DZ, rolling his neck. "And check this place out! Did you guys notice that it's floating on the top of the ocean? And those glowstone blocks down there are gnarly!"

"From what I understand," said Charlie wisely, "those glowstone blocks illuminate the water underneath the base so that if anybody tries to attack them from below, they'll see it coming. They've got lookouts positioned in rooms made of glass under the water, watching for enemies attacking them from below."

"That's a pretty smart design choice," said Stan, impressed by this ingenuity. "You know, we always just tell people to build stuff and let them do their own thing with it, but we should really check some more of this stuff out sometime! I mean, this is really sick!"

"Yes, we're quite proud of it," replied a soldier with a corporal badge, walking up to them. "And we'll be happy to give you a full tour of it once your visit to the Mushroom Islands is complete. However, as of now, it's time for curfew. Please follow me to your quarters, and we will wake you up tomorrow morning to escort you to your meeting with the commander."

As he said this, Stan realized just how tired he was. Whether it stemmed from the fight earlier that day or the sailing under the hot sun that had preceded it, Stan felt totally burned out. One look at his comrades told him that they felt the same, and so they nodded in assent as they followed the corporal into the complex and toward their bedrooms.

The next morning, Stan was on edge as he followed another soldier toward the briefing room where the commander was meeting them. It wasn't that Stan hadn't gotten any sleep.

Quite the contrary—he now felt refreshed, alert, and on full guard.

However, Stan's dreams last night had been filled with horrible nightmares. Stan could vividly remember reliving horrible scenes from his past all throughout the night. Over and over, he watched in anguish as Archie was blown apart in the courthouse explosion, as a throng of players scrambled desperately to outrun the wave of lava coursing down the seats of the Spleef arena, and as Oob's chest was punctured by the teeth of his mutated kin.

And it wasn't just his fights with the Alliance that had plagued Stan's dreams. He'd relived the tragic events from months before throughout the night as well. He was helpless to stop the Adorian Village from burning to the ground. He was defenseless as Jayden's brother, Crazy Steve, was felled before him. He was powerless to stop King Kev from landing an arrow in Avery's head. And this was the emotion that was the most pronounced throughout the night: helplessness. He had realized, the instant he woke up, that being helpless against the Noctem Alliance was what he was most terrified of.

The straight-up fighting was easy. Well, not easy, but Stan knew what he had to do, and how he would have to do it. But the Noctem Alliance's true strength was that they made him feel powerless. And that, thought Stan, was why it was so crucial that this mission succeeded. They finally knew, for sure, where the Alliance was. They were the ones with the element of surprise now, and they had the ability to catch the Alliance off guard. The importance of getting this assault right could not be overstated.

At last, the soldier led the three players to a door, which he gestured them through. Stan walked in and found a room very similar to the council room back in Element City. It was a featureless stone brick room with a square conference table in the middle. A player sat at the farthest end of the square table. Though he was wearing an army uniform, he had long, unkempt black hair and a similar beard. His face had clearly been cut up and scarred many times, and he wore a black eye patch over his left eye. When he saw the three players, he leaped to his feet.

"Blimey! Be it that time already? Well, good mornin', Cap'n Stan. 'N' ahoy, Councilmen Charlie 'n' DZ," the player said. It was impossible to tell what accent this player spoke with, although it sounded vaguely Irish.

"Hello . . . ," said DZ slowly. He was, like the others, a little put off by this player's speech pattern.

"Dismissed, Private!" he bellowed, and the soldier escort left the room, closing the wooden door behind him. The player walked over to Stan with what could only be described as a spastic, energetic swagger. He grasped Stan's hand, shaking it up and down vigorously as he said, "Me name be Commander Crunch o' th' Grand Elementia Navy. How're ye doin' on this fine day?"

"I'm pretty good," replied Stan, and he glanced at Charlie, catching an incredulous look. *This* was the brilliant commander of the Elementia Sea Base?

"Wonderful! I be glad t' hear it!" Commander Crunch exclaimed, a giant smile breaking across his face. "'N' how about ye, Councilman Charlie? Councilman DZ?"

Charlie opened his mouth to respond, but before he could, DZ cut in and said, "Okay, I have to ask. Where did you get that accent from?" Stan sighed in exasperation. Leave it to DZ to pose the question that everybody wanted to ask but wouldn't.

However, far from being insulted, the commander gave a jolly chortle.

"Oh, Lord! Ye're a spitfire, aren't ye! Well, t' be truthful, I don't natter like this by choice. One day, I was messin' around wit' th' settin's o' Minecraft, 'n' I accidentally changed me language t' th' Pirate settin'. Since then, I haven't been able t' get it back t' English. T' be honest though, 'tis kind o' grown on me. Especially given me name 'n' all."

"So let me get this straight," said DZ as Stan and Charlie pieced together what he had just said. "Your name is Crunch? And you're commander?"

"Aye," Commander Crunch replied.

"Well then," replied DZ with a snicker, "I guess you miss the good old days when you were a captain, eh?"

"I 'ave no idea wha' ye're talkin' about," replied the commander straightly.

"So wait, you can change your language settings to Pirate?" asked Stan, amazed. "Why would they program something like that in?"

"It beats me. Same reason they programmed the giant flyin' firebreathin' Jellyfish, I suppose," the commander replied, shrugging.

"Anyway, that's nah wha' we be here t' natter about. I received a message a while back from th' council in Element City. So ye wants t' look fer soldiers o' th' Noctem Alliance hidin' on th' Mushroom Islands, do ye? 'N' ye wants t' disguise th' operation as jus' a normal visit from President Stan?"

"That's correct," replied Charlie. "And I know that you know why it's essential that we keep up that facade."

"Excuse me," interjected Stan in an irritated fashion. "But could somebody please explain to me why it is we can't just put the island on lockdown? You know, just have soldiers search in every nook and cranny? I mean, we have the entire force of the military at our fingertips. Why can't we do that?"

Commander Crunch looked at Stan incredulously, then

turned to face Charlie and DZ.

"How in th' name o' Davy Jones' locker does he nah know about th' Mushroom Islands Doctrine?" Crunch asked.

"We wrote that part of the constitution," replied DZ. "He sat out for it."

"Don't worry, Stan," said Charlie kindly. "I'll explain it for you."

And with that, Charlie began to explain the situation to Stan, as DZ and Commander Crunch grouped together and began to discuss the logistics of the attack.

"Back when King Kev controlled Elementia, the Greater Mushroom Island, the bigger of the two of them, was settled by people who wanted to escape King Kev's oppression. They called themselves the Mushroom Tribe, and they vowed to survive there without ever interacting with the modern world. They could do this because of the Mooshrooms, mushroom-cow hybrids that lived on the islands and provided an infinite source of mushroom stew for the people to eat.

"When the people in Elementia learned about the Mooshrooms, they realized that they were valuable, and tried to steal them from the Mushroom Islands for years. They were never able to, though. The tribesmen defended the Mooshrooms with their lives, and developed a hatred of Element City and the modern world. This kept going on until Adoria sent Jayden out to the island, and he managed to trade a few modern materials to the tribesmen in exchange for two Mooshrooms, which the village could breed and sell.

"However, as soon as they got their hands on the modern materials, some of the tribesmen decided they were sick of living a simple life and that their home would be a great place to open a resort. This started a civil war in the Mushroom Tribe, which went on at around the same time as our rebellion against King Kev. In the end, the Mushroom Tribe divided into the Greater Tribesmen on the Greater Mushroom Island, and the Lesser Tribesmen, who moved to the smaller Lesser Mushroom Island and opened a resort.

"The Lesser Tribesmen love us because the people of Element City come to the resorts. The Greater Tribesmen hate us for the years of stealing from them, and for supporting the Lesser Tribesmen with our tourists. When we were putting the constitution together, we realized we had to keep tensions between the two islands as low as possible, so that's why we put a law into the constitution about the Mushroom Islands. The law says we're not allowed to have any sort of military on either Mushroom Island unless one of them attacks our citizens. That's why we can't bring soldiers there."

Charlie finished his explanation, and there was a moment of silence as Stan processed everything. As he did, a few questions came to his mind.

"So . . . no military operations are allowed on the islands

because of that law? And we're getting around the law by saying I'm just visiting, and that I have a right to bring bodyguards with me?"

"Yes," replied Charlie, nodding.

"Okay," replied Stan. "So here are my questions. First, why don't we just rewrite that law? It seems stupid to keep it intact, especially now that the Noctem Alliance is there!"

Charlie snorted. "Stan, do you have any idea how people would react if they found out that we changed more of our own laws just for the sake of advancing this war? They'd go crazy, they'd say we don't care about the constitution, and they'd start protesting again! And even if we tried to keep it secret, it would just get released by the leaker."

"Okay, okay," said Stan hastily. "So have we done any investigations on either of the Mushroom Islands yet?"

"Yeah," said Charlie, nodding. "The ambassador of the Lesser Mushroom Island has used their local police force to comb the entire Lesser Island. They haven't found anything. Regardless, we're still going to do our own investigation. The team that the Mechanist put together for your bodyguards are skilled in detective work as well as fighting."

"Yeah, I knew that," Stan replied. He had been aware that the assault team was composed of specialty forces, the best of the best in all areas of the military.

"One last question. Why would the Noctem Alliance pick

these islands to set up their base on? I know the 'no-military' law would be a perk for them, but Lord Tenebris probably guessed that we'd find a way around it. And when you take that law out of the picture, then the Lesser Mushroom Island is pretty much controlled by Elementia, and the Greater Mushroom Island is filled with people who hate outsiders. I don't think either of those places would be a very easy place to make a base."

"Well," replied Charlie. "I'm going to assume that they're on the Greater Mushroom Island for now, since it isn't civilized and there are a lot more hiding places because it's so much bigger. I think the Noctem Alliance probably set up the base in secret, probably underground somewhere. And if they used Invisibility Potions, then it would be really hard for the Greater Tribesmen to see them. The Greater Mushroom Island is going to be really hard for us to search, though, not only because of that law, but the fact that we're going to have to deal with the Greater Tribesmen ourselves while we look for them."

Stan nodded reasonably. He could see that the Specialty Base, if it was indeed on the Greater Mushroom Island, would be very difficult to attack, especially without arousing the suspicion of the Greater Tribesmen. And if word got back to Element City that Stan was interfering on a protected Mushroom Island . . . Stan doubted that even the Mechanist's brilliant speechwriting would be able to quell the outrage. This operation would have to be handled with total precision and dexterity, and no room for error.

"Oi!" came a shout from Commander Crunch as he barreled over, interrupting the break in the conversation. "Are ye finished wit' all o' yer redundant explanations, Councilman Charlie?"

"I think I'm all caught up," said Stan to Charlie, nodding in assurance.

"Then yes," replied Charlie to the commander.

"Brilliant! Well, I be sorry t' say that I 'ave jus' received some bad news from one o' th' scallywags under me command," said the commander, who, despite delivering bad news, delivered this message with unchecked vivacity.

"Ugh." Stan sighed. "And what is it?"

"I've looked all around me pieces o' eight, in th' logs," he said, somehow excited yet downcast at the same time. "But alas, couldn't draw up one single map o' th' Greater Mushroom Island."

"And we don't have any in Element City, either. I checked before we left," spat DZ bitterly. He turned to Charlie. "Charlie, you had all those papers, do you have a map of the Greater Mushroom Island?"

"Well, I did have one that I got from the Adorian Village," said Charlie bitterly. "Unfortunately, it kind of got destroyed when you guys destroyed my boat and DZ stabbed it in half with a sword."

"DZ!" exclaimed Stan in exasperation.

"Hey, don't go yelling at me, Stan, you went along with the idea too!" DZ shot back.

"Don't go gettin' angry yet, me laddies," laughed Commander Crunch, slapping Charlie on the back and knocking him to the floor. "Wrath ne'er helped nobody. We'll simply see if th' Lesser Mushroom Island has one, 'n' if nah, then we'll jus' 'ave t' play it by ear."

Charlie raised a blocky finger and opened his mouth in protest, then closed it.

"Well . . . ," Charlie said after a moment, "I don't like it, but I guess if it's our only option, then it'll have to do. And actually," he continued, his face lighting up as an idea dawned on him, "what if we tried to enlist the help of the tribesmen? You know, tell them that dangerous people are hiding out on their island, and that if they help us find them, we can get rid of them."

A moment of silence greeted this proposal, as Stan, DZ, and Commander Crunch, all with varying degrees of knowledge about the situation, mulled it over. Finally, Commander Crunch, ever excited but now slightly hesitant, spoke.

"Well . . . I suppose that if we were t' sell it t' th' natives that way . . . 'tis possible that they might help us . . . 'n' seein' as we'd 'ave no maps o' th' island otherwise, says I that yer plan be our best option."

Stan and DZ, after a moment, nodded in agreement.

"Fantastic! We 'ave a plan. I'll go inform me crew. We leave at high noon!" exclaimed Commander Crunch before almost skipping with excitement out of the room. DZ followed him, doing his own little dance as he walked. The excitement in the air was pronounced. Before long, they would be in combat once again. Charlie was about to follow DZ when he felt a hand on his shoulder. He turned around and found himself looking at Stan.

"I have to admit, Charlie," said Stan, an eyebrow slightly raised, "I'm kind of impressed. You came up with the idea to attack an island that we know nothing about, to try to find a base guarded by Alliance members, all while trying to enlist the help of a tribe of players that are hostile to outsiders. That takes some guts to want to suggest that. I honestly never would have thought you'd want to do something like that. What changed?"

Charlie sighed, and looked Stan in the eye. "Stan, the Noctem Alliance is at war with us. They've attacked our civilians, they've lured us into traps, they killed one of our council members and friend, and they mutilated Oob and his family. The Noctem Alliance is the bane of the world of Minecraft, and if blindly invading that island is the fastest way to get rid of them, then that's what I'm doing."

And with that, Charlie shrugged off Stan's hand and walked out the door, leaving Stan flabbergasted in amazement at what his friend, whom he had once believed to be a coward, was now thinking.

CHAPTER 25
THE TWO TRIBES

Kat was sitting alone in the common room of Element Castle. The redstone lamps that lit the room had been turned off, and the windows had been closed by the Mechanist's redstone shutters. The only light in the room was the flickering glow of the fireplace, casting eerie shadows around the walls. But Kat was not focused on that. She was sitting in a comfy chair, absentmindedly running her fingers through Rex's hair and staring into the fire, reflecting on what she had just experienced.

Not for the first time, Kat and Rex had gone into the Cold Front, to an Elementia encampment located between two strategic command posts in the Ender Desert. Kat was supposed to be training privates, soldiers newly drafted into the army, for their first mission in combat. What she hadn't been expecting was a Noctem sneak attack right in the middle of the briefing.

Kat had instructed the new recruits to fall back to the encampment, only to find that the fighting was happening in there as well. A full-out battle was going on in front of the main building of the encampment, and the air around the base was clouded with dozens of hues of used splash potions. Kat had quickly ordered the terrified trainees to run to the nearest secure Elementia base, fighting off the opposition as they went. Then, she drew her sword and charged into the wave of troops coming toward them, Rex beside her. Though not totally convinced that she was capable of it, Kat had resolved to take on all the troops outside the base herself, hoping to buy the trainees time to escape.

Kat and Rex took down as many of the Noctem troops as possible, sword slashing and teeth gnawing. They greatly outmatched the black-suited soldiers in combat skills, but there were just too many of them. In the end, the Noctems had won the base, leaving the few remaining soldiers inside directing Kat to flee. She had yelled at trainees to run too. But when she did, only three of the group of thirty had followed. The others had been cut down by the Noctem Alliance.

The loss of twenty-seven players was on Kat's mind now as she watched the pixelated flames dancing in the Netherrack fire pit. Although Kat had managed to get the three trainees safely to the heavily fortified railroad base nearby, the remaining twenty-seven players, so new to the world of Elementia, were now gone from it forever.

It was at that moment that Kat had realized just what the implications of this war were. The majority of the citizens in Element City were lower-level players, and therefore, the same was true about the players who were conscripted into the war. And if Elementia was sending lower-level players into combat against the Noctem Alliance who wanted them eliminated . . . then could that possibly mean . . .

The door slammed open and Kat jumped up with a start as the Mechanist strode in. "Kat! There you are. I have some important information."

Kat reeled for a moment, shocked at being so abruptly snapped from her chain of thought, but she quickly recovered. "Okay," she said, nodding. "Lay it on me."

"Okay, but first, I have a question. Have you seen Blackraven anywhere? I need him to be here, but nobody's seen him anywhere since yesterday morning."

Kat shrugged. "I dunno. Doesn't he usually just do his own thing when he's not at the council meetings? He's probably out in the city somewhere."

The Mechanist sighed. "Well, I'm sure I'll find him soon. Anyway, on to the more pressing order of business. We just received word from the Elementia Sea Base. Stan, Charlie, DZ, and Commander Crunch have left the base and are probably on the Lesser Mushroom Island by now. The messenger reported that, tomorrow morning, they're going on a 'diplomatic tour' of the Greater Mushroom Island. And you know what that means."

"The attack is going to happen tomorrow," said Kat, in awe. It was finally happening. The Noctem Alliance was about to fall. The war was about to end. Before long, no more innocents would be killed.

"And we're going to be ready for it," the Mechanist said valiantly. "Kat, tonight, all the council members are going to suit up and join the soldiers on the two fronts. At the crack of dawn tomorrow, we're going to launch an all-out strike against all of the Noctem Alliance's strongholds simultaneously. If all goes according to plan, the Noctem Alliance's control over their territory should fall at the same time that Stan and the others take out their leaders, and the Noctem Alliance will finally be destroyed."

"I'll tell the others in the castle," said Kat as she stood up, her mind racing with all the preparations that would have to go on throughout the night. Rex leaped up too, his tail wagging in excitement. The Mechanist nodded, and with that, he rushed out the door to find Blackraven.

"Ah, th' sea," said Commander Crunch with a sigh, his eyes glazed over with wonder. "So mysterious, so beautiful. So . . . uhh . . . wet. Our tale begins in . . ."

"Uh . . . what are you talking about?" asked DZ, looking a little put off in the boat adjacent to the commander.

"Wha'?" said Commander Crunch. He had almost forgotten that anybody else was with him on the boat trip to the Lesser Mushroom Island. "Oh, uh, sorry, I lost meself thar fer a moment. But don't ye reckon 'tis beautiful?" He took a deep breath through his nose, and gave a shudder of pleasure. “Blisterin’ barnacles, I love th’ crisp smell o’ th’ salty sea air . . . th’ gentle rockin’ o’ th’ ship . . . ’n’ naught but cerulean ocean as far as th’ eye can see!”

“Uh, Commander?” interjected Charlie meekly, as if he were afraid of how the commander would respond. “We’re . . . uh . . . not in the middle of the ocean. We’re not surrounded by water as far as the eye can see. In fact . . . we’re, uh, pulling into the Mushroom Island harbor right now.”

The commander stared at Charlie, blinked twice, and looked around. In a rush, his senses returned to him, and he became aware of the two islands that sat directly in front of them. The commander finally managed to get out, “Right ye be, me lad . . . Blimey . . . How did I nah see that . . . ?”

As Commander Crunch stared at the harbor in bewilderment, Charlie turned back to look at Stan and DZ, both of whom wore expressions of exasperation equal to his own. “Are you guys sure that this is the world-famous, brilliant commander of the Sea Base that everybody always talks about?”

“Well . . . uh . . . I mean . . . ,” sputtered Stan awkwardly before finally collecting his thoughts. “Blackraven looked up a lot of specs on this guy before we chose to let him in on this plan. I mean, sure, he might be a little bit eccentric, but come on, haven’t most great minds in the history of the world been a little nuts?”

"Well, of course! I mean, look at me!" exclaimed DZ. "I'm brilliant in about every thinkable way, and I'm cr-cr-crazy!"

"Well, I guess you're right . . . ," said Charlie slowly. *Still, though*, he thought as the fleet of fourteen boats pulled into the harbor, *I'm gonna be keeping my eye on him.*

As they pulled into the harbor of the Lesser Mushroom Island, Stan was floored by how different it was from what he had imagined it. Stan knew that the island had fairly recently adopted all the luxuries of Minecraft civilization, and he had imagined an island composed of basic structures, beginning to build upward toward greater things.

What Stan had not expected to see was a full-blown city situated atop a hill, full of towering buildings made of blocks of gold, diamond, lapis lazuli, and other precious gemstones. He hadn't imagined the flashing lights that, even during the daytime, seemed to make the entire island glow with radiance. As the fleet docked in the harbor, pulling up alongside the wooden docks, Stan found that he had to shield his eyes from the blinding light from thousands of redstone lamps flashing on and off around the island. It was so bright, in fact, that Stan had to squint to see the form of a player walking down the dock toward them.

"Ah, President Stan and company!" exclaimed the player in a deep baritone, taking a small bow. Stan could see that he was dressed in shades and a tuxedo, and had a wide, very white smile. "Welcome, one and all, to the Lesser Mushroom Island, the premier locale for fun, relaxation, and enjoyment in Elementia! From our hotels to our fine eating establishments, you'll never feel more at home than you do right here! I trust that you've all had a pleasant trip?"

Sheesh, Stan thought, *what is this guy trying to sell?* "Yeah, it's been pretty good," he replied politely, before stumbling backward in surprise as Commander Crunch rushed forward.

"Sorry, laddy, but we 'ave no time fer formalities, we be on a tight schedule," the commander interjected with invigorated importance. "I trust ye know why we've come here?"

"Ah, yes, you must be the . . . eh-hem . . . famous commander of the Elementia Sea Base," replied the player, looking rather uncomfortable. He had clearly heard of Commander Crunch's peculiar tendencies before. He recovered rather quickly, though, and smiled his toothy grin once again. "Very well then, I shall be hasty. I am aware that you are here for a presidential inspection of the islands. My name is DanPitch, but you can call me Danny, and I will be your escort for as long as you are here on the Lesser Mushroom Island.

"Before we enter the island, however, I must ask why you have brought troops with you," Danny said, gesturing to the players standing behind Charlie, armed with diamond swords at their hips, bows on their back, menacing scowls on their faces. "I'm sure that you, Mr. President, are aware that, by law, no military operations are allowed on this island?"

"Shiver me timbers!" bellowed Commander Crunch in outrage, causing all in the vicinity to jump in surprise. "Be ye really so squiffy as t' reckon that we would violate that law? Do ye honestly reckon that these troops are here t' carry out some sort o' attack?"

"Dude, calm down!" cried Charlie, looking at Commander Crunch in alarm. As the commander sputtered in annoyance, Charlie calmly turned to face Danny, who was looking petrified at this maniac in his care.

"Danny, as I'm sure you know, Elementia is at war with the Nation of the Noctem Alliance. Under the constitution, the president is allowed to bring bodyguards with him for personal protection. I assure you that these soldiers," he continued, gesturing to the threatening warriors, "will not be doing any kinds of military operations while we're on these islands."

"Oh, well, that's a relief then!" exclaimed Danny, eyebrow twitching as he struggled to maintain his smile. He had clearly been shaken up by Commander Crunch's outburst. "In that case, I shall escort you to the Town Hall. Come along now, follow me!"

And with that, Danny set off down a pathway of gravel that led up the hillside and toward the city. The others followed close behind. As Stan walked, he noticed that the ground surrounding the gravel was not grass, but rather some sort of gray, stringy, fibrous material. Tiny gray particles were drifting out of the blocks and into the air, before being carried away by the wind. It gave off a somewhat earthy smell. Stan hustled to the front of the group and asked Danny what it was.

"Oh, pay no attention to that, President Stan," replied Danny hastily and with a disgusted look, as if embarrassed by the presence of the gray blocks. "That's just mycelium. It grows naturally here on the Mushroom Islands. I can assure you, though, President Stan, we're well aware of how unsightly and odorous it is, and we're doing all we can to rid our island of it."

"Really? I don't think it's that bad," replied Stan with a shrug. "And don't mushrooms grow really well on mycelium?"

Danny looked mortified, and almost offended. "I will have you know that we members of the Lesser Mushroom Tribe are a civilized people, President Stan. We refuse to lower ourselves to eating fungus off the ground, like those savages on the Greater Mushroom Island. Any and all mushrooms that we eat here are obtained in a much more refined manner, by shearing them off the Mooshrooms that call this island home. I assure you, President Stan, that when you sampled the delicious mushroom delicacies from this island, they were not made from ingredients yanked from the dirt."

Geez, thought Stan, *these guys take their image really seriously.* "But, I mean, come on!" he exclaimed. "You guys are the Mushroom Tribe, you have things here that can't be found anywhere else in Minecraft! Why aren't you proud of them?"

Danny's head slowly turned around to face Stan, though he never stopped walking forward. He had an irritated expression on his face.

"President Stan, forgive me for saying this, but you sound exactly like the savages who live on the Greater Mushroom Island. We civilized folk of the Lesser Mushroom Island used to conform to that belief as well, but we have realized that the Mushroom Islands are, in fact, a revolting and hideous place. We have evolved beyond the belief that the Mushroom Islands are sacred or even special, unlike the idealistic savages on the Lesser Island.

"Through our own hard work, we have transformed the Lesser Mushroom Island from nothing into the greatest resort town in the history of Minecraft. We have tried to talk with our brothers and sisters of the Greater Island, but they refuse to see reason. Whenever we try to help them adopt progress, they berate us, and conflict ensues. For a tribe that claims to put so much stock in the natural beauty and harmony of the world, it seems quite hypocritical that they attack us like that.

"The Mushroom Islands may be unique, an environment unlike any other in Elementia, but, just like any other environment, it is our duty to improve it, as we have done here. . . . And this is a truth that the degenerates on the Greater Island simply refuse to see."

Danny finished his response and Stan paused, not entirely sure how to respond. Thankfully, he was spared from doing so as Danny started speaking again.

"Oh my," he said, looking around as he realized they had reached the entrance to the city. "I'm sorry, President Stan, I went off on a tangent there. But anyway, we're now approaching the main street. Feel free to admire our city as you follow me."

Stan didn't have to be told twice. When they finally reached the top of the hill, he could see directly down the main street of the city that had been built on the island. The buildings stretched dozens of stories into the sky, and the precious gemstones that he had seen from the outside made up the front of the buildings as well. And it wasn't just a few buildings, either. The entire city was made out of precious mineral blocks.

There were players as well, hundreds and hundreds of players. Stan was shocked to see just how many of his citizens were either living on or visiting this island. The streets bustled with players traveling between the resorts, and there were vendors lining both sides of the streets, trying to peddle their products. Stan saw Commander Crunch giving them all pointed dirty looks.

While the city had seemed bright from the outside, now that they were in the heart of the metropolis, the blinding light outshone the sun. Everywhere you looked, redstone lamps flashed on and off, spelling out the names of casinos and hotels, with the light reflecting off the mineral blocks and becoming so bright that it made Stan's eyes water.

"This is quite an impressive town you got here," said Charlie, painfully opening his eyes to glance at Danny, who seemed unfazed, totally used to it.

"And bright, too," replied DZ, cringing even with his hands over his eyes.

"Oh, thank you," replied Danny, sounding rather bored, as if seeing tourists blinded was nothing new to him. "And don't worry about the light, your eyes will adjust soon enough. And besides, you're only here for today."

"I mean . . . just . . . ouch!" exclaimed DZ, opening his eyes to look at Danny for a moment, only to instantly squeeze them shut again. "How did you possibly manage to get all these precious materials?"

"Oh, it was quite simple, really," replied Danny, completely ignoring DZ's grunts of anguish. "You see, after we let go of our barbaric way of life and adopted modernism, we mined out the entire underside of our islands, and traded what we found in Element City in order to gain enough resources to turn our island into a resort. As people started to come to the islands, we used the revenue to improve upon what was already here, which in turn attracted more people to come and ended up giving us more profit. It's a cycle of profit, and has given us more and more power to distance ourselves from our simpleminded brothers and sisters."

"Wow," exclaimed Charlie under his breath, and Stan drew his attention away from Danny's monologue to listen. "Have you ever met somebody so snobbish?"

"Not really," exclaimed Stan with a bemused look over at Danny, who was still talking, although nobody was really listening. "I mean, he's going on about the Greater Tribesmen like they're worthless. To be honest, I think it's kind of hard to listen to."

"Testify," replied DZ, dropping his head into the conversation. "Matter of fact, I think that the idea of the Greater Tribesmen is kinda cool. You know, just some dudes and chicks living out on the island with nature and no modern stuff. Kinda reminds me of livin' out in the Ender Desert back in the days before I met you people. It was pretty sweet. I mean, don't get me wrong, I love you guys," said DZ hastily, seeing the looks on Stan's and Charlie's faces. "And that is the reason that I left, 'cause I wanted to help you free Elementia from the king. But I gotta admit, I do miss the simple life sometimes."

Charlie chuckled. "Haha, speak for yourself, DZ. I don't know about you, Stan, but I'm perfectly happy living with all the modern luxuries Minecraft has to offer. If you ask me, we've earned it." And with that, Charlie turned forward again, immediately shielding his eyes against the direct lighting. DZ was about to do the same when Stan spoke.

"Hey, DZ, I have a question."

"Shoot."

"Were you serious about wanting to go back out into the desert?"

DZ, who had been grinning since they had entered the city, suddenly faltered in expression. After a moment, he spoke. "Well, you see . . . look, Stan, it's like this. You, Charlie, Kat, and everybody else are my best friends, and it's awesome hanging out with you. And I know that you need my help to run the city and all. And even if you didn't, it's something that I really enjoy doing. I honestly love my life on this server, I really do.

"It's just . . . every now and then, I miss how simple everything was out in the desert. There was no war, no conflict, not much of anything. It was just me, by myself, living a life of solitude, and it was never boring, 'cause I was constantly fighting mobs and nomads and crap just to stay alive. And when I joined you guys, I made a conscious choice to leave that life behind in order to do the right thing.

"And a few times, I'd remember the reasons that I left the city in the first place. Like in the middle of the Battle for Elementia . . . There was a point where I couldn't fight anymore, 'cause I knew that it would only lead to more violence in the future. And it has. I mean, look what we're doing now. I realize now that it was the only way, that there are some people who only speak the language of force. But I didn't have to deal with any of that in the desert. So yeah, sometimes I wish that I could just spend, I don't know, a week or so back out there."

As DZ gave a sigh, Stan looked at his friend with a newfound respect. Stan had always known that underneath DZ's manic and hyper coating, there was a person who was very intelligent, exceptionally skilled at fighting and tactics, and an all-around great guy. But what Stan had never realized was that, even deeper than that, DZ was troubled by the state of the world around him, and constantly in an existential crisis as he tried to find his place within it. As he realized this, Stan found that he needed to understand his friend better, and he immediately knew what had to be done.

"Then go back," Stan said quietly.

DZ threw back his head and laughed. "Haha, good one, Stan. . . . Didn't you hear me just freaking say that . . ."

"No, DZ, I'm serious," said Stan. "When we get back to Elementia, I want you to take some time off, and go back out into the desert to live your old life again for a week or so."

Stan had never seen DZ as totally caught off guard as he was in that moment. His jaw dropped and his eyes flew open in a state of total shock. Finally, after a minute, DZ responded. "Are you . . . are . . . are you serious, Stan?"

"That's what you want, isn't it?"

"Yeah, more than anything, but . . ."

"And after we wipe out the Noctem Alliance, the desert's gonna have plenty of free space, right?"

"But the council needs . . ."

Now it was Stan's turn to laugh as he said, "DZ, listen, I'm the president of Elementia. If I say that you're taking a vacation, you're taking a vacation."

"Oh my God! Thank you so much, Stan!" replied DZ, elation on his face. "I can't believe it! Is there any way I can thank you?"

"Actually, there is," replied Stan with a smile. "I know this trip to the desert is something you really want, so I would completely understand and respect if you said no to this . . . But is there any way I could go out into the desert with you? To be honest, some time away from the politics and everything else once this war is over would be just what I need."

"Of course!" exclaimed DZ with a smile. "You're one of

my best friends, Stan, I'd be happy to teach you everything I know about surviving out there."

"Well, good," replied Stan as he looked DZ in the eye and returned his smile. "I look forward to it."

"So it's a deal?" asked DZ, sticking out his hand.

"Deal," replied Stan, firmly grasping DZ's hand and shaking it.

DZ opened his mouth to say something else, but before he could, they were stopped by a sudden boom.

"Halt in yer tracks!"

Immediately, Stan crashed into DZ, who crashed into Charlie, who crashed into Danny, who crashed into all the heavily armed soldiers walking in front of him, creating a haphazard pile of players. As Stan hopped to his feet, he ran up to the front of the line, seeing Commander Crunch perfectly idle and stroking his beard, a deadly serious look on his face.

"What is it?" demanded Stan in alarm.

"That feelin' . . . ," whispered the commander, uncharacteristically quiet and fearful. "I know that feelin'. . . . A feel o' bad tides ahead, a feelin' o' dread. . . ." His eyes were bulging now, his tone the highest level of urgent. Stan was terrified to hear what was causing the commander to feel such horror.

"It feels . . . like someone . . ." And then all at once, the commander whipped around behind him, diamond sword drawn, and bellowed, “wants to sell me somethin’!”

Stan let out his breath, rolled his eyes, and inspected the space where the commander was pointing. As he expected, there was nobody there. In fact, Stan noticed with exasperation, it was the only stretch of road on the entire street *not* lined with vendors.

“If you’re through with your psychotic episode,” said Stan politely, looking up at Commander Crunch, “could we be on our way now?”

“What? Oh, yes . . . er . . . of course,” replied the commander as he sulked forward, followed by a terrified Danny, and an exasperated Stan, Charlie, and rabble of soldiers. DZ was about to join the line, when out of the corner of his eye, he saw two players dressed in business suits pop their heads out of a nearby alley. They looked around nervously and then took off, running away from them. As DZ looked, he saw that they were carrying stacks of books that read *Quest for Justice: An Unofficial Minecraft-Fan Adventure.*

DZ looked confused for a moment but then shook his head, rolled his eyes, and jogged to catch up with the others.

CHAPTER 26
THE GREATER MUSHROOM ISLAND

Early the next morning, Stan's boat drifted forward, cutting sharply through the stagnant ocean water. The massive rising cliffs of the Greater Mushroom Island were silhouetted against the light blue sky of the rising sun. This morning had not been like other mornings; Stan was totally awake. He had gotten an extra-long rest last night. He was now fully awake despite the early hour, ready to take the Noctem Alliance down once and for all.

After Commander Crunch's outburst the previous day, the rest of the day on the Lesser Mushroom Island had been pretty boring. They had quickly arrived at the embassy, and Commander Crunch, DZ, and Charlie had talked with the ambassador long into the night about formalities and procedures (which Stan was frankly getting really sick of). Stan, meanwhile, had sat there, growing more and more impatient. As soon as they arrived at the high-class hotel Danny had selected for them, Stan barely had any time to admire it before he turned in, eager to get plenty of sleep for the next day.

Now that day was finally here, and at the crack of dawn, Stan, Charlie, DZ, Commander Crunch, and fifteen highly armed, specially trained task force members had climbed into their boats and set sail. They

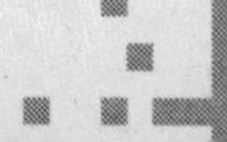

had set out across the strait of water, about fifty blocks wide, which separated the two Mushroom Islands.

The short trip was eerie. The farther they moved away from the Lesser Mushroom Island, the more the constant noise and light generated by the city faded away. And as the boat ride went on, an ominous silence became more and more pronounced, and it seemed to dominate the airspace more than noise ever could. The island's appearance only added to the foreboding atmosphere surrounding it. The land-mass was totally devoid of all human creation, leaving only a mountainside of gray-and-brown mycelium blocks dotted with tiny red and brown mushrooms. It was one of the creep-iest things Stan had ever seen, even in broad daylight.

The fifty-block boat ride was over quickly. Before Stan knew it, they had reached the shoreline of the Greater Mush-room Island. Stan looked up the cliffside. He couldn't see the sun, and the spores let off by the mycelium hung in the air, tinting the light gray. It gave the entire island a feeling of gloominess.

Stan heard a loud noise behind him and whipped around, startled. However, Stan let his breath out when he saw that the sound was nothing more than Charlie, who had come in toward the shoreline too fast, shattering his boat on contact with the mycelium coast. As a soldier helped Charlie onto the island, Stan reassured himself that one lost boat was no big deal. They had plenty of spares for just such an occasion. And, at that thought, it occurred to Stan to check his arsenal yet again before they ventured onto the island.

Stan was carrying the same gear he had worn when he engaged King Kev in combat nearly five months ago atop the Element Castle bridge. He was decked out with a diamond chestplate and helmet, and his diamond axe. Two iron axes were strapped to his back as secondary weapons should his diamond axe be lost or destroyed. Attached to his belt were Potions of Healing and Swiftness, and in his inventory sat a bow and a stack of arrows. Also within his inventory were miscellaneous items that he had on hand should something unexpected happen.

Stan looked over at his friends and comrades, and saw that they were also well-equipped. Everybody in the party wore a diamond chestplate and helmet, with the notable exception of DZ. He insisted that he not be weighed down, and only wore his leather armor emblazoned with the green Zombie team colors. DZ was equipped with no less than three swords, which he had held on to since his days in the desert and refused to upgrade: one diamond sword with no enchantments, one diamond sword with the Knockback enchantment, and one iron sword with the Fire Aspect enchantment. DZ also had a bow and arrows, as did Charlie, who himself had a diamond pickaxe on each hip. Commander

Crunch was armed with a single gleaming diamond sword, which Stan knew had a Sharpness enchantment on it, and the soldiers had a wide assortment of weapons dependent on their preferences.

As soon as everybody had disembarked from the boats, Commander Crunch whispered loudly, in a voice that was excited yet also official sounding, "President Stan, are ye ready?"

"Yes, Commander," replied Stan. "Lead the way."

And with that, Commander Crunch started walking up the side of the mycelium cliff, zigzagging to find the path of least resistance. It was a tiring climb, as the crew weaved back and forth across the one-block-high jumps that led to the top of the cliff. When Stan reached the top of the rise, he had to bow his head, breathing heavily from ten minutes of climbing straight up. When he finally did look up, he gasped, amazed at the landscape before him.

While it hadn't been apparent from the shore, Stan could now see that the entire Greater Mushroom Island formed a sort of bowl, with mountains rising in a circle around the island coast and a flat plain in the middle of the ring of cliffs. The entire ground was totally covered in gray-and-brown mycelium, with pools of water, and occasionally lava, punctuating the plains. From high above, Stan could see red animals wandering around the plains, which he could only assume were the Mooshrooms.

But what caught Stan off guard most of all were the mushrooms. There were mushrooms of the tiny red and brown variants dotting the mycelium as far as the eye could see. Stan had expected that. What he had not expected to see were the giant mushrooms, dozens of blocks high, which rose up out of the mycelium across the entire island, like trees in a forest. These mushrooms also had brown and red variants, but were significantly different from one another. The red types seemed to be slightly more common than the brown. They were about the same size and shape as a house in an NPC village, with red mushroom blocks dotted with white spots forming an overhang over a thick white stalk. The brown mushrooms were much taller than the red ones, and instead of hanging down like the red ones, the brown mushrooms featured a single platform of brown mushroom blocks that sat atop a huge, one-block-thick white stalk.

Stan only had a few seconds to take in this amazing, unique landscape before he heard the powerful voice of Commander Crunch.

"Ok, that's enough, scallywags, stop gawkin' at th' island. Ye'll 'ave plenty o' time t' do that as we be walkin', which we'll 'ave t' do handsomely if we be t' reach th' Greater Tribesmen by nightfall."

"Wait," said Stan, confused, "I thought that we didn't

have any idea where the Greater Tribesmen were, so how do you know where to walk?"

"Oh fer th' love o' Davy Jones's locker, me lad . . . I mean, President Stan," bellowed the commander in exasperation. "Weren't ye listenin' at all durin' th' meetin' last night? Ne'er mind," he said sourly, shaking his head in disdain, as Stan feebly opened his mouth to respond. "I know th' answer, so I guess I'll tell ye again.

"We dunno where they be, but th' ambassador thinks that, since th' Greater Tribesmen hate th' light 'n' sound that comes from th' Lesser Island, they will likely be at th' far end o' th' island, 'n' since they've been fightin' wit' th' Lesser Tribe, I reckon that th' Greater Tribesmen will prolly be livin' on th' high ground somewhere. So, all thin's considered, I reckon that they be prolly on or around that peak o'er thar."

Commander Crunch pointed his grimy, blocky finger up toward a mountain at the far end of the Mushroom Island. It was the highest point as far as the eye could see, and situated on top of a plateau. Stan was impressed. The commander may have been insane, but this was a pretty good deduction.

"Now, if thar ain't any more ignorance t' deal wit', let's go, we be wastin' daylight! *Mountain, ho!*" cried Commander Crunch, his voice reverberating around the cliffs as he marched down into the bowl at a brisk pace, which the others had to hustle to keep up with.

Stan found it ironic, and slightly annoying, that although Commander Crunch was constantly yelling scorn back at them, such as "Faster, ye dirty bunch o' landlubbers," the one time that they stopped on the way to the mountain was on Commander Crunch's behalf. This was when they passed a herd of Mooshrooms, and Stan got a good look at the cow-like creatures for the first time.

The Mooshrooms were essentially the same size and shape as cows, and they made the same noises, but that was where the similarities ended. The Mooshrooms had a cowlike pattern of color, but were bloodred where the brown should be. Red-and-white-dotted mushrooms sprouted up out of the creatures' backs and appeared to be growing directly into the animal itself. But what Stan found creepiest were the eyes. The eyes of the Mooshrooms were pure black, and had a dead and glazed-over look to them. It seemed to Stan almost as if the mind of the animal was being controlled by the fungus, as opposed to its own volition, as he saw no life in those black, empty eyes.

Commander Crunch, apparently, saw these disturbing-looking creatures as the absolutely perfect way to cut their journey to the mountain in half. Convinced that it was the best option, Commander Crunch wasted a half hour of their time trying to mount one of the Mooshrooms and ride it like a horse, despite repeated protests by the others that it was a waste of time. Eventually, after the twelfth time that Commander Crunch was bucked off the Mooshroom, he finally screeched at the herd, "Fine, then! Be that way!" His face was red, possibly with embarrassment, but more likely with genuine rage. "Ye're a bunch o' dirty, squiffy beasts anyway! We can get thar perfectly fine without ye!"

"As we've been telling you for the last half hour," mumbled DZ under his breath in disgust.

"Honestly," said Charlie, shaking his head as he whispered to Stan and DZ, "doesn't he have to be stupid somewhere else?"

"Nah till four, Charlie," replied Commander Crunch with a sly grin, apparently having overheard them.

And with that, Commander Crunch walked on. Stan, DZ, and Charlie looked at one another incredulously for a moment, before determining simultaneously and wordlessly that it wasn't worth questioning, and they followed.

By the time the episode with the Mooshrooms was over, they were about halfway across the plains, and the sun was starting to dip into the afternoon position. As they trekked on, Stan felt increasingly anxious. There were giant mushrooms everywhere, far more imposing now than they had seemed on the cliffs. He had difficulty keeping himself from imagining Greater Tribesmen jumping out from behind every stalk, bent on taking them hostage. The terror of running into the tribesmen in this way only added to the eerie environment of the island, alongside the spore mist that hung in the air and the odd stretchy sound that the mycelium made underfoot.

Stan's only consolation was that the Noctem Alliance was about to go down for good. Based on some calculations run by the Mechanist, they had determined that all of the Noctem Alliance's available forces were now fighting on either the Hot Front or the Cold Front. That meant that, while the higher-ups of the Noctem Alliance were indeed hiding on the island somewhere, they would likely have no guards, and would be forced to take on Stan and his men themselves. The fight would no doubt be difficult, as Caesar, Minotaurus, and presumably Count Drake would be there, all of whom were exceptionally powerful fighters. And Stan still wasn't sure what to expect from Lord Tenebris.

In any case, though, they had a team of nineteen highly skilled fighters on their way to fight what was probably a team of eight or nine. They had the element of surprise as well. The odds of victory were definitely in their favor.

And that was just here, fighting the leaders of the Noctem Alliance. As they were walking, all the leaders of Elementia were launching an all-out attack with the full force of the Elementia army on both fronts. If all went according to plan, by the end of the day, the Noctem Alliance's leaders would be dead, and the war would be won on both fronts. In fact, with any luck . . .

"Halt!"

The sudden shout from up front snapped Stan out of his thoughts. He jolted to a stop, nearly crashing into DZ and Charlie, while the special forces came screeching to a stop behind him. Stan furiously marched his way up to the front of the pack, where Commander Crunch was still frozen in place with his blocky hand raised.

"You'd better have a good reason for stopping . . . ," Stan started to spit out, but he was unable to finish when he saw what was in front of them.

They had walked all the way across the valley without Stan even realizing it. Now they stood atop the plateau, with the peak of the mountain high above them, and the sun setting over the panoramic ocean view behind them. Scattered between the giant mushrooms stood a crowd of players, all staring at Stan and his crew with horror, surprise, and contempt.

There were about fifty players, and it seemed they hadn't seen civilization in quite some time. All of them were covered in a thin layer of spore powder. Many of them held bowls in their hands, some of which were filled with a brown liquid that Stan could only assume was mushroom stew. However, twenty of the players were empty handed. Far from looking shocked and horrified, they stood in fighting stances. Stan didn't imagine that they would be able to stand up to any player with a weapon. However, he still didn't want to fight, so he willed himself to remain calm.

A single player walked forward. He was skinned identically to Stan, but his entire outfit was darker. The expression on his face was that of disapproval of the highest degree.

"Who are you people?" the player demanded, quietly yet more powerful than a yell. "Why do you come to our island with weapons?"

Stan stepped forward, mustered up his courage, and, after clearing his throat, spoke. "My name is Stan2012, and I am the president of the Grand Republic of Elementia. I am here on a Presidential Visit to inspect your island."

Sounds of outrage erupted all throughout the crowd.

"And you brought troops with you? It is illegal for you to carry out military operations on our island, President Stan," seethed the player, his eyebrow twitching. "In the name of the Greater Mushroom Tribe, of which I am the chief, I demand that you and your cohorts leave immediately, or we will be forced to take action against you."

And with that, the twenty fighters closed in on Stan and his friends, their blocky fingers clenched into fists. Stan wasn't sure what to make of this. Did they honestly think they could take them in a fight, unarmed? Commander Crunch surged forward in a rage.

"Ye idiotic savages! I'll 'ave ye know that under th' law . . ."

"Commander, calm down," said DZ, grabbing Commander Crunch by the arm and throwing him backward as the eyebrows of the chief knitted and a scowl crossed his face. "Let me handle this." And with that, DZ stepped forward to address the chief face-to-face.

"Honorable Chief of the Greater Mushroom Tribe, we ain't gonna carry out any type of military operation on this island. The Mushroom Islands are still part of the republic, I'm sure you know that, and so President Stan has the right to carry troops with him here, especially in a time of war."

"What war?" demanded the chief, his eyebrows shooting up as whispers suddenly broke out in the group of tribesmen. "What are you talking about?"

"The Republic of Elementia has been fighting against a terrorist group called the Noctem Alliance for the past month. They have attacked us on multiple fronts, and we are engaged in an all-out war with them."

"And what does that have to do with us?" asked the chief skeptically.

"Well, we have reason to believe that the leaders of this group, the Noctem Alliance, have been hiding on the Mushroom Islands. We have already conducted a search of the

Lesser Mushroom Island, and we found nothing."

"You are being deceived!" exclaimed the chief as mutters of disparagement and disgust broke out. "If there is an evil organization present in these islands, then it is being harbored by those ignorant, materialistic demons on the Lesser Island! They are lying, no-good animals who snuck away from us, and have destroyed the sanctity of the Lesser Mushroom Island for nothing more than the evils of capital gain and greed! Surely, such a despicable agenda would go hand-in-hand with an organization bent on taking over this server! And furthermore . . ."

"Enough!" cried Charlie, cutting off the chief's tirade. "Look," he continued, once the chief had finally stopped breathing heavily from his rant, "it's not the place of the president, or the republic, to get involved in quarrels between you and the Lesser Tribesmen. But it is our job to destroy the Noctem Alliance. The organization is sly and devious, and isn't afraid to use tactics like sneak attacks and Potions of Invisibility to win the war. The Noctem Alliance is determined to destroy everything that we hold dear, and it will surely come after both Mushroom Islands next if it is not destroyed.

"All we are asking is for your help to find out if there are any members of the Noctem Alliance hiding on this island. If there are, then we'll get rid of them, and if there aren't, then nothing changes. Do we have an understanding?"

The chief threw back his head and gave a dry laugh. "Ha! Of course we have an understanding. We're not like those traitors on the Lesser Island, oh no, we respect our president and share your enemy as our own. We actually have integrity. And actually, now that you describe this . . . Noctem Alliance . . . to me, I think they might be here, and I can point you to where."

Stan's heart lifted, and he stepped forward to join the conversation. "Really? That would be hugely helpful. What do you know?"

A shadow crossed the chief's face, accentuated by the sun finally dipping behind the horizon, bringing darkness to the world around him.

"Many of my people have reported unnatural disturbances to me, all of which come from there, President Stan," the chief said solemnly, and Stan's line of sight followed the chief's pointing finger to the top of the peak rising high above the plateau. "Atop Mount Fungarus, there have been troubling signs. Loud noises of an unnatural sort. And on that cliff that you can see right beside the cave entrance, a sort of . . . shimmering . . . that we have only hypothesized to be some sort of glitch, or perhaps something more."

TNT, thought Stan gravely, *and Potions of Invisibility.* The Specialty Base had been constructed up there, by hollowing out the top of that mountain.

"Many of us have wanted to go up and explore that cave atop Mount Fungarus," the chief continued. "However, we have not found it wise. Throughout our fighting with the monsters of the Lesser Tribe, we Greater Tribesmen have developed great unarmed player-to-player combat skills, developing the style to the point where we are able to fight unarmed to the level of master swordsmen." *Well*, thought Stan, *that explains a lot*.

"However, in the dark of the cave, monsters will spawn. Evil mobs cannot spawn on mycelium, and so we, on the Greater Island, have never had to deal with them. This also means, however, that we are not skilled at combating them, and so we have seen fit to avoid the darkness of the cave altogether."

"Thank you, Chief," said Stan, stepping forward and extending his hand, which the chief tentatively shook. "Thanks to you, we'll be able to take down the Noctem Alliance quickly, and we'll be out of your hair."

"Chief," said Commander Crunch in businesslike fashion, "I suggest that ye evacuate yer scallywags from th' area. Thar's a good chance that they will try t' escape, 'n' if they do, then we do nah want any hands o' yer tribe gettin' hurt."

The chief nodded and gave a grunt of assent, before turning to face his people, who had been listening to their conversation with a mixture of awe and confusion. He briefly explained the situation to them, and ordered them to move down the mountainside. Within minutes, the plateau was cleared, and the Greater Tribesmen were nothing more than specks down in the valley below.

Stan looked away from the tribesmen and over at his men. Charlie, DZ, and Commander Crunch were staring at him, deadly serious looks on their faces. The fifteen men huddled behind them wore the same expression.

"It's time, isn't it," said Stan, after a deep breath. It wasn't a question. They all knew what was about to happen.

"Yes, sir, it is," replied DZ. He looked around at everybody. "Is everyone ready?"

Eighteen heads nodded as one.

"Ender Pearls at th' ready!" ordered Commander Crunch, and, in one motion, nineteen Ender Pearls were pulled out of inventories and sat in their respective owners' hands.

"All right," ordered Stan in tones of steel. "Let's finish this."

And, in one motion, he pitched the Ender Pearl as hard as he could toward the sky, aiming at the slight outcrop of rock directly outside the cave near the peak of Mount Fungarus. As soon as he did so, there was a flailing of limbs and arms as eighteen more Ender Pearls were pitched sky high. Stan closed his eyes and prepared himself. After a moment, Stan felt his feet leave the ground as he rushed through space at breakneck speeds until his feet finally hit stone.

CHAPTER 27
THE TRAITORS

Stan's first realization atop the stone platform was a feeling of déjà vu, as immediately after he landed, all he was aware of were the projectiles flying all around him, bouncing off his chestplate and helmet. It was all Stan could do to sprawl to the pressure plate–covered ground and bellow "HIT THE DIRT!" repeatedly as loud as he could, hoping that the others would be able to duck in time to avoid the barrage of arrows. Indeed, the air was soon punctuated by the sounds of teleportation, shouts of pain, and players dropping to the ground all rolled together into a wild cacophony.

Stan looked up toward the source of the fire. He saw that the entire group had landed on a grid of pressure plates, and he noticed the redstone wire that ran across the ground toward a row of arrow dispensers. In one quick motion, Stan awkwardly dragged the blade of his axe across the ground, severing the glowing redstone dust lines from the dispensers and cutting off the entire flow of arrows instantly.

Stan pulled himself up off the ground, aware of the constant clicking noise being generated from the pressure plate–covered ground around him. As he looked around, Stan saw that, to his relief, there had been no serious injuries from the trap, with the

diamond armor taking most of the damage. Only one of the soldiers had taken an arrow to his knee, and he quickly remedied the injury with a Potion of Healing.

As the group recovered, Commander Crunch walked up to the front of the pack. After glaring into the mouth of the cave for a moment, he gestured them forward. As Stan began to walk into the cave, axe now drawn, he noticed very quickly that this was not a normal cave. Immediately past the mouth, the cave entrance suddenly became very square shaped, with cobblestone patching up certain places in the otherwise pure stone wall. Furthermore, Stan could see a light at the far end of the tunnel, growing brighter and brighter the farther they walked. His heart began to race. They were getting close.

Every soldier had his eyes peeled and was scrutinizing every nook and cranny of their surroundings, on high alert to detect any more booby traps. Commander Crunch seemed to be particularly finicky, twitching around as he surveyed the premises. The walk down the squared-off cave went off without a hitch, however, and the group soon reached the source of the light.

As Stan looked around the brightly lit room, he was incredibly unnerved by the lack of anything of interest. The room was large and shaped like a cube, with a five-block drop down from where they were standing to the floor of the cube. The ceiling was high, and the entire cubic room was lined with torches. There was one element, however, that immediately caught everybody's attention: two cobblestone staircases, at both of the back two corners of the room, that led out of sight.

Stan looked over at the others. DZ and Charlie looked bewildered, while Commander Crunch leaned over to Stan and whispered in his ear, "We needs somebody t' go down thar 'n' see if th' coast be clear."

Stan opened his mouth instinctively to protest, but then closed it. The commander was right after all. As much as Stan hated throwing one of his soldiers under the bus, he knew that somebody would have to go down there first, at the very real risk that they could die instantly. Stan accepted with a heavy heart that, though he would gladly go down himself in their place, as president, he was too important to do something so risky.

And so Stan nodded his head and looked at his men. All of them showed expressions of grim determination, showing that they all seemed up to the task. And so Stan pointed at the soldier nearest to him and said, "You, go down there and scout out the scene."

The soldier stepped forward and nodded. Stan couldn't remember what this soldier's name was. He thought maybe it was Josh, but he couldn't remember clearly. This player had pale skin and brown hair, and the little bit of his shirt visible under his armor revealed a red shirt with a *Star Trek* logo on it. The soldier stepped forward to the edge of the ledge. He took a deep breath, drew his diamond pickaxe, and jumped down the five-block drop to the ground.

The instant the soldier landed, there was a rapid series of clicks and whirs, and the wall with the staircases in them opened up, revealing a window. In a flash, a whirling blue blur flew out of the window, and before the soldier could even react, the flying diamond sword knocked the soldier to the ground. Three arrows flew from the window and found their way into the soldier, the last of which caused a ring of items to burst out around him.

Stan's emotions were on a roller coaster in a matter of seconds. He was livid that his soldier had fallen and furiously wanted revenge. At the same time, though, he was relieved that this member of the Noctem Alliance, shrouded in shadows, wasn't particularly skilled, having killed the soldier in such a clumsy way. Then, after a click, the lights illuminated in the window to reveal the smug face of Caesar laughing. Stan was a little surprised that Caesar had had to knock the soldier down in order to get a clean shot at him, but this emotion was drowned out by the beast in Stan's chest roaring in simultaneous triumph for finding Caesar, and hatred and desire to take him down.

"Well, well, well," simpered Caesar in his upper-class accent. "It's nice to see that you've finally decided to show up. Minotaurus!" he suddenly shouted. "They're here!"

Another series of clicks and whirs, and out of the wall underneath the window opened a hole two blocks wide and three blocks high, out of which burst Minotaurus in all of his giant, muscular terror, double-bladed diamond axe in hand. "Oh yeah!" he bellowed. "I'm ready to fight!"

Another equally powerful wave of rage crashed into Stan like a locomotive. Caesar may have been the mastermind and organizer of the Noctem Alliance, and he may have caused the deaths of Archie and hundreds of other Elementia citizens with his terror attacks and his war, but Minotaurus had taken Sally away from him. Now, on a fair playing field, it was time for Stan to take his revenge.

"We have no time for your games, Caesar!" bellowed DZ across the courtyard, a vein pulsating in his forehead. "Come down here and fight us like a man!"

"Oh, I don't think that will be necessary," replied Caesar, in an infuriatingly mundane voice. "You see, I am simply the tactician of the Nation of the Noctem Alliance. Minotaurus is the powerhouse. If you'd like to fight, he will be more than happy to oblige you," to which Minotaurus gave a wildly enthusiastic nod. "However, I will tell you now that you will have to get through both of us if you wish to challenge Lord Tenebris."

"Har har! So that's yer great last stand?" Commander Crunch laughed, mockery dripping from his voice. "Fightin' us all by yourself 'n' alone?"

Caesar then proceeded to give the most maniacal, evil laugh Stan had ever heard, which made his blood curdle, before responding, slyly and slowly. "My dear Commander . . . whoever said that we were alone?"

All at once, Stan suddenly found himself flying forward with no warning and no explanation. He teetered for a moment before tumbling head over heels toward the stone courtyard, his arms flailing in panic. He landed with a thud on the stone floor, and a lightning bolt of pain shot through his body for an instant, leaving a slight ache behind. The sounds of moaning and groaning around him suggested that he had not been the only one to fall, and a quick look around confirmed this. His entire team now lay on the ground in various states of disrepair, struggling to get back on their feet. Stan was flabbergasted. How had they been pushed down there? But then, within the next ten seconds, it all clicked into place, and in Stan's mind, everything made terrible, horrific sense.

All around the perimeter of the room, players were appearing in poofs of purple smoke, and when the smoke cleared, Stan recognized the spore-coated and empty-handed fighters of the Greater Mushroom Tribe, all staring directly at Stan and his men. Stan then watched as an Ender Pearl flew directly over his head and landed in front of Minotaurus, and in a puff of smoke, the chief of the Greater Tribesmen appeared, a grim sneer on his face.

"Are you ready?" the chief yelled up to Caesar as Stan and his teams stood paralyzed with white shock.

"Attack at will," Caesar replied, almost lazily.

And with that, all fifty members of the Greater Mushroom Tribe charged forward, converging toward Stan and his men.

Stan found no need to order his men to counterattack. At that moment, every member of Stan's team had one thought and one thought alone: it was time for these unarmed traitors to die.

As the blades came out and the members of the task force started to gang up on everybody two-to-one, Stan set his sights on Minotaurus, who was charging into battle with his axe spinning like a sideways helicopter rotor. Right as Stan was about to catch up to Minotaurus, though, a punch from somewhere to his right slammed into Stan's head. He reeled for a moment, and wildly swung his axe to the side, forcing the Greater Tribesmen's chief to hop backward away from him. The two simultaneously recovered, and their eyes locked.

"What do you think you're doing?" bellowed Stan in fury.

"You said you were on our side!"

"Well, I'm sorry, President Stan, I truly am," replied the chief, bouncing back and forth on the balls of his feet while he cracked his knuckles. "But that's just the way it is. You have your agenda to keep, and I have mine!" And on the last word, he threw another punch at Stan's head, which Stan quickly ducked under and counterattacked with the axe.

Stan fought his hardest, determined to make the chief pay for his betrayal, but he had never fought anybody like this before. It was well known that Stan was by far the best axe fighter on the server now, but the large weapon with far range seemed to be countered quite nicely by the chief's empty-handed fighting style. Stan's blows were fast, hard, and accurate, but the chief always managed to slip in through the tiniest cracks in Stan's offense and land a punch or kick on some part of his body.

Try as he might to fight, the chief was too evasive for Stan to hit, and the constant barrage of landed kicks and punches were wearing Stan down quickly. All it took was one slow attack and the chief's foot launched Stan's axe into the air, and another square punch to the face sent Stan flying across the room, landing beside his weapon.

As Stan's dizziness from the blow subsided, he could make out the chief sprinting toward him, his blocky hand raising a fist for a final blow. As quickly as he could, Stan swigged a Potion of Healing from his belt, feeling instantly better, and he scrambled across the ground to retrieve his axe. Before the inevitable barrage of kicks and punches could land, however, Stan heard a grunt of pain from behind him.

He snatched up his axe and spun around, only to see Charlie, now fighting the chief. Stan watched the fighting for a moment and saw that Charlie's pickaxe was able to get in quickly and effectively. In fact, Charlie's fighting style was similar to empty-handed combat, with the diamond pick as an enhancer. No sooner had Stan thought this than Charlie's pickaxe grazed the chief across the arm, and one kick in the stomach later the chief was in a crumpled pile on the ground. Aware that he was being watched, Charlie wiped his brow, whipped around, and addressed Stan.

"Your axe isn't a good match up to their style, Stan! We'll take care of them, you take down Caesar and then Minotaurus!" Charlie jabbed his finger over to the corner of the room, and then rushed back in to finish off the chief.

Stan looked where Charlie was pointing. He noticed Caesar sitting up in his window, watching the battle with glee, while below him, the two staircases stood completely unguarded. *This is my chance!* Stan thought triumphantly as he sprinted toward the stairs. *I can catch Caesar off guard and finally take him down!* Stan ran as fast as he could, and was about to climb onto the first step when suddenly, another player emerged from the stairwell, blocking his way.

Stan was too stunned to do anything. He couldn't believe what he was seeing. He knew this player, quite well, actually. He easily recognized the black body, beady white eyes, and splash of yellow on his face. Stan was barely able to speak, he was so confused.

"Blackraven, wha . . . *oof*!"

Blackraven had whipped a diamond sword out of his inventory and had struck it across Stan's chest.

The diamond armor absorbed the hit, and the blow only caused Stan to stagger backward. But the mental shock of processing what had just happened was too much for Stan to handle. His battle instincts told him to raise his axe to counter two more swings, and to swing back in retaliation, causing Blackraven to feint backward, but he still couldn't work out why.

"Blackraven . . . ," said Stan, dazed. "What . . . what the . . . what are you doing?"

And then, for some inexplicable, horrible reason, Blackraven gave an evil grin and replied, "Something that I've wanted to do for a very, *very* long time, Stan."

And with that, Blackraven lunged forward, his sword outstretched and his eyes blazing with fire.

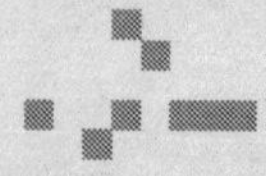

As determined as Caesar was to oversee this battle like the dignified leader he was, he couldn't help but laugh merrily when he saw Stan and Blackraven fighting. Stan was completely, horrifically astounded. Caesar had been waiting for months to see how Stan would react when he finally found out that Blackraven had been the spy in the midst of the council, and this reaction was everything Caesar could have hoped for.

Caesar readily admitted that Stan was one of the most dangerous fighters in Elementia, or even in the whole of Minecraft. But his complete and utter shock at seeing Blackraven's true nature had caught Stan completely off guard. It was a testament to Stan's skill that he was able to repel Blackraven's full-on attack, even when it seemed that his defense was almost robotic, like he was too stunned to defend himself properly. But soon enough, Blackraven would break him, and Stan2012 would finally be handed over to Lord Tenebris.

As Caesar inspected the courtyard, he saw, to his delight, that the other fights were going equally well. The task force had never expected, and could never have prepared for, a fight against the best hand-to-hand combatants in the server. Several of the president's so-called "handpicked task force" had already fallen, and the remaining soldiers were quickly becoming overrun by the sheer number of tribesmen. Even that stupid brute Minotaurus was managing to be useful. He was engaging DieZombie97 with apparent ease, despite the fact that the acclaimed Spleef champion was dual-wielding.

Caesar was beside himself. This operation had gone perfectly from start to finish, from the second Blackraven had told him about the incoming task force, to the battles that they were primed to win handily. *Pat yourself on the back, Caesar,* he thought with satisfaction. *You've done well.*

The slam of a door behind Caesar snapped him out of his blissful train of thought. Caesar turned around, locked on the player in the doorway, and his eyes widened in surprise and ire.

"Leonidas? What are you doing . . . What in the—"

Caesar was forced to dodge quickly to the side as an arrow flew from Leonidas's bow, coming within inches of Caesar's shoulder. Caesar whipped back with an iron sword drawn to face Leonidas, who had notched another arrow and was holding it steady.

"What do you think you're doing? Have you gone mad, man?"

"No," replied Leonidas. His tone was merciless and his eyes cold, dark, and furious. "I came to my senses."

And with that, a flurry of arrows began to fly from Leonidas's bow, straight at a terrified Caesar.

"You seem . . . surprised . . . to see me . . . Stan," said Blackraven almost casually as he swung his diamond sword back and forth. The hint of demonic pleasure in his voice as he spoke was what finally snapped Stan out of his stupor and allowed him to speak.

"So . . . so . . . it's you?" Stan said, not believing what was coming out of his mouth as he blocked Blackraven's attacks. "You . . . you're the spy?"

"Catching on rather slowly, are we?" said Blackraven with an amused snicker. "It doesn't surprise me. You're not a very intelligent person, Stan, if the way that you've been running Elementia is any indication."

"What are you . . . ?" asked Stan drearily. It seemed almost surreal that he was having this conversation at all, let alone having it in the middle of a fight.

"You had the potential to make Elementia great, Stan," said Blackraven, suddenly sounding angry to an alarming degree. "But you squandered that potential, just because of your incessant need to protect lower-level players!"

Stan still didn't know what Blackraven was talking about, but that last sentence made something snap within Stan. Now, he was glad he had his axe in hand, not to defend . . . but to kill. Suddenly, and without warning, Stan gave a savage war cry as he shifted into attack mode. His axe flew fast and furious, jabbing, cutting, swiping, glancing hit after hit onto Blackraven's diamond chestplate. It only took a few seconds before Blackraven was on the ground, his sword clattering away. Stan stood over him and was about to drop the axe into Blackraven's chest when he suddenly gave a shout.

This shout was an odd, indescribable noise, and it was so peculiar that Stan was distracted by it for a moment, only to have Blackraven leap to his feet and punch Stan in the face. He spun around, in a daze yet again, and became vaguely aware of Blackraven pouring something down his throat before barreling toward Stan. Stan raised his axe to attack, but Blackraven was already upon him, and had pinned him to the ground.

Stan struggled to move, and saw that Blackraven had wisps of blue smoke curling off his body. A Potion of Swiftness. As he became aware of that, Stan also became aware of gray smoke pouring out of the walls and spreading over the battlefield. Immediately, he panicked. It was a cloud of Potion of Slowness, sure to knock him out. He immediately grabbed a Potion of Swiftness from his hip, but Blackraven was too fast and knocked it to the floor, shattering it. There was nothing Stan could do. He only had an instant to freak out before the cloud rolled over him, and his last vision was of Blackraven, pinning him down and leering at him.

It was all Caesar could do to dodge the constant stream of arrows that came shooting rapid-fire out of Leonidas's bow. He was too shocked to think, but he tried to remember anyway. There was a technique for approaching an archer with a sword, but what was it? Caesar couldn't remember. He hadn't been on the battlefield for so long.

"Why have you betrayed me, Leonidas?" Caesar demanded desperately, ducking behind a wood plank block on the floor to catch his breath for a moment. "Surely you know that, if you strike me down, you shall bear the full weight of the retribution of Lord Tenebris?"

As Caesar said this, he heard Blackraven's signal from outside the window. As luck would have it, he was crouching right next to the activation lever. Caesar yanked down on it hastily before turning his attention back to Leonidas.

"I'm not afraid to die, Caesar," Leonidas retorted, sending an arrow toward Caesar's leg, which he just barely managed to move in time, "because if I do, it'll still be ten times better than bein' in the Noctem Alliance."

"How . . . how can you say that?" Caesar breathed in horror. "How can you bear to speak ill of the greatest organization in the history of Minecraft!"

"Oh! I don't know!" bellowed Leonidas, a vein pulsating in his head as he sprinted over to the block Caesar was hiding behind and stared down at the Noctem chancellor with venom. "Why don't ya ask . . . the prisoners' village!" And on the last word, he let the arrow fly at Caesar, who managed to roll out of the way with a look of pure fear streaming down his face.

Leonidas refused to let up the barrage, and notched another arrow. "Or ask the people at the Tennis Machine!" And another arrow flew. "Or the Spleef finals!" Another arrow flew. Leonidas took a deep breath and locked onto his target, who was desperately sprinting for the door.

"Or how about . . . *the NPC village*!"

Suddenly, Caesar felt a stabbing pain as the final arrow found its way into his arm, and he fell to the ground, bellowing in agony. Soon, two more arrows followed, followed by a constant barrage of arrows, all sinking, one by one, into Caesar.

Leonidas slowly walked over to Caesar, an arrow notched in his bow. He became vaguely aware of a cloud of vapor rising into the air surrounding the battlefield outside the window, but chose to ignore it, instead reveling in the sweet taste of victory and justice. The head of the Noctem Alliance, who had organized the murder of the prison villagers, the Elementian citizens, and his family, the NPC villagers, was now chock-full of arrows, looking up at him feebly. Nothing in the world could spoil this moment.

There was one thing left to do, though, before putting Caesar out of his misery. Leonidas crouched down next to Caesar's trembling body and said, "I have to admit, Caesar, I'm a little bit surprised that ya didn't put up more of a fight.

I thought ya were supposed to be a world-class swordsman. Ya know, maybe I can say this in a different way . . . a way you'd be more familiar with. . . . Oh, I know!"

And with that, Leonidas stood up, pulled back the string of his bow, and took aim.

"You've disappointed me," Leonidas said simply.

And with that, he let the arrow fly.

There was a moment of silence, the airspace filled only by a hissing sound coming from outside the mechanized window. Sweat dripping down his face and adrenaline coursing through his veins, Leonidas glanced out the window.

A cloud of gray gas had filled the air around the battlefield, and was hanging in the air throughout the cave. Leonidas could see the unconscious forms of Stan, Charlie, DieZombie97, five members of their task force, and thirty members of the Lesser Mushroom Tribe lying spread out across the battlefield. Only three figures remained standing, all of them having wisps of blue smoke rising from their bodies. Minotaurus was conversing with Blackraven and the chief, but when Leonidas glanced at him, he seemed to sense it, and returned the glance.

Leonidas froze for a moment, staring back into the eyes of Minotaurus. There was a long pause, where the two comrades who had worked together for months under the ruthless eye of Caesar held their gaze. Then . . .

"Look! Up in the window!" bellowed Minotaurus, his deep baritone echoing around the chamber. "It's Leonidas! He's not supposed to be here!"

Blackraven and the chief whipped their heads around to face Leonidas, and their eyes popped. Then, Blackraven shouted a command, and the three players rushed toward the stairwells.

Leonidas cursed under his breath. In his ecstasy over the death of Caesar, he had grown careless and let himself be seen! Now they would all know who had killed their leader, and Leonidas would become the most hunted player in the whole of Elementia. Leonidas didn't let himself dwell on it, though. He couldn't take on all three of them at once—he had to escape. He told himself that, as he fled, he would think of some way to gain the trust of Stan and his army, and fight back against Lord Tenebris.

And with that, Leonidas spun around, opened the wooden door that he himself had closed just moments before, and ran out of the room.

CHAPTER 28
ATOP MOUNT FUNGARUS

"So his death was, admittedly, quite unexpected."

"That's very unfortunate. You will find the one responsible, I assume?"

"As a matter of fact, we know who is responsible. . . . It was one of our own, who turned on us. He will be brought to justice soon, I assure you."

"Hmmm . . ."

Stan's eyes fluttered as he began to stir. His brain still felt the effects of the Potion of Slowness on the battlefield. He became aware of voices relatively close to him.

"Once again, I would like to thank you for your help, my friend. This would not have been possible without you."

"Do not call me your friend, Blackraven . . ."

That name caught Stan's ear, and instantly, his head felt much clearer. Stan opened his eyes and saw that he was sitting in a tiny cobblestone cell, barely large enough to stand in. He was sprawled out on the floor, his head against an iron door. Beyond the iron door, voices spoke in hushed tones. The voice of the chief of the Greater Tribesmen continued.

". . . we are on uneven terms, and we will continue to be until you hold up your end of the deal."

"Don't fret, my esteemed Chief. It is being attended

to. As we speak, an entire legion of the Noctem Alliance's finest troops is headed this way, bound for the Lesser Mushroom Island."

Stan's stomach clenched, and he began to sweat in panic as he continued to listen.

"Once they arrive, we will help you overthrow the police and declare martial law on the island. The Noctem Alliance will capture the citizens of Element City still on the Lesser Island and hold them hostage. Then, the Lesser Tribesmen are yours to do with as you choose."

"I can't wait. Those traitors have had it coming to them for a long time."

"If you would like, Chief, the Noctem Alliance would be happy to destroy the city. I know that it is your wish to return the islands to their rightful state of nature, and as your newfound allies, it would only be right for us to help you."

"Thank you, Blackraven. That would be very helpful to us."

"It is my pleasure, friend. Now please do me a favor and see how your men are faring down below. I have a feeling that our captives will be awakening soon."

"Yes, sir," replied the chief, and Stan heard a pair of footsteps grow fainter and fainter.

Stan continued to lay on the ground for a few minutes. His heart was racing as he processed what he had just heard, but he was determined not to reveal himself. Blackraven had assumed that he had been unconscious. Stan wouldn't let him know he had heard such valuable information.

Finally, after about five minutes, Stan pulled himself up to his knees, and then to his feet. He could now see a set of iron bars on the back wall of the cell, behind which were blue skies and clouds. He was clearly high up in the sky. Then, Stan turned around. He stared through the small window atop the iron door, and the beaked face of Blackraven was staring back at him.

"Hello, Stan," said Blackraven with a devious smile.

Stan did not respond. All he could do was stare Blackraven down through the iron cross over the window, daggers of contempt shooting from his eyes.

"I see that you're awake," Blackraven continued with a smug grin. "I hope that your cell is to your liking."

Stan still refused to answer. He didn't think that he could. It felt like a sea of acid was building up in his stomach.

"Oh, and if you were by any chance thinking of punching your way out of here, I'm afraid that you'll be severely disappointed." Blackraven's smirk grew larger still. "We have Greater Tribesmen standing guard over every block of the tower. If you try to run, you will get nowhere."

"I'm not going to run," Stan finally spat out.

"Oh, I'm sure you're going to want to reconsider that,"

replied Blackraven with a chuckle. "Especially when you hear what we've done to your friends."

That was all it took. Stan flew forward, smashing his face into the window of the door, snarling like a rabid animal. "What are you talking about? What did you do to them? Answer me!" Stan demanded.

"Oh, don't fret," chuckled Blackraven, outrageously whimsical in tone. "They're still alive . . . for now." His grin grew even larger as he spoke, while the horror on Stan's face quickly grew in poignancy.

"We're not going to kill any of them until they give us some information that we dearly need. And you will not suffer at all, Stan. I know you're far too unintelligent to know anything of true importance. You'd rather just let your friends do all the planning for you, assuming that what they decide will be for the best. That, my friend, is the sign of a truly pathetic leader.

"So, for that reason, you will not be tortured. However, I know for a fact that all three of your comrades know valuable information about the security of Element City, information which I was unable to coax out of them when I sat alongside you all on the council. And so now, I am forced to obtain the information the hard way. I must admit, Stan, that Charlie has proved himself to be quite resistant to the torture so far. We haven't gotten a word out of him yet. Rest assured, however, I shall break him eventually. Charlie, as well as DZ and Commander Crunch."

Words could not describe the sheer, undiluted levels of rage and hatred swelling within Stan. The revulsion threatened to send Stan's body into spasms while Blackraven casually discussed the malicious torture of Stan's friends. And the fear and horror were real too, as Stan imagined all the terrible, terrible things the Noctem Alliance was surely doing to Charlie at that very moment.

"What about the others?" choked out Stan, his breathing shaky and a sob of pure malice caught in his throat. "My men? What have you done with them?" bellowed Stan as Blackraven held his entertained smirk.

"We've been teaching the Greater Tribesmen how to use bows and arrows to take down moving targets," replied Blackraven happily. "You'll be happy to know that they're getting quite good at it. I suspect we'll be out of targets within the day!"

Stan's heart clenched yet again. His men were being shot down as he spoke, his best friend was being subjected to persecution, and DZ and Commander Crunch were surely in cells just like his own, awaiting the same fate. And it was all because of the player staring at Stan through the window.

Finally, Stan stopped stewing in despair for long enough to return the glare. There were no words to describe what he longed to say to Blackraven, the player he now hated more than Caesar, more than Leonidas, more even than Minotaurus. Finally, Stan willed himself to speak.

"Why, Blackraven?" Stan asked, trying not to let his feeling of utter defeat sound in his voice. "When I first met you, five months ago, you took me in, along with Charlie and Kat, when nobody else would. How did you go from that . . . to this?"

Stan was then genuinely surprised to see a shadow cross Blackraven's black-and-yellow face. He took a deep breath, and then spoke.

"As I'm sure you know, Stan," Blackraven said, his voice sounding oddly solemn, "I was nearly killed by a lynch mob the day after I took you in. I had prepared for such an occasion when I built my store, and I sought refuge in an underground bunker I had built. What I had not expected was to be discovered by riot control when they looted the remains of my house after dispersing the mob.

"I was brought before Minotaurus, and he sentenced me to execution after the Proclamation Day ceremonies. My crime was evading arrest, but I knew they really just wanted me dead for harboring lower-level players.

"I'm sure you remember the events of that Proclamation Day quite clearly, Stan. After you shot King Kev, and riot control burned down the Adorian Village, King Kev knew that he had to do everything he could to find you. When he learned that I was the one who had protected you, and I was in his custody, King Kev waived my death sentence on the condition that my life now belonged to him.

"With all his vast resources, it wasn't long before King Kev discovered the resistance forces massing in the ruins of the Adorian Village. He sent in a spy who determined that they were working with you to take him down. King Kev saw his opportunity to use me, and sent me into the militia as a spy whose goal was to gain the trust of the militia and report information back to Element City.

"At that point, I was still under the misguided and preposterous notion that lower-level players were equal to the upper-levels, and they were worth preserving. For this reason, I only fed King Kev false information, or else information which I deemed to be trivial. And as you know, the battle was won by the Adorians, and you took over Element City as president. I was quite pleased with myself. I was in a position of great comfort. I was on the winning team, and could easily gain the trust of the enemy should King Kev's remaining followers return."

"But why did you turn, then?" asked Stan, utterly bewildered. "Why did you join the Noctem Alliance, instead of becoming a spy for the council?"

Blackraven's face took on an ugly look, and now it was

his turn to glare at Stan in contempt.

"The fact that I joined the Noctem Alliance, Stan, is one hundred percent your fault."

Stan was shocked and mortified. "What are you talking . . ."

"You had so much power, Stan," Blackraven cut in bitterly. "You were in control of an entire world, and your only enemies were too weak to do a thing to oppose you. Your citizens were so enamored by your leadership during the rebellion that they would have blindly followed any command you gave them.

"And what did you do? Did you put all your citizens to work to gather enough resources to make Element City a powerful force? No! Did you give yourself enough power to ensure that you could accomplish any of your goals on a whim? No! No, you didn't, Stan! You were so focused on protecting the rights of your people that you became blind to the possibilities you had at your fingertips!

"Compassion is a blinding thing, Stan. As admirable a quality as it is, there are times when it must be shelved for the greater good. You have never done that! You are a weak leader who would rather empower your people than your country! People are ephemeral, Stan. No person will last forever, because they will die, they will leave Elementia, and they will leave you! But empires . . . empires can last forever!

You had the ability to strengthen Element City to the point where it would never die! You had the resources, you had the capabilities!

"And what did you do? You sacrificed that chance in order to promote kindness. Fleeting, mortal kindness. And you refused to let your compassion go for the sake of empowering your nation! And now it's too late, Stan. We now live in the age of the Noctem Alliance, and the republic will soon be overshadowed by an organization to which compassion is alien!

"I tried to help you, Stan. I tried to convince you and your friends to pass laws that would enable you to build Element City into a superpower. I tried to convince you, for once in your life, to put your ridiculous care for the lower-level players and the NPC villagers aside. You wouldn't, though. And I soon realized that you never would. I knew I had to try to run for president. I knew that others would be bound to see it my way. But no. You were reelected yet again, by selfish, lower-level players who would rather live empty, unfulfilling lives than to build an empire that would last for years.

"It was then that I knew I had to turn. I had received a notification from Caesar in secret a few days before the election, telling me to join up with the Noctem Alliance in Nocturia. I didn't want to. I truthfully disagree with many ideals of the Alliance. But the Noctem Alliance has ambition.

They aim to create an empire that will last for eons in this fair land of Elementia. And if I couldn't turn your country into my vision for the future, then I knew the Noctem Alliance would. They won't halt greatness for the sake of protecting their people. And that, Stan, is the reason the Noctem Alliance is the greatest organization in the history of Minecraft."

There was a moment of silence as Stan processed all that Blackraven had just said. Finally, he managed to speak. "So . . . that's all you wanted, this entire time? To create an empire that would last forever?"

"That is all I have ever wanted," replied Blackraven darkly.

"And . . . you've been working against me and my friends from the inside this entire time?" Stan asked weakly.

"Oh, Stan," replied Blackraven with a dry chuckle. "You truly are in your own tier of ignorance. Surely you must have noticed that I was the catalyst for all that has weakened Elementia and strengthened the Noctem Alliance. Whose idea was it to add the reenactment of the battle to Elementia Day, allowing the perfect opportunity to strike fear into the heart of the city? Who handed control of Brimstone Prison to the Wither Skeletons, knowing full well that they would revolt against you at the slightest provocation? Who slipped materials to Count Drake in secret, so he could escape when you entered his room? Who helped you develop your plan for striking the Specialty Base, knowing full well that Caesar would be told exactly what was coming, and how to counter it?

"I must admit, though," said Blackraven, a cocky look on his face, "that my most brilliant idea was to leak council information into the city. The general public is a fickle animal, Stan. It can build you up and tear you down on a dime, depending on how you use it. And leaking your secret plans to the people ensured that they would never trust you again. And so it was that your people, who you had worked so hard to help, were now against you, and fighting among themselves. The order of chaos in Elementia was complete."

As Stan reeled in shock, Blackraven's smile grew back to maximum size, enjoying every moments of his ex-leader's struggle. Finally, Blackraven spoke again. "It is time for me to go, Stan," said Blackraven. "I have an audience with Lord Tenebris, and then I must oversee the end of Charlie's . . . er . . . persuasion. I shall take care of DZ next, and Commander Crunch soon after. And then . . . well, let's just say that Lord Tenebris has special plans for you." And then, with an amused chuckle, Blackraven turned on his heel and walked down the hallway until he was out of sight.

Stan was too overwhelmed to think properly. So much information had been thrown his way—so much was falling into place—and Stan was furious with himself for being blind to this plan, this horrible plan that had taken place right under his nose.

"Hey . . . Stan . . . Can you hear me?"

The voice was near silent, barely audible over the constant stream of gale winds outside the iron bar window, but Stan would recognize that voice anywhere. He bolted upright.

"DZ? DZ, where are you?"

"I'm over here," came the muffled reply. "In the cell to your . . . uh . . . left, I think."

Stan immediately scurried over to the left wall of his cell and pressed his ear up against it. "DZ? Can you hear me?"

"Yeah, I can hear you," the voice sounded out, still muffled but much clearer. Stan could now hear that DZ sounded tired and hurt, and lacking all his usual vivacity.

"DZ? What happened to you?"

"Nothing, I'm fine . . . ," and Stan heard a grunt of pain come from the other side of the wall. "Well . . . actually, no, I'm not. Those tribesmen messed me up pretty bad during the fight."

"Just hang in there, DZ, you're gonna be okay," said Stan, his heart beginning to race as he realized what must have happened. "Um . . . DZ . . . how much of that talk with Blackraven did you just hear?"

"All of it," replied DZ weakly, followed by a series of powerful coughs. Stan winced as he imagined DZ's body racked with spasms. "So they're planning to torture me, eh? Well, they're outta luck. I'm not gonna break easily." It sounded like every word was painful, but Stan needed to keep the discussion going. Time was running out quickly.

"DZ, we've got to get out of here. We need to find Charlie and Commander Crunch. Do you know where Crunch is?"

"No idea," rasped DZ in response. "And Stan . . . I don't think we're all gonna be able to . . ." Another round of coughs sounded off. ". . . escape. I've watched . . . the guards patrolling this place while you were unconscious. There are a lot of them, and neither of us is in any condition to fight."

"So you're just gonna give up?" cried Stan in horror.

"No. I'm gonna compromise instead . . . there's a difference . . . ," DZ replied weakly.

"Wait . . . what does that . . . ?"

"It means," replied DZ, "that I have a way to escape. But it'll only work for you . . . me, Charlie, and Crunch are gonna have to stay here."

"What? What're you . . . how will . . . ?"

"It's pretty simple, really." Another round of coughs echoed around the chambers. "They frisked us when they put us in here to take all our items away. But I used . . . this old trick I know . . . and managed to sneak some stuff in. Unfortunately . . . it's only enough stuff to get you out. Just you."

"No!" cried Stan. "I'm not letting you do that! You can't just sacrifice the three of you for my sake!"

"Shut up!" rasped DZ, followed by more coughing. "Do you . . . want them . . . to . . . hear?" His voice was wheezing now. He was clearly in a lot of pain. "You're not . . . sacrificing yourself, Stan. Charlie and Crunch are both . . . pretty tough players. I'm sure . . . they'll manage to survive. As long as . . . Lord Tenebris needs info . . . outta them, he'll keep them alive."

"But I can't just let them live on in misery like this when I walk free! And what about you?"

"Listen to me, Stan!" said DZ, his weak voice suddenly very stern and authoritative; Stan was compelled to obey. "You are the president of Elementia. It's your job to . . . be there for your citizens in a time of need. And they have never needed you . . . more than they do right now."

"But . . ."

"No buts, Stan. We came here with the goal of destroying the . . . Noctem Alliance. You need to escape from here. . . . We may have lost today . . . but the war isn't over yet. As long as you're here . . . you're our only hope, Stan."

"DZ, don't make me . . ."

"Stan, I want you . . . to listen to me . . . very carefully." There was a moment of silence before the gasping wheeze of DZ's voice came back. "In all these months . . . that I have known you . . . when have I . . . ever . . . let you . . . down?"

There was yet another moment of silence. Then . . .

"Trust me, Stan. Crunch and Charlie . . . they'll be fine. And as for me . . . this is what I want. You're my . . . best friend, Stan. Please . . . do as I say."

There was a long, poignant pause, filled with the loudest silence Stan had ever experienced. And then . . .

"Okay, DZ," replied Stan, his voice defeated. "Tell me the plan."

"You'll know what you need to do . . . when the time comes, Stan. All I need you to do now . . . is back away from the wall," DZ wheezed.

Stan robotically backed away from the wall. It didn't occur to him for a second to disobey. He was already in the process of forcing his brain to figure out how to escape. All his instincts were screaming at him to argue with DZ, and not leave until he could get all four of them out alive. Stan knew that DZ was right, though. If he had an opportunity to escape alone, he would have to take it. Stan wondered where they were. Naturally, he assumed they were still somewhere in the Specialty Base, but he still had no idea where. Atop Mount Fungarus, perhaps. But if that was the case, then he still had no idea how he was going to get off the . . .

Stan's train of thought was cut short by the explosion.

Waves of light, sound, and pain crashed over Stan. It felt like being pushed through a Nether portal painfully slowly. The blast forced him into a corner of the cell, contorting his entire body into the pinnacle of pain. The light was blinding. Stan couldn't see a single thing, and the sound of the blast rung in his ears so that all his vital senses were offline.

Stan wasn't sure how long he lay there afterward, his entire body screaming in pain. In the wake of the supernova, Stan seemed to lose all sense of time as well. Finally, however, he slowly drifted back toward the world of the living, his sense of sight and sound slowly turning back in at the cost of the pain intensifying into pure agony. Stan became vaguely aware of the blue sky above him, blocky clouds drifting not far overhead. The sound of the wind was whipping intensely now, and a siren blared far off in the distance.

Stan forced himself to his feet, wincing with every motion. He painstakingly looked around, and his heart stopped.

The blast had left a gash in the side of the complex, which, from what Stan could see, was situated at the peak of Mount Fungarus. In front of him was a drop straight down to the ocean, hundreds of blocks below. The walls of the cells were gone, the floor was now patchy with holes, and stray cobblestone blocks lay everywhere. And lying in the center of it all, where the cell adjacent to Stan's had been, a figure lay sprawled across the floor, a glowing diamond sword and a ring of flint and steel sitting beside him.

Immediately, all the pain in Stan's body evaporated. He no longer felt the sting of his body, nor the frigid lash of the wind around him. All he felt was dumbstruck shock as he staggered forward, almost in a trance, and he fell to his knees next to DZ's body. Then, as if sensing that he had arrived, DZ's eyes flickered and, with great effort, opened.

"Wha . . . what did you do?" gasped Stan. He was finding it impossible to breathe.

"I . . . got you . . . out . . . didn't I?" croaked DZ, his breath raspy and uneven and his chest heaving with every word. "That's . . . what I . . . promised. . . ."

"No . . . ," said Stan, loudly now, as he leaned down and grasped DZ's shoulders. "No, this can't be happening," he moaned.

"It's . . . okay . . . Stan . . . ," DZ said, a faint smile on his face. "You're . . . free . . . now. . . . And so . . . am I. . . ."

"NO!" shouted Stan, jerking DZ's shoulders in desperate fury as tears rolled down his face like waterfalls. "DZ, don't you dare die on me!"

"Ssshhh . . . ," whispered DZ, his breathing growing fainter by the second. "Stan . . . don't worry . . . about . . . me." DZ's face was serene now, with no cares in the world. "My . . . time in . . . Elementia . . . was . . . great . . . thanks to . . . you. . . ."

"DZ, no," moaned Stan, his entire body shaking now as grief swirled around him like a vortex.

"I just have . . . one last . . . request. . . . ," said DZ, his voice barely audible over the wind.

"Yeah," Stan choked out, perfectly attentive through his grief.

"When . . . you win . . . the war . . . I want you . . . to go . . . into the desert. . . . Stay there . . . for a week . . . let go . . . of your problems . . . and . . . remember . . . me. . . ."

And with a look of wholeness and peace on his face, DZ gave one last heave of his chest as his body faded away.

Stan knelt there for what seemed like an eternity. He could not move his hands from the place where DZ had lain just moments before. He could not cry anymore. He could not move. He couldn't think of anything, besides DZ's parting words, and the overwhelming fact that DieZombie97, the one player he had known almost as long as Kat and Charlie, was now gone from Elementia forever.

As Stan realized this, he suddenly became acutely aware of the sirens in the background, and angry shouts growing louder and louder. At once, all Stan's grief morphed into passion, a red passion of combined sadness, fury, and lust for vengeance. Stan closed his eyes for a moment. DZ was dead, but he was still alive. The Republic of Elementia still stood, and it was in greater danger now than ever in the history of the server. Stan knew what he had to do.

"I promise you, DZ," Stan said to himself through gritted teeth as he knelt in the bombed-out ruins of the prison atop

Mount Fungarus. "I will return to Elementia, and I will rally my people behind your memory to win this war once and for all."

Stan glanced down beside him and saw the items still lying on the ground. DZ's glowing diamond sword, with the Knockback enchantment, lay beside him on the ground. With a resolve of steel and a new level of drive, Stan snatched the sword in his blocky right hand and stood up. He walked forward, past the holes in the floor, and stood at the precipice of Mount Fungarus, overlooking the ocean hundreds of blocks directly below.

The journey ahead of me will be difficult, thought Stan. *It's a long road back to Elementia, and the Noctem Alliance will be out for my blood. I doubt the city will be able to help me. If Blackraven was telling our battle plans to the Alliance this entire time, then our assault on Nocturia has definitely failed, and the city will be fighting for its very existence at this moment. The republic is in peril . . . and it needs me.*

As the voices grew louder, Stan gave one final glance at the ground where DZ's body had lain for the final time. He felt no more grief. Surely it would return throughout his long trek back to Element City. For now, however, Stan's grief was dormant, giving way to a drive and passion he had not felt since he had shot the arrow at King Kev all those months ago.

All at once, the voices behind him became crystal clear. Stan heard his name being shouted out as he clutched DZ's sword, took a deep breath, and jumped off the edge of the cliff, plummeting toward the ocean below.

CHAPTER 24
THE HOSTAGES

For the first time in recent memory, the council room in Element Castle was completely and utterly silent. This was not solely due to the lack of members, although just five of the eight council members sat around the conference table, and the presidential seat sat vacant.

It was the Mechanist, the elected interim leader of the council until Stan's return, who had called the council meeting to order. This was to be expected. The offensive against the Noctem Alliance was now resolved, and a report on the condition of the fronts was necessary. However, now that the formalities and introductions were completed, nobody was willing to say the first word. The grim aura of the room clearly reflected the similar mood of what each of the players had to say about the situation on the fronts, and nobody seemed willing to break the news first.

Finally, after several minutes of uncomfortable silence, the Mechanist spoke.

"As you all know, the fighting forces of the Republic of Elementia launched a full-out assault on the forces of the Noctem Alliance today. Each of you in this room were on the front lines leading the charge."

There was a dismal murmur of assent around the room.

The Mechanist sighed. He knew what was coming, and didn't want to hear it any more than any of the other council members. He decided to get the less painful discussions out of the way first.

"First and foremost, does anybody have any idea where Blackraven is?"

The silence around the table rang.

"Bill, Ben, and Bob, I want an all-points bulletin out on him as soon as this meeting is over," ordered the Mechanist, gesturing to the three solemn police chiefs leaning against the wall.

"Second, is there any new information on the status of the assault on the Specialty Base?"

Four heads shook around the table, and Ben replied gravely, "We haven't heard anything about the status of the attack, although we had expected we would have by now. I guess there's nothing we can do except wait for information."

The Mechanist nodded in agreement, his face full of melancholy. "Keep in mind, everybody, there is still a very real chance that the assault went off perfectly, and that the leaders of the Noctem Alliance may well be disposed of already."

Dead silence greeted his statement, and the Mechanist wasn't surprised. He knew that all the officials in the room shared his gut feeling that that was not true. Finally, the Mechanist sighed. He knew the time had come, and reluctantly gave the command.

"Chief Bill, you were the commander of the assault on the Hot Front in the Nether. Please give a report on the status of the operation."

Bill slowly stood up straight. His unwillingness to speak was palpable. Finally, though, he began his report. "The assault began as planned. We managed to push the Noctem forces back toward Brimstone Prison, which they were using as a base of operations. However, it wasn't long before they revealed that they had Oob with them. As it turns out, the Zombie villagers are able to command Nether mobs as well. The Wither Skeletons and Zombie Pigmen formed an impenetrable defense around the prison, while the Ghasts laid down suppressive fire to prevent us from advancing.

"We were unable to drive forward because the Noctem soldiers seemed to know every move that we were going to make, and countered them perfectly. They managed to push us back fast and hard, until I eventually had to order a retreat back through the Nether portal and into Element Castle. We destroyed our Nether portal, so that the Noctem Alliance wouldn't have a way directly into the castle. That being said, the assault did cause us to lose all ground that we had gained in the Nether, and the Noctem Alliance now has unilateral control over the entire dimension, with no way for us to get back in."

Bill gave a deep breath as he finished his speech, and the hearts of the entire room sunk. They knew the assault hadn't gone well, but they were still not ready to hear it. Jayden and G in particular appeared sour and dejected. They had fought alongside Bill on the front lines of the Hot Front. The assault had been a disaster, and the Noctem Alliance now had the unrestricted ability to travel wherever they needed to go.

"Chief Ben, you were the commander of the assault on the Cold Front in the desert and tundra surrounding Nocturia. Please give a report on the status of the operation."

The Mechanist used the exact same words he had used with Bill, yet the tension was far higher now. All the council members had been in the city since the assault, and they had all heard the terrible rumors flying around like wasps since the assault had ended. Ben looked like it pained him simply to open his mouth, and Bob and Kat, the other commanders of the Hot Front, wore expressions of pure pain, which only increased the awful anxiety of the other players.

"Our assault began in a very similar way," Ben finally began. "We managed to crush a lot of their resistance as we pressed forward, closing in on Nocturia. As soon as we neared the city, however, an absolutely massive wave of forces poured out. Most of them were armed players, but there were also a good number of Creepers, who completely ignored the Noctem troops and targeted our men. I'm sure that Mella or Stull had trained them in Nocturia, and that one of them would have been out there alongside the mobs had it been nighttime.

"In any case, we were completely overwhelmed. The Noctems fought hard, and the Creepers inflicted huge damage to our numbers, so much so that we were forced to fall farther and farther back. We lost command post after command post across the tundra and into the desert. We tried to fight, but we were far too overwhelmed and could only watch as the Noctems took important positions like railroad stops and high grounds. They pursued us all the way back to the forest, and we were forced to make a full-on retreat back to the Adorian Village."

Suddenly, Ben let out what sounded like a choked-back sob. There were tears in his eyes, and it was clear that he was on the brink of saying something incredibly painful.

"Before long, the Noctem troops converged on the Adorian Village. We tried to fight it out in the street for a while, but then . . . we were overwhelmed. We realized we were the last fighting forces available in Elementia, and that it was our duty to protect as many citizens as possible so . . . so . . ." Ben took a deep breath before continuing. ". . . we were forced to leave the volunteer trainers and lower-level players in the village at the mercy of the Alliance. They're most likely going to be used for hostages.

"As of now, our forces have mounted a very sturdy defense around the walls of Element City. Our walls are mounted with auto-turret defense, underground TNT mines, temporary lava-walls, and enough other deterrents to make an attack by the Noctem Alliance on the city foolish and impossible. However, as of right now, the Noctem Alliance has control over the Adorian Village, Diamond Bay, and the woods surrounding Element City and, by extension, the entirety of Elementia itself."

The news sank into the council room slowly, in waves of comprehension. It wasn't until a full minute after the announcement that everybody in the room fully grasped the magnitude of what had happened. The assaults had failed on all fronts. The Noctem Alliance now had control over the entire server of Elementia except for Element City. And Element City now stood bunkered down on the defensive, preparing to fight for its very survival.

"What about the soldiers at the bases out in the country?" asked Jayden desperately. "You know, at the Sea Base and the Jungle Base . . . aren't they still around?"

Bob shook his head sadly. "No, they're not. After Stan and the others left the Sea Base, we called all the soldiers in from all our outposts so we could have the strongest assault possible. The soldiers that we have guarding our city . . . that's all we have left."

Silence followed the announcement. It wasn't surprising, but still nobody knew what to say. What could they say? An organization led by the remnants of King Kev's army had, in less than a month, taken control over what was essentially the entire server. And now, they had no extra soldiers on standby to combat them.

The silence was finally broken by a door opening behind them. All heads turned to see a soldier walking into the room, a book clasped tightly in his blocky hand.

"What's your business?" the Mechanist asked.

"I'm here with a message," the soldier replied tiredly. "A Noctem soldier walked up to our wall under a white flag and delivered this book to us. The title is *The Current Situation* and the author is Blackraven100."

There was a sharp collective intake of breath around the room. The Noctem Alliance had delivered a message bearing Blackraven's name?

Since Blackraven's disappearance days before, they had all wondered if it were possible. There was always a possibility that it could be a coincidence . . . or perhaps Blackraven had been captured by the Noctems, and this was his ransom message. . . .

Ben took the book from the soldier. As he skimmed the pages, his eyes widened, then shrank into sadness. Finally, after a long pause, he read the book out loud.

The Current Situation, by Blackraven100

A Message for the Council of Eight

Greetings, Council Members. This message is an informational notice for you, so that you may know of my true allegiance to the Noctem Alliance and its glorious leader, Lord Tenebris. I have told all your plans and battle tactics to my colleague, Caesar894, which is the reason for your assault failing so spectacularly, as I am quite confident it is sure to do.

In the past days, I have taken a permanent leave for the Specialty Base of the Noctem Alliance, where I was able to capture President Stan, Councilmen Charlie and DZ, and the commander of the Elementia Sea Base during their attempted attack on the base. Currently, we are holding all four of them in a high-security prison in an undisclosed location. In due time, we will have certain demands that you will have to comply with if you would like to keep your friends alive.

In the meantime, it is my personal recommendation that all members of the council, as well as the police chiefs, turn themselves in to us. The Noctem Alliance is not an evil organization. Should you surrender, you yourselves shall be executed as enemies of the state, but your subjects shall be allowed to live under the ordinance of the Noctem Alliance. We do not wish to kill civilians. Our aim is simply to put lower-level players in their rightful places.

Know, Council Members, that the longer you fight this war, the longer we will continue to kill your players. We hate to do this as much as you hate us doing it, but only you have the power to stop it.

Sincerely yours,

Blackraven100

The silence lingered, but the shock wasn't nearly as much as one might expect. So much terrible and horrific information had entered the common knowledge of the group in the past ten minutes that this newest information only left them drained. There was no more room for shock anymore. And besides, nobody was truly surprised anyway. Since Blackraven's untimely and unexplained disappearance, seeds of suspicion had been growing in each of the council members for days, and so the confirmation of their notions served more as a dull blow to the stomach than a slap across the face.

The more prevalent feeling in the room was that of suspense, as each of the council members realized the same thing. Blackraven's note had made an offer to them. They could turn themselves in to halt the fighting entirely. The ability to end the war now was in their hands.

There was even more silence still as the group mulled over the idea in their heads. And then, finally, when she could bear it no longer, Kat leaped up from her chair and onto her feet, and all eyes turned to her.

"I call for a vote," said Kat, her eyes flashing with zeal as she spoke the first words since the end of Blackraven's note. "All in favor of turning ourselves in to the Noctem Alliance, raise your hand."

Kat looked around the table. All members of the council matched her expression. Not a single hand was raised in the air.

"Good," said Kat, "because even if you had voted for it, I would have fought you tooth and nail. And do you know *why*? Because we are the Grand Republic of Elementia. We stand for the principles of equality and liberty for all of our citizens, regardless of background or level. If we were to turn ourselves in, we could stop the fighting, but for what? A server run by the Noctem Alliance? Run by the same principles that we all fought to destroy just a few months ago?

"I don't know about you, but as for me, as long as the Noctem Alliance is alive, I will never stop fighting them. Justice is a cause that deserves to be fought for, and injustice is something that must be eradicated from Elementia forever. Right now, the forces of our enemy have pushed us back to the brink of collapse. The new players of the Adorian Village are being held as hostages. Our four friends are being held captive by the Noctem Alliance. We are closer to the brink of destruction now than we have ever been, so we have to fight harder than we ever have before, not just to stay alive, but to destroy our oppressors once and for all."

As Kat finished her speech, she looked around the table. There had been no dramatic shift in the mood as she had spoken, yet something had changed. There was an element in the air that hadn't been there before. Kat couldn't put her finger on what it was. Maybe it was hope, maybe it was determination, maybe it was unity. But Kat knew she was not alone, and that as long as at least one of them stood, all was not lost for the future of Elementia.

CHAPTER 30
LORD TENEBRIS

Blackraven was having trouble hiding his giddiness. The time had now come, the time Blackraven had waited for since he had first joined the Noctem Alliance all those months ago. Even the fact that he was sitting alongside the idiot bull-man Minotaurus couldn't put a damper on the sheer elation Blackraven was feeling.

Blackraven had just made his allegiance to the Noctem Alliance public, causing all of Stan's forces to reel in shock. The information he had relayed from Element City had helped the Noctem Alliance gain control over the entire server of Elementia, with all of the republic's forces being pushed back to one stronghold. Due to his brilliant planning, the Alliance now had four high-ranking government officials as well as an entire village of lower-level players to bargain with.

There was no doubt in Blackraven's mind that he was now Lord Tenebris's favorite servant. The fact that he was being called to an audience with Lord Tenebris clearly indicated that at long last, Lord Tenebris would use his own divine might to bestow wondrous powers upon Blackraven.

The one thing that confused Blackraven about the entire situation was the presence of Minotaurus beside him. Despite being in the Alliance since its inception,

Minotaurus was nothing more than an exceptionally powerful grunt, with little to no brain power to speak of. That being said, Blackraven was sure there was an explanation.

Of the four of them who had first joined the Alliance, only he and Minotaurus were left. Caesar had been betrayed and murdered by Leonidas, who was now on the run, a fugitive from both the republic and the Alliance. Perhaps, in light of all that was going so well, Lord Tenebris was feeling generous, and had decided to bestow powers on to both of the remaining founders. *Yes, that seemed reasonable*, Blackraven thought with a smile. *Who knows, perhaps Lord Tenebris will order us to test our new powers by hunting and destroying Leonidas.*

There was a faint click, and the iron door swung open. Blackraven's heart gave a leap, and he jumped to his feet. It took every ounce of his self-control not to sprint out of the waiting room and into Lord Tenebris's chamber. Instead, he walked in respectfully, took his position in the middle of the chamber, and sunk reverently to one knee, with Minotaurus doing the same beside him.

In due time, Blackraven sensed a presence in front of him. A moment later came the deep, calm voice.

"Greetings, my friends."

This was the cue. Blackraven raised his head, and looked toward the source of the sound. It was dark in the back of the chamber, with no light to speak of. Blackraven could barely make out the outline of a player standing tall within the blackness. Blackraven's heart raced. As far as he knew, Lord Tenebris had never revealed his appearance to any players, even within the Noctem Alliance. However, Blackraven had a suspicion that today might be the day.

"Greetings, your highness," replied Blackraven, his voice as humble as he could manage.

"Yeah, greetings, sir," Minotaurus's dumb-sounding reply came alongside him.

"I would like to congratulate you," the voice of Lord Tenebris said. "Due to your efforts over the past weeks, the Nation of the Noctem Alliance is now by far the largest and most powerful that it has ever been. For this reason, you have earned the satisfaction of I, the great and powerful Lord Tenebris."

Blackraven shuddered. This must be a dream! He was being directly praised by Lord Tenebris himself! Words could not describe his excitement.

"I am a benevolent leader," Lord Tenebris continued, "and therefore, I see fit to reward my followers for their loyalty and hard work. This is why I have called you before me, the Great Lord Tenebris, on this day. It is time for you to receive your reward."

Blackraven was focusing every iota of energy he had on standing still. This was the most exciting moment of his life.

"I shall begin with you, Minotaurus," Lord Tenebris announced. A moment later, an arm extended out of the darkness. It was a typical blocky Minecraft arm, with tan skin and a turquoise sleeve extending just beyond the point where darkness enveloped the arm's owner.

Blackraven watched in awe as the arm extended straight out, straight toward Minotaurus. The bull-man closed his eyes and took a deep breath, and began to levitate into the air. As he rose higher and higher, Blackraven's anticipation escalated at an exponential rate. He was positive that some sort of divine essence would fly out of Lord Tenebris's hand, endowing Minotaurus with the power of a deity.

Instead, the fist of the hand clenched. Minotaurus's head flew backward, and a ring of items burst out around him before his body fell to the ground in a crumpled heap.

No sooner did Blackraven comprehend what had just happened to his colleague than he found himself levitating into the air by some unknown force, a hand outstretched from the darkness toward him. Blackraven felt no rush of divine power enter his body. Rather he felt as though a hand was clasped around his throat. He tried to raise his arms, only to find that they had been pinned to his side by the unseen power.

"My lord," breathed Blackraven uncomprehendingly, "what are you doing?"

"You have earned my satisfaction, Blackraven," the emotionless voice rang out from the darkness. "Therefore, this will be painless."

Then, all at once, Blackraven felt his head moving backward at the speed of light, and everything went black.

Lord Tenebris glanced down at the bodies of his two remaining followers, lying on the floor alongside their rings of items. Lord Tenebris was, truthfully, sad to see them go. Blackraven had been a great asset in the grand scheme of things, while Minotaurus had been unwaveringly loyal, if also relatively useless. Lord Tenebris did have an agenda, however. Allies never stayed true allies for long in the game he was playing. Besides, Lord Tenebris had always preferred to work alone, something far more reasonable now that Blackraven had done his job.

As soon as the bodies and items of the two players had despawned, Lord Tenebris called in his next conference.

Lord Tenebris found a good deal of amusement in the fear and awe displayed on Captain Drake's face as he entered the chamber. It was not altogether surprising, though. Never had a player so low-ranked as the captain been called in to conference with the great and powerful Lord Tenebris before. This would soon change, however. Lord Tenebris had plans to promote the captain to the rank of general soon, as he was now short three of them.

"Greetings, Your Excellency," whispered Captain Drake in a deep bow.

"Greetings, Captain," replied Lord Tenebris. "Now, present to me your reports on the conditions of the prison and the front line."

The captain faltered for a moment. Lord Tenebris saw a glint of horror in his eyes before he began to speak. "Well . . . your highness, um . . . The front line is holding up most excellently. . . ."

Something has gone wrong in the prison, I know it, Lord Tenebris thought. He knew himself to be acutely decisive, and he knew how to read a conversation.

"What has gone wrong in the prison?" Lord Tenebris asked, his voice still unemotional as ever. "I assure you, Captain, that whatever punishment I shall give you for your error, it will be far worse should you withhold information from me. I suggest telling me the truth, and the entire truth."

The captain stammered and sputtered for a moment before finally taking a deep breath, looking straight at where he judged Lord Tenebris's eyes to be, and gave the report.

"There was some sort of explosion in the high-security block. It killed Councilman DZ and allowed President Stan to escape. Councilman Charlie and Commander Crunch are still detained."

As Captain Drake winced in preparation for the inevitable blow, he couldn't see that Lord Tenebris, still shrouded in shadows, was not angry. In fact, he was delighted.

So, Lord Tenebris thought. *DieZombie97 is dead. And Stan is still out there somewhere. I guess that my fun isn't quite over yet.*

"Captain, I am charging you with no punishment . . . yet."

Captain Drake looked up, hardly daring to believe his ears.

"I am charging you with the responsibility of finding and capturing President Stan on your own. I want him alive. If you succeed, then you shall have no punishment."

Captain Drake fell down into a full bow, sobbing in relief.

"Oh, thank you, merciful Lord Tenebris, you are far too kind. I deserve a leader far less merciful than you."

"This is true," replied Lord Tenebris nonchalantly.

"I . . . I do have one question, however," replied Captain Drake, looking up. "I understand that, as of your last announcement, you appointed me the new head of the Noctem Alliance's armies. Do you still wish me to command the armies while I carry out this task for your majesty?"

Lord Tenebris's face slowly broke into a huge grin.

"That will not be necessary, Captain," said Lord Tenebris slowly.

"Then . . . who will be the new commander of the armies?"

Lord Tenebris gave a slow, spine-chilling laugh before responding.

"That, my Captain, shall be myself. I have determined that I have been a dormant player in this game for far too long. The republic is in critical condition. I intend to bleed them out, to keep them in their position for as long as I can, and to watch them suffer. And I want to see it firsthand."

And with that, Lord Tenebris stepped forward, out of the darkness, and into the light of the chamber.

Captain Drake's jaw dropped.

Lord Tenebris looked almost identical to a new player. He had dark brown hair, a turquoise shirt, and blue pants, the standard look for a Minecraft player unchanged by skins. On whole, he bore a striking resemblance to President Stan. Except for the eyes.

The sinister, empty, white eyes.

TO BE CONTINUED...

DON'T MISS THE
NEXT EXCITING ADVENTURE!

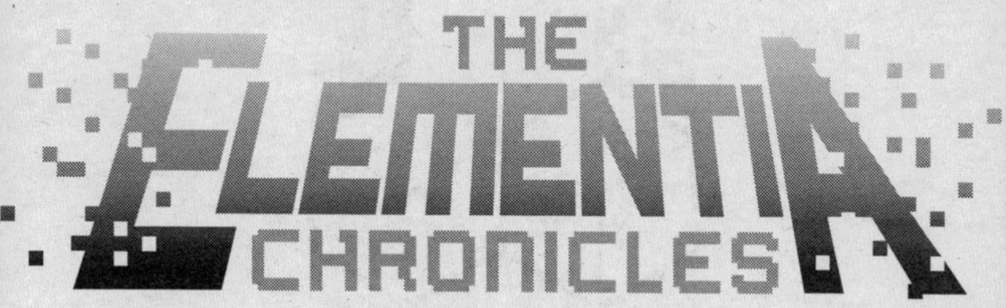

BOOK THREE:
HEROBRINE'S MESSAGE

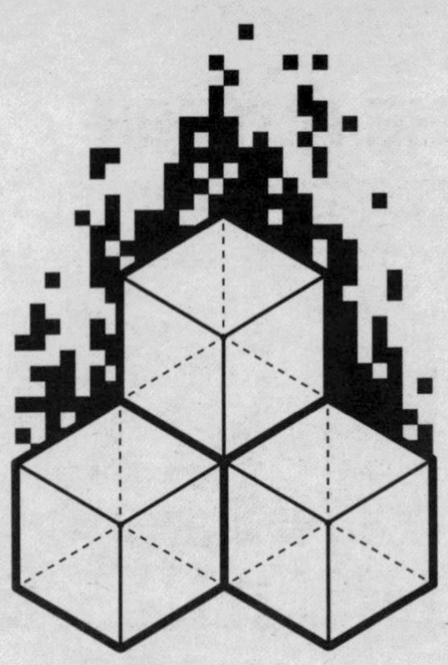

It is a dark time on the Minecraft server Elementia. The fates of all are in the air, and none are certain what the next day will bring. Isolated from his country, President Stan must make his way through the countryside of Elementia, which is controlled by the forces of the Noctem Alliance and the evil mobs they command. To return home and lead Elementia to victory, Stan must embark on the most perilous quest he has ever faced. He will team up with unlikely allies, and search through the entirety of Minecraft, even beyond the server of Elementia, to find the guidance and power he needs to destroy the Noctem Alliance once and for all. Will Stan be able to overcome the adversity and peril around every corner? Or will a new threat . . . a dark, sinister, and mythological force . . . change everything? Find out in the epic conclusion to the Elementia Chronicles saga.

FROM THE AUTHOR

Thank you for reading *The New Order*. I hope you enjoyed it. If you did enjoy it, please tell your friends, and write an online review so that others can enjoy it too.

—SFW

CONNECT WITH SEAN

: www.sfaywolfe.com

: www.facebook.com/elementiachronicles

: @sfaywolfe

Links to buy Sean's paperback and ebooks are on his webpage.
Links to Sean's online games can also be found on his webpage.
Go to **www.goodreads.com** to rate and/or review this novel.

ACKNOWLEDGMENTS

First, I would like to thank all the fans who have showed their support for *Quest for Justice*. Your enthusiasm and the ways that you have shown it to me are the number-one inspiration and drive that keeps me writing.

I would like to thank HarperCollins for publishing my series. It takes a really special company to take on a seventeen-year-old with a Minecraft fan-fiction.

I would like to thank Pamela Bobowicz, my editor, who has helped me turn the Elementia Chronicles into the best series it can be, and respected my opinions in the process.

I would like to thank my grandmother, who has always been there for me throughout my life, and will always provide me with a 100 percent honest answer to anything I ask her.

I would like to thank my brothers, Eric and Casey, for providing me with their support and keeping me motivated and (when I need it) humble over the past two years.

I would like to thank Rick Richter, my agent, who reached out to me and offered to help me share my ideas with the world. He has been of invaluable help to me, always providing me with advice, answers, and anything else that I need throughout the process of working on the Elementia Chronicles. For that, Rick, I offer you my sincerest thanks.

And last but not least, once again I would like to give special acknowledgment to my mother and father. They keep me on track, they keep me motivated, and they never fail to go out of their way to help me pick up the pace when I'm slacking. Without their undying support, the Elementia Chronicles would never have left the hard drive of my computer. For that, I cannot thank them enough.

P.S. I would also like to thank my cat, Boo, for ceasing his attempts to take a nap on my keyboard while I am typing. This change in behavior has made writing significantly easier and for that, Boo, I thank you.